# Bloodstone

## Written in Stone

By: RJ Ladon

Three Ravens Publishing
Chickamauga, GA

Published by Three Ravens Publishing
threeravenspublishing@gmail.com
160 Park St. Chickamauga, Ga 30707
https://www.threeravenspublishing.com



Credits:
Bloodstone Written in Stone was written by R. J. Ladon
Cover art by Dawn Spears www.dawnydawny.com
Bloodstone Written in Stone by: R. J. Ladon, 1st edition, 2020
Trade Paperback ISBN: 978-1-951768-11-9

Dedicated to all my friends and family
Who provided encouragement, support, and
threats (you know who you are)

In Memory of Judith and Alex

# Chapter 1

The bars fit snugly over Kragnor's shoulders, pinning his wings against his back. There wasn't enough space to leverage the metal apart. For four days, he hadn't found a weakness in the forged steel. Others around him were also trapped in six-foot crates, unable to do more than turn in place. The past two days, more caged akitu were added to the damp, dank room. How many more? Kragnor was unsure.

Soon they would be destroyed by the will of Pope Boniface. They were to be heated over the flames of a blacksmith's forge until the metal of their cages turned white. Then the cell and akitu inside were to be quenched in the coldest water available. Kragnor didn't know if his body could withstand the sudden and explosive change in temperature. He suspected that even if he survived, the pain of a million cracks would be excruciating.

Akitu were considered demons by the Catholic Pope. All Boniface needed to see were the horns, wings, and tails to know they were evil. With his divine influence, he demanded the faithful to destroy or capture all akitu. The culling began in the daylight hours while akitu slept. Some were tossed from their perches on tall buildings where they shattered on the ground. Others, too ancient to be killed by a fall, were pressed into cells in their slumbering state.

Kragnor opened and closed his fist, flexing his fractured forearm. It was healing. A wrestling match with friend and mentor Basal caused the damage. He grunted, frustrated with his predicament. A healed fracture would help little if he were to die tomorrow.

A man in brown robes entered the room, an oil lamp hanging from one hand. Kragnor caught his scent: Friar Francois. He had worked with the man in the past, teaching him languages and the time before human history. A time that Pope Boniface insisted didn't exist. Kragnor snorted. He'd liked Francois until recently. Until he was deceived and captured by the man in brown robes. His lip curled into a feral snarl.

He heard the growls from the other akitu in the room. "Betrayer!" someone shouted.

"Please," Friar Francois begged. "I was forced to comply with my Pope. Under penalty of death."

"How many akitu died in the name of your God, of your Pope?" asked a female. "How many of our bodies lie beneath or within Notre Dame's construction?"

"That is why I have come. This madness needs to stop. I cannot free your bodies, but I can free your souls."

"Catholic nonsense!" An akitu growled behind Kragnor.

"No!" Francois pulled something out of his leather pouch. He held it high for everyone to see. It looked like a smooth river stone with cuneiform writing etched on one face. "Basal helped me prepare these vessels for your souls. For your freedom with akitu spells."

Basal was an ancient akitu, perhaps the first of their kind. Kragnor thought he died or escaped the Pope's culling.

"If Basal is here, bring him before us," someone requested.

"I dare not. If anyone saw Basal…we both would die."

Cries of discord and disbelief broke from the other akitu.

"Please, I must save at least one of you. Will none of you trust me?" Francois sounded like he might cry. He, too, was desperate. Perhaps, guilt ate at him.

"I will do it," Kragnor said. The others grew silent.

Friar Francois moved to stand before Kragnor's cramped cell. The human held a green and red bloodstone, offering it to Kragnor. "What do I do?" he asked the Friar, whispering with trepidation.

"Touch it. The spells were already cast."

"Then what?"

"Your soul will enter the vessel, and your body will turn to stone as if you were sleeping."

"How do you know?"

Francois showed Kragnor an onyx stone with cuneiform etched on it. Life pulsed within. "Basal went first."

# Chapter 2

Megan Petrov studied the boring wooden mannequin that stood before her; it barely looked human. She saluted then struck her defenseless opponent with the rattan practice sword, first to the head, then the leg, then a twist to smack the waist. The sound of rattan on wood echoed through the empty gym.

"Excellent, Megan." Nikolai tapped the wooden mannequin with the rattan sword in his hand. "Again." His English was perfect, but his Russian accent was thick.

"When do I get to fight a real person?"

"You fight me every day." Nikolai was a tall, strong man, topping six foot two and two hundred pounds. "I'm a real person." He bounced on the balls of his feet. The blade in his hand swept in front of his face and torso like a shield. "I'm ready when you are."

"Let me clarify, when can I fight someone other than you?" She blew her sweaty brown hair out of her eyes. Megan was half his size and weight and, when it came to experience, she had far less to draw upon.

"When you can strike the pell without fail, blindfolded." Nikolai narrowed his eyes. "Again." He tapped the mannequin impatiently.

Megan repeated the kata-like exercise. Head, leg, waist. Head, leg, waist. She felt her body fall into the rhythm. Her breathing relaxed. Head, leg, waist. Head, leg, waist.

She closed her eyes. Her body kept the beat and time. Head, leg, waist. She felt her body move out of place, and she became uncertain of where her strike might land. She adjusted her positioning and swung again, head, leg, nothing. Her swing went wild. She stumbled.

She snapped open her eyes. Nikolai was against the wall, near the mannequin, but not close enough to move it. "What happened?"

"You lost confidence in yourself." Nikolai frowned. "You second-guessed your footing, and you readjusted what didn't need adjustment." He shook his head, disappointment written on his face. "This is why you can't hit me. You are too busy fighting yourself."

Megan lowered her weapon. He was right. "Can we stop for the day?"

"Nyet. It's not good practice to stop a lesson on a sour note." He tapped the mannequin. "You will continue until I say you are done. Open your senses, reach out, as I taught you. Trust yourself. You have more than sight at your disposal."

Megan frowned but nodded. "As you say, Weapons Master."

"Again," Nikolai commanded.

Megan inhaled fully then exhaled, willing her body to function like a finely tuned instrument. She addressed the mannequin and began the three-strike dance. Megan settled into the horseman's stance, keeping her joints loose, and let muscle memory control her movements. In her mind's eye, she turned the boring wooden frame into a monster's likeness, including fur and curved horns. Megan closed her eyes, imagining the beast held a rabbit, gripping it with sharp claws.

Desire to save the helpless rabbit sharpened her senses. Megan saw each hit, felt the face, leg, and waist. Each strike rattled the weapon in her hand, numbing her palm and wrist. Still, she continued striking that imaginary terrifying face and hulking body. With each hit, Megan felt a little stronger, faster, and confident. A growl rattled deep in her throat. She would become a whirlwind of death.

"Enough!" Nikolai commanded, breaking her focus.

Startled, Megan stopped and turned to the sound of his voice.

"Very good. You did twenty in a row, perfect. You may hit me yet."

Megan bowed to Nikolai. "Thank you, Weapons Master."

"Run five miles and go home." Nikolai nodded to the track that wrapped around the outside of the vaulted room.

Megan bowed again. "Thank you, Weapons Master." She held her smile and waited for him to turn away. It's unwise to smile with confidence or pride in front of Nikolai. He would give her more to do.

Around the outside of the training area was a two-lane track. Running there was more enjoyable than the treadmill, even though the only view was gym equipment, the boxing ring, and Nikolai.

Megan loved running. She could think while her feet pounded the cork-covered track. Mentally, she set the pace to light exertion to work out the kinks from training, then let her mind wander. The last time Megan imagined a bully, she did very well on the shooting range. With the addition of a helpless victim, her reaction felt more potent, more powerful. Nikolai often instructed her to visualize to improve her skills. Did he intend for her to turn the pell into a rabbit-wielding monster?

Her mind moved to other instructions during the school day. Megan received a math and science assignment to finish for the next day. The English teacher assigned a long-term English paper for the following week. Bonnie was required to work with her on the project. Megan enjoyed spending time with Bonnie during school hours, but her father wouldn't understand after-hours fraternizing.

Artem never allowed Megan to have friendships because they were unnecessary and dangerous. "Friends can be duplicitous, and you will let your guard down around them."

He felt the same way about phones, forbidding the devices to leave the house. "We can be tracked and hunted with a phone." He often lamented the discontinuation of the landline. Even though Megan never saw signs of danger, she kept her phone connected to the scrambler when talking to anyone, even Bonnie.

Megan finished her run and headed to the showers. The locker room was small, with thirty lockers and two private bathing areas. After drying off, she put on her school clothes, loose-fitting jeans, and a sweatshirt, including a light jacket with special weapons. Hidden in the seams were six-inch steel needles. They worked as both lock pick and shiv.

She threw her sweaty gym clothes in her bag. On her way out, Megan passed Nikolai and a male client. "Good night Nikolai," she said.

Nikolai nodded in return. "Come back Wednesday after school." He cleared his throat. "Mr. Smith is willing to teach the intricacies of wiring."

Megan inclined her head in greeting. There had been many "Mr. Smiths" teaching skills at Nikolai's gym. She studied this Mr. Smith. He held his shoulders square, his posture was good, and defined muscle was visible under his too-tight tee-shirt. He was confident, maybe too confident, probably ex-military. "I will ask Father." She left the building without glancing back.

Wiring to ex-military could be anything from installing a bomb or setting up security to preparing snares and setting traps in the field. Her father would know if the training was worth attending.

The "gym" Megan attended was an unassuming building outside Avalon's city limits. Nikolai owned the building and trained a select few people, all of whom were much older than her. She seldom saw the other students, only their vehicles. Megan climbed into her small blue Honda, one of two cars in the lot.

Nikolai and Megan's father, Artem, had a partnership many years ago in Russia. Megan never knew what exactly it entailed, other than the Russian mafia was involved. Nikolai came to America a few years after Artem acquired asylum with the United States government.

From an early age, Artem insisted Megan received the best training possible, and in his eyes, only Nikolai would do. Megan didn't remember when her training started. It seemed as if she always practiced with swords and guns.

# Chapter 3

Kevin Arkis unslung his backpack, setting it in the grass at the edge of the sidewalk. He leaned forward, kissing Annie Brown's strawberry flavored lips lingering on the subtle taste. He pulled back, grasping her free hand. "I've got to go. Tonight is my first night at Grandma's."

Annie's pixie-cut blonde hair gave her an innocent appearance. "I'm actually dating a boy that has moved out of his parent's house." She giggled, bounced on her toes, then looked up at Kevin through long lashes.

Kevin's heart raced. "I didn't move out. Grandma needs help."

Annie bit her bottom lip, pouting. "Don't ruin my fantasy." She toyed with the purple crystal on her necklace, adjusted her bookbag, and backed toward her front porch. "My door is always open." Annie jerked her head to point at her second-floor bedroom window. She blinked her long lashes coyly. The cape cod style house had windows dormered out over the roof.

Filigree enhanced, wrought iron posts supported the porch roof, perfect for climbing.

He felt his heart flutter. “I will if I can.” Kevin watched for a moment as Annie disappeared into her house. He swung his backpack onto his shoulder and walked to Grandma’s.

Annie lived in an upper-class neighborhood. Her house had a few acres of property that butted up to the Turtle River. All the homes along the river were expensive, opulent, or had many acres. Some residences had all three.

As the streets moved away from the river district, the housing turned moderate to reasonable. On the far southern end of Avalon were inexpensive new family homes and a couple of trailer parks.

Kevin and his family lived a dozen blocks from Annie in an older neighborhood that was a mishmash of architectural styles. His parents owned a ranch style home while his grandmother, who lived behind them, owned a craftsman. Their backyard shared a fence and gate.

Kevin opened the front door, stepping into the living room. Grandma sat on the couch, watching her favorite talk show. Rapscallion, the big white tomcat, lay beside her. Her shoulder-length bobbed hair was dark with a few streaks of silver. She wore jeans and a red sweatshirt that said, 'World's Greatest Grandma.' She smiled at Kevin. "Good, you remembered."

"Of course, Grandma, how could I forget?"

"Grandma? Grandma?" She scowled at him with feigned anger. "Enough of that. If we're going to be roommates, you will call me Ruby." She smiled. "It'll be nice having a man in the house again."

Grandpa Joe died unexpectedly five years ago when Kevin was thirteen. Shortly after his death, Grandma was diagnosed with the early stages of dementia. She was put on medication right away, which helped maintain her freedom for those years. However, recently, her doctor identified her habit of seeing and forgetting things in the evenings as Sundowners. Her daytime behavior seemed unchanged.

Kevin nodded absently. The idea of calling Grandma by her first name was strange. He climbed the stairs to his new bedroom. He slept in the room countless times in the past as a guest. Now, it was his to decorate as he saw fit. His backpack was placed near the old wooden desk, a remnant from when his father was a child. The posters, books, blankets, and clothes were all his father's. Most of them were outdated, but some things were popular again—posters with iconic video games and movies decorated the room. When Kevin was a kid, he thought they were ancient. Now, he had new respect, a fondness, for the retro images.

Kevin studied the old oak dresser and sighed involuntarily. He needed to move his father's junk out to make room for his clothes and games. The bed was quickly covered with clothing as he set out items to organize. Kevin eyed the underwear and socks, wondering if they shouldn't be tossed, or maybe burned. He shrugged, not caring either way. From inside the closet, he grabbed the few remaining gaudy shirts, adding them to the pile.

He opened the attic door, the third door in his room. The stairs creaked underfoot, but Kevin continued in the hope he would find a box or empty wardrobe to toss the clothes in. Cedar, mothballs, and mouse droppings created an ambrosia that permeated the lofted room, reminding Kevin of long-lost summers exploring his grandparent's house.

Four windows allowed enough light to see. Books, shelves, cabinets, tables, blankets, and boxes stood in organized rows. Everything was stacked in an orderly fashion and marked with words or symbols. Some of those symbols were runes, while others represented planets and the zodiac. Grandma organized her belongings with the signs of Wicca, her religion. While Kevin didn't know what the glyphs meant, he avoided some boxes due to the symbol's shape. *Was that symbol for Taurus or the image of Satan?*

Sheets covered furniture and full-length mirrors along the back wall. Absently he wondered if any of the mirrors had special powers. He decided against removing the sheets, just in case. Kevin checked a few unmarked boxes, but everything was full. He sneezed from the haze of dust motes and grime he kicked into the air.

Ready to give up, he walked back to his bedroom. Against the knee wall that surrounded the stairwell was an enormous wooden box with a domed lid. Inside, Kevin found a few old outfits, but most of the box was empty. "Perfect." Kevin fetched his father's nasty, outdated clothes and unceremoniously tossed them into the trunk. Afterward, he trotted down to the main floor.

"Rap, do you believe that? Darn, kids have no respect." Grandma pet the cat as she watched a news report about graffiti in downtown Avalon. She glared at Kevin. "I hope none of your friends would do that to public property." She pointed to the painted image of an eye with a slit-like pupil put on park benches and slides in a playground.

"Of course not." Kevin frowned. All he had was Annie, all he wanted was Annie, and she would never do that. "I'm going to fetch my stuff. I'll be back in a few minutes."

"Okay, dear." Ruby waved her hand to acknowledge she heard him.

The grandfather clock in the hallway between the kitchen and living room chimed 4:45. He loved the reassuring thrum.

Kevin slipped through the kitchen and out the back door into the backyard. Ruby loved to garden and kept her raised beds in a herringbone pattern. During spring and summer, flowers, shrubs, and herbs filled almost every open space. Now only perennials and mulch were left. Ruby enjoyed playing in the dirt even if there were no weeds to pull or seeds to plant. She used to become depressed in the winter until she discovered mushrooms and cultivated them in the basement. Over time she added culinary and medicinal herbs to her basement garden. The greenery thrived under UV lamps.

He walked under the old sprawling bur oak. The branches were gnarled and twisted. The tree used to give Kevin nightmares when he was little, but now it reminded him of Halloween. Within its protective canopy was a fancy clubhouse Grandpa and Grandma made for Kevin's father, Jerry. As a child, Kevin was too afraid of the tree to use the magnificent fort. His triplet sisters, however, never had a problem and played in the structure often.

Kevin opened the chain-link gate at the back of Grandma's property and stepped into his parent's yard. His mother had little time left in the day to maintain a garden like Ruby. Instead, her backyard was the domain of the girls. They had an enormous jungle gym, with slides, swings, monkey bars, and a climbing wall. It was enclosed by edging and filled with wood chips. Recently the girls were ignoring the play equipment, using the clubhouse instead.

He walked into the kitchen of his parent's house. Donna looked up from chopping vegetables. "Hello, Kevin."

"Hi, Mom. Can I use a laundry basket to bring some clothes to Grandma's?"

"Sure, dear." She continued chopping. "Oh, Kevin, why don't you and Grandma come over for supper? The girls would love it if some things didn't change."

"Seriously? I haven't even been gone for a day," Kevin whined. It'd be challenging to see Annie if he still had to play big brother to his kid sisters.

"They love you, Kevin. One day you'll appreciate that."

"That's not what I meant." Kevin stomped into the laundry room and grabbed a basket. He walked to his bedroom, set the basket on the floor, and dumped his clothes inside.

"Do you think Mom would let me sleep in your room?"

Startled, Kevin turned quickly. "Inez, you love scaring me, don't you?" His sister lounged on his bed. Her long dark hair cascaded over her shoulders.

She smiled at him. "I'm not Inez; I'm Mina."

Kevin laughed. "Liar."

Inez frowned. "Dad falls for it all the time."

Kevin added his deodorant to the basket. "I'm not Dad. Besides, you three aren't identical."

"What?" Inez sat up, indignant. "We are too. Our teachers can't tell us apart. Or the doctors and dentists. Or Father Pat."

"Oh, I've heard stories about you three causing mischief at school and church. But you've got your differences. Your teachers only need to pay attention." Kevin scanned his bedroom. "What else do you think I should take?" His eyes fell on his video game system and laptop.

Inez slid off the bed. "You're next door." She placed her hands on her hips. "If you forgot something, come and get it." She left Kevin's room, shoulders square, nose in the air.

"Did I piss you off or something?" Kevin shouted to the open doorway.

Her fist appeared with the middle finger erect. The hand vibrated with intensity.

"Love you too, Inez."

"Jerk." And the fist was gone.

"Does this mean you won't carry my gaming system?"

# Chapter 4

Kevin and Ruby entered his parent's house through the rear door. Setting the empty laundry basket on the floor, Kevin pushed it towards the laundry room.

Donna kneaded a ball of dough. “Good, you’re here. Would you please go in and play a game with the girls?” She tucked the dough's edges under itself until it was round and taut and then placed it in a bowl. “Kevin, put the basket away. Don’t leave it there.”

Kevin sighed, disappointed she’d noticed. He grabbed the basket and put it with the others.

Mina, Tess, and Inez sat on the living room floor. Each girl had five cards. Even though the eleven-year-old triplets had similar facial features, their mannerisms and clothing styles were vastly different. Kevin never understood why people couldn’t tell them apart.

“What are you playing?” Grandma asked.

“Rummy,” Mina replied.

“Who’s winning?” Kevin asked

"Me, of course," Mina said, tossing her long black hair back, looking smug.

"It's no fun playing games with her," Inez said, pointing at Mina. "She always wins."

Tess nodded in agreement. "Please play with us."

"All right," Grandma said as she settled on the floor next to the girls. "Let's spice things up a little by adding another deck." She snapped and pointed at Kevin. He turned and looked in the cabinets until he found a blue-backed deck to go with the red one in play.

"But that's not how you play Rummy," Mina protested.

"We're not interested in rules; we're interested in having fun," Grandma said.

Tess nodded. "Yeah." She moved closer to Grandma and leaned on her.

Kevin handed the cards to Grandma and then sat between Mina and Inez.

Grandma added the blue deck to the red, shuffling the cards like a dealer from Vegas. She bridged the cards a few times and dealt seven to everyone. "Okay, to make this more interesting, we're using more cards per hand. All flushes and mates must be of the same color. So, if you have four Jacks, they all better be black or red. The same with your flushes. Understand?"

The girls said, "yes," in unison. Mina pouted.

"Good," Grandma said. She picked up her cards and spread them in her hand, arranging them to her liking. She smiled. "I have an excellent hand. Anyone interested in a bet?" She reached into her bra and pulled out a five-dollar bill.

"Grandma, you know Mom doesn't like betting," Mina scolded.

"Fine. Mina, you go first." She returned the bill, frowning.

The clanking of plates and cups on the dining table prompted Kevin to shout, "Mom, do you need help?"

"No, no. You're helping by playing with the girls."

"Okay," Kevin said under his breath. He wanted to move things along so that he could visit Annie.

A mumbled response came from the dining room, followed by the clatter of silverware.

"Leave her be, dear. If she wanted help, she would ask for it." Grandma nodded. "Your turn."

Kevin chuckled. "Am I going too slow?" He found Grandma's itch to play games and gamble almost comical. With slow deliberation, he arranged his cards and then pulled a new one from the draw pile. He looked at it then eased it in and out of his hand, placing it in different locations, only to put it into the discard pile. Each of his movements seemed to push Grandma deeper into a state of frustration and anxiety. "The look on your face is priceless," Kevin said. The girls laughed.

"Shush and play." A hint of a smile tugged on Grandma's lips.

Inez drew a card, and the game resumed with stifled giggles from the girls. They played a total of three hands, with Tess, Inez, and Grandma, each winning. As Grandma shuffled the next hand, Mom called everyone to the table.

"But Dad isn't home yet," Tess whined.

Mom entered the living room. "He said to get started without him."

"Okay, Mom," the girls whined in unison.

Roast chicken, garlic mashed potatoes, gravy, mixed vegetables, and freshly baked bread sat on the table. It smelled wonderful. The girls perched three-abreast on a bench with Kevin and Grandma sitting on the opposite seat. Mom sat closest to the kitchen.

Grandma grabbed the mashed potatoes to add a spoonful to her plate.

Mom cleared her throat, giving a piercing stare to Grandma. “Grace first.”

Grandma grunted, setting the bowl and ladle down. She took Kevin’s hand, then reached across the table to grasp Mina’s, completing the circle.

Mom said the traditional Catholic prayer, with Kevin and the girls joining in, “Bless us, O Lord, and these, thy gifts, which we are about to receive from Thy bounty. Through Christ, our Lord. Amen.”

Grandma mumbled a Wiccan prayer under her breath. “Corn and grain, meat and milk, upon the table before me. Gifts of life, bring sustenance and strength, I am grateful for all I have.”

If Mom heard what Grandma said, she gave no indication. “Okay, everyone, dig in.” She never approved of Grandma Ruby’s Wiccan practices, but she wouldn’t make a scene at dinner. Everyone tucked into the delicious food. Only the sounds of appreciation filled the room. Mom often dreamed of opening a restaurant or food truck. Kevin was confident she would be a success.

The front door opened with a thud and then reclosed. The girls brightened at the sound. "Daddy," they squealed, turning in their seats to race toward their father.

"Stay at the table and eat," Mom snapped.

"Aww." The girls turned back, frowning. They huddled together, talking in their secret language, a combination of simple syllables and hand gestures. Mom disapproved of the communication. Kevin suspected they used it openly to make her mad.

Everyone at the table ate quietly while they listened to the noises Dad made. He dropped his lunchbox and shoes near the door and shuffled down the hall into his bedroom. Drawers opened and closed. Zippers were undone. He farted, then stumbled into the kitchen, mumbling something unkind about Tom, who was his boss. The refrigerator opened, followed by the pop and hiss of a bottle top.

Dad entered the dining room, wearing grey sweats and looking exhausted. He kissed Mom on the cheek. "Dinner looks great, Donna." He passed the girls, patting them on the head, and sat at the table. Dad placed his beer next to his cup and reached for the chicken.

Mom grunted. "Jerry, you need to say grace."

Dad looked first to Mom and then Grandma Ruby, who sat next to him. He bowed his head and mumbled a prayer. Kevin didn't hear what prayer he said but suspected it was Wiccan. Dad grabbed the overflowing bowls and platters, piling meat and vegetables on his plate.

"So how was your day, dear?" Mom asked.

"Awful. My stupid boss wants us to work more hours." Dad shoved mashed potatoes into his mouth but continued to talk. Most of what he said was muffled and distorted by the food. He drank some beer then continued. "Fast, he wants, and accurate." He waved a drumstick in the air. "He has no clue. Fast I can do. Accurate I can do. But both?" Dad's laughter had a tinge of mania to it. "Accuracy always suffers when I increase speed." He stuffed the drumstick in his mouth and spoke around it. "The man is an idiot."

The girls giggled.

"Dad, you sound crazy," Mina said while she poked at her vegetables.

"Crazy?" Dad appeared offended. "I'll show you crazy." He crossed his eyes, flopped his hands around, and made grunting sounds.

The triplets giggled louder.

"That sounds like something I heard before. The mating call of a sasquatch." Grandma Ruby nodded. “That’s right. A sasquatch.” She leaned forward, toward the girls. “I saw it a couple of months ago, in the woods down the street.”

“Do you think this is an appropriate conversation for the girls?” Mom asked.

“I do. It’s vital information.” Grandma retorted.

Mom looked at the clock, then sighed. “Your Sundowners wouldn’t allow you to know real from imaginary. Not to mention your history of LSD.” She said the three letters like they were some cryptic code that only adults knew.

Grandma waved her hand casually, dismissing the comment. “It was late that night,” she continued telling the girls. “I was out for a walk. The stars and moon were beautiful. I saw the beast lurking behind a tree, at Miller Park, like it was trying to hide from me.”

“May Jesus save your soul,” Mom said to Grandma.

Grandma Ruby shot an angry glance at Mom, then turned her stare to the girls, with a smile and twinkle in her eyes. “The squatch was nothing compared to the gnome that lives in my garden. He tells me all kinds of secrets. Like the boy, Tess has a crush on.”

Tess’s eyes widened. The triplets gasped and moved their heads closer together.

"Okay, okay, enough of this nonsense. It's getting late. You all have school tomorrow. Now get ready for bed."

"Aww, Mom," Tess and Inez whined.

"She's right. You didn't finish your science homework," Mina said scathingly and pointed to Inez.

"Tattletale," Inez shouted, smacking Mina.

"Girls!" Mom barked. "You'll get your showers in, get ready for bed, and if there's enough time, you'll work on that assignment, Inez. In fact, I want her to shower first." She looked at the silent triplets through narrowed eyes. "Now, say goodnight to Grandma and Kevin."

The girls grumbled but quickly hugged Grandma and Kevin before running down the hall, arguing about who got the shower second.

"In two more years, they'll be teenagers." Mom put her face in her hands. "I don't know if I'll survive." She sniffled behind her fingers. "They set off smoke bombs in the boy's bathroom today. Yesterday, Tess and Inez copied Mina's science report. I thought I could go back to work soon, but I'm not so sure. Most days, I'm at their school talking to the principal or teachers."

Grandma Ruby frowned sympathetically at Mom. “Come on, Kevin. Let’s clean the table, and we can get out of Jerry and Donna’s hair.”

Kevin nodded in agreement. He wondered if moving out of the house helped Mom. She seemed more frazzled than before. But if he hadn’t, then she would be taking care of Grandma as well as the triplets.

# Chapter 5

The drive home was uneventful. Avalon was a quiet town of twenty thousand. Megan's father often referred to the city as a bedroom community. There were no factories or large businesses, which forced residents to either telecommute or work elsewhere. Still, Megan watched the rearview mirror and made sure she didn't have a tail.

Large trees hung over Megan's brick driveway, their autumn colors vivid red, yellow, and orange. The setting sun turned her white house to a soft pink. She clicked a button on her car's console, and the center garage door opened.

Her father's car was absent, which wasn't unusual; she figured he wouldn't be home for another hour. He worked in Chicago, and the commute time varied. Megan grabbed her gym bag, backpack, and the bug-out bag from under the car's passenger seat. She entered through the kitchen door by punching in the six-digit number.

As she walked in, she tossed her gym clothes in the laundry room hamper. The cleaning lady washed clothes twice a week. Megan never saw her, but the house had a distinct pine smell on cleaning day. The chemical smell at the gym was similar. She often wondered if the same service cleaned both places.

Megan set her bookbag on a stool in the breakfast nook, then untied her bugout bag, unrolling it into a flat mat with many pockets. She fetched the cleaning kit off the top of the refrigerator, where she left it two weeks before. She turned on the small kitchen television. The PBS channel was playing a repeat of *Nature - Worlds Most Wanted Animal*. The episode was about the pangolin, a small, bipedal anteater, whose scales are worth a fortune on the Chinese black market. The story initially thought the pangolin would become extinct quickly, but the adorable creature soon caught hearts everywhere, which produced laws to save the animal and its habitat.

Megan's phone rang.

"Hello."

"Good, I caught you. Did you go to the gym today?"

"Aerobics." Megan pulled her SIG Sauer P250 .40 caliber from a pocket in the bugout bag. She dropped the magazine, racked the slide to eject the round in the chamber, then field-stripped the pistol. Because the weapon stayed in the car, it was subject to vast temperature changes and humidity. Moisture and rust were ever-present enemies. The idea of a stainless pistol crossed her mind once, but the high shine would be a liability.

"I ought to go with you some time. What's that noise? Are you watching TV or working on your car's engine?"

"You can hear that? You know me and my science shows." Megan set the gun chamber on the table quietly to lessen Bonnie's growing suspicions.

"Sure do. What is it this time? Wait, let me guess, something on PBS?"

"That's where the best shows are. I love *Nova* and *Nature*." Megan ran a microfiber cloth over the disassembled pistol, picking up trace amounts of moisture.

"Did you get a chance to look over the English assignment yet?" Bonnie asked.

"It's not due until next week. I'm working on math and science tonight." With a cloth-covered dowel rod, she plunged the chamber.

"We're supposed to work on it together."

"I know." Megan's father wouldn't allow Bonnie in the house. "What are you thinking?"

"Can you come over tomorrow night?" Bonnie's voice went higher as if expecting a negative answer.

"I'll have to ask. But I don't see why not."

"Uh, okay." Bonnie sounded sad as if Megan already said no. "I gotta go," she said, and the call ended.

Megan sighed. She would find a way to work with Bonnie on the English assignment. Megan reassembled the SIG Sauer P250 and slid it back into its pocket. She rifled through the other items to make sure they were there. Megan had three passports, with her picture and three names. The photos would need replacing soon. For money, there were six different forms of currency and numerous credit cards. The cards and the passports were for emergencies. They could only be used once, and they were expensive to replace.

Inside a pouch were a few precious-metal coins and gems, small items that could be swallowed and retrieved later. Lastly, a bowie knife with a hollow handle. Inside were waterproof matches, paracord, and a thin draw saw with two pull loops that could double as a garrote.

When she was little, she thought everyone behaved the way her father did, with fear and paranoia driving every move. But, as Megan aged and saw more of the world, she realized that her father was one of a kind. Was he right? Was there a price on his and, by proxy, her head? Did the Russian mafia really want them dead? Or was he overreacting? Did she lie to her friends because she was protecting them and herself? Or was her father delusional?

Megan wasn't sure, but she was afraid to find out. What if her father was right? What if Megan broke their seclusion, and Artem was killed as a result? She shuddered at the thought of losing her father. Even though he could be cold and distant, Megan still loved him. He and Nikolai were all she had. Her mother died when Megan was two. She didn't remember her, except for the smell of floral perfume and the sound of her lilting voice. Her father implied the Russian mafia had something to do with her death.

She rolled up the bug-out bag and set it in her bookbag, trading it with her school laptop and a library science book. Megan opened the computer, pulled up the school website, and began her math homework. She paused when she heard the garage door open, and Artem's car drove into the garage.

He entered through the kitchen. "Dobryy vecher moy sladkly," Artem said, greeting his daughter in Russian. He patted her head like any doting father. His eyes flickered to the gun cleaning kit. "Please put that away when you are done. If anyone saw that…" He sighed, like a parent who told their disobedient child the same thing hundreds of times.

Even though no one came to their house to see the kit, Megan obeyed. "Of course, Father." She collected the equipment and took it into the pantry, where she pushed a small screw and listened for the click. The back wall moved slightly. She pulled the door open and walked down a set of spiral stairs.

This section of the basement had guns on the walls and shelving filled with ammunition. The walls and ceiling were lined with two-inch steel plates to protect from incoming projectiles, including EMP's. The room was a faraday cage; no listening equipment could penetrate the steel barrier. It was a safe room for ten people, not that anyone was ever home to use it.

On the wall near the stairs was a security panel to control critical lifesaving systems. At a push of a button, all the windows would release a steel curtain for complete protection from outside assault. Another regulated the sprinkler system in case of fire. Still another released sleeping gas to fill the first-floor rooms. Megan considered the overabundant protections, suspecting they would never be used. She set the cleaning kit on a file cabinet and returned to the kitchen and breakfast nook to finish her homework.

Artem hummed and danced as he moved around the kitchen, looking for ingredients and tools. The sizzle of meat and the knife cutting through lettuce and tomato told her they were having hamburgers. Her stomach grumbled in response.

Megan smiled. Her father might be strict, but he was a clown while cooking. Artem flicked the salt and pepper shakers off his biceps and caught them. Once and awhile, he'd look to see if she watched. Artem was in his late forties, but his blonde wavy hair didn't show a lick of grey, giving him a younger appearance.

"Dorogoy, will you come to the museum before mid-November? I have picked a few wonderful items for Halloween and Day of the Dead. I'd very much like you to see them." Artem finished cooking the patties and assembled two burgers, then carried the plates to Megan.

Megan pushed her homework aside and attacked the hamburger ravenously. Artem brought two glasses of milk and set them by the plates.

"Hungry? Did Nikolai work you hard this afternoon?"

Megan nodded, her mouth full, savoring the juicy meat and sweet veggies.

"He told me your skills with a blade have become quite good."

Megan grunted. Nikolai didn't seem all that pleased from her point of view. She swallowed. "There was a Mr. Smith there who's teaching wiring on Wednesday. Do you think I need this class? I've already had training with traps and bombs."

"I will speak to Nikolai." Artem tapped the edge of his plate. "Was Mr. Smith American or Russian?"

Megan shrugged. "I don't know. He didn't talk. He just stood there, but I think he's ex-military."

Artem finished eating in silence. When they finished, he picked up the plates and cups and put them in the dishwasher. He left the kitchen and went into the den.

He returned a few minutes later with a briefcase. “I wanted to show you some of the interesting objects I gathered for this year’s Halloween Exhibit.” Artem worked for the Field Museum in Chicago as a curator. His line of knowledge was Neolithic tools and art. For the past few years, he was responsible for the Halloween exhibit. He scoured the world for objects and folklore that surrounded traditional Halloween aspects. Witch’s items for casting spells, tarot cards, cauldrons, wands, spell books, crystal balls, and the like. Voodoo and zombies were also a big draw for the museum. For Day of the Dead, skulls, coffins, and Latino art were favorites. Sometimes he found extraordinary items, most of which were from other countries. These items had to be borrowed or purchased. Either way, it cost the museum cash or trade.

Artem popped open his briefcase and pulled out some pictures. Megan took the papers and fliers. Some collectors purposely advertised, making their items available for museums to rent. They created glossy flyers with beautiful images to entice museums, but many of the items were props from movies and were not real witchcraft or voodoo items.

Megan tapped a picture of a broom, wand, and cauldron. “I think these came from a movie.”

Artem frowned. “I was afraid of that.” He drew a red line through the picture. “I will remember for next year.”

“It’s already on display?”

He shrugged sheepishly. “It’s only for this month, and Halloween items are subject to opinion. You really ought to come and see the display. It is quite grand. You might even be proud of your old man.”

“I *am* proud of you.” Megan squeezed her father’s hand, smiling up at him. She looked through a few more photos before spotting an anomaly. “This is from an even older movie.” It was a shield made of what looked like dragon scales and a long lance.

The red line made its way across that picture too.

“This is neat. I’ve not seen anything like this before.” Megan pointed to a picture of many fist-sized stones with what appeared to be cuneiform or ogham writing on them. “What are they?”

“Those are protection stones. Witches used them when casting a strong spell. It would protect them from retaliation from a rival witch."

"Really? That isn't how witchcraft works." Megan scowled at him.

"I know, but that is what the brochure says." He tapped the paragraph under the photograph. "Does it matter?" Within the article was the headshot of a beautiful Chinese woman. Under the picture were the name Tai Lu and her contact information.

"Yes! You should be educating the public, not spreading lies."

"Because your opinion matters, I'll figure out what these stones are and put a disclaimer next to their exhibit. I'm sure their real purpose is far less interesting." Artem rubbed under his nose.

Megan laughed. "Where did they come from?"

"China. Tibet, to be exact."

"I didn't know Chinese had witches. I thought they were shaman."

"You can't think that way. The collector is from China. The stones could be from anywhere. I'd love to translate the inscription." He sounded wistful. "When we rent items like this, we are unable to touch them. If they are damaged, I could lose my job." He reached in the briefcase and pulled out velvet gloves. "I am not allowed to touch anything unless I'm wearing these."

Megan touched the gloves; their white surface shifted color slightly when she moved the piling with and against the grain.

"Was there anything else in the photos that caught your eye?"

"You know me. I love a beautiful spellbook." Megan pointed to a photo of *The Green Witch's Grimoire*. The leather-bound book was aged and a little battered, but that was what drew her eye. "Imagine what this ancient book has seen."

# Chapter 6

Kevin opened the adjoining gate, which squeaked in the moist air. "Shhh." Grandma held up her hand. "Do you hear that?" Frogs and toads sang approval to the humid evening. Perhaps it was their farewell to the last warmth of summer. She moved to one of her raised beds. "I can hear him."

"Him? Who?" Kevin strained his eyes, looking into the shadows of twilight.

"Benny, of course." She moved the leaves of a hosta plant. "There he is." She squatted, wrestled with something, and then stood with a big fat toad in her palm. Grandma talked to it, nose to nose. "What's wrong, Benny?"

"Burrup," said the toad.

"Can't it wait until morning? I'm with my grandson."

"Burrup," demanded the toad.

"Now?"

"Burrup," repeated the toad.

"Okay, okay." Grandma gently placed the toad at the base of the hosta plant and rearranged the leaves. She turned her attention to Kevin. "We can't waste any time. You heard what he said." Grandma rushed into the house.

Kevin rolled his eyes. He sighed and slowly followed grandma inside, wondering if her dementia took her over the cliffs of insanity. Cookbooks and recipe cards were scattered across the kitchen cabinets. In the living room, books and magazines were haphazardly tossed to the floor.

"Found them!" she cried, holding a deck of cards triumphantly in the air. She removed the rubber band and pulled her bobbed hair into a ponytail. Grandma walked toward the kitchen, shuffling the cards, bringing them to her lips, and mumbling.

She sat at the small two-person table, spoke to the cards, then with eyes closed, drew three, laying them in a row—first, the Tower. Second, Death. Third, the Ace of Cups. She placed the deck on the table and opened her eyes. "Death? That can't be right." Her hands trembled.

"Grandma," Kevin implored. "Sorry…Ruby. You told me once that the Death card was good and didn't mean real death."

"Did I?" Grandma Ruby's hands twisted in her lap. "I don't remember." She sighed. "I hate getting old."

"Don't you have a book?"

"Yes. But I don't need it. I can remember. The position of the first card signifies the past." She pointed to the tower card. "The second represents the present." Her finger touched the death card and lingered. "and the third defines the future."

"I'd feel better if we got your book and made sure."

She bit her lip. "You're right." Grandma stood and went upstairs. At the top landing, she paused and looked to her bedroom on the left. Then turned towards Kevin's room.

"Where are you going?"

"The attic."

"I was just up there; it's pretty full. Will you be able to find the book?"

"Sure, sure. I marked the boxes." Grandma Ruby waved her hand to dismiss the question and walked through Kevin's room into the attic. She went straight to two cardboard boxes marked with a blue star. "Here you take this one. I'll take the other."

"To where?"

"Your bedroom." Grandma took her time walking down the creaking attic steps. "I need your help, so it's best you learn about Wicca."

They sat on his bed and rifled through the boxes. Grandma found the Tarot book and flipped through the colorful pages. "Here's the page we need." She set it between them on the bed and pointed to the diagram. "The three-card spread is for the past, the present, and the future. I thought I remembered that right."

Kevin leaned forward. Under the three-card spread was another picture described as the Celtic Cross. It had a total of eleven cards in the layout. Each card represented part of the problem or solution to a specific question. He was fascinated. Could cards tell you your future?

Grandma Ruby picked up the book and skimmed through the pages to find the descriptions of the cards she drew. She marked each page with her fingers. "The tower stands for disruption and unexpected events. I pulled it first, so it describes the past. I think this is for the loss of my beloved Joseph and my dementia diagnosis; both events have disrupted many things." She looked at the next page. "I pulled death second, which represents the present. It means change, not death like you said. Your moving into my house has changed my life. Change for you and the entire family too." She sighed and looked at the last page. "And the last location is to predict the future, the Ace of Cups. That card signifies love. Not just any love but finding new love. I haven't been in love since Grandpa Joe." Grandma Ruby's eyes misted, and a tear rolled down her cheek.

Kevin stared. Unable or unwilling to see her as a person who desired physical love as much as he did. He always saw her as Grandma, a position in his childhood that transcended that need. A person who thrived on the hugs, kisses, and devotion of her grandchildren.

"I know that the Death card isn't bad. But I might forget that tomorrow." She sighed. "Kevin, I need you to help me when I forget and panic like I did tonight."

"What about Mom? She would freak if she knew. You know how religious she is."

"Nonsense. There is nothing evil here. Look at it, you'll see. Besides, you don't have to tell her. It could be our secret." Grandma jumped to her feet, excitedly. "I think I'm going to make something for dessert."

Kevin looked at the alarm clock. "It's almost nine."

"So? I'm hungry." Ruby trotted downstairs, a spring in her step. From the banging and clanging of pots and pans, she was preparing to feed an army.

Kevin's phone rang. He pulled it out of his pocket. "Hello?"

"Can you get away?" Annie asked, her voice low and husky.

Kevin swallowed. "I don't know. Grandma's upset, and I'm worried about her."

"Aww, aren't you the sweet grandson?" Annie's voice changed; she didn't sound sincere. "So, what's going on?"

"She's making a dessert, and from the sound of it, she's making it from scratch. While she's doing that, I'm looking through some of her old magic things." Kevin patted the boxes.

"Magic? Like abracadabra?"

"I'm not entirely sure." Kevin opened one of the boxes and started to remove items. "I've got a lava lamp, a pipe, a mirror, feathers, dried roses, a bag filled with rocks, and another filled with herbs."

"Rocks? Herbs?"

Kevin dumped the rocks out of the bag. "The rocks look like crystals, green, white, and there is a big purple one, like the one you wear. The herbs are in a bundle; I don't know what they're for."

"Is it pot?" Annie prompted, sounding excited.

Kevin opened the bag and sniffed. "No, I don't think so. The smell reminds me of New Age Gifts and More. You know the store downtown that sells books, crystals, and incense?" He pulled out a wooden box. "I found a bunch of small candles in all kinds of colors."

"What are they for?"

"I don't know."

"Don't you have some books that will tell you?"

"Yea, that's the other box." He stood and hovered over the smaller box. "Well, tonight, we used the Tarot book." He absently patted the book on the bed. "There's *Healing Herbs*, *Candle Magic*, *Mirror Magic*, *Wand Magic*, *Witches Grimoire*, *Book of Shadows*, *Gemstones*, *Spirit Animals*, *Gods and Goddesses*, and *Herbal Grimoire*. The other books are plain, no titles."

Annie chuckled. "Are any of them her diary?"

Kevin looked at the untitled books, remembering Ruby's comment about love, feeling a bit queasy by the idea that Grandma and Grandpa would need a diary. "That's a disturbing thought. I'm afraid to look."

"I'd let you read my diary."

"Would you?"

"Absolutely," Annie said. "I guess you'll have to come over to see." Her voice cracked.

Kevin shifted the phone to his other ear. "I'll call you after Grandma goes to bed. Then we can talk, and maybe I can come to see you."

"Promise?"

"I promise, Annie."

"Okay." She hung up.

Kevin put his phone on the bed. He picked up the *Book of Shadows* and opened it to a random page. He skimmed the words and flipped pages. Rituals and spells filled the paper. Ruby dog-eared some pages and marked sections with a rainbow of highlighter colors, stickers, symbols, and arrows. Other areas had notes on the page edges. Her handwriting was tight and clean.

He put the *Book of Shadows* down and tried another book, *Gemstones*. High quality, glossy pictures of stones, gems, and crystals filled the thick, heavy pages. The book seemed to cover every rock found on the planet. About halfway through the book, in the center, near the spine, a section of pages had a square cut out. Within was a wooden box with the words "protection stone" written on it.

A beautiful picture of a lapis lazuli was cut nearly in half, and the words under the photo were damaged. It appeared that the box was inserted into the book after printing.

"Kevin, dessert is done," Grandma shouted up the stairs.

He closed the book, left it on his bed, and went downstairs.

Grandma left the hot pan of brownies on the stove. "Would you please cut a couple of slices and put them on plates? I'll get the ice cream." She opened the basement door, turned on the light, and disappeared down the stairs.

Kevin cut the brownies into squares and placed the warm treat on the plates. They puddled chocolate sauce. The oven clicked on. Kevin turned it off, then looked toward the basement door and the sound of footsteps.

Ruby carried a plastic gallon bucket of ice cream.

"Grandma, you left the oven on."

"Did I? Wouldn't be the first time." She laughed. "It's never been a problem. I always notice sooner or later." She set the ice cream on the countertop and pulled off the lid.

"The brownies aren't done." Kevin pointed to the pooling sauce on the plates.

"That is the way it is supposed to be, dear." Grandma placed a scoop of vanilla ice cream on top of the dessert. "Try it. You might like it."

She pushed a plate and spoon into Kevin's hands, then took one and sat at the table.

The ice cream melted, joining with the chocolate sauce at the bottom of the plate. Kevin sat at the table. Reluctantly he ate a bit of brownie and ice cream. The chocolate combined with the vanilla well. Kevin was surprised by how delicious it was.

Grandma cleaned her plate, set it in the sink, then took the ice cream back to the basement.

"Ruby, I forgot something at home. I'm going to run over there." Kevin placed his empty plate into the sink and then left out the back door.

# Chapter 7

Inez sat at the dining room table, completing her homework, grumbling. Mina and Tess sat at the other end of the table with a chessboard between them. Mina was winning, of course, but Tess didn't care. She pushed her pawns at Mina. It appeared that she was trying to pin Mina's pieces, not take them. Mina slaughtered the pawns with no sign of mercy. Tess rolled her eyes at Kevin as if begging him to save her.

"Where's Mom and Dad?" he asked the triplets.

"Dad's in the den. Mom's—around," Inez said, shrugging. "Wanna see some magic? I can make her appear if I stop doing my homework."

"Don't you dare, young lady." Mom swept into the room.

"It was an empty threat, Mom. Kevin's looking for you." Inez smiled and blinked at her as if to say, "I would never do such a thing."

Mom looked at Kevin. "What's wrong?"

"Grandma made a dessert…"

"You got dessert? Not fair! Where's mine?" Erupted the complaints simultaneously from the triplets.

"Would you hush? I'm trying to talk to Mom."

Mom used her hand to indicate that Kevin should continue.

"Well, I think the brownie was underdone. It oozed all over the plate. And she left the oven on."

"Did you eat it?" Inez asked.

"Yes."

"Did it taste bad?" Tess asked

"No, it was quite good."

"Then it was her lava cake, not a brownie." Mina finished. "She loves to make that recipe. Bring some over next time."

"What about the oven?"

"I've left the oven on too." Mom shrugged. "Especially if something distracted me. Did she get a call or email or something that might have bothered her?"

Kevin nodded. The death card messed with her, but he knew better than to mention Grandma's Wiccan practices. Not to Mom.

"This is why we wanted you to help with her. I can't help your grandma; I have the girls and their after-school activities. Plus, we can't afford a caregiver." Mom smiled apologetically. "We're going to pay you to help Ruby with little things around the house and to keep her safe. You did well, telling me about the oven, but all by itself, it doesn't mean much. Hopefully, between you and her medications, we can keep her out of a home. I think once you get into the rhythm of living with her and her crazy habits, it'll be like having your own apartment."

"Yea, I suppose," Kevin said, feeling like he tattled on Grandma over nothing. "That's why I agreed to this idea from the beginning."

"Good, good." Mom looked from Kevin to the girls. "Why don't you and Ruby come over for supper every night? I don't think the girls are ready for you to move out. And it'll give you a chance to keep me apprised of what is going on."

"Good idea," Kevin admitted.

"You ought to get back home. The girls need to get to bed."

"Wave to us from your new bedroom, Kevin," Inez requested.

"Yea," agreed Tess and Mina.

"Take your toothbrush; I'm sure you forgot it." Mom narrowed her eyes, knowing well that her son would prefer his teeth fall out than be minty clean.

Kevin stepped into the kitchen. The house was quiet and dark. The television's glow brought Kevin into the living room where Grandma sat in a recliner watching a drama. Rapscallion slept on a shelf behind the couch, his white fur capturing the colorful flashes.

Grandma hit mute on the remote. “What did you forget?”

Kevin shook his toothbrush and a bottle of shampoo. “I’m going to take a shower then go to bed.”

“Well, goodnight then.” She clicked the remote, and sound filled the room.

Kevin kissed Grandma Ruby on the head and went to his room. He opened the heavy curtain and waved to his sisters. They waved back excitedly. He closed the curtain, gathered the shampoo and toothbrush, and left his room to take a shower.

Upon returning, he began to box the books and items on his bed. But curiosity got the better of him. He examined everything more closely before packing them away.

Inside the *Book of Shadows*, there seemed to be an organization of color to the comments.

Green ink was used for healing spells. Beside them were notes and initials and dates, usually followed by another comment and year. The second notation indicated the usefulness of the incantation or herb.

Ruby used red ink for love and purple ink for protection spells. Purple seemed to be on every page, followed by the initials M.I.T. Mina, Inez, and Tess? Kevin wondered. He decided that it was impossible. The date following the initials would have made them weeks old. Some of the dates were before they were born.

Kevin finished clearing the bed of Wicca objects, stuffing everything back into their boxes. Something tugged in his subconscious mind. He returned to the purple comments written in the margins. Stretching out on the bed, he flipped through pages. Gradually his eyes glazed, and he fell asleep, holding the *Book of Shadows*.

Kevin strolled to Annie's house and knocked on the door. After a moment, the door opened. Annie's mother wore a bathrobe and had a cup of coffee in her hand.

"Good morning."

"Morning," Kevin said. "Is Annie home?"

"You just missed her. She left for school about fifteen minutes ago. She was distraught, saying someone was supposed to call her last night. That wasn't you, was it?" Annie's mother narrowed her eyes, studying Kevin.

"Oh, no!" He turned, jumped down the porch steps, and ran toward the school. Before Kevin completed a block, he was panting. He slowed to a walk, feeling embarrassed. He was young; running shouldn't be difficult.

Kevin arrived at school before the first bell. Annie was outside in Commons Square, a park-like area with benches, tables, and trees. She wore a short skirt and ruffled shirt, the one that opened and showed off her cleavage if she wanted. She talked with Tony, her ex-boyfriend, who leaned against a maple tree. A portion of the leaves had turned flaming red, reminding everyone that it was October.

Tony stared at Kevin while talking to Annie. Her face was in profile. He nodded in response to a question. She smiled, then rubbed his chest. Annie turned to look at Kevin as if she knew he was there. She laughed and leaned into Tony.

Kevin turned away from the scene, entering the school. "I know she wants to piss me off.

But why, Tony? He's such an ass." Randomly he punched a closed locker.

"Kevin Arkis, to the office, now!"

Kevin jumped, then looked to the voice. Principal Walters stared at him from under his bushy eyebrows. "Yes, Principal Walters. I'm sorry, Principal Walters." Kevin walked to the office and waited impatiently.

The first bell rang. Everyone entered the front doors and walked toward the office before going left or right down the halls to their classes. Kevin was on display in the glass-encompassed waiting room.

Principal Walters removed his sports jacket and stood in front of Kevin. "Are you having a bad day?"

Kevin nodded.

"That is no reason to destroy school property."

"I didn't destroy anything." Kevin tried to defend himself. "I just punched a locker, instead of punching…a fellow student." His shoulders fell.

"I see. Do you have your temper under control, Mr. Arkis?"

"Yes, I believe I do," Kevin said.

"Good." Principal Walters looked at the clock. "The second bell hasn't rung. Get to your first class." The principal turned to leave, then paused. "Let's not meet in the hallway like that again, Mr. Arkis."

Kevin nodded. He entered Psychology in a rush, just as the second bell rang. Tony sat in the front row, flanked by Chad and Vin, his best friends. The last thing Kevin wanted was to be in the same room as Tony.

Vin and Chad laughed, punching Tony's shoulder as if congratulating him.

Kevin moved to the rear of the class.

Mrs. Anderson came into the room and announced, "We have a section review, short answer test today." She pulled a stack of papers and handed them to the head of each desk row. "Please take one and pass the rest back. You'll have the entire hour to finish. Take your time and be sure of your answers. This test will be weighed heavily on this semester's grade."

Kevin rolled his eyes. All he had on his mind was Annie, not Carl Jung, Sigmund Freud, or Friedrich Nietzsche. He pulled out a pen in preparation but doubted he would do well.

# Chapter 8

Megan parked her blue Honda in front of Bonnie's house. She turned off the engine, walked onto the porch, and rang the doorbell.

Bonnie opened the door. "You know I walk to school. Why pick me up?" She backed up and waved Megan in. Bonnie was blonde and almost a foot taller than Megan's five foot four. She wore a flower print shirt and tight-fitting jeans.

"I wanted to make plans to work on the English assignment."

"I have a phone." Bonnie shook the phone, as emphasis, then put it in a small purse that hung from her shoulder.

"I wanted to see you. Talking on the phone is so impersonal."

"That sounds like something your father would say."

Megan shrugged. "The apple doesn't fall far."

Bonnie laughed. "It sure doesn't," She picked up her book bag from the counter and headed out the door. "What are you thinking?"

"I'm free most nights between five and seven, except this Wednesday," Megan said. They climbed into her car.

Bonnie sat in the seat and leaned into the center console, popping it open. She pushed the passenger seat back to give her long legs space. "Tonight works for me." She shrugged. "Thursday and Friday are open, too, as far as I can remember." Bonnie closed the center console and shoved the exposed items back under the seat. "Sorry about that. My legs are too long." She smiled sheepishly.

Megan licked her lips, her eyes darted to the floorboards under Bonnie's long legs, then to the keys. "Tonight, it is." She started her car, and they drove the three blocks to school. If Bonnie saw the bugout bag, she didn't recognize what it was. *But what if she had?* Megan parked the car, and they walked toward the school together.

The first bell rang. They entered the school side by side, surrounded by a mass of students. Kevin Arkis was in the office, sitting in the fishbowl. Bonnie elbowed her in the ribs. Megan couldn't help but smile. He sure was cute.

Principal Walters seemed to enjoy showing off his latest naughty child by leaving him or her in the widow-enhanced lobby. As if Principal Walters could instill good behavior by putting bad on display.

Megan shook her head. “We are in high school, not grade school; I wonder if he knows.”

A few nearby students snickered.

Bonnie whispered in Megan’s ear. “What happened? He doesn’t get into trouble.”

Megan shrugged.

They often compared notes on Kevin. It was silly to behave like a lovestruck freshman when they were seniors, but for now, they only had other seniors to occupy their free time.

“Bathroom,” Megan said as she slipped out of the stream of students. Bonnie followed.

Annie Brown leaned on a sink, getting as close as possible to the mirror, putting on eyeliner.

Megan’s lip curled involuntarily. She shot a glance at Bonnie, who nodded. They each took a stall, out of sight of the mirror, and closed their doors stealthily. Hopefully, the bitch would leave soon.

Annie’s phone rang. She looked around the bathroom then answered it. “Yea?” there was a pause. “No, I didn’t.” Pause. “Yes, I know. Soon, I’ll have him.” Pause, then a sigh. “Yes, the sisters. Look, I got it, okay?" She turned off her phone, checked her lipstick, and left.

Megan and Bonnie exited their stalls simultaneously. Bonnie was laughing behind her hand.

"Did you hear?" Megan asked.

"Oh, yea. Annie's got a new sucker on the line." Bonnie rolled her eyes.

"I wonder who's stupid enough to date her? I thought she had the reputation of a black widow."

"Don't forget succubus," Bonnie added, frowning.

"Exactly." Megan shook her head. "How does she do it?" She pulled her hair back into a ponytail, using the mirror to catch the strays.

"Must be magic." Bonnie's eyebrows furrowed in thought.

"I know that look," Megan said.

"What?" Bonnie gave Megan an innocent expression.

"You want revenge."

Bonnie smiled. "I do, oh God, I do. But how?"

"You could steal this boy she has on the line," Megan suggested.

"No, that won't work. Once Annie has her claws in them, they're puppets. Look at Tony." Bonnie swallowed hard. "And Chris."

Megan frowned, placing a hand on Bonnie's shoulder. "I miss Chris too." She dropped her hand. "And I used to like Tony. I remember when he was sweet."

"Exactly, we have to do something to Annie." Bonnie cracked her knuckles. "Maybe we ought to break her pretty face."

"I like the way you think." Megan nodded. "Come on. We're going to be late for first class."

# Chapter 9

By lunch, Kevin was a wreck. He messed up the Chemistry Lab as well as the Psychology test. And he lost Annie, the one girl he thought he could love and marry.

He sat alone at a table with his hardly touched pizza. He gazed at Jarrett and Matt, longing to sit with them and talk about the latest video game. Since Kevin started dating Annie and ignored their warnings, they refused to acknowledge his existence. Maybe he could win back their trust. Kevin poked the rectangular-shaped pizza with his fork, hardly interested in eating.

Annie slid into the bench beside him. She touched his lips with her finger. "You know Kevin. You made me upset last night. You promised me that you were going to call, maybe even show up in my bedroom. But you didn't. I felt awful falling for your empty promises."

"I know, and I'm sorry. I have all these new responsibilities, and I failed you. Grandma needs me." Kevin sighed, feeling like his explanation was inadequate. "I'm sorry. I'll do better."

"I forgive you, Kevin. This time." She turned to face him, displaying her cleavage. The purple charm on her necklace nestled between her breasts. She reached up and brushed his cheek with her fingertips. "Will you come to see me tonight?"

Kevin felt a weight lift from his shoulders, and the pit of his stomach unclenched. "Oh, yeah, tonight, no matter what."

Annie smiled at him, looking through her lashes. Kevin was hers.

After school, Annie and Kevin strolled to her house, hand in hand. They walked along the bike path at Miller Park. From the wooden bridge that spanned thirty feet across Miller Pond, they stopped to laugh at the antics of the ducks and geese.

He fell into the depth of her eyes, pulling her close, he kissed her passionately. She ensnared his senses. He would do anything she asked.

Annie pushed him away. "Not here, Romeo." She looked towards the playground where children played, and parents watched. "Let's go home." She took his hand and guided him away from the busy park. Her determined stride and pace slowed at the sight of her house.

Her mother sat on the porch. "Where have you been? You were supposed to be home thirty minutes ago. You forgot about your appointment, didn't you? We have to leave now if we're to salvage it. Hurry!"

Kevin leaned in and hugged her with the unsaid promise of seeing her after dark. As he walked home, his backpack felt heavy, like lead weights slowed him down. Every step away from his true love was grueling. He mounted the porch steps to grandma's house and opened the door.

Grandma lay back in her recliner as usual, but something was wrong. Her face contorted in a grimace. Rapscallion sat in Ruby's lap. His emerald eyes were transfixed on her as if he were trying to help.

"Grandma, what's wrong?" Kevin dropped his backpack by the door and rushed to her side. Thoughts of Annie fluttered from his mind like autumn leaves.

"I fell, and I think I broke my wrist." Her swollen arm had an off-putting purple color.

"When? Where?"

"This morning, in the basement."

"You've been home all day with a broken arm?"

Ruby chuckled. "It's a funny story. I was harvesting my mushrooms, and I slipped in a puddle. I landed on my hand and didn't think much of it. But as the day went on, I noticed some swelling and discoloration, so I took a pain pill from the medicine cabinet." Ruby waved her unhurt arm. "and in no time, I fell asleep in my chair."

"Why didn't you call Mom? Or an ambulance?"

"Well, I just woke up now when you stomped on the porch." Ruby shrugged like a child who did something wrong. "Can you drive me to the ER?"

"Of course. I need to run to Mom's and let her know we won't make it to dinner."

"Take your time. I'm not going anywhere." Ruby laid her head back. Her face ashen and contorted. With her good hand, she stroked Rapscallion's fur.

Kevin ran next door. The last thing he wanted to do was take his time. He made a promise to Annie, if he messed up again tonight, he would lose her forever. Probably to Tony, the worthless jerk.

He burst into the kitchen. "Mom, Mom."

"Laundry room, dear."

"Grandma fell. I need to take her to the hospital."

Mom looked up from folding a towel. "What happened?"

"She slipped and fell. I think she broke her wrist."

Mom's eyes flashed. "Why didn't she call me? I could've helped her."

"She said she took a pain pill and fell asleep."

Mom grunted. "Find out what kind and let the attending physician know so they don't give her anything that might interact. Also, let them know about her dementia medications too. Might want to take all her medication bottles, so you don't have to write it all down."

"Okay, thanks, Mom." Kevin was out the door and back to Grandma's.

Kevin snuck into her bathroom to collect medications. Inside the mirrored cabinet were many different bottles. He knew the three drugs she took for dementia. Unknown pills filled the other containers. He tossed them all into a bag, in case one of them was the pain pill. Kevin returned to the living room. "Can you stand?"

"Rap, get down, please." The white cat jumped off her lap and moved to the couch.

Grandma held out her good hand. "It'll be faster if you help."

Kevin pulled and was surprised by how little she weighed. He guided her out of the house and to the car. The drive to the hospital was quiet except for Grandma Ruby's sudden inhale of breath whenever there was a bump in the road.

A plump lady sat at the Emergency Room admitting desk. She set her magazine aside as they approached. Her stern stare settled on Ruby's pain-contorted face. "What happened?"

"Broke my arm," Grandma said through clenched teeth. "And this idiot doesn't know how to drive softly." She struck Kevin with her good hand.

"I said I was sorry."

"Name and birthdate." The woman prompted. grandma rattled off the information the woman needed to check her in and start the paperwork. "Okay, please have a seat."

"You picked a good day to fall." Kevin nodded to the mostly empty waiting room. An elderly gentleman and a small family with a sick baby were the only other patients. After thirty minutes of waiting, a nurse appeared and called "Ruby Arkis." She and Kevin went from the waiting room to a patient room, where they continued to wait. Kevin sat in a hard plastic chair, and Grandma laid back in the bed and drowsed.

A nurse in blue scrubs came in and took Grandma's vitals. She looked at Kevin. "I'll need to know the medications she's currently taking."

Kevin produced the bag of medication. "I am positive she takes these three for her dementia." He set three bottles on the small table next to the bed. "But she told me she took a pain pill, and I don't know which one it is." He dumped the rest of the bottles on the bed between Grandma's feet.

The nurse frowned. She looked at a few of the bottles and set them aside. "These are expired, and not just by months, by years. They should be destroyed." She frowned at Kevin. "You need to figure out what she needs and get rid of the rest." The nurse shook a bottle. "This pill interacts with her dementia medication. Who is responsible for her?"

"I guess I am," Kevin said, feeling overwhelmed.

"You?" The nurse tilted her head and looked at him again. "How old are you?"

"Eighteen."

The nurse looked surprised. “You’re taking care of her all by yourself? Have you finished high school?”

Kevin shrugged. “I’m taking care of her, but I’m still in school. A senior, I’ll graduate this spring.” He swallowed hard then continued in a rush. “My parents live next door. So if there are problems, we can get help.”

“I see.” She sighed. “Well, let’s get these meds sorted out now.” The nurse pulled up Grandma’s chart on the computer and cross-referenced her prescribed medication with the bottles on the bed. She made a pile of the ones that were not needed, expired, or interacted with her current prescriptions. “I’ll have the attending physician double-check.” The nurse turned to leave. “A technician will be in soon to take her to x-ray.”

After nearly four hours in the ER, Grandma gained a bright pink cast and a prescription for painkillers. The doctor and nurse reduced the medication Kevin brought in to six bottles. The doctor wouldn’t discharge Ruby until she and Kevin told the doctor what her pills were for and what time she needed to take them.

"I'm hungry," Grandma complained when Kevin pulled out of the hospital parking lot.

"Me too." Kevin agreed. "What sounds good?"

"Burgers." She grinned. "Something better than a drive-through. I'm buying."

"Deal." Kevin pulled into a nearby family restaurant called Sophie's. The diner was a family favorite. When he was younger, Mom, Dad, and the girls would stop for pancakes after church. Sometimes friends from the congregation would join them. He helped Grandma ease into a booth then slid in across from her.

When their burgers arrived, she pointed to her cast and pushed the plate toward Kevin. "Would you please cut up my sandwich?" As he cut, she dipped her fries in ketchup and slurped them from her fingers. "Would you cast a spell for me?"

"Excuse me?" Kevin looked over his shoulder. If anyone he knew heard her, the news would get back to his mother.

"Would you cast a spell of protection for me?" Grandma Ruby gestured to her broken arm with ketchup covered fingers. "So, I don't get hurt again?" She looked at him sideways and then continued eating.

"I don't know anything about spells," he said quietly, leaning close to the table. Kevin looked around for familiar faces as he tried to hide in his seat. His eyes caught on the nearest table. Did he know them? Did they know him?

"Nonsense. You have all my spell books and my Grimoires." Her voice raised. "My tarot cards too. You can make any spell you wish. And I need a protection spell."

Kevin wanted to hide under the table. "Grandma…Shhh," he whined. "Okay, okay, I'll do it."

"I told you to call me Ruby."

"Ruby, please can we talk about this at home?"

"Talk about what?" Grandma ate more fries, one at a time. Her glazed eyes blinked at him.

Kevin pulled the car into the driveway. He helped Grandma Ruby into the house and settled her in her favorite chair.

Kevin pulled out his phone and dialed. "Hi, Mom."

"How'd it go? How's Ruby?"

"She broke her wrist and came home with a bright pink cast."

"Did you eat? I can bring something over."

"Thanks, Mom, but we ate on the way home. It's late, and we're exhausted."

"I understand. Thank you for calling and letting me know. Sleep tight."

"Night." He turned off his phone and put it on the charger in the kitchen. Kevin walked into the living room to check on his grandmother.

"Kevin, I need help with a shower," she said, half dozing in the chair.

"You're half asleep. Can't that wait until morning?"

"No, the doctor said I might need a shower right away if I feel itchy."

"And you feel itchy?"

"Yup." Grandma Ruby tilted her head back to look at Kevin. Her drug-addled eyes rolled in her head, comically.

Kevin laughed. "Okay, I'll help. Where are the cast bags?"

"The box is in my purse." She flung her unhurt arm to point at the front door.

How can she remember the doctor's orders and where the cast bags are, but not the fact that she offered to pay for dinner? Kevin pulled a sack and a rubber band from the box. "Let's get this done."

Grandma Ruby attempted to stand but fell back into the chair. She grinned and held out her arm. Kevin helped her stand then guided her to the bathroom, where she swayed like a willow branch. “You’ll have to undress me.” Her eyes widened, and she snickered. “I can’t believe I said that.”

“Grandma!” Kevin rubbed his face, feeling awkward. He took a deep breath, letting it out in a huff. “Let’s take this slowly. Where are you itchy?”

“My arm.” She patted the cast.

“The cast can’t get wet.”

She looked at Kevin with puppy eyes and a trembling lip.

He smiled. “Don’t worry. I’ve got this.” Kevin put a washcloth under warm running water, wrung it out, and wiped Grandma’s elbow and fingers. “There. All better.”

She looked at Kevin with drugged adoration. “Thank you.”

“Can you get to bed?”

“Sure.” For the first time since Grandpa Joe’s death, Grandma slept in her bedroom, not the living room recliner. She flopped on the king-sized bed and snored.

Kevin climbed the porch post's metal filigree design and knocked on Annie's dark window.

She pushed aside the curtain and opened the glass.

"I know it's late. Sorry I didn't call."

"Shut-up." Annie attacked him, kissing him, hugging him, and pulling him into her bedroom. They made out on her bed. Her lips tasted of strawberries, and she smelled as sweet. Annie touched, kissed, and caressed him in all the right places. She pulled at Kevin's clothing, tearing away his shirt.

He was surprised; they had only been dating for a week, but he didn't stop her from exploring his body.

Stomping and voices on the stairs startled Kevin. He sat up, expecting Annie's parents to open her door any second. He grabbed his shirt and bolted out the window. He slipped off the porch roof and took his time walking home.

As he walked home, Kevin's mind raced. He wondered if he really could cast a spell for Ruby. Would it keep her safe? Would he have more time with Annie?

His one true love.

# Chapter 10

Megan walked stealthily down the hallway, her Smith and Wesson SD 9mm pointed up. She checked her six, then advanced down the hall. The door to her left was open. She poked her head in the room and quickly withdrew. Three people. Two men were facing the television, and a woman stood in the kitchen.

She shot the woman first, then the men in quick succession. Clean kills, headshots.

Megan continued moving through the hallway. The door to her right was closed. She quietly tried the knob, but it was locked. She shot the door and jamb at an angle to shatter the wood and disable the lock. Megan threw her weight against the door and forced it open, falling into the room, landing on her side. She shot two men from her prone position.

A buzzer sounded, and a red light flashed. Megan stood, released the magazine, and popped the chambered round. She glanced up at the room that overlooked the course. Nikolai nodded to her from his perch. Megan walked back down the hall and dismantled the Smith and Wesson on the table. She cleaned it and then stood, waiting for Nikolai's assessment.

"Very good," Nikolai said when he entered the range. "You cleared one more room than you normally do" He looked at the pistol, reassembled it, and put it into the safe. "Your father will be pleased to hear this progress."

"Nikolai, what would you recommend I do to remove a threat from school?"

"Threat?" His eyebrows furrowed.

"Well, she isn't a threat to me personally. But she hurt others in the past."

"I see." Nikolai stroked his chin. "This is why you did so well today. You always do better when there is a bully at school. I noticed this when you were little. But you can't rely on anger to focus your mind."

"Is there anything I can do?"

"You should meditate before you practice again."

"That's not what I meant." Megan folded her arms.

He shook his head, a smile on his lips. "If you take direct action, you could endanger your father and yourself." Nikolai put his arm around her, directing her to the exit. "But you can do other things."

"Like?"

"You can look into her past, and if she has some black mark on her record, you could bring it to the attention of the school." Nikolai turned to face her. He smiled. "And if you are smart like I know you are. You'll do it anonymously."

"But that only means she'd be removed from the school." Megan patted the sides of his face. "She hurt my friend. I'd like her to suffer."

Nikolai shrugged. "Accidents happen every day." He stared at her with narrowed eyes. "Accidents."

Megan looked down and nodded. "Thank you for setting me straight."

"I'd rather you do some digging instead of direct action. Mistakes can happen even if it's an accident." Nikolai kissed her on the forehead. "Now, hit the showers. I have another client coming in."

Megan rang the doorbell. Mrs. Schumacher opened the door and peered out. "Good evening, Megan." She stepped aside for Megan to enter. Her blonde hair was up in a bun. She appeared to be Bonnie's aged twin. "Bonnie said you were coming over for a study session."

Megan nodded. “English assignment.”

“I don’t envy you girls. I never did well in English.” Mrs. Schumacher turned to face the stairs. “Bonnie, Megan is here,” she shouted.

Bonnie bounded down the stairs. “Mom, can we get some snacks?”

“In your room?” Mrs. Schumacher looked at Bonnie and Megan. She raised her eyebrows.

“Yes. Please,” Bonnie begged.

“Fine, fine, just remember to bring your garbage and plates to the kitchen.”

“Thank you, Mom, you’re the best.” Bonnie hugged her.

“Plates and garbage.” She reminded the girls.

Bonnie ran into the kitchen and collected a few chip bags and two cola cans. “Come on. I want to show you something,” she said to Megan, then ran back up the stairs.

Megan looked at Bonnie’s mother and shrugged, apologizing for her daughter. This behavior was another aspect of American life that was different from Megan’s. She would never presume it would be alright to eat, much less with a friend, in her bedroom. Her father would find that behavior rude.

Megan strolled up the stairs. She had never been in Bonnie’s room before, but it was easy to find. It had posters of boy bands tacked to her wall, pop music playing, and smelled vaguely of perfume.

Bonnie sat on her pink four-poster bed. “I thought you might change your mind and not come over at all.” She patted the bed beside her. “Come, sit.”

Megan pulled out the English assignment and set it beside them.

Bonnie smiled. “You thought we were going to do homework?”

“We’re not?”

“Well, it isn’t school assigned, exactly.” Bonnie shrugged. “But it’s still homework.” She went to her door and closed it, and then she turned up the music. “What are the plans to mess up Annie’s face?”

“I didn’t give it much thought.”

“Well, I have!” Bonnie paced. “After what she did to Chris and me. I’ve been shopping for a voodoo doll and brass knuckles.” She punched her right fist into her left hand.

Megan assessed her friend. Bonnie was thin. In fact, fragile might describe her better. “Where have you been shopping? I’ve never seen a store like that in town.”

Bonnie’s eyes lit up like she had a joke to tell. “I’ve heard rumors about a business in town that teaches assassins. How to blow stuff up and take people out." Bonnie swiped her finger across her throat. "Maybe we can hire one of the students." She laughed and rolled her eyes. "Oh, my God. I'm kidding. You should see the look on your face. My dad told me when I asked him about brass knuckles. He knows I'm serious, and he says something stupid like that."

How would Bonnie's dad know about Nikolai's business? Megan forced herself to look at Bonnie and smile. "That does seem pretty far fetched. Maybe in a big city like Chicago, but here?"

"Who are you kidding? You took that story, hook, line, and sinker."

"Yea, I suppose I did." Megan shrugged. "If there were an assassin business, would you take some classes?"

"Defending myself is one thing, but going out to hunt people, that's completely different." Bonnie shook her head. "I don't think I could do that."

"All right, killing Annie is out of the question." Megan winked at Bonnie. "So, what's the plan?"

"I think we need to find out what sucker she has on the line." Bonnie scratched her head. "Which means finding out her schedule so that we can track her moves at school. I think I can do that. It'll take a day or two."

"You know how to get her schedule?" Megan was surprised that someone might have a skill she could exploit. She was astonished that Bonnie was that someone.

"Not exactly." Bonnie smiled a devilish grin. "But, I do work in the office during study hall." She wagged her eyebrows. "Mrs. Granger isn't very attentive when I use the computer under her log in."

"Well, Mrs. Granger isn't the brightest," Megan agreed.

"I plan to do what I normally do, file, proofread the newsletter, and see if I can find the schedules." Bonnie shrugged. "It's just a shot in the dark. But, if I do find it, I can't print it."

Megan nodded. "You could write it down on a notepad."

Bonnie pursed her lips. "I'm not sure that would work."

Megan pushed up the sleeve of her sweatshirt. "If it were me, I'd write it on my arm."

"First of all, I don't wear clothes like that. Second, I could take a picture." Bonnie shook her phone.

"What's wrong with what I wear?" Megan stood and straightened her shirt.

Bonnie raised an eyebrow. "Really? You're never going to attract a guy with that unflattering shirt. You're swimming in it."

Megan nodded. "I know." Her father would never let her date, no sense in dressing for disappointment.

"You've always been shy about your body. It's alright. You don't have to wear something that would make you uncomfortable."

Megan regularly wore loose-fitting clothing. Wearing tight clothes and showing off her shape would draw too much attention. Her job was to keep her head down and keep a low profile, at least until she graduated and moved out from under her father. "Okay, we have a plan to find Annie's target. We can start that tomorrow. You know, I did come over for a reason. We really should start the assignment." She picked up the handout sitting on Bonnie's bed.

Bonnie frowned. "Fine, where do you want to start?"

After deciding who would work on which sections of the project, they wrote an outline. The process took much longer than Megan anticipated.

"What time is it?"

Bonnie turned her phone over. "Almost seven."

"Crap, I've got to go. I told my dad I'd be home by seven." Megan grabbed her portion of the English assignment and put it in her book bag. "We'll work more on it tomorrow."

"Thursday or Friday, remember?" Bonnie corrected.

Megan remembered the lesson with Mr. Smith. "That's right." She tossed the bag over her shoulder and headed downstairs. She entered the foyer and left through the front door. Megan was surprised that neither Bonnie nor her mother walked Megan to the door. Was that rude or just ignorant? Do they really believe they're safe?

Her eyes darted down the street. Parked under a streetlamp was a dilapidated, tan, four-door Honda Civic. There was something familiar about it. Maybe she saw it in passing yesterday. She frowned, trying to remember.

Megan climbed into her car and drove past the sedan, taking mental notes. Single male occupant, late fifties, reading a newspaper and eating an apple. The vehicle had a logo on the door, hinting at something official, but she couldn't read it.

The man didn't seem to notice or care that she drove by. Still, Megan felt the flush of adrenaline as panic and paranoia took her mind. Was he a tail or lookout? She backtracked, taking side roads to her house. Did she have reason to be afraid, or was she thinking like her father?

Megan entered her house through the kitchen. Most of the rooms were dark. She heard movement in the back by the den. Artem walked out, holding a novel. "Are you alright? You look like you've seen a ghost."

"I saw a strange car on the street and…" she fidgeted. "I got scared."

He closed the book with a snap. "Tell me."

Megan described the car, the star-like logo, and the man inside.

"Where was this?"

"Four hundred block of Maple Street." Megan swallowed; she couldn't lie; he would know. "I was at Bonnie's."

"Bonnie? Who's that?"

"A girl from school, we were working on our English assignment."

"A friend?" Artem scowled. "No friends. They lead you to temptation and trouble."

"It's only for homework." Megan looked at her feet. She understood the problem of friends. Friends ask questions. She might say too much.

"Dorogoy." Artem hugged her tight. "I'm trying to protect you."

Megan nodded; her head rubbed against his chest.

"You can finish this homework, but in a public place, like the library or restaurant." He pushed her back and lifted her chin to look in her eyes. "Yes? Promise?"

"I promise."

# Chapter 11

Kevin slipped through the back door, into the kitchen, quiet as a mouse. Snoring came from the living room. Before Kevin left the house, Grandma was asleep upstairs. He figured the bed would be more comfortable than the recliner. Clearly, he was wrong.

Flashes of color and light emanated from the muted television. Grandma Ruby curled her unhurt arm around Rapscallion, hugging the big white tomcat close to her stomach. The bright pink cast glowed under the television's radiance. Kevin pulled a throw off the back of the couch and laid it across them. Grandma smacked her lips and tugged the blanket closer to her chin.

He climbed the stairs to his room. Through the open curtain, he could see the dark window of the triplets' bedroom. He hated to admit it, but he did miss all three of them. Maybe even Mom and Dad. He tugged the curtains closed and sat on his bed. Kevin looked in the boxes

Grandma gave him the night before. Was it only one night? It seemed like a week had passed.

He opened the *Book of Shadows* and started to rifle through the pages, trying to find a protection spell. There were more spells for protection than he imagined: protection from bad luck, protection from enemies, protection from family and friends. "I wonder what kind of protection Grandma needs. She broke her arm, but that was an accident, not someone out to get her."

Kevin read some of the spells; they seemed simple enough, short rhymes with the intent of the incantation described within. "It's an affirmation. We studied something like this in Psychology class. If that's what a spell is, then Grandma needs to cast it. Not me."

He continued to dig through the books. He picked up the gemstone book, opened it, and remembered the strange box hidden near the binding. Sure enough, it was there, not a figment of his imagination. He opened the book completely, laying it flat on his bed. He pried the box free from the pages. The craftsmanship of the box was beautiful, the seams barely visible.

The stone inside was greenish. It had red lines running through it, like veins, nourishing it. Kevin held it up to the light and noticed a scratch on the surface. No, more than one scratch, a series of lines and wedges along the outside of the round stone. He rubbed his finger along the marks; they were barely there. The design seemed to start on the outside and swirl inward, wrapping around, getting smaller. The stone under his fingers felt smooth like slippery plastic.

He tossed the rock, feeling the weight of it. In the Gemstone book, he found a stone that looked close to what he had in his hand. Bloodstone. "That sounds ominous."

On a whim, he flipped open the *Witches Grimoire* and found runes and other unnamed writing forms. The scratches looked similar, but they weren't right. He sighed, disappointed that he couldn't find a way to translate the words. At the same time, he was proud that he did discover it was writing of some kind.

Kevin looked at the red light of his clock, grabbed his boxers, and headed into the bathroom for a shower.

"Kevin, Kevin!"

He woke with a start. Did he miss his alarm? Kevin blinked and sat up.

"Kevin," Grandma Ruby called again.

"Coming, coming." Kevin tossed aside his blankets and trotted downstairs. "What's wrong?"

"My arm, it hurts. I need my painkillers." Grandma's eyes were swollen and red. She held the bottle of medicine in her hand, struggling to open the top.

"Why didn't you call me sooner? You look like shit."

"You need to sleep too. You have school in just an hour or so." Grandma looked sheepish.

"You're important too, Ruby. You have needs. I'm here to help you." Kevin took the bottle from her and opened it. He pressed a pill into her hand and grabbed the cup of water on the nearby table.

Her tears lessened. Grandma tossed the pill into her mouth, chasing it with the water. "Thank you, Kevin, for more than just the medicine." She squeezed his hand with her good one.

"Sit back and relax until your medication starts working. I'll make breakfast." Kevin smiled but was uncertain of what to make. Mom always cooked every meal at home.

He checked the refrigerator and saw eggs and bacon. Perfect. It took a little digging until Kevin found the pots and pans. He turned on the stove and cooked the bacon first. Once done, Kevin scrambled six eggs in the bacon grease. He placed two plates on the counter, four strips of bacon, and half the eggs for each. He added a fork, then delivered them to the living room.

The morning news show was on television. The camera zoomed in on Beth Gibbons, the anchor for the station. "Breaking this morning, a dozen teens were arrested last night behind Hair of the Dog, a popular bar in downtown Avalon. Their crimes range from misdemeanor vandalism to grand theft. Avalon, a city once known for its quiet streets and retirement homes, has recently become a haven of adolescent criminals. The mayor and county sheriff will be holding a meeting at town hall tonight. Channel KVEW has exclusive access and will broadcast at ten."

"Stupid teenagers. Back in my day…we didn't get caught." Grandma Ruby grinned mischievously. She accepted the plate, setting it on her lap, and dug in. "Oh, my, you're a good cook."

"Probably because I used the bacon grease to fry the eggs." Kevin grinned between bites.

"Indeed. That would do it."

Kevin noticed the slightly glazed look in her eye. "Medicine must have kicked in?"

"I think so; I feel better at any rate. Thank you."

"Why do I feel like the parent today?" Kevin mumbled. "Ruby, please don't do any gardening while I'm at school. The doctors don't want you going up and down stairs while you're using your pain pills."

"I know."

"Promise me."

"Okay, Kevin, I promise, I won't go into the basement today." Grandma Ruby blinked at him. "Will you water for me?"

"I'll take care of it tonight." Another program started on the television. Kevin realized it was the top of the hour. "Dang it, I'm late." He grabbed the empty plates and left them in the sink. He ran to his bedroom, where he collected his book bag and the rock with the curious writing.

He ran down the stairs and said, "I'll see you this afternoon, Ruby."

Annie was on the sidewalk, arms crossed, and pacing. “It’s about time!”

“I know, I’m sorry.” Kevin stepped beside Annie. “Ruby couldn’t get to her medicine.”

“Ruby? She had better be your grandmother.” Annie glared at him as she continued stomping.

“Yes, she wants me to call her Ruby.”

“You sure spend a lot of time with her.”

“That’s my job; my responsibility. I live with her.” Kevin stopped and grabbed Annie’s arm spinning her around. “Why are you behaving this way? You knew about this arrangement.”

“Why are you taking her side?” Annie rubbed the crystal on her necklace.

“You know she can’t afford a caregiver.” Kevin frowned. Why was Annie behaving like a jerk?

Annie pulled away from Kevin, then continued walking toward the school. “I know, it’s just…”

“What?”

“If she weren’t around, you could spend more time with me.” Annie blinked and looked up at Kevin, leaning into his side.

“Yes, I could.” Kevin smiled at the thought of spending hours with Annie after school. Her beautiful smile, her sexy body, and the way she always smelled like strawberries. “I would love to. But I can’t.” He looked down at her pouting face. “Why are you so upset this morning? I thought you liked my grandmother?”

Annie pulled away from Kevin; she looked at her hands. “I don’t know. I guess I’m jealous.”

“Jealous? What have you got to be jealous about? She’s my grandmother.” Kevin touched Annie’s nose. “You’re my girlfriend.” A sudden thought occurred to him. “Think of this arrangement with my grandmother as practice. I’m practicing how to be a husband. I made her breakfast this morning, bacon and eggs.” He grinned.

Annie snorted a laugh, then looked away from him.

They walked hand in hand, approaching the front door of the school.

“Um, Kevin, I won’t be sitting with you at lunch today. I have an ap…meeting. I have a meeting. I can’t miss it, or Mom will be pissed. I’ll be back after lunch, and we can walk home. Together.” Annie squeezed his hand.

“What kind of meeting?”

“Don’t you trust me? It’s just a meeting.” Annie dropped his hand and stomped into the school.

# Chapter 12

Megan drove to Bonnie's house in the morning. The tan Honda Civic was gone. Maybe she'd imagined it. She chuckled at the thought, even though the fear felt real only hours ago.

She tromped up to the stoop and rang the doorbell.

Bonnie stepped out. "Were you planning on giving me a ride again today?"

"Yes." They walked to the car and got in. "My father found out I was at your place, and he got mad." She started the car and drove off.

"Did you tell him we were doing homework?"

"Of course. He thinks we'd be better off in the library."

"How the hell did he find out?"

Megan shrugged. She pulled into the school parking lot.

"Well, he isn't wrong. The library could help us with homework and give us some privacy." Bonnie raised her finger. "And we could use their computers. Do you know how hard it is to get on the internet at home?" She pulled her phone from her jacket pocket. "I know I could use my phone for research." She slipped it back, smiling devilishly at Megan. "But not for hacking."

Megan shot a glance at the cars parked near them, feeling paranoid. "Hacking?" The words came out in a whisper.

"I'm only going to get one shot at getting Annie's schedule. If I fail, I'll have to try something else."

Megan turned off the car and placed her hands on the steering wheel. "We could work on our English assignment too."

"What, are you crazy? Hacking is way more fun." Bonnie opened the car door and headed into the school.

Megan shook her head, smiling. She trotted after Bonnie. "Hey, wait up."

Megan sat at a corner lunch table, back to the wall, watching both doors. She was waiting for Bonnie to make an appearance. She bit into her daily protein bar; it had all the nutrition she needed for lunch. Her lip curled. "Tell that to my stomach," she complained.

She pulled a worksheet from her backpack and continued her math assignment. She wrote an answer and tapped the pencil's eraser end on the tabletop, three fast taps, followed by three slow taps, repeating. Maybe someone would answer her call for help, but she doubted any student in this school knew Morse code. She set her pencil down.

Bonnie plopped beside her with her lunch tray in hand. The meal made fast food look healthy.

“Are you really going to eat that?” Megan pointed to the sandwich with an unknown breaded patty in the middle.

Bonnie bit into the sandwich, chewing with her mouth open, exaggerating the disgusting sandwich.

Megan picked up her book bag and pretended to throw up into it.

“That never gets old.” Bonnie dropped her head onto Megan’s shoulder. She continued munching on the sandwich.

“If you’re going to eat that, please, over there. It smells awful.”

“Plug your nose. I have to tell you a secret.” Bonnie twisted her head to look at Megan. “I did it.” She breathed heavily on Megan.

"You what?" Megan shouted, then pushed Bonnie away.

"I succeeded!" Bonnie shouted, jumping out of the seat and spiking her half-eaten sandwich on the table. White bread fell away, and the meat substance hit the table like a hockey puck.

The cafeteria fell silent, and all eyes were on Megan and Bonnie. The girls laughed, leaning on each other, pointing at the sandwich, gasping for air. Talking resumed, and the buzz of the lunchroom went back to normal. They cleaned the mess and left the cafeteria.

The girls ran to Megan's car and climbed in.

"What happened?" Megan asked.

"Not much to tell. I brought Annie's schedule onto the monitor and took a picture of it." Bonnie shrugged, wrinkling her nose. "I was a bit disappointed at how easy it was." She showed Megan the image of the schedule.

Megan scanned the information at the top of the page. "We could still go to the library. Look at the header." She waited for Bonnie to examine the schedule. "I wonder why her last name is different from her parents."

"Adopted?"

"Not unless her parents gave her up or died recently." Megan racked her brain for Annie's parents' names, but they didn't come. "Do you remember her parent's names?"

"Yea, it's…" Bonnie leaned forward and put her head in her hands. "When Annie stole Chris, I went to her house. I talked to her mom." She shook her head as if trying to will the names to come to the surface of her brain. "Why can't I remember?" She turned to stare at Megan. "Let's go to the library tonight."

"Shit. I can't. It's Wednesday."

Bonnie frowned then nodded. "I suppose you can't get out of it?"

"No, I made a promise." Megan folded her arms. She had a sudden urge to defy her father and do what she wanted. *Like you'd disobey your father.*

"Tomorrow night. It can wait until then." Bonnie said, interrupting Megan's thoughts.

Megan drove into Nikolai's parking lot. She parked on the side of the building, then stepped to the trunk, where she pulled out a blonde wig, fit it, and walked in the building.

Nikolai sat at the front counter.

"Good afternoon. I'm surprised to see so many cars."

"It's good business." He smiled. "Remember the rules?"

Megan nodded. "Questions directed to the instructor only. No names, don't ask, don't give."

Nikolai smiled over his steepled fingers. "Class has already started." He gestured with his hand.

Megan opened the door and walked through. The lights were dim with a spotlight on the instructor. He was the same Mr. Smith that Megan had seen talking to Nikolai the other day. She found an empty table with a single chair. She looked around at the other students, curious. Everyone sat at individual tables, and the room was dark, except for the spotlight. The lighting, and the apparent disguises, made it difficult to identify anyone with certainty.

Only two other women were in the room. The rest were men. No surprise there. However, the fellow directly across from her looked like the man in the Honda Civic from the other night. She narrowed her eyes, trying to remember. His grey hair and light, stubbly beard matched his eyes. He was thin, neither strong nor scrawny, and he was bold enough not to wear any disguise.

"Any questions?" The instructor asked. He had finished soldering a wire to an electronic board, a marshaling board if she remembered right. No one responded. Most wanted to keep their anonymity. If they had questions, they might hire the instructor for a private lesson.

Mr. Smith continued talking. Megan saw the style of timing device many times in the past. The instructor was from the U.S. military. The application he taught appeared to be old information. Feeling bored, she looked at her fellow students again. The man across from her looked back with a hard-lingering stare. Megan stood and left the room. She felt the man's eyes follow her.

Nikolai was at the front desk. "Everything alright?"

"No." Megan shook her head. "Something's wrong. I don't know." Megan looked back at the closed door. "You've always told me to trust my gut. My gut told me to leave."

"One of the students?"

Megan nodded. "I thought I saw him the other night. He might be following me." She stepped away from the desk and left the building.

She leaned her back on the door, taking a deep breath, opening her senses, making her feel hyper-vigilant. Crickets chirped, the air was humid, and the scent of mold prominent. Her feet on the pavement crunched on stray loose gravel.

She climbed in her car, took off the wig, and drove home. As she drove, she entertained the idea of getting Bonnie and going to the library. She decided against it because Nikolai would tell Artem what happened, and her father would wonder why she didn't come straight home.

Megan pulled into the garage and turned off her car. She relaxed. She was home. Where was her father? She went inside and found him watching television. "Did Nikolai call?"

"No." Artem muted the television and turned to face his daughter. "Should he have?"

"I don't know." She looked at her feet and fidgeted with her keys. "I could be overly cautious."

Artem nodded. "That's okay, better to be cautious than dead." He turned off the television and patted the couch next to him. "Tell me what happened."

Megan sat. "I went to the lesson, and I thought I recognized the man in the car from last night. What's weird is he seemed to recognize me too." She shuddered. "I may have over-reacted because no one has ever *looked* at me during a class before. Not like that."

"I see." Artem went into the kitchen, where Megan heard him on his phone. "Nikolai, it's me. What happened? I see. Can you verify? I see. Good. Very well." He reappeared and sat on the couch next to Megan.

"Dorogoy, you did the right thing. Always follow your gut." Artem hugged Megan and kissed her forehead.

"What about the guy?"

"Everyone at the lesson has been checked, vetted, and confirmed. A diligent process was conducted to ensure the safety of anyone who goes to the gym. Nikolai is standing behind that procedure."

"Are you saying I over-reacted?"

"Who am I to say? You did the right thing." Artem hugged her again. "I'm proud of your decision. You came home alive."

She stood and went to her bedroom. Megan wanted to confide in Bonnie, but the phone was in the kitchen. She wasn't allowed to take it to school, in her car, or to her room. Artem always told her she couldn't have friends because they were dangerous. Megan hated uncertainty and fear. Was the man a threat? Was it just her imagination? She couldn't wait to take control of her life once she graduated and moved out.

She stopped the car in front of Bonnie's house. Her father would be displeased with the amount of time she spent with her friend. Megan gripped the steering wheel tightly, resting her head on her hands.

Bonnie knocked on the passenger door window. "You okay?" She shouted through the glass.

Megan looked at her and smiled. She unlocked the door.

Bonnie sat with her book bag in her lap. "You'll never guess what I found last night."

"You went to the library without me?" Megan clutched at her heart like it was breaking.

Bonnie rolled her eyes. "Of course not. I searched from home."

"From home? That's not safe." Megan covered her mouth. "Aw, shit, I'm sorry, that's something my father would say. Let's try that again." She fluffed her hair and cleared her throat. "What did you find?" She tried to be supportive but couldn't get her father's paranoid voice out of her head.

"Annie has a criminal record." Bonnie bounced in the car seat, barely able to keep in her excitement. "She's eighteen. Everything is online, including her juvenile record. It's public."

Megan stared at Bonnie, speechless. Annie was more dangerous than she imagined.

"Everything," Bonnie repeated, wiggling her fingers like some magician. She frowned. "Come on! Aren't you going to ask any questions?"

"Sorry, I…I guess I'm in shock." Megan turned over her engine and slid the gear into drive. "Tell me everything."

"At least ten endangering-a-minor charges. Although I have no idea what that means. The Fredricks adopted her this past summer. I can't find anything on her birth parents, the Browns. It's like they turned to mist and blew away."

Megan parked the car and turned off the engine. "What's that mean? Did her parents die, or did they give her up?"

"There is no record. Nada." Bonnie held up her finger. "Better yet, why did the Fredricks adopt her when she's eighteen? Can you even be adopted at that age?" She raised her eyebrow.

Megan tapped her bottom lip. “Could it be because she’s still in school? It sounds like we need to do more research. How do you feel about going to the library tonight?”

“I’m in!” Bonnie opened her door. Megan followed, and they walked into the school together.

Megan’s eyes narrowed as she spotted Annie walking with Tony to his locker. She poked Bonnie and nodded in Annie’s direction. “Feel like eavesdropping?”

“Let’s do this,” Bonnie said. She glanced down the hall to spot teachers.

The girls walked together to a section of lockers near Tony’s. Bonnie picked one at random and rolled a combination. She tried three numbers and lifted the handle. It didn’t open. “Damn it,” she said aloud, thumping the locker.

Megan turned so her back faced Annie, which allowed her to listen in and block what Bonnie was doing.

“I don’t like it any more than you, but I have to do it today,” Annie said.

“What about the fish? He’ll be suspicious.”

“Fish? Really?”

"Would you prefer, flunky? Bootlicker?" Tony disapproved of whoever Annie was chasing.

"Look, he's only a means to an end. I have to get in the good graces of his sisters."

"Why not just go after the sisters directly?"

"Because they're not in high school, and you know my talents don't extend to females."

"Hey!" A big guy slammed his fist into the locker Bonnie was trying to open. "What do you think you're doing? This is my locker."

"Is it?" Bonnie grinned. She looked at a piece of paper and then glanced at the locker number. She said, "Oh, I'm sorry. You're right. Won't happen again."

"Damn right, it won't!" The big guy pointed up the hall. He leaned into Bonnie and whispered, "Get."

Bonnie squealed and trotted off in the direction he pointed.

Megan followed on Bonnie's heels, looking back. Annie stared daggers at her and Bonnie. "Shit." Megan moved to Bonnie's side. "We've been made."

# Chapter 13

He walked into Russian History, the last class of the day. While the course was interesting, it was merely a device to boost Kevin's GPA. There were a few tests, but they only counted for ten percent of his grade. Participation and engagement received more percentage points. It was an easy A.

The final bell rang, and the students bolted for the door, except for Megan, a quiet girl who kept to herself. Mr. Mulligan leaned over her and pointed at a map on her desk.

Kevin approached the teacher. "Mr. Mulligan, I found a stone in my Grandma's attic. It appears to have writing on it. Do you know what the writing is?"

Mr. Mulligan gave Kevin a sideways glance. "Did you try to find out for yourself?" His finger remained pointing to the word Tunguska on an old map of Russia.

"Yes. I looked at the books I had. I know they aren't Runes."

Megan looked up at what Kevin said. “May I see it?” She held out her hand, pushing the map aside to make room.

Kevin wrinkled his brow.

“If anyone is going to know, it’ll be Megan, here,” Mr. Mulligan said. “Her father works at the Field Museum in Chicago.”

Reluctantly Kevin handed over the stone.

Megan rolled it over in her hands. She looked up at Kevin, squinting. “Have you ever been to the Field Museum?”

Kevin shrugged. “Yea, sure, I guess. I went with the school. All-day field trip.”

“Recently?”

“Fifth grade. Seven years ago.”

Megan nodded. “Someone from China let the museum borrow their collection of stones for Halloween. They look identical to yours.” She smiled. “I almost thought you stole one.”

“Me? Steal? You’ve never met my mother.” Kevin smiled, chuckling. “She’d kill me.”

Her eyes widened. “You’ve got strict parents too?”

“Not strict exactly. My mom’s got high expectations.”

Megan gave him a half-smile, tilting her head slightly. “So, if you didn’t steal it, where did you find it?

“Inside my grandmother’s book.”

“Inside a book?” Megan leaned forward, interested.

Kevin sat at the desk near hers. “The book was titled *Gemstones of the World*. Inside was a box with that stone.”

“Was the stone labeled?”

“The box had “protection stone” written on it.”

Megan’s eyes lit up. “Did it?” She cleared her throat. “Does the gemstone book have anything to do with witchcraft?”

Kevin frowned. His eyes darted between Megan and Mr. Mulligan. Could he say? People were funny about religion. “It’s part of my grandmother’s Wiccan things.”

Megan nodded. “The Chinese owner said the stones are a witch’s protection talisman. But I don’t think they know anything about Wicca. My father is itching to find out what is written on the stones, but he isn’t allowed to touch them. May I get a rubbing?”

“Sure, I guess.” Kevin shrugged.

She laid paper over the rock, and with her pencil, rubbed the side of the lead on the paper. The carving's dips and valleys appeared white, and where the stone remained, carbon from the pencil marked the paper. “Oh, nice,” she said as she turned the stone and continued the rubbing. "See the pennant or arrow shapes?"

"Yes."

"This is cuneiform writing. That's how cuneiform got its name. It means wedge-shaped. Sometimes people mistake it for ogham, which is Old Irish and completely different." Megan finished the rubbing and handed the stone back to Kevin.

Kevin felt his heart leap. "Can you read it?" He looked at the stone and back to her paper, which was much clearer.

"Well, it's not that easy," Megan stated.

"Cuneiform is complicated." Mr. Mulligan interjected as he went to the board. "It's five thousand years old. You could try and translate it, I suppose." He marked a few symbols on the board. "Each mark or group of marks make up a syllable or sound. But sometimes they're words and not sounds at all. You won't know either way unless you know the subject of the text.

"To make matters worse, they didn't use a space between words or sounds. So it is hard to know where words begin or end. The language should be either Sumerian or Acadian, but there is no guarantee. Odds of you finding someone who can speak either of those languages and translate it into English…well, they're slim. At least, around here, it's slim."

Kevin looked at Megan. "What about your father?"

Megan narrowed her eyes and frowned. "He can translate Sumerian and Acadian, but don't get your hopes up." She looked at the board. "What Mr. Mulligan said is true. The hardest part will be figuring out the subject matter. But to find the subject, you need to know the language and make some assumptions. It's a chicken and egg situation. Which comes first?" She shrugged. "I can show him the rubbing and let you know."

"Thank you." Kevin turned to leave. "How long do you think that will take?" He'd paused in the doorway to look back.

"I don't know, but I'll bug him because I'm curious too. There's something special written there."

"Really?" Kevin asked. Something special could be something worth money.

"Don't get too excited," Mr. Mulligan said. "Might be a grave marker or a tax decree."

"Still, that would be fascinating," Megan said. "A Neolithic grave marker would be one of a kind. Most cuneiform was written on clay tablets. Someone took time to write something important on that stone. Don't lose it. It could be valuable."

Kevin reached down and touched his pocket, feeling the weight of the stone that was cradled there. He smiled, feeling like his luck changed, then turned to leave.

"What are you smiling about?" Annie stood in the frame of the history room door. "Who's that?" Her eyes narrowed as she looked at Megan. "I think I know her."

Megan hunched over the map on the desk. Mr. Mulligan's head was next to hers as if they were hatching a bank heist. "That's just Megan," Kevin said.

"Really? *Just Megan*?" Annie stared hard at him, hands on hips. "What were you doing, talking to her? She looks like the girl who was with Bonnie, the slut."

Kevin walked away from the History classroom, bristling. What the heck was wrong with Annie? She's been a bitch all day. Wasn't this a free country?

Annie grabbed Kevin's shirt and stopped him. "Well, are you going to answer me?"

"First, you complain about Ruby, and now you're threatened by Megan? I don't even know her. Mr. Mulligan introduced us today, five minutes ago." Kevin grabbed Annie's shoulders and searched her eyes. Her red splotchy face and narrowed eyes said it all. "Why are you so mad today? Does it have anything to do with that *meeting* you had earlier?"

Annie opened her mouth to say something, but then her eyes closed and shook her head. She jerked away from Kevin and ran into the nearby bathroom.

Kevin threw up his hands, then followed her. He sat on the floor in the nearly empty hallway and patiently waited for Annie to reemerge. A shadow crossed over him. He looked up, and his mood darkened further. "What do you want?" Kevin expected Tony to say something inappropriate about Annie.

Tony shrugged then leaned against the wall. "What everyone wants, peace, love, and happiness."

Kevin clambered to his feet. "What?"

Tony folded his arms. "You wouldn't understand." He looked away.

The bathroom door slammed against the wall. Annie stomped out. "I thought I heard your voice. You'll be happy to know; it's done." She stepped into Tony's space. "I'm done."

"What is going on?" Kevin looked from Tony to Annie.

"I don't want to talk about it," Annie said.

“She…” Tony started, pointing at Annie.

“I said, I don’t want to talk about it!” She shoved Tony, bouncing his shoulders off the wall.

Tony held up his hands in defeat.

“Kevin. Can I get your phone number?” Megan walked toward him, oblivious to what was going on. She looked to Kevin, Annie, and Tony, confusion then understanding crossed on her face. “So, I can let you know what my father finds.”

“You!” Annie turned her attention and anger to Megan. “What the hell do you think you’re doing? How dare you talk to my boyfriend.” She pulled her arm back as if to strike Megan.

Megan stepped toward Annie, crowding her space.

Annie seemed to realize she couldn’t hit Megan while she stood so close. Uncertainty crossed her face, and her hand dropped.

Megan’s eyes narrowed, and she spoke softly. “You touched him. You can keep him.” She confidently stepped back from Annie and walked away.

Annie grimaced then leaned over. Her hands gripped into Kevin’s arm, pinching him. “If you ever talk to her again, I’ll…kill you.” She gasped, held her stomach, and ran back into the bathroom. Kevin thought he heard Annie vomiting.

"That took balls." Tony watched Megan walk down the hall. He seemed disappointed.

# Chapter 14

Megan climbed into her car. Her mind lingered on Kevin. What the hell was he doing with Annie? She hit the steering wheel and took a few deep breaths, steadying her nerves. After a few minutes, she started the car and headed to Bonnie's house.

Kevin wasn't Annie's type. He wasn't gorgeous. He was cute. He wasn't rich. His family was poor. His grades weren't high, nor was he an athlete. He didn't participate in drama or art club. He didn't do anything that would normally attract attention from Annie. He was the normal, average high school boy. That's why Megan and Bonnie kept an eye on him. For them, Kevin was the perfect distraction from senior year.

Annie's only friends were the string of boys she dated. Not men, boys. Only a child was foolish enough to fall into her trap. Tony was in line right before Kevin. Before Tony, there was Mark, Vincent, Nick, and countless others. But

Tony seemed to have a higher place in Annie's heart than the others.

When school started sophomore year, Annie burst on the stage as the catch of the town. There was something special about Annie. She had charisma that no one could resist. Not that any of the guys complained, they all seemed happy to do her bidding.

It was too bad Kevin was involved with Annie. Soon, he'd be just like the mass of guys before him. Dating Annie was a curse, not the honor they all thought.

Megan parked and climbed the steps to Bonnie's front porch. She heard a shuffle along the sidewalk. A man in his thirties walked alone, eyes on the ground, hands in his pockets. Further up the street, a twig snapped. It was quiet. No dogs barked, no cars, it was too silent. Instinct forced Megan to investigate the broken twig. Nothing except for the smell of soil and mold. She went back to Bonnie's house and climbed the porch steps.

She knocked on the door, then turned and watched the man walk down the sidewalk, rocking back and forth like a pendulum. He didn't lift his head and watch where he walked. He was too young to be the man from the tan car. Still, his presence bothered her. Megan shrugged it off; her mind and her senses were playing tricks. The air felt dense and moist. The door opened, and Bonnie stepped out.

Megan held up her hand. "Just a minute." The hair on her arms rose. Something was off. She blinked her eyes, trying to clear them. Was that additional movement? She frowned. Her gun was in the car. A lot of good it did there.

Bonnie stepped next to her. "What's going on?"

"Get back inside. Lock your door," Megan demanded. The man who walked down the sidewalk doubled back. "Do it now!" She hissed at Bonnie. Her fingers worked at the seams of her light jacket, pulling the steel needles free. Her ears twitched, was there another person behind that tree?

"Why?" Bonnie had one hand on her hip. "I thought we were going to the library."

"Go!" Megan settled in a fighting stance, low and ready, watching the man approach, suspecting another hiding nearby. The man's eyes snapped upward and locked on hers. She felt transfixed; she couldn't look away, couldn't move. "Go," Megan repeated, but it came out as a breathy sigh.

"I'm not going anywhere until you tell me what the hell is going on!" Bonnie said.

Pounding feet landed on the wooden porch behind Megan made her tense, but she couldn't move her eyes off the strange man at the bottom of the stairs in front of her. A second attacker. She tried to turn, but her body seemed compelled to face the man on the sidewalk.

Bonnie screamed, and she fell to the porch floor.

"I have a message for Bonnie. Stay out of Annie's business," the second man said behind Megan. Bonnie screamed again as something substantial connected with her flesh.

Megan felt her anger ripple across her body, like the vibrations of a tuning fork, breaking against her brain in a crescendo. She threw the four-inch needles into each of the man's eyes. The hold he had on her broke. With the tension gone, she fell forward, rolled, then jumped to her feet, turning to face Bonnie's attacker.

The other man wore all black, and there was something odd about him too. Megan could feel it. "You're going to come to a sticky end, my pretty," he said, licking his lips. His creepy eyes spasmed in their sockets as he looked at Megan. "You're next."

"Perhaps, you'll be next," Megan hissed. She jerked her head in the direction of the man sprawled on the sidewalk.

The man looked to his motionless companion and roared with fury, sounding more animal than human. His lip retracted, displaying sharp teeth.

A man with a Mossberg 500 tactical shotgun burst out of the house. “What the fuck is going on?” He racked a round into the chamber and aimed at the man’s torso. “What did you do to my daughter?”

The man stood tall. He raised his hands. “Teaching a lesson.”

Bonnie’s father clicked off the safety, secured the shotgun to his shoulder, and pulled the trigger. The buckshot barely had time to separate while leaving the chamber. Nine marble-sized pellets struck the man center mass. He flew off the porch, landing on his back.

The bark of the shotgun sounded muffled to Megan. She expected an echo off the houses in the neighborhood, but it never came.

“Sally, did you call 911?” Bonnie's father yelled. He lowered the shotgun.

“They’re coming,” Sally said, stepping on the porch. “They’re coming.” She saw the man lying lifeless. “Oh, Howard, you could go to jail.”

“Self-defense.”

Bonnie moaned.

Mrs. Schumacher bent by her side. “Bonnie? Darling.”

Bonnie’s eyes blinked then opened. “My stomach.” She pushed her body up with one arm and retched.

Megan noticed Bonnie’s legs didn’t move with the effort of vomiting. She looked at the man’s heavy work boots. “He’s wearing steel toes.”

Bonnie groaned, falling forward.

Mrs. Schumacher tried to move her daughter’s face out of the vomit.

“No, stop!” Megan bent and pulled the vomit away from Bonnie’s mouth and nose. “He might have broken her back. If you move her, you could make it worse.”

Sirens broke the stillness, followed by a dog bark, then another.

# Chapter 15

Kevin walked with Annie to her house. He leaned in for a goodbye kiss. Annie grabbed the back of his neck, holding him, kissing him hard. She moaned, moved closer, rubbing his thigh with her leg. Annie released him, looking up at him through her eyelashes. She bit her bottom lip, eyes dilated. Without a word, she took the front of his shirt and pulled him toward her door.

Kevin followed. He balked, looking down the street toward his house.

"Come on, Kevin, my parents won't be home for a couple of hours." She turned his head back to her, pulling him into a lingering kiss.

They parted breathlessly. Annie smiled, rubbing the charm on her necklace.

"I want to, Annie. I really do." Kevin stammered.

Annie's smile disappeared. Her eyes narrowed.

"I have to check on my grandma. If I don't, I'll be distracted. I don't think either of us wants that." Kevin sighed and stepped away from Annie.

"You need to grow up, Kevin. Your grandma won't be with you forever, but I could be." She opened her front door and stepped into the foyer. "The decision is yours."

"I'll be back."

"I might not be here." She slammed the door.

Kevin hurried home. Thoughts of Annie kissing Tony flitted about in his imagination. He shook his head, not wanting to believe she would cheat on him.

He ran up the porch steps and entered the living room.

Grandma Ruby rushed into the room and pushed Kevin aside, slamming the door. "He'll get out," she whispered. She looked behind the curtains.

Kevin looked at Rapscallion, sleeping on a bookshelf. "Who?" he whispered.

"Mr. Tibbles."

Kevin stopped in his tracks. "Ruby, Mr. Tibbles isn't here anymore; he's gone."

Grandma spun and turned on Kevin. "You let him out?"

"No, no, I didn't." Kevin dropped his book bag and held up his hands.

"Well, if you didn't let him out, he is here somewhere. I just saw him." She tried to get on her hands and knees, but her broken arm wouldn't let her. "Here, kitty, kitty, kitty," she trilled.

"Ruby," Kevin touched his grandma on the shoulder. "Have you eaten today?"

"Just my pills."

"Ruby," Kevin took a deep breath. "The doctor said you have to eat a sandwich or something when you take your medication."

Grandma stopped searching for her cat and looked at him with big doe eyes. "Did he?"

"Yes, he did. Let's get you something." Kevin took her hand and guided her into the kitchen, directing her to the small table while he opened a couple of ravioli cans. He dumped each into separate bowls and then set them in the microwave.

When the timer dinged, he pulled the bowls out and sprinkled shredded cheese on top. He set a bowl and fork before his grandmother and the second before the other chair.

Kevin watched and noticed that her eyes became less wild as she ate. "How are you feeling, Ruby?"

"I'm doing fine. Did you know I broke my arm yesterday? Hurts like the dickens."

"I know, Ruby. I took you to the hospital."

"Oh, yes, that's right." She reached across the small table and squeezed Kevin's arm. "Now I remember, you drove, and we picked up hamburgers afterward." Her hands went to her mouth, eyes full of mirth. "And you helped me with my shower." She giggled like a girl.

Kevin felt his cheeks burn hot. "I only washed your arm."

"Oh, Kevin, it's all right. You don't have to make up stories." She grinned. "So, how was school?"

"Good, good," Kevin commented. "I walked my girlfriend, Annie, home and was going to hang out with her, but I wanted to make sure you were okay. After what happened yesterday and all."

Grandma Ruby's eyes twinkled. "Oh, I was in love once, but that was a long time ago. That love died with your Grandpa. You should see her after you eat. You know if you cast that spell of protection for me, you'd have more time with her because then I would be safe."

Kevin took another bite. "I've read some of the books you gave me, and it seems the spells are personal. Almost like you should do the spell."

"I need you to do the spell so your youth and strength can help look over me. To keep me safe. If I did the spell, it would be my youth and strength, which is non-existent." Grandma Ruby knocked on the hard-outer coating of her cast.

"Oh, I guess I didn't read far enough into the books to understand that part." He scooped the final bits of ravioli into his mouth. Kevin looked at her half-eaten bowl. "Can you tell me about that crazy orange tabby you had?"

"Mr. Tibbles?" She lifted her eyebrows. "What is there to tell? He passed about five years ago."

Kevin sighed in relief. "When I came home, you were trying to find Mr. Tibbles. You said you saw him and were looking under furniture, and well, you scared me."

"Did I now?" Grandma scratched her head. "Stupid dementia."

"I think it was because you didn't eat with your medication."

"You think so?" She shoveled more into her mouth.

Kevin shrugged. "Hard to say. You've seen things before that no one else has."

Grandma Ruby looked crestfallen. "Really? Do you all think I'm nuttier than squirrel droppings? I'll have you know I'm fine." She looked up at the clock. “Look at that; my show is on.” She squeezed Kevin’s hand. “Go see your girl.”

Kevin smiled at the thought of spending time with Annie. “I’ll only stay for an hour or so.”

“Take all the time you need.”

Kevin stepped onto Annie’s porch and rang the bell. He waited a few minutes, pressing his ear against the door. Nothing. He climbed the corner post of the porch and got onto the roof. He went to Annie’s window and knocked.

The curtain moved aside. Annie stared at him, surprise evident on her face. She opened the window and screen. “I didn’t think you’d be back.”

“I told you, I would.”

Annie laughed delightedly. “Get in here.”

Kevin slid through the window. Annie sat on her four-poster bed, patting the mattress next to her.

“I’m glad I went home. Ruby was in bad shape. But I got her some food, and now she seems good. She told me to come and be with you.”

"Doesn't she know to eat?" Annie looked incredulous. "Everyone knows to eat."

"Her pain medications are strong. I think they were making her see things." Kevin shrugged. "She asked me to cast a spell on her to keep her safe. Then we'd have more time."

"A spell? Are you serious?" Annie fell back on the bed, laughing. She caught her breath then said, "Of course you should do it. Make the old hag happy so we can be together."

"Old hag?"

"Shhh." Annie reached out a hand and pressed a finger against his lips. "You read too much into things." Her hand slipped off his mouth, down his neck, and then stopped on his chest. She gripped the shirt and pulled him toward her.

Kevin let her. Thoughts of Annie calling his Grandmother a hag ran through his mind, but he didn't want a fight. Especially at a time like this.

Annie ran her fingers through his hair. He kissed her on the mouth, then moved to her neck. She grappled with his shirt, pulling it over his head. Kevin sat back, letting his eyes drink in her beauty.

A car in the street honked. "Get out of the way!" an angry man shouted.

Kids shouted obscenities at the driver.

Kevin looked out the open window. “I think it’s your dad,” he said to Annie.

She smiled coyly. “It’s alright; Dad watches television after work. He won’t come upstairs for hours.” She wrapped her arms around him.

Kevin moved closer, kissing and caressing her. Thoughts of Annie’s father being nearby concerned and excited him.

Annie’s dad cursed. “Yea? Well, I know your parents.” The car revved and moved into the driveway. The engine turned off, followed by the sound of the car door slamming shut. The front door of the house opened and closed with such force Annie’s windows shook. “Annie? Annie!” Feet pounded on the stairs. “Annie, so help me. You better be home.”

“Shit, get out, get out,” Annie hissed, shoving him toward the small window.

Kevin dove through the window, making it onto the roof before Annie’s dad threw open the door.

“You have a lot of explaining to do, young lady.”

Annie drew the curtain but didn’t have time to close the window. “What’s the problem, Dad?”

Kevin sat close to the dormer. He heard his shoes scrape the shingles. He had to hold still, or her father would notice. Kevin held his breath, clutching his shirt to his chest.

"Where is your purse?"

"Here. What are you looking for?"

"I need to see your wallet." Annie's dad sounded panicked.

"Is this about money? Really?" Annie laughed.

"Just give me the wallet."

"I've got private stuff in there."

"Oh, no, you don't. Sit!" Annie's door slammed shut. "Here is your credit card." He paused. "You can't lie and tell me it was stolen, like last time." Another pause. "A six-hundred-dollar payment to a woman's health clinic? What was that for?"

Annie cried, intense, sobbing tears. "You…wouldn't…understand."

"Oh, Annie," his voice soothed. "Try me."

Annie's sobs sounded muffled like she was crying into her father's chest. Annie said something, but Kevin couldn't make it out.

"Birth control? Six hundred dollars? What kind of fool do you take me for? You're grounded. You can spend the rest of the night on the couch, sulking."

Kevin heard Annie's father continue to scold her, but the voices were getting smaller. They were probably going downstairs. He climbed off the roof and headed home. Six hundred dollars. His eyes went wide as he figured that it was likely what an abortion cost. Who was the father? Tony? Kevin tried to dismiss the thought, but it kept rising to the surface. As he walked toward home, his gut twisted and turned, wrenching him into dark thoughts. His phone rang. “Hello.” His voice cracked.

“Kevin, I need you now more than ever,” Annie said through gasping sniffles.

“What about the abortion you had? Whose was it, Annie?” Kevin yelled into the phone.

“Before we got together, I was…” Annie broke into a fit of crying. “I was raped. It wasn’t a good time in my life. I got drunk at a party and woke up naked.” She sniffled. “But now, I have you. You’re good to me. You showed me how a real boyfriend treats his girlfriend.”

“So, you don’t know who the father was?”

“No. That is why I did it. I needed to start over. I knew you were the one. I want to be with you forever.” Annie paused, “I can’t believe I said that it sounds so corny. But it’s true. I want to marry you.”

“Marry?” Kevin stopped on the sidewalk. “You want to marry me?”

"Well," Annie said quietly. "Yes, I love you."

"I don't know what to say."

"Tell me you will come to my house tonight and make love to me."

"What about your father? Your mother?"

"Don't come over until after ten; they'll be asleep by then," Annie said.

"I'll be there." Kevin turned off his phone and slid it into his pocket.

Annie loved him.

# Chapter 16

Megan parked her car in the garage, grabbed her backpack, and went into the house. Her father waited in the kitchen, disapproval on his face. "You're late." He swung his keys around the ring and caught them.

"I take it you heard."

"Of course, I heard. This community is small. News travels fast." Artem walked into the living room and motioned for her to follow. "I took the liberty to pack your things."

"You what?" Megan put her bookbag down and placed her hands on her hips. "Why?"

"You were attacked by the mafia. It's time to go." He picked up two suitcases and took them into the kitchen.

Megan sat on the couch and crossed her arms.

A few minutes later, Artem returned. "We don't have time for this nonsense. We need to leave. Now!"

"The attack was on Bonnie, not me. She almost died. Did you hear about that?"

"Bonnie? Who is Bonnie?"

"We were working on English homework together. Remember?"

"Friends are dangerous. See, now we are on their radar."

"Whose radar? I suppose you think the Russian mafia are after Bonnie?"

"Um, well." Artem sat on the couch next to Megan. "I just want to protect my daughter."

"You have. By having Nikolai teach me, you probably saved both our lives tonight." Megan leaned against his side, hugging him.

A phone rang. Artem went into the kitchen. "Yes, I see. All right." He came back into the living room. "You're right. Someone named Howard is in custody for killing a man. But the police have two bodies." He looked at Megan and raised his eyebrows.

"What?" She shrugged. "I had to."

"Did you give a statement?"

"No, they told me to go home. The police will be in contact tomorrow. That's another reason why we can't just leave." Megan placed a hand on his knee. "I would look guilty of something. Then we'd be fugitives in this country too."

Artem bowed his head. "You're right." He shook his head. "You shouldn't have gotten involved. This is what I mean when I say friends are dangerous."

Megan stared at her father. Was he serious? "Are you saying I should've let her die? That I should let those evil men walk free to kill others? When I have the power to stop them?"

"What I am saying is if you didn't have this friend, you wouldn't have to make that decision."

"Yea, she would have died, and I wouldn't be any wiser," Megan said sarcastically.

"Exactly." Artem smiled as if this was the lesson every child needed to learn.

Megan looked into her father's eyes, wondering if he was always cold and uncaring. "There's another reason why we can't go." She reached into the book bag and pulled out a semi-crumpled piece of paper.

He took the paper from her and straightened it. He flattened it as much as he could without smearing the pencil rubbing. He turned the paper, twisting and examining it. The longer he studied the writing, the more excited he became. "Is this real?"

"I took the rubbing this afternoon. As far as I know, it is real."

"But it could be a fake," Artem said.

“Sure, I suppose. But why would anyone fake a stone with cuneiform writing?”

“Because if it is real, it’s worth millions.”

“Millions?”

Her father nodded. “Millions. So, there is a reason to be suspicious of such an item.” Artem turned the paper, smiling. It seemed that Artem had forgotten about the trouble at Bonnie's house.

“I doubt Kevin would know. It’s not common knowledge.”

“Kevin? Who is this Kevin?” Artem scowled.

“He’s a boy from school.” Megan tried to placate her father with the simple statement, but he frowned further. “Kevin asked the history teacher about the writing, and I got involved. Especially when I saw the stone. I thought he stole it, but he said he found it in his grandmother's Wiccan things.”

Artem smirked. “I told you, it’s a witches stone.” He relaxed and looked at the paper again.

Megan sighed in relief. “Do you think the Chinese group would be interested in adding to their collection?”

"I don't have to think. Tai Lu told me, if anyone has a stone like hers, that she would buy it."

"Wow." Megan paced; her mind awash with thoughts. "Why are they worth so much? Can you read the words? What do they represent?" She wanted to ask a few more questions, but her father raised his hand.

"First." Artem opened his left hand. With his right, he pulled the erect pinky into the palm. "They are worth millions because Tai Lu has a huge bank account, and she wants all the stones that look like this. And before you ask, I don't know why."

He pulled his ring finger in toward his palm. "Second. All the stones have the same engraving." He sighed, looking at Megan, expecting another question. "Alright, I'll translate it if it pleases you. Now that I have a rubbing that ought to be easier to accomplish."

Artem added his middle finger. "Third. The inscription says, and I quote, "The stone shall protect the bear till the end of time."

"The bear?" Megan raised her eyebrow. "Bear?"

"Tai Lu and I agree that it must have meant bearer, or the one who holds the stone." Artem smiled. “You didn’t think it meant an actual bear, did you?”

“You never know. We have seen some unusual items listed in cuneiform.” Megan frowned and repeated the quote, tapping her hand. “That’s only twelve syllables.”

Artem shrugged. “Some things can be lost through translation.”

“I know, I know, Sumerian or Acadian is not one for one with English. Still, it ought to be close. Shouldn’t it?”

“You always want a mystery.” Artem chuckled. “The syllable count ought to be within a tolerance of two for every ten. For twelve, you ought to have a tolerance of two or three.”

Megan cracked her knuckles and leaned back on the couch, feeling smug. “There are over thirty syllables, assuming I broke the cuneiform correctly.” She handed the folded paper to her father. “Look for yourself.”

Artem’s smile fell. He opened the paper and counted. “You’re right.” He dropped the paper to his lap. “Why would Tai Lu lie about the inscription?” He folded the paper, stood, and put it in his pocket.

“To hide something,” Megan said.

“Okay. But why lie about something that I can figure out?” Artem rubbed his chin.

"What if they don't know it is a lie? They say a sucker is born every minute. Might be this collector is a sucker?"

"Perhaps and perhaps not." Artem paced, tapping his bottom lip. "While the Field Museum has an object, it is not under the nose of government officials. If a collector wanted to hide something of value, it would be easier to hide if it were out of the country. China isn't exactly a friendly government. This Chinese collector could be quite wise." Artem smiled at his daughter. "Looks like you have your mystery."

Megan rubbed her hands together. "We could use the computer and translate it now." She stood and moved toward the study.

"Wait." He held up his hand, then dropped it. "No, no, go ahead. It'll be fine; they won't care about stones or cuneiform. They will assume I am working."

Artem's home computer was museum purchased and owned. It was connected to the museum system through a network, allowing him to work from home. He rarely used the machine and often wouldn't allow Megan to use it either.

Megan ran into the study and turned it on. It had been unused for so long it had an update.

She knew her father worried about the U.S. government or Russian mafia listening to his phone calls, bugging the house, or watching online. The worry seemed unjustified; no one cared what he or she did. No one was watching. Their computer was linked to the museum, not the outside world. It had no search engines or other software to navigate. As far as Megan was concerned, no one could possibly know the computer was in use.

After the computer came on-line, Megan looked at the syllables for each of the cuneiform marks. She tried Acadian first, but her first translation didn't work. All that appeared was a string of sounds, not words. Megan attempted another series of words but found nothing. Feeling a little frustrated, she tried Sumerian, but that resulted in a similar gibberish answer.

Artem entered the den, left a sandwich and iced tea near Megan, and left the room. She ate absently as she attempted to figure out the puzzle. The stones in the museum were from China. They could be written in Mandarin or Mongolian. Megan tried her assumption, but the other languages didn't work any better than the first two. The carving on Kevin's stone was old; she was sure. The language could be from something older than Acadian or Sumerian. But, newer? English? She doubted it but tried anyway. Nothing.

She placed her head into her hands and sighed. Megan returned to Acadian and tried more words.

"Dorogoy, it's midnight. You need to get to bed," Artem called down the hall.

# Chapter 17

An old tan, four-door sedan was parked outside Grandma Ruby's house. On the driver's door was a strange star logo with the letters AKG. Both the logo and the lettering were in a tone that was only a few shades lighter than the vehicle itself. None of the neighbors owned the ugly car, he would have remembered. An unfamiliar man sat in the driver's seat, reading a book and drinking from a thermos.

Ruby met Kevin on the porch. "Good, your home. Your mother wants to have dinner with us tonight."

"But we already had ravioli."

"I told her, but she wouldn't hear it. She wants us to come over."

Kevin sighed. "Do you know who that is?" Kevin hiked his thumb over his shoulder toward the ugly vehicle.

"Oh, that's Johnny." She smiled, looking fondly back at the car.

"What's AKG?"

"When I asked him. He showed me his badge and said, 'It's just a multi-government agency, with no jurisdiction or governing country. Got any coffee?'" A wistful smile crossed her face.

Kevin frowned at his grandmother. "What the hell, Gran…Ruby?" He turned to look at the tan car. Johnny lifted the thermos and drank. "Tell me you didn't give him coffee."

"Of course, I did."

Kevin rolled his eyes. "What's he doing here?"

"Trying to catch a smuggling ring. But I don't think he told me the truth."

Kevin nodded. "I'm not sure anything he said was true. He doesn't know you. You could be the neighborhood gossip."

Grandma threw her head back and cackled. "I am the neighborhood gossip!" She grinned, eyes twinkling.

Kevin steered her into the house. "I want to cast that spell tonight. Do you think you can help me?"

"You need to do the spell for me, remember: strength and youth."

"That's not what I mean. I need help writing the spell. But I was going to take care of it."

Grandma nodded. "Let me think about it." She wrapped her good arm around Kevin, and they walked out the back door. "Oh, wait. Johnny told me to lock up the house." She shrugged, looking at Kevin's disapproving face. "What? Not like it's a bad idea."

"But the front door is unlocked." Kevin pointed out.

"Is it?" She stood on the back stoop, thinking. "Bah, it'll be okay. Johnny's out there."

"Hey, wait for me." Inez scrambled out of the treehouse; she stopped beside them. "I can see into your bedroom from up there. The whole thing! We'll have to get walkie-talkies." She skipped away from them, opening the gate.

Kevin looked at his sister, appalled at what she might see if he had Annie spend the night. He made a mental note to keep the drapes shut.

The three of them walked into the empty kitchen. Laughter and conversation came from the dining room. In the middle of the table was a huge pan of lasagna, flanked on either side by garlic bread. Even though Kevin ate recently, it smelled so good; he felt starved.

"You're late," Mom grumbled. Her eyes snapped on Inez. "And where have you been?"

Inez shrugged. "The treehouse."

"I shouted for you to come in an hour ago." Mom's eyes narrowed dangerously.

Inez shrugged again. "I must not have heard."

"I bet *not listening* is what happened," Grandma whispered and then ruffled Inez's hair

Inez giggled then sat next to her sisters.

"How did things go this afternoon?" Mom asked Kevin.

Kevin decided not to tell his mom about the missing Mr. Tibbles incident. "I think everything went okay. But honestly, I'm at school for seven hours. Would it be too much to ask if you checked on her at noon?" Kevin felt a kick from under the table.

He looked at Grandma Ruby. "What? I want to make sure you eat lunch. I don't think you ate today."

"Mother," Dad scolded.

Grandma rolled her eyes. "I'm older than the lot of you. I don't need any mothering."

"Grandma," the triplets whined in unison. "We don't want you hurt again."

Kevin didn't know if the girls were cute or creepy. He shuddered. Creepy, he decided.

Grandma sucked in her breath and cooed. "Oh, my babies." She smiled sweetly at the girls. Then shot a narrow gaze to Dad than Mom. "Alright, I relent. A noon phone call will do. But that's it. Kevin is doing fine." She patted his arm. "Just fine."

After dinner and countless games, Kevin and Grandma headed home. While passing under the clubhouse, Kevin felt like they were being watched. He turned to see the triplets at their window waving.

Grandma tried to open the back door, then sighed and dropped her hand. "I knew there was a reason I don't lock my doors." She beckoned to Kevin. "We'll have to go through the front." They walked along the dark side of the house. "Watch your step, don't squash Benny."

"I'm watching," Kevin reassured her, even though it was too dark to see, and that Benny was a figment of her imagination. They climbed onto the porch and entered the house.

Grandma Ruby looked over her shoulder to the tan car and waved at Johnny. "I'll be right back," she said, then ran to the car and leaned into the window. She returned, chuckling. "I love it when plans come together." She waved her hand. "Would you please get the books?"

Grandma sat on the living room floor and laid them out to read the covers. She opened the

Witches Grimoire searching for something specific. Occasionally, she nodded and said something under her breath. Finally, Grandma looked up from the book. "We need to write our ideas down. Do you have a notebook?"

Kevin ran to his room and returned with a new composition notebook.

Grandma Ruby wrote instructions for him to follow.

1. *Must be naked.*
2. *Must have four candles, pink, mint, light blue, and yellow. Each one must be at north, south, east, and west.*
3. *Pour a circle of salt.*
4. *Light the candles.*
5. *Cast your spell at precisely 9 pm. (listen for the grandfather clock)*

Kevin looked over her shoulder, reading the instructions. "Naked? Are you serious?"

"I'm always serious," Grandma said. "Clothing blocks the energies of the spirit. Those coming and going."

"Four candles, does it matter what color points north? Where is north anyway?"

Without hesitation, Grandma pointed toward the television and the wall where it hung. "It doesn't matter, but if you want to do it right, ask the candles which one wants to be north."

"*Wants to be north*?" Kevin looked at his grandmother like she was crazy.

She nodded. "Hover your hand over the candles and think or say north and touch the candles. One of them will volunteer to be the north candle. Do the same with the south, east, and west. Trust your grandmother. You'll see."

Kevin rolled his eyes. *It's no wonder Mom thinks Grandma is a nutter.*

"Oh, this is a good one." Grandma tapped a spell in the book. "Look." She pushed it toward Kevin.

Kevin read the passage then asked. "Do I chant this once or twice? Or more?"

"Once. But you'll need more than just words. You'll need some earth and a bowl of water. The sky is all around; you won't need that, and the candles provide fire." She thought for a moment. "Make sure your window is open to allow the sky and Goddess to see and hear you."

"Goddess?" Kevin wondered if he was doing the right thing. "Feels like I'm betraying God."

Grandma squinted at Kevin. "The Goddess is mother nature. If a Wiccan spell is to work, she must give her blessing. You're helping me. God will understand, and if he doesn't, he's not worth your time."

Insulted at first, Kevin stared at her. But she was right. Wicca wasn't his belief system; he was helping. He wouldn't be in trouble with God. "What about the girls? Inez said she could see in my window. I'll be naked."

"She can only see into your room from the clubhouse." Grandma reminded him, chuckling. "Besides, it'll be nine. Your mother will have seen to it that she's sleeping."

She pointed to the ceiling of the living room. "Your room is right above this room. I'll be down here, casting my spell. If we both start at the chime of nine, we will build a spell column. Two is better than one, of course, three would be best." Ruby tapped her steepled fingers together. She looked toward the front door. "When you're done with your spell, go to bed. I don't want you to come downstairs. I'll be naked too." Grandma hid her embarrassment behind her hand, then snickered. "In the morning, we can discuss how things went. If the spell worked or if we need to do something more." She glanced at the clock. "Please bring everything to the kitchen."

Kevin set the books on the kitchen table. Grandma dug in a cupboard; she had four small glass bowls on the countertop above her head. "Two for you, and two for me."

"I only need one."

"One?"

"I'll use a rock instead of earth." Kevin thought the protection stone made logical sense to use in the spell. He felt the weight of it inside his pocket. "I have the perfect stone for the spell."

"Indeed?"

Kevin nodded. "Indeed."

"Take a container of salt and go upstairs. Get ready." Ruby pointed to the cabinet above the stove.

Kevin opened the cabinet. Inside were many glass jars with salt written on them. He pulled out two, leaving one on the stovetop. He caught sight of the time on the green digital display, 8:36. "We have about twenty minutes."

"Would you fetch four candles for me?"

"Sure." Kevin ran to his room to pull candles from the other box. They were about three inches long and thin like a standard taper candle, only shorter. When he returned, Ruby had already created a large circle of salt on the floor. "Why is your circle so big?"

"It's a big spell." She took the candles and shooed him away.

Kevin ran up the stairs, opened the curtains, and lifted the window. He pulled the short, stubby candles from the box, taking his time, asking each one if it was a north candle. As ridiculous as he felt asking them, he was shocked when the light blue candle volunteered. The yellow wanted to be south, green east, and pink west. Kevin laughed as he placed each candle, wondering if he was as nutty as Ruby.

He placed the bowl with water on the floor next to the stone from his pocket. Kevin took off all his clothes, feeling foolish, and poured a circle of salt. He sat back on his heels, waiting for the grandfather clock to chime nine. The open window allowed a cool breeze to caress his skin.

As the chimes rang through the house, Kevin lit the candles. When the clock became quiet, he stood, with the bowl in one hand and stone in the other, held out from his body like the arms of a scale.

Kevin called out the spell Ruby picked out for him:

"With the strength of water,
With the endless sky,
With the eternity of earth,
With the intensity of fire,
Bring forth the power of protection."

The stone and water grew warm. Kevin smiled, pleased that something obvious happened. That pleasure turned to worry as the water steamed. That must be perfectly normal. He squatted and gently placed the bowl on the floor.

Only by removing the water did Kevin notice the heat and weight of the stone. "What's happening?" He tried to drop it, but it held fast to his flesh, melting into his palm, disappearing. "No, no, no!" He gripped his wrist as if he could stop it, staring fearfully. The heat felt pleasant as it traveled to his extremities. Kevin relaxed, feeling euphoric.

The warmth reversed course and pulled itself together near Kevin's heart. It felt heavy sitting there. The pleasant warmth that enveloped his body grew stronger, building into burning heat. Kevin leaned forward, holding his chest. He tried to scream, but only a moan escaped his lips.

His eyes watered.

Air would not come.

Panic attacked his brain. *Run,* it told him. He stood. A cord of pain ripped down his spine. He fell. Blackness covered his sight, and his mind became silent.

# Chapter 18

Kragnor stood, slowly opening his eyes. He reached long and far with each limb. He stretched his wings, feeling his tendons scream with tension. "Focus," he grunted to himself. He closed his eyes and continued reaching without the distraction of the strange objects surrounding him. Mentally he felt the extents of his body, fingers, toes, tail, and wingtips. He stopped his mental cataloging. Something was wrong, different.

Kragnor focused on the room and objects closest to him. On the floor were four burning candles and a circle of salt. Some things never change. He extinguished the candles. Too much wood and cloth to leave them unattended. Not that flame would hurt him. No, but other things live in buildings, humans, mice, bats, and insects.

His eyes adjusted to the starlight entering the open window. Spread around the room were human trappings, furniture, clothing, blankets, and art on the walls. The artwork was strange and flat. It wasn't made of canvas, paint, and wooden frames; instead, paper and ink were used. Whatever it was, it was starkly different, shiny, and smooth. The smell was wrong. Kragnor sniffed again. No, this place smells and feels wrong. He trembled with misgiving. This is not where I slept last.

Muffled rumbles filled his head. Thunderstorms? No, it doesn't sound right, more like the drone of a beehive. Warmth stirred around his legs, and the strange smell intensified. He snorted with distaste.

The window. He preferred nature to human-made things. Kragnor pulled his wings tight against his sides and back, passing through the narrow pane and onto the roof. Kragnor backed away from the edge, the streetlight, and detection from prying eyes.

The night air was cool, but here the odd smell was more potent. The air was dirty, like a busy city. Oil and metal ambrosia hung heavy, and the wind didn't lessen the scent. The insistent rumble continued. He stood on the peak of the roof, rising as tall as his body would allow. In the distance, the white and yellow lights of cars and trucks moved, slithering north. Red lights shifted south. Could this be a fire serpent? Perhaps two, intertwined? The animal didn't appear natural. It followed the same course and made noises Kragnor never heard before.

How much did he not know?

The wooden structure he stood on was small, almost delicate, and the nearest building was set apart, with open space, an old oak tree, shrubs, and grass. There were no tall or bulky structures, nothing to imply city. Still, the greasy odor clung to Kragnor's nostrils, indicating otherwise.

The lights from the neighboring building didn't flicker the way oil lamps or candles did. Yet it seemed as if light filled the entire building. The streetlamps didn't waver either.

A young male and female, dressed for chilly weather, walked down the sidewalk arm in arm. They looked at the lower level of the house he stood on. Their faces expressed surprise, followed by wonder. A small thud from behind made Kragnor turn. A lithe shadow dropped from the oak tree. It ran to a nearby house and climbed through a window, a young human female.

Kragnor looked to the sky. These stars are different, not unfamiliar; no, the viewing angle was different. The last time he saw them, they were bright and beautiful, and the Milkyway splashed across the abyss. Kragnor blinked and grunted. The stars were dull like a thin black cloth covered his eyes. The difference in brightness unnerved him. What happened to make the sky lighter? Did the planet move away from the stars? The idea seemed unlikely, even impossible.

Three bright blinking stars moved in conjunction with each other. Their movement was against the rotation of the constellations. They were slower than a shooting star, yet more brilliant, rumbling Kragnor's chest as they approached and passed. Could it be a dragon? With riders who carry lights? Kragnor felt like that was a ridiculous idea, but it was one he could understand.

Another grumbling sound approached, low and close to the ground, on what appeared to be a road. Two bright lights grew with the sound. The shine was the right height for a horse and carriage, but no horse pulled that fast or made that sound. No light could be that bright. There was no smell of horses. He watched the horseless carriage race past, growling, and vibrating as it went. Red lights chased it.

The constant rumbling he heard before and the smell of oil and steel made sense. How long did he sleep? He looked to the stars, imploring them.

He tried to remember the last human city he saw. Paris, yes, that was its name. He scratched his head. What human year was that? He grunted. A small earthy chuckle escaped his lips. What human year was it now? Often, after sleeping for a year or more, it took days to remember the little things. He needed seclusion from all these new and strange objects if he were to focus and remember.

He needed his home in Ninab, where he could meditate. Where the sounds of mother earth vibrated and where his torans lived. Toran were portals that would take him almost anywhere on the planet. Anywhere, and yet he felt this land was new. His lips pulled back from his teeth, showing a feral grin. He was both afraid and excited.

Kragnor descended from the roof slowly. The materials that made up the house were soft, like wood and tar. Carefully he moved back into the room, hoping to find the human who resided there and to receive answers. Humans always had answers. They were not always correct. Still, he could learn something, even if it was opinion.

After slipping through, he pushed the window down. It moved fast and struck the casing. The glass shattered, and many pieces fell from the frame. Kragnor picked up a shard. He rubbed his finger along the edge. Feeling alone and confused, he pulverized the glass in his fist.

Kragnor closed the curtain. The rod fell off its brackets and lay at an odd angle. He snorted, turning away from the window. Why was everything so fragile?

Even though he didn't require heat during the winter months, Kragnor noticed a temperature difference between the room and outside. Yet, there was no fireplace. Magic?

The bed was small, with wooden posts at each corner. Someone important must live here, as beds are expensive. But only a single someone as the bed was too small to hold more than two.

High on a shelf, as if in a display, were a few books. Kragnor hooked one with his clawed finger and pulled it from its companions. On the leather spine and cover of the book was written, "Lord of the Rings," in beautiful cursive. English, he grunted to himself. French was spoken in Paris. *Could I have moved from France to England while I slept?*

He turned the idea in his mind. France and England are not so far apart that it would be impossible. But with horses and wagons, and then boats, it would take almost a month for humans to do so. He had not slept for more than a day in centuries, especially with the… Kragnor huffed in frustration. His memory flitted away like a moth in the night.

He carefully opened the book and read the text. It was indeed English, but the language had changed significantly. Human language evolved from year to year, new words added, and old words removed from the vernacular. Some texts didn't change at all. Religious scriptures often took time to change, if they changed at all.

Was this text religious? He read more, his mind adjusting to the changes in language. Kragnor decided the book was a legend. It lacked the notations and verses of scriptures. His brow knitted. The changes from the English he knew to this English indicated centuries had passed.

Centuries. That explained why his memories were unformed.

Kragnor slid the book back with its brothers. Stone bookends held them in place. The brown and white streaked alabaster seemed to mock him, sitting high on the shelf, silently witnessing. "How did I fail to see you?" he whispered. Kragnor took the stone and cradled it. His finger caressed the smooth glassy surface. "Salutations, young one," he said softly, more with his mind, than his voice. The stone didn't respond. It should communicate, but it did not.

Kragnor focused, pressing the palm of his hand to the alabaster surface. Images of the room fluttered in his mind. He saw himself and then a young man. He refocused, playing the picture back, but the stone's memory jerked through time. One second the boy was there, then he was, then both gone. Kragnor went deeper into the memories, noticing the same breaks of time throughout. He discontinued the link with the stone and turned it in his hands. Under the glassy surface was a crack that spider-webbed through the entire bookend. He glanced at its twin; it too was broken in a mirrored fashion. Kragnor frowned and huffed his dissatisfaction. The imperfection was probably a beauty mark and selling point to the human who found it. But to him, the splintering break was a hindrance. The stone couldn't share its memories or communicate properly. He set it back on the shelf.

Three identically stained oak doors led out of the room. Kragnor selected one and opened it. Sweet odors rolled down a set of stairs. Wood, dust, mice, bats, paper, and old fabrics tossed their smells into the air, enticing Kragnor to join them. Cedar and oak, old, familiar friends. As he climbed the creaking stairs, the treads bowed under his weight. His claws clicked and scratched the surface. He gripped the walls to help relieve the burden on the stairs.

Kragnor's eyes adjusted, allowing him to see in pitch dark. Objects, both strange and familiar, covered the room. It was the smell that comforted him, bringing forth memories, long hidden. He smiled, feeling content.

Here he could meditate.

Here he could remember.

He opened a cedar chest, allowing the scent to wash over him. The fabrics inside the chest were old. Under his rigid and unyielding fingers, the clothing tore. Carefully he pulled the items free of their companions and lifted them to his face, breathing in deeply. He pulled the rest out of the chest and laid them on the floor in a rough circle, a nest. Kragnor lay on top and among the fabric. He pulled the open chest closer, tipping it on its side, placing his head inside, breathing in the aromatics.

He closed his eyes, trying desperately to remember what event led to his emergence here. What was the last thing to happen? He focused on what he last remembered. A cathedral. Oil lamps. Candles. Open-air. Night sky. Stained glass. Metal bars. An urgent summons. A friend. A trick. A trap. Broken trust. Boniface. Francois. Death. Hiding. Courage. Fear. Prison. Escape. Images and thoughts flashed in his mind, but they were unformed.

Broken thoughts and broken memories, like the bookends.

# Chapter 19

Kevin threw an arm wide and stretched. Clunk. Panic filled his mind. He was in a box. A coffin? He looked down at his body. No, only his head was in a wooden chest. He felt the scurry of little feet running across his body. Four small grey shapes ran into a corner.

He pulled his head out of the chest and sat up. Cardboard boxes were askew, not the organized rows of the day before as if a small tornado had gone through. Kevin blinked, trying to think. I cast a spell for Ruby, and then I was going to see Annie.

Annie!

Kevin stood. When the blankets, fabrics, and clothing fell to the floor, a cool breeze brushed across his skin. He was naked. “Oh, come on. What the hell?” He went to the stairs and noticed fresh scratches on the walls and treads. He reached out, touching the sharp gouge in the stair. His index finger fit into the gaping wound. “Why do I feel like this is a practical joke?”

The broken window and toppled curtain were evident as the cool air touched his skin. The circle of salt was scattered and kicked around. The candles were snuffed and left on his desk. His closed laptop was not where he left it. "I don't remember putting those there. Who else was in my room last night?"

He dressed, found his phone, and stared at the time. Collecting his book bag, Kevin ran down the stairs and found Ruby on the couch. She was sleeping, her naked arm and shoulder hung out of the blanket.

Kevin shook her awake, holding her blanket in place. "Are you alright this morning? I have to rush; I'm late for school."

"Are you late now?"

"Yes"

"Then, rushing won't make a difference." Ruby yawned and stretched, exposing more skin.

Kevin turned away, not wanting to see naked grandma bits. He rushed to the kitchen and rifled through the cabinets taking a few granola bars. He jogged to school. Kevin's thoughts turned inward. He was worried about not seeing Annie last night. She'd probably be hanging out with Tony again. Kevin sighed heavily, then readjusted his backpack. As he entered the school grounds, he realized he ran the entire distance and was not breathless.

He stopped at the office to get a note for his first class.

"Good morning, ladies."

The secretaries looked at him with pleasant smiles. "What is going on, Kevin?" Mrs. Renfro asked. Her black hair was in a bun with five or six pencils stuffed to hold it in place.

"I'm late; I need a pass to go to psychology class."

Mrs. Renfro tsked at him, then smiled. "I don't think you've ever been late before, Kevin. Your mother told us you're helping your grandmother." Mrs. Renfro smiled at Mrs. Granger. "That's so sweet. I hope my grandkids are as good as you." She handed him a slip of paper. "Here you go, dear."

"Thank you," Kevin said, then slipped out the door and trotted to his class. He opened the door, crossed the room, gave Mrs. Anderson the note, and then took his seat.

From the moment he entered the room, he felt the stare of Tony and his cronies. Whenever the teacher went to the board to write something, Tony would turn and smile at Kevin. A smug smile. The smile of a criminal. Vin and

Chad seemed to be in on the joke. They often nudged Tony and snickered.

Did Tony know what happened last night? Did he cut scratches in the stairs? Or break the window? Kevin stared daggers into the back of Tony's head.

Mrs. Anderson gave an assignment, and the bell rang. Kevin rushed to his locker, dropping off his bookbag. He scanned through his phone and tried to contact Annie. She ignored or blocked him on every social site. "Damn it!" he swore under his breath.

Kevin stood in the cafeteria line to grab his food. The room was buzzing with kids talking about an attack on a girl named Bonnie. She was severely injured and ended up in the hospital under police protection. Her father killed the attacker, shooting them with a shotgun. Megan was there and either killed a second attacker or saved Bonnie's life. Speculation flew. Why was Bonnie attacked? Who was shot? Was her father a hero, or did he shoot Bonnie's boyfriend?

Across the room, he spotted Annie sitting with Tony. Not just sitting with him but hanging on him and snuggling into his arm and shoulder.

Kevin was disgusted. He walked over and said, "We need to talk."

Annie spun around.

Kevin closed his eyes and shook his head; something was wrong. Annie looked different, like a curtain or mist surrounded her. Annie's facial features were distorted, maybe even ugly. He backed away.

"Talk?" She laughed. "No. Look after you didn't make good on your promise to come over at ten, I went to your house. I looked in your front window. There were candles, and I could hear lovemaking. Hell, I could see lovemaking. I don't know who you were with, but I bet it was that bitch, Megan." Annie blinked back tears and pouted like someone kicked her puppy.

To Kevin, her charade looked fake, staged.

"You can have her. I don't need you; I have Tony." Annie brushed Tony's face with her hand. "But then again, I've always had Tony when I wanted him. Haven't I, babe?"

Tony smiled devilishly at Kevin and wagged his eyebrows. Tony met Annie's eyes. "I'm at your service." He bowed his head.

Kevin looked closer at Tony; he too looked different, like he was drunk or drugged. "Are you saying you were with him when we were dating?" He felt betrayed, and yet her revelation didn't bother him. As if, deep down, he knew. Why didn't he care?

Annie batted her eyes at Kevin, then shrugged. "He's good at what he does. You're..." she touched Kevin's cheek, "...nothing but a pretty face, and an amateur, and, well, a girl has needs." Annie laughed.

Kevin backed up, bumping into a kid eating at a different table. Even her touch was different, repugnant. What was wrong with him?

"Look, I think you've made him mad," Tony said. "Let's go to my car and make out."

Annie smiled at Kevin and shrugged. She slipped her arm around Tony's waist, and the couple left the lunchroom, in total comfort, like they were lovers for years.

More confused than hungry, Kevin left his food and exited in the opposite direction.

Kevin sat on the stoop outside the gymnasium, his back to the glass doors. He listened to the dull sound of basketballs striking the floor or bouncing off backboards.

The unpredictable thuds helped Kevin think. What the hell was going on? He cast a spell for

Ruby last night, and things changed. *Why don't I care about Annie, like I did yesterday? I was all but prepared to die for her. I was going to go to her house and make love to her.* Kevin shuddered. He didn't want anything to do with her. She was poison; he could feel it, smell it, taste it. Tony could have her.

The door behind him swung open quickly, striking the wall. "You're a hard person to find."

Kevin turned; it was Megan. She looked different too. Cleaner, no, that wasn't right. Clearer. *Yes, I can see her more clearly.* Like she was hidden in shadow before. Hidden? Kevin closed his eyes and shook his head again. He rubbed his head with his fingers, half expecting to feel bumps and bruises of an injury.

Megan plopped down on the stoop beside him. "My father wants to see your stone. He says if it is genuine, he would like to buy it. It could be worth millions. I was shocked."

Kevin opened his eyes. "Wait a minute. What?" He looked critically at Megan. Her clothing was not lavish or expensive. Nothing fancy, no brand names. Nothing to show off her shape. Nothing beautiful like Annie owned. Nothing like Annie used to flaunt her sexuality. Instead, Megan looked sincere, honest, courageous, and beautiful in her own way. "Your father wants to buy my stone for millions?"

Megan nodded. A smile plastered on her face. "Yes, can you believe it?"

"No, actually, I can't." Kevin put his face into his hands. He shook his head, trying to clear it. "Does your family have that kind of money?"

Megan's smile fell. She stood and backed away from Kevin, pulling on her plain sweatshirt and crossing her arms. "Of course, we don't." She stepped on the stoop and opened the door. "The museum is interested. My father would broker the deal." She walked through the door and let it slam shut behind her.

"I'm sorry," Kevin shouted at the closed door. But Megan didn't hear; she was on the other side of the doors and hurrying away.

# Chapter 20

Megan ran down the hall, away from Kevin and the thumping basketballs. What was he thinking? Why would he say that? Everyone was acting strange today, including him.

From the time she walked in the door, people stared at her. At first, she thought she was delusional, but she caught them from the corner of her eyes a few times. It was creepy. Maybe they found out she was at Bonnie's house when the attack happened.

Was Bonnie alright? Megan sighed. She hadn't heard anything, nor would she while at school. She went to the office. Mrs. Renfro was at the counter. Perfect. "I'm leaving early. I can't concentrate today," she said, wiping her eyes.

"Little surprise there, with what happened to Bonnie." Mrs. Renfro leaned forward as if Megan would fill her in on the details.

"Does everyone know?" Megan placed her laptop on the chest-high counter.

"Only what was on the news this morning, dear." Mrs. Renfro smiled. "No one knows everything except Bonnie and, perhaps, you. You were there, weren't you? You and Bonnie are as thick as thieves."

Megan nodded. She let a tear slip down her cheek. "I don't know how she's doing. I don't know if she'll live. They said they would call, but I haven't heard anything." She wrung her hands helplessly.

"You poor, dear. I bet you'd feel better if you went to see Bonnie."

Megan nodded. "But, my father…" her lip trembled.

"There's no reason for your father to know. I'll make sure you're marked present for the rest of your classes." Mrs. Renfro made a tsking sound, disapproving of Megan's father. "Now, you go and see your friend, and let me know how she's doing."

"I will. Thank you." Megan threw a pathetic smile at Mrs. Renfro. She collected her laptop and left out the front doors.

After driving for thirty minutes, the hospital complex loomed before Megan. Various sized buildings and parking lots intertwined, creating the heart of the hospital. The pristine grounds were covered in trees, sculptures, flowers, benches, and meandering trails. The hospital's core belief was that healing started with nature. Staff and volunteers guided the sick and injured along the trails while some patients participated in yoga and Tai Chi. Inside were more trees and plants for those who could not leave the buildings.

Megan found Bonnie's room on the third floor. A police officer with Timms written on his nametag stood outside Bonnie's door.

The officer stopped Megan. "Name?"

"Megan Petrov."

The man looked at a tablet. "I see. Do they know you're coming?"

"I don't know. Probably not."

Officer Timms grumbled then knocked on the closed door. "Visitor?" A moment later, the door opened, and Bonnie's mom peered out.

"Goodness, Megan. Why didn't you call?" Mrs. Schumacher beckoned for Megan to enter the room. The officer closed the door after her. Bonnie's mom took the chair next to the bed.

"I left school early so I could see Bonnie. I didn't think to call." Megan shrugged. Bonnie was in bed, lying on her back. Her legs were in a sling, with a weight attached. Bonnie appeared to be sleeping or drugged. "Is she alright?"

"Her back is broken, but there was no damage to the spinal cord. She must be quiet and still for a week. Then they'll x-ray again to determine if surgery is needed, or if she's healing well on her own." Mrs. Schumacher moved some hair out of Bonnie's face. "They sedated her. But it doesn't matter. She doesn't move much when she's awake." Mrs. Schumacher moved Bonnie's phone and rested her arm on the table.

"Oh," Megan was disappointed. She wanted to talk to her friend.

"The doctors say the prognosis is good." Mrs. Schumacher smiled. "I'm glad you were there that night. She could have been in worse shape."

"Worse?" Megan frowned. *Wasn't this bad enough?* "Is that why there's an officer outside her door?"

Bonnie's mom nodded, sobbing. "They don't know why she was attacked. They're afraid there could be another."

Megan knew why Bonnie was targeted. Annie. They started digging into Annie's past. Bonnie must have found something. Megan frowned. Something worth killing for. Her thoughts turned to her father and his paranoia that teetered on the insane. Something in Annie's life pushed her to that point too. But what?

Megan went to Bonnie's side and grasped her hand. She leaned forward and whispered to Bonnie, "I will find Annie's dirty little secret and take her down." She stayed in that position for a few minutes hoping Bonnie would respond.

Megan stood and made for the door.

"Leaving already? But you've just arrived." Mrs. Schumacher moved to the door as if to block Megan's escape.

"Is everything okay?"

"I'm scared. Scared for my daughter. Scared for my husband. Scared for the future." Tears streamed unabated down her cheeks. Her hands went to her face as she sobbed uncontrollably.

Megan stood glued to the spot. Her father acted irrationally from time to time, but he never became a sobbing mess. Not like this. Tentatively, Megan stepped toward Mrs. Schumacher and placed her arms around the woman she hardly knew.

Bonnie's mom leaned into the hug, sobbing even more. Eventually, she ran out of tears. Sniffles filled Megan's ears.

How could Annie have this kind of power? The longer Megan stayed, the angrier she became. What started as a harmless game turned very serious. Megan directed Mrs. Schumacher to a reclining chair and settled her in place, covering her with a blanket.

Megan looked from mother to daughter. How could she help? Nikolai would know. She opened the door to leave only to have the officer stare back.

"My superiors want you to make a statement." The officer said.

"Are you asking me to stay?"

"Yes." The man shrugged. "Wait in there." The officer indicated Bonnie's room.

"They're sleeping. I'll sit out here." Megan sat in a chair relatively close to the officer. The small table next to the chair had some magazines on it. She picked one and riffled through the pages. After a few minutes, a blonde woman in a brown pencil skirt approached.

"Megan Petrov?"

Megan nodded.

The woman pointed to a man in jeans and a button-up shirt. "This is Detective Karter Stanton, and I'm Detective Leanna Wayne." The man lifted his jaw to Megan.

"No offense, lady, but weird things have been going on. I'll need to see your ID." Megan closed the magazine and leaned back in the chair. Artem and Nikolai taught Megan her rights from a very early age. At any other time, she would deny the detectives any conversation until she had a lawyer present, but she was curious, and they seemed lax.

The detectives displayed their badges.

"What can I do for you?" Megan asked.

"We need you to make a statement about the events that occurred last night," Detective Wayne said.

Megan held up her finger. "One minute, please." She entered Bonnie's room and picked up her friend's phone, returning to the hallway. "Okay, where did you want to talk?"

"At the station," the woman said.

"Am I being charged with a crime?" Megan asked.

"No," Detective Stanton unwrapped a piece of gum and popped it in his mouth. His partner frowned at him.

"Then here will be fine. I want to be nearby if Bonnie needs me."

The detectives agreed. "Where?"

Megan remembered passing an alcove on her way to see Bonnie. She led the detectives there.

The doorway opened into a sitting area set inside a corner of the building. The windows were tinted, but the trees and park-like setting were beautiful. The room itself was small, with clusters of barrel chairs and ferns scattered in groups. Megan chose a chair that faced the entrance, opened Bonnie's phone, activated a recording program, and set it on a small table.

The detectives watched her. “What’s that for?”

“Miranda rights apply to you too.” Megan smiled and pressed record. “I don’t like being misquoted.”

“Clearly, you have a better assessment of your rights than the average citizen,” Detective Wayne stated.

Megan offered nothing and waited for their questions.

The detectives sat in the chairs opposite Megan. “Can you describe the events that occurred last night between the hours of three and six in the afternoon?” Detective Stanton looked at Megan expectantly.

“Without counsel to advise me? No.” Megan shook her head.

“Look, all we’re trying to do is understand the timeline of the events.” The woman smiled sweetly. "Don't you want the person who attacked your friend to come to justice?"

Megan frowned. "This line of questioning is open-ended. Either ask me a direct question, or I am leaving."

The woman frowned in return. "How did the man on the sidewalk die?"

"I am not a pathologist. That's a question your coroner should answer." Megan shrugged.

The detectives looked at each other, expressions unreadable. From behind them, a figure entered the room from the hallway. It was the man from the Honda Civic. Megan stiffened.

"Excuse me, Detectives. Officer Timms told me you were interviewing Megan Petrov." The man looked from the detectives to Megan and winked. "This is ill-advised."

"Who the hell are you?" Detective Wayne stood and stepped closer to him. Detective Stanton was slower to get to his feet.

The man pulled his badge and gave it to them. "Johnny Conner."

Detective Wayne studied the badge then shoved it into Johnny's chest. "AKG? I've heard stories about you guys taking over investigations." She shook her head as if uncertain. "Is that what you're doing here? You've no right."

"You'll find that it's you that's lacking rights. Megan here is under the protection of the United States Asylum laws. You will have to go through the right channels to interview her. Which, I suspect you haven't. That means anything you gathered today is inadmissible." Johnny put his badge away. "Second, you have no case. The bodies you had in the freezer were reported missing, among other anomalies."

Detective Wayne frowned. "That's right. Now I remember the stories. Seems that weird brings AKG out of the woodwork. Like cockroaches." Her lip curled, and she punched Stanton's arm. "Damn it, Stanton, you need to back me up."

Detective Stanton grabbed his arm. "Hey. What do you want me to do?"

Detective Wayne rolled her eyes. "Nevermind." She pointed at Johnny. "We're not going to take the back seat on this one. I don't care if AKG is international. We're going straight to the top."

"Sorry, detectives, only doing my job."

Detective Wayne flipped him off. "So are we." She left the waiting area with detective Stanton following in her wake.

Megan sat rooted to her chair. She slipped the phone off the table and put it in her pocket while the recording app still ran.

Johnny turned and dug into his pocket, withdrawing an envelope. He tossed it on the table. “Nice trick, but next time make sure they are silver or, better yet, jade.” He nodded, then left the room.

Megan snatched the envelope, opening it. The two needles from her jacket were inside.

# Chapter 21

Megan drove back to Avalon, stopping at Nikolai's gym. She pulled into the parking lot to see one car. Nikolai ought to be alone. She entered the building and stepped up to the empty front desk.

A few moments later, Nikolai emerged from one of the many doors that lined the waiting room. "Megan, you're not scheduled today."

"I'm not here for training. I need the name of a good hacker. Someone I can trust."

"Megan, Megan," Nikolai shook his head and placed his arms around her. "You know I trust all my contacts. That trust can be extended to you. I would never let any harm come to you." He kissed her forehead then led her through the door he emerged from.

Nikolai had a small apartment within the gym. In the first section was a wall of cabinets. From one, he pulled out a cell phone. Inside were ten or more, waiting to be used. She assumed they were burner phones.

Nikolai punched in a number from memory. “It’s me, Nik. I have a favor to ask. I see. No, it is for a dear friend. Okay.” He handed the phone to Megan.

Megan placed the phone to her ear. “Hello,” she said tentatively.

“No need for pleasantries. Tell me what you need.” The voice was American and female, probably from the northwest region.

“I need the background of Annie Brown, Avalon, Wisconsin. She’s eighteen, give or take. Be careful.”

“I always am. I’ll give my findings to Nikolai.” She hung up.

Megan handed the phone back. “Now what?”

“Now, we wait.” He put the phone back in the cabinet and waved Megan into his apartment. “Come sit, tell me what’s happening.”

Megan sat on the purple loveseat facing the small television. Nikolai sat in the wooden rocker, leaning forward, expectant. She sighed. He trusted her. She could be honest with him, even if her father would get involved in one way or another. “Remember the other day when I asked you about removing a threat at the school?”

Nikolai frowned with concentration. "Um, yes. I suggested an accident. Did I not?"

Megan nodded. "And research." She shook her head. "Bonnie was attacked last night. And all we did was research."

"You are certain it was the 'threat'?"

"Yes, the attacker gave a verbal message, giving a name to the threat."

Nikolai leaned back in the rocker, pushing himself back and forth by lifting and dropping his toes. "It's never wise to trust information from an attacker when it is freely given."

"I agree, but I believe he thought we were going to die."

"Is there anyone else who knows you were *researching* this threat?"

"Me, Bonnie, and you."

"Where was this research done?"

Megan frowned as she made a realization. "Bonnie's home or the library. Both would have pointed back to her address."

"Instances like these are why I leave the research to others. Then there is no trail back to me." Nikolai steepled his fingers.

"There was no reason to think we were in danger. The threat goes to high school with us."

"You go to that school." Nikolai pointed out. "Technically, you are just as dangerous, maybe even more so than this threat of yours. If you can be trained, so can others." He looked at her down his nose.

Megan understood. She had become complacent and trusting of her place in school. "This is America," she protested. "It's supposed to be safe here."

"Is it?" Nikolai folded his arms. "You've gotten soft. You were unprepared. You had a friend who was a burden in a time of crisis. You didn't consider the threat to be real. It was just a game to you." Nikolai shook his head, disappointed. "We've taught you better than that."

Nikolai was right. She failed Bonnie. A tear ran down her cheek. "This is bigger than one threat." Megan looked at him. "I killed a man, and Bonnie's dad killed the other. But the bodies are missing from the morgue."

Nikolai's eyes widened in surprise. "You did? Explain." A tug pulled at his mouth.

Megan recounted the attack, the silence like being in a bubble, the feeling of helplessness as her body seemed to be held in a vice, and the toss of needles into the man's eyes, breaking the hold.

"And the other?"

"Bonnie's father shot him from a few feet away in the chest with a Mossberg 500 tactical shotgun."

"Was there a hole?"

"Hole?"

"In the man's chest? Did he fold in half? Was there a lot of blood?"

Megan thought back to the moment but could only remember the man flying backward off the porch. "No, I don't think so."

A phone in the cabinet vibrated. Nikolai answered it. "Nikolai." He was quiet and motionless for a few minutes. "Yes, I understand. Thank you. Good night." He returned the phone and sat back in the rocking chair.

"Annie Brown was raped and nearly murdered three years ago. Her parents took her to a camp for Distressed and Troubled Teens. She returned to Avalon alone. Her parents went missing."

"Bonnie was researching Annie's parents the night before she was attacked. Do you know what happened to them?"

"No one seems to know. Two camp counselors adopted Annie and returned with her."

"I know her parents, I've talked to them, but for some reason, I can't think of their names or what they looked like." Megan shuttered at the strangeness of losing a selected bit of memory when she could remember it existed but not get to it.

"Camp DaTT has a reputation for rehabilitating young women, helping them become stronger and more capable than before. Since she returned, Annie has gained a police record, robbery, intimidation, attempted murder, and arson, to name a few. She's never been sentenced, never done time, always receives probation or a slap on the wrist. Almost always, a man takes credit for her indiscretions. Even when there is evidence of her guilt, video, witnesses, and DNA."

"Sounds like this camp creates criminals," Megan said.

Nikolai nodded. "It might be creating more than criminals. You said the dead men are missing from the morgue?"

Megan nodded.

Nikolai leaned back in the rocking chair, pulling on his chin. "Back in the Mother Land, there are stories old women tell children. Where women turn into wolves, where the dead walk among us, and where people control others with their voice. Perhaps they're not stories."

Megan's mind spun. All those boyfriends, they would kill for her. "Yes. There are boys in the school that will do anything for Annie. But this is real life, not legend. Zombies aren't real." She shrugged, thinking Nikolai's stories from Russia were just that, stories.

"Myths and legends have a sliver of truth." Nikolai scowled at her. "I'm not talking about zombies. That is a Haitian myth. I'm talking about something different and more powerful." He stood and paced, murmuring in Russian. Nikolai stopped and looked at Megan. "We have to bring your father up to speed on this one. He knows much about these Russian myths."

Megan groaned. *Coming to Nikolai might have been a bad idea.*

# Chapter 22

When the last bell rang, Kevin rushed to his locker to find Annie and Tony kissing passionately.

"Okay, enough of that," said Mr. Olsterholtz. The teacher didn't stray from his room's doorway. "You know the rules, no public displays of affection. Take that home."

"I plan to Mr. O," Tony said with a smirk. "I plan to."

Annie grinned. "We could visit the nunnery instead." She shot Kevin a wink and blew him a kiss as Tony pulled her down the hall.

Kevin was confused by his lack of feelings. Why wasn't he pissed? Annie was trying to bait him, but inside, Kevin didn't care. He opened his locker, grabbed some books for an assignment, and then moved as fast as the crowded hallway would let him.

Kevin jogged home, feeling invigorated, alive. The tan AKG car was down a different street. Johnny was in the driver's seat, drinking coffee. He saw Kevin and raised his mug in greeting. For a guy on a stakeout, he sure was conspicuous.

He crossed the street and stopped. “Hi, Johnny. You still on a stakeout?”

Johnny grabbed Kevin’s shirt and pulled him down closer to his car window. “Did Ruby tell you that?” He shook his head. “Well, this is no good if everyone knows.” He let go, fuming.

Kevin straightened his clothes. “Why did you tell her of all people?”

“She gave me coffee and treats.” Johnny cleared his throat. “And well, I could always use help. These stupid assignments don’t give me much to go on. I have the whole town to investigate, to look for,” his fingers racked the air, “something suspicious.”

“Suspicious? That’s vague.”

“Tell me about it. But I get paid whether I find anything or not. So, here I am, getting paid, drinking coffee, and reading a book. I can’t say anything else is going to happen.” Johnny laughed and took a drink from his cup. “Not like it would be the first time I got paid to get fat.” He rubbed his thin belly.

Kevin straightened as if to go.

Johnny grabbed his arm. “Do me a favor. Let me know if you see or hear of anything strange.”

"Yea, sure." Kevin made to pull away but changed his mind. "There was a rumor at school about someone getting attacked, and they are in the hospital. Someone else, maybe two, were killed."

"I know about that one. I've investigated it. It's suspicious but not the right *suspicious*. At least that's what my boss tells me." He shrugged then gave Kevin an appraising look. "You're in pretty good shape. You jog every day? When I was young, video games were my life."

"I suppose." Kevin shrugged. "I usually walk. Today I'm in a rush."

"Then you better get moving. Tell Ruby I said hi." Johnny picked up his phone.

"Yeah, sure," Kevin said. Johnny was right. Kevin never ran, not in school during gym, not anywhere. And yet he was running and not out of breath. He shook it off as weird. But suspicious? Suspicious enough to tell Johnny about it? He chuckled then pumped his legs, running faster than he thought possible. His house was only two blocks down the street and around the corner. When he reached the porch, his breathing was calm, not ragged like it would have been a couple of days ago.

Maybe it is suspicious; he ought to say something to a doctor. *Hey, doc. I'm in excellent shape, and I have no reason to be.* Kevin smiled at the ridiculous thought. Maybe there's a disease that makes people feel better than average.

Kevin opened the door and entered the front room.

Ruby was watching her program and looked up at his entrance. "You're home early."

"Am I?" Kevin shrugged. "I ran home. Oh, I saw Johnny, he said to tell you hi."

"Did he now?" Ruby smiled, brushing her hair with her fingers.

Realization struck Kevin between the eyes. The comment from Annie about coming over and seeing lovemaking made sense. "Grandma, err, Ruby, are you involved with Johnny?"

Ruby sat up in her chair and straightened her shirt. "So, what if I am?"

"But, but, you're so…"

"Old?" Ruby suggested. She laughed. "I might be older than you, but I'm not dead." She continued, snickering.

"What the hell? You've only known him for a day."

"And you've dated your Annie for how long?

"One week." For a moment, Kevin thought about telling Ruby that they broke up but decided against it. She was right, he was willing to have sex with her, and he didn't even know her.

Ruby's eyes twinkled with delight. "Hypocrite."

Kevin went upstairs with vivid and disturbing thoughts of Johnny and Ruby in his mind. He shook his head to remove them.

The Wicca boxes were on his bed. He saw the Gemstone book and opened it. The container was missing, but the square hole was still there, so at least he wasn't completely crazy.

"Did I remove the box and stone?" Kevin's brain was not cooperating. "I think I did. I took it to school and showed the teacher and Megan." He ran the events through his mind as he continued to look in the boxes. He placed all the items on his bed one at a time, no stone.

"Wait a minute. When I first showed Megan, she told me the stone might have value and to keep it safe. Then when I stepped out the door, Annie was right there. I bet she heard. I bet she knows it's worth money, and I bet she told Tony."

Kevin punched his bed. "Of course. That is why she tried to get me in bed. She wanted to get me out of my clothes to get the stone. I can't believe I'm that big of an idiot." He shook his head, suddenly remembering. "She never got me out of my pants, her father interrupted us. Tony must have come and stolen the stone. He broke the window and scratched the stairs. I bet I can get it back if I go to Annie's tonight."

Donna was in her kitchen, gathering plates, cups, and silverware. "Kevin, good. Set the table." She held out her arms. Kevin took the plates and carried them to the dining room.

Ruby went into the living room to play games with the girls. From the dining room, one of the girls said, "Is Kevin here too?" The voice was high and timid for one of the girls.

Kevin placed the plates and cups delicately, trying to eavesdrop, but nothing more was said. He finished setting the table and entered the living room. Inez stood and ran into the kitchen, calling, "Mom, do you need any help?"

"What's wrong with Inez?" Kevin asked Tess and Mina. They shrugged.

"That's weird. Is Inez scared of you?" Ruby shuffled the deck.

"I don't know." Kevin eyed the remaining triplets, who had begun talking in their made-up language.

Ruby sighed. “Well, I don’t think there will be any games tonight.” She moved to the couch.

Eventually, Inez reappeared, sitting with her sisters, and their private talk resumed. All three of their heads shoved together, whispers and gestures flew.

“Dinner is ready,” Donna said.

Kevin and Ruby went to the dining room and sat.

“Girls, dinner,” Donna said.

“Donna,” Ruby said. “Something has upset them.”

Donna put her hands on her hips. “This is ridiculous. I don’t have time for their nonsense.” She raised her voice so the girls could hear. “If they don’t come to dinner, then they’ll have to wait until breakfast to eat.” She sat and scooped spaghetti onto her plate.

“Let me see if I can talk some sense into them.” Ruby left the dining room.

Kevin took some spaghetti, eating because the normalcy was comforting. He didn’t want the girls afraid or mad at him. He loved them.

Ruby returned, shaking her head. “They want to wait until their father’s home.”

“Or until I leave?” Kevin suggested.

Donna reached out and patted his arm. “It’s okay, Kevin. Your father won’t be home for another ten minutes. Just eat. You know they get this way sometimes."

"Yea, but usually I'm in on the joke. Not the butt of it." Kevin set his fork at the edge of the plate.

Ruby patted his leg. "Perhaps we ought to take a doggie bag. Besides, there is plenty to eat at home." She looked at Donna. "The girls could use the nutrition."

"You're right." Donna conceded. "Leave the plates. I'll get them."

Ruby said in a loud voice. "Thank you, Donna, the meal was excellent, but Kevin and I have to go." She and Kevin left out the back door and walked home.

While in Ruby's garden, Kevin stopped. "I think I know what happened. Inez saw the spell I cast last night. She saw me naked."

"Oh," Ruby covered her smile with her hand. "I don't know why that would scare her. If anything, she would've made fun of you." Ruby placed her hand on Kevin. "Thank you for reminding me. You did a fabulous job. I feel a tremendous weight off my chest. I feel so good. I haven't taken my pain medications." Ruby spun in a circle as if rejoicing. Suddenly, she stopped and looked under some hosta leaves.

"What are you doing?"

"I wanted to thank Benny. Ah, there you are." Ruby moved the leaves aside. Kevin saw a small chubby person wearing a red cap, a yellow jacket, and a white beard. Ruby's shoulder obscured the rest of the gnome.

Kevin stumbled backward, shaking his head. He tripped on a raised bed, dropping on his butt.

"Are you alright?"

"I don't know." Kevin took a few deep breaths trying to calm himself. "The Benny I saw the other day looked like a toad. Today I see a tiny man. Am I going crazy?"

Ruby narrowed her eyes. "Come inside, don't worry about it." Ruby led the way, numbly Kevin followed.

"Sit, sit." Ruby directed Kevin to the small kitchen table. After a few minutes, she pressed a hot cup of cocoa into his hands. "I can't say I've heard of this happening before."

"What?" Kevin sipped the coca absently.

"Normally a gnome lets their presence become known in small bits, to let the human brain come to terms with their existence. I had plans to introduce you to him, but I needed his permission to do that, and it could take years." Ruby sipped at her cup. "You could be a born-witch. But knowing your mother's religious background, I find that hard to believe."

"I only went to church because Mom made me. It wasn't like I wanted to go." Kevin smirked. "Half the time, I fell asleep."

Ruby laughed at Kevin's admittance. "Still, you were in the church and on the grounds. If memory serves, you worked there too."

"Worked?" Kevin nodded. "Oh yea, I was an altar boy for a couple of years."

"No gnome would show themselves to you with that kind of stink."

"Stink?" Kevin raised his eyebrows.

Ruby waved her comment away. "You wouldn't notice it. It's more of a feeling than an odor."

"Are you saying that this is normal?"

Ruby thrummed her fingers on the table. "I wouldn't say it's normal, per se. It took me years to see a gnome, and that was with help. It took you a day, and you weren't ready. Perhaps casting that spell last night awoke the inner warlock in you." She took a drink, then shook her head. "Seems odd. I'll make some calls."

Kevin stood. "Thanks for the cocoa. I might go out. Get some fresh air and clear my head." He stepped to the back door.

"To see Annie too?" Ruby said with a wry smile. "Don't stay out too late. I'm worried about you. Now, if you see bigfoot while out, try not to scare him. He's a sensitive soul." Kevin stared at his grandmother. Benny existed, could bigfoot? What if Ruby wasn't crazy?

Kevin went into the back yard and dialed Annie's number. No answer. He pocketed the phone and jogged to her house. Could Ruby be right? Did he awaken his inner warlock by casting a spell? That seemed like a ridiculous idea. At the same time, it made perfect sense.

Annie's light was off, and her parents' cars were in the driveway. He climbed onto the roof and looked in her window. The moon illuminated the room well enough to see she was not home.

Kevin pulled out his phone to check the time. Almost nine. Annie could be at Tony's. He climbed down the porch post. He looked up Tony Meleta but found three different addresses. Kevin sighed and decided to try the closest house.

As he jogged, he imagined Tony and Annie hovering over the stone, talking about how they would spend their fortune. On the corner of Bluff and Knoll sat some earth moving equipment. Orange striped wooden horses with flashing yellow lights protected a yellow backhoe. The ditchwitch parked next to it had its signature chainsaw arm replaced with a large circular blade used to cut cement and blacktop. A rectangular section of the road was gone. A metal divider sat in the hole, holding back the earth. It looked like a water or gas line was being replaced.

Kevin skirted around the construction area. A sudden twist in his stomach made him stop. He thought he was getting a cramp. His temperature rose quickly. The hair on the back of his neck and arms stood tall. Pain ran along his spine from his hips to his shoulders. Ripping and tearing sensations made him cry out. He fell to his knees and passed out.

# Chapter 23

Kragnor stretched and noticed he was not in the attic where he fell asleep. He stood outside under a streetlight with torn and bloody clothing in piles at his feet. He bent, picked up a scrap, and sniffed. Memories of the previous night flickered in his mind. The wooden house with the warm and comforting room filled with wonderful smells and mysterious objects. Why was he not there upon awakening? How did he arrive at this location?

He dropped the cloth scrap and examined his surroundings. The ground was hard under his feet and talons. It looked like square blocks of grey stone, it felt like stone, but it didn't talk like stone. Nearby a long dark path with painted yellow and white lines ran from east to west. It smelled strongly of tar.

A persistent yellow light flashed. Candles and lamps didn't blink, not like that. Kragnor hopped, spread his wings, and glided to the light source. It was connected to a short four-legged wooden structure. Another stood next to the first, each blinking at a different rate.

Behind the lights was a grand machine. It was gigantic like the Persian water machines or Islamic wind machines, but with neither water nor sails were present, something else powered it. A cup-like scoop hung off an arm at one end and an even bigger flat scoop on the other. Kragnor tapped it with his claw, clanging the metal under the paint—human-made stone.

Stone was born of the earth, melted in magma chambers, formed by pressure and millennia, until it was one stone, one voice. Manstone, or metal, was also born of the earth, but humans heated it in their furnaces, purifying it, quickening mother earth's creation from millennia to hours. Manstone had many voices, many stories, but there's always a prominent voice in the chorus.

Kragnor touched the surface, allowing his mind to open, to listen. He pushed the quiet voices aside and focused on the loud, nearly singular voice.

The machine showed images of the holes it dug and filled. It shared the sounds of humans discussing cars and trucks and massive equipment that moved rocks and soil. Kragnor was impressed by the pictures and words in his mind. Humans have progressed. Two ideas stuck in his thoughts, a flat spinning masonry blade that could cut rock. And a strange substance called dynamite that was placed in the drilled holes, and then the rock exploded, flinging boulders and pebbles everywhere.

These machines and tools were weapons against his kind. In the past, if a human wanted to kill an akitu, they had to wait for slumber and drop them from a height tall enough to shatter granite. The density of an akitu body often didn't allow the body to crumble, only crack, and healing happened with time. Kragnor's body had scar lines from such cracks. Not from attempts on his life but the stupidity of youth. Wrestling and feats of strength were games all akitu partook in.

He removed his hand and his mind from the metal. A smaller machine sat next to the grand device. It had the masonry blade attached to its arm. Kragnor moved closer, fascinated, poking the flat surface with his claw. It didn't seem any more dangerous than a sword or ax. Curious, he spun the blade as he witnessed in the metal's memory, then touched the narrow edge with his fingertip, and it bit into his flesh. A burning sensation started at Kragnor's finger and screamed up his arm. He was familiar with pain, but this tool sent fear into his heart. It could kill him.

A vehicle approached, exposing Kragnor in the beam of its lamps. A head appeared, and a bright flash of white covered his body. Instinctively he lifted his wings to protect his eyes.

"Holy shit! Did you see that? Turn around." The car screeched to a halt and reversed.

Kragnor opened his wings and kicked into the air. Within a few beats, he flew above the car, houses, and trees. He inhaled and found the direction of the house that matched the smell of the torn fabric. His wings stretched, encompassing the air and pushing down, Kragnor gained lift.

The spires of a church caught Kragnor's eye. He flew closer, landing on the bell tower. The shingles slipped and crumbled under his weight. Kragnor dropped his hand to anchor to the roof. But he punctured through, tearing off the outer layer. He pushed off, not wanting to cause more damage to the building. The tower groaned. Kragnor plummeted to the ground, then opened his wings, stretching them taut, turning the fall into lift.

Kragnor circled the church, recognizing the cross symbol. It brought back feelings of fear and apprehension. A memory bubbled to the surface, and just as quickly, it was gone.

On one side of the church was a balcony that appeared to be stone. He landed. The structure took his weight, but it was not the stone he expected. It was like the road, stone but not stone.

The grounds below the balcony contained a cemetery but no gardens, no statuary, or brethren. Kragnor jumped to the grass, his wings folded behind him, like a cape. There wasn't a fence or gate around the cemetery, allowing him to walk among the gleaming headstones. To Kragnor, they were jewels.

These stones laid directly on the earth, level with the soil. They were thin and long. Nothing like the headstones Kragnor remembered, tall, elegant, and beautiful. Still, it was apparent that they were stone.

He placed his hand on a stone and felt it awaken. "Greetings, my child."

The stone expressed confusion, followed by the wonder of ignorance.

"Hush now, child. I need you to tell me what you have experienced."

Following Kragnor's guidance, the stone shared images of sad human faces staring down at it. Flowers came and went. Grass grew. A chisel and hammer scratched and cut its face. A whirling saw blade cut the slab free from its birthplace. And the blackness and the gentle hum of mother earth. The stone expressed happiness to tell its story.

"Thank you, child, now sleep," Kragnor told it. He pulled his hand away and read the date inscribed on the stone. 1912-2010. The years startled him, drawing old memories of Paris to the surface. The last date he remembered was 1298. Kragnor checked more headstones, discovering the most current year was 2025.

More than seven hundred years.

He moved around the cemetery looking for weathered stones, knowing they would have seen more. He found a statue. He smiled, but the figure didn't respond. He touched it, but it was silent. The statue was another object made from particles of stone, sand, and slurry. Kragnor snorted, shaking his head. What happened? Where are the brethren?

Kragnor listened to the lives of many more stones before he determined the cemetery to be too young to provide useful information. The sun made the eastern horizon glow. Birds began their morning chorus.

Feeling uncertain and overwhelmed by the time that passed, Kragnor wanted to be back at the house. He didn't know if the world was safe for an akitu. Kragnor leaped into the air, caught the wind, and flew to the house from the night before.

Knowing that the house was weak, he landed gently, then entered the broken window. Kragnor crawled across the floor and up the stairs into the attic. He curled up into the nest of familiar objects and smells, pulling them close, enjoying their weight.

Kragnor's mind turned and twisted. How could he figure out what happened? Where could he go? A different church or cemetery, an older one. Perhaps a bigger city.

His mind was filled with stone statues, mausoleums, and headstones. Feeling at peace, Kragnor slept.

# Chapter 24

Kevin opened his eyes and blinked a couple of times. "The attic?" He shoved the objects off his body. Somewhere in the mess, a bell chimed. He sat up, feeling something odd on his head. He reached up and pulled a long strand of cobweb out of his hair. Rolling the web into a ball, Kevin noticed a thin cut on his fingertip, not much more than a paper cut. Wouldn't be the first time he cut his finger and forgot the details.

He stood, letting loose the old quilt that covered him. "Naked? Again?" He sighed heavily and walked to his bedroom.

Kevin racked his brain but couldn't figure out how he got home. The last thing he remembered was trying to find Tony's house. He looked for his phone but couldn't find it. It was in his pants from last night. But his clothes were nowhere to be seen. The clock radio read 7:00. He got dressed and left the house through the back door without waking Ruby.

Kevin ran to Annie's house then retraced his steps, jogging. A woman and a dog ran on the other side of the road. He remembered the earth moving equipment but little else. He slowed and scanned the ground, looking for his phone. A pile of cloth sat near the corner. The pattern on the fabric looked like the sweatshirt he wore yesterday. Kevin swallowed hard as icy fingers crept up his spine. He kicked at the pile with his foot, moving the clothing aside. Jeans and shoes were underneath, everything was shredded, everything was his. Was that blood?

He grabbed the clothing, afraid that someone else might find them, and walked home. Kevin squeezed the pockets and found his phone undamaged. Where the sweatshirt and jeans were torn, the edges were bloody. What could do that kind of damage? He rolled his shoulders but felt no stiffness or pain. What if the blood came from someone else?

His thoughts flickered to the newest movie. Werewolf? The films always show a horrendous transformation, pain, blood, and gore. Each time the human turns to a beast, the beast is hungry and kills. Kevin's stomach flipped. He ran the rest of the way home. He checked his torn jeans' pockets for any loose change or keys and tossed the destroyed clothing in the garbage can before entering the back door.

Ruby was drinking coffee at the kitchen table. "Where were you?"

"Went for a jog." Kevin wiped his brow.

"In jeans?" Ruby looked at him sideways. "You must not have gone far. You're not even out of breath."

Kevin laughed at the oddness of the situation and what he wasn't telling her. Instead, he said, "It was too cold for shorts." He opened the refrigerator and poured a cup of milk. "Ruby, what do you know about werewolves?"

"I saw the latest movie, and it was awful."

"That isn't what I mean." He gulped a mouthful of milk and sat at the table. "I mean, like Buddy. Do you know anything about werewolves, like you do gnomes?"

Ruby looked at Kevin, really looked. "Is there something wrong, Kevin? Are you okay?"

Kevin drank more, his leg bounced. "I don't know." He looked at his hand, holding the glass. "I think I broke my bedroom window. But I don't remember." His leg bounced faster.

"Look at me." Ruby gripped his forearm.

He looked up, catching Ruby's eyes. They twinkled with amusement. "A broken window doesn't mean you're a werewolf."

Kevin opened his mouth to mention the torn bloody clothing. The scratches in the attic stairway and waking up naked every morning. But he changed his mind. No sense in worrying her until he knew for certain. "I know, I know."

"You can check the internet or the library. I don't know very much about movie creatures."

"How about your books?"

"My books are religious, not mythology," Ruby said, looking offended.

"I'm sorry." He looked down at his glass. "If it's all the same with you, I'd like to go to the library."

"Sure. Would you like to use the car?"

"No, that's fine, I don't mind walking. I need to think." Kevin finished his milk and set the glass in the sink. He opened the back door to leave.

"Don't you want some breakfast?"

"Nah, I'm not hungry." Kevin left and walked toward the library.

He walked a few blocks before he noticed the flashing lights of police cars. A wave of panic washed over him. Did they find a half-eaten body? He broke into a jog and stopped in front of St. Stephen's Catholic Church. The police were talking to Father Patrick McCobbe, a bald man in his late fifties.

The cops closed their notebooks, entered their car, and drove away. Kevin approached the priest. “Good Morning, Father.”

“Hello, Kevin. I haven’t seen you at mass for a couple of weeks.”

“I’ve been helping my grandmother.”

“Oh, yes, your mother mentioned that.” Father Patrick watched the police cars disappear. “Come.” He turned and walked to the church. “See there?” He pointed to the belfry. “Vandalism?”

Kevin squinted. The roof of the belfry was torn and cut, as if a sword-wielding knight attacked it. The brickwork also seemed damaged. Kevin moved his head side to side. “How could someone get up there to do that kind of damage?”

“I don’t know.” Father shrugged. “There are no stairs to the top of the belfry. That was part of the plan. We wanted to avoid accidents or misplaced ideas.” He rubbed his bald head.

“I’ve seen a tree fall on a roof and do damage like that,” Kevin suggested.

The priest shook his head. “I don’t have any trees close enough or tall enough.” Father Patrick pointed to the old trees in the cemetery at the back of the property. The young trees near the sidewalk were barely fifteen feet tall. “What

I'm thinking is, the contractor I hired to roof the church did a shoddy job." He picked up a section of wooden sheathing with shingles attached to it. "But why didn't I notice that damage before this morning?" He handed the evidence to Kevin.

The break in the wood was bright yellow-white, not the gray of aged wood. Two parallel marks were on the shingles' surface, and they looked very similar to the cuts in the attic stairway. Kevin put his finger into the slice. It seemed just as thick too. "A bear attack?" Kevin suggested, then laughed.

"I thought the same. It looks like something attacked the roof. Which only begs the question—why?"

"Why?"

"Yes, what did the roof do to the bear?" Father Patrick slapped Kevin on the back and erupted in laughter.

Kevin rolled his eyes. "I know that's a crazy thought. But it does look like claw marks." He handed the partition of the roof back to the priest.

Father Patrick took the section. "I have to call my insurance. I'll check to see if they cover bear attacks and let you know." He chuckled and walked to the church entrance. The building had a broad set of stairs that cascaded from the double front door, getting wider at the bottom.

“One thing is for sure,” Kevin mumbled under his breath, “a werewolf can’t fly to do damage like that.” He turned to resume his stroll to the library and noticed the ugly tan AKG car.

“Hey, Kevin.” Johnny waved Kevin over to his car.

“Now, that is suspicious. For once, the agency knew what they were talking about when they sent me here. However, I was expecting a young female to be involved.” Johnny pointed to the roof. “Fascinating.” He looked at Kevin as if waiting for the admittance of guilt. “There was an incident on the road near Knoll and Bluff. Someone called 911 and claimed to have seen a demon. He even had a picture. But, of course, it was blurry.”

Bluff and Knoll? The clothing. Kevin swallowed hard, then composed himself. “Father Patrick and I concluded that a bear got mad at the roof and attacked it. What we don’t know; is why.” Kevin smirked at the absurdity of the earlier conversation.

“Or,” Johnny suggested, “How he paid the eagle to fly him up there.”

“Yea, that too. Maybe he was offered a salmon?” Kevin laughed but abruptly stopped when Johnny didn't join in. "You aren't serious?"

"About the eagle and bear? No." Johnny grabbed Kevin's shoulder. "If you hear or see anything, please tell me. And I mean anything." He let Kevin go. "There could be something in it for you." Johnny jumped into his car and drove into the church parking lot.

"Oh, gosh, I could get rewarded for turning myself in. I don't think so." Kevin continued to the library, convinced that somehow, he damaged the roof and was photographed.

# Chapter 25

Megan walked out of her bathroom. Her freshly washed hair dampened her shirt. She smelled bacon and headed to the kitchen, mouth watering.

"Morning Dad."

Artem chewed on a strip of bacon as he cooked on the stove. "Eggs are almost done."

She sat at the breakfast nook and heaped food onto her plate, hash browns, bacon, French toast, and orange slices. "This looks delicious."

Artem placed two sunny side up eggs on Megan's plate and then his own. "Nikolai and I had a long talk last night."

Megan groaned.

"Why did you hide this from me?"

"I know you hate it when I have friends. That's what I was hiding. The attack on Bonnie was unexpected. I'm still not sure I fully understand why it happened."

"You're right, I'm not happy. Friends are trouble. As to why your friend was attacked, she found something she was not supposed to find."

Artem shrugged and placed a large piece of French toast in his mouth.

Megan nodded. "Yes, but what could possibly elicit such a response?"

He pointed at her with his fork and shrugged. "We can only guess. You both might still be in danger. For now, we want you to behave normally, go to school, and do your best to avoid this, Annie." Artem waved his fork around. "Nikolai has his best people digging further, and a few extra to watch your back."

Megan fought the urge to roll her eyes. Her father found a way to babysit her. He wouldn't allow her to visit Bonnie to tell her she was in danger. "Did you find anything on the cuneiform written on the stone?"

Artem patted his shirt pocket. "No. Every language I tried came up with nonsense."

"Could the stone be a hoax?'

"I double-checked; the pattern appears to be the same as the other stones. If it's a hoax, it's quite elaborate." He tapped his fork on the plate. "I'm not sure who would benefit."

"Can I use the computer to try some more languages?"

"I think we have used all the languages in the world, including the dead ones. But why not?" Artem placed a hand on Megan's arm, preventing her from leaving the table with her plate. "After breakfast."

Megan snickered, stuffing bacon in her mouth. She hoped to contact Bonnie through the computer and some social media sites but had her doubts. Her dad's computer only allowed searching of the records and data inside the museum. Maybe she could figure her way through the server and onto the internet, but she was no hacker. Megan finished breakfast, cleaned off her plate, and set it in the dishwasher.

The doorbell rang.

Megan ran to answer. She expected a book delivery and hoped this was it. But it was the man from the tan car, Nikolai's gym, and the hospital.

The man looked at her, nodded, and said, "Hello, Megan, I'd like to speak to Artem."

Megan shifted uncomfortably. He knew her father's name. Nikolai never shared names. "He's not here."

The man removed his sunglasses and tucked them into his jacket pocket. He placed his hands on his hips, exposing the gun on his side. "I know Artem is home." He paused for a second. "Well?"

Megan swallowed hard. “Dad!” She knew there was a tone of fear in her voice. She hoped it would warn him.

Artem hurried down the hall; upon seeing the man, he slowed. “What do you want?”

“We have given you and your daughter asylum, and in return, we expect cooperation.” The man removed his hands from his hip, holding his hands open before him.

Artem looked to Megan, “Go.”

Megan looked to the man at the door then to her father. She went into the kitchen, then snuck into the living room, which was adjacent to the front hall and doorway. She listened and waited.

“I’m Johnny Conner.” The man said.

“I repeat, what do you want?” Artem’s voice was cool and collected.

“Your computer and your house are bugged,” Johnny said.

“I know.” Artem offered nothing. This was his way. He was required to assist the United States government, but he wanted them to work for it.

The man at the front door sighed. “Can I come in?”

“No.”

Megan could imagine the man at the door, smacking his head or covering his face in frustration. But when he spoke again, he sounded just as calm as her father, which was worse.

"As you wish. I have intelligence that tells me your computer was accessed looking at information on cuneiform, stones, and a variety of languages."

"That computer only accesses the Field Museum. There is no search engine on it. I work for the museum as a curator; my job is Neolithic in nature. Neo means new and lithic means stone."

"I understand what Neolithic means, sir," Johnny said.

"Cuneiform writing is also within my job description. I often have to look up hieroglyphs of all types, not just Egyptian."

Johnny's shoes scuffed on the cement porch steps. He was fidgeting. Megan smiled; she felt that way, too, when her father was not forthright with her.

"Sir, there has been activity in Siberia and China. I'm afraid you and your daughter may be in danger. If your computer connects directly to the Field Museum, that may be where the leak is located."

"What kind of activity? Your government promised us protection."

"Yes, we did, and that's why I'm here. Whatever it was you looked up in the past day or two seems related to the activity spike. I hoped you'd tell me what your research was so that we could identify if the threat is legitimate."

There was a long pause, and Megan wondered if it was time to come out of hiding or if the man was still there.

"Who are you?" Artem asked. "What government agency are you with?"

"AKG."

"I want to see your credentials." Another pause, and then Artem burst out laughing. "Asylon Kryptos Gignoskein. Is this a joke? Sanctuary of Hidden Knowledge. That's a riot. You tell the FBI, CIA, or whoever you really work for that they got me. Jokes on me. Very good." His laughter stopped suddenly. "Now go."

The front door slammed shut. Megan assumed it was on the face of Johnny. She moved from her hiding spot and went to her father.

"That's the man I saw in the car on the street and again at Nikolai's gym. What's going on, Dad?"

"Either someone is trying to get to us, or this is an elaborate joke." Artem held his hands in front of him and bounced his splayed fingertips on each other, thinking. “There is something familiar about Asylon Kryptos Gignoskein,” he mumbled under his breath. “Don’t use the computer anymore. If you need to research, go to the library. But even there, don’t use the computer and use your alias when checking out books.” Her father grasped her shoulders. “Pack your car with essentials and keep a burner on you.”

Megan nodded. “Yes, father.” She’d had an alias for years; it included everything. Name, passport, social security, and birth certificate. She didn’t know where they came from, only that they were hers. This alias was like her shadow. It was always with her, not like the cold identities that she carried in her bugout bag. If she and her father ever had to leave the city, state, or country, she was to go by Sara Higgins until their new identities could be established.

Megan was excited about going to the library. Apart from the museum, it was her favorite place to be. She felt comfortable among the books. The smell of an old book reminded her of the fun times in the museum. It would surprise the average teenager, but there are books and information that are only available at the library. Some things were considered too old or irrelevant, and they never made it online.

Megan went to the pantry and down into the safe room. She picked up a small black backpack and placed a burner phone, gasmask, a bottle with a water purifier, and a first aid kit into the bag. The Sara Higgins driver's license and passport were slipped into her back pocket. Mentally she touched on the items in her car's bugout bag. She topped off her backpack with two boxes of .40 ammunition.

She climbed the stairs, and the safe room door closed behind her. Artem was in the kitchen. "I'd like to try the library to see if they have anything on cuneiform and languages."

Artem nodded. "Only use the burner in emergencies. Be back in two hours. I'm going to stop at the gym and ask Nikolai about this AKG official."

She grabbed her jacket and car keys. The small backpack couldn't be hidden with the bugout bag; it would be too obvious. She collected the bugout bag and put them both in the trunk.

Megan entered the library through the double doors. Even though it wasn't as big or fully stocked as the big city libraries, she loved this library. It was once a three-story farmhouse built nearly one hundred and fifty years ago and had five or six extensive additions. Each room was decorated according to the genre of the books inside.

One of her favorite rooms was horror. Scattered among the books on the shelving were skulls, ravens, spiders, hourglasses, wolves, bats, and owls. Sometimes the exotic items were on sale, made by a local artist or taxidermist. She browsed, looking at the decorations and the books. Two novels attracted her attention. Megan selected them in case her father refused to let her leave the house again.

The fantasy room had a dragon mural on the ceiling. The only way to fully appreciate it was to lay on the carpet and gaze. Which was dangerous because no one looked down once they entered. A woman sat in the window nook, reading a novel.

Next to the fantasy room was science fiction. There was a fabulous mural in this room too. Nebulas and spaceships were the highlights. At the edges of the ceiling were silhouettes of famous fight scenes. In the occult room, two young girls looked at a book on witchcraft. A cryptozoology text was open near them. Megan smiled, remembering when she was curious about the oddities of life.

She walked across the hall to anthropology and history. Megan dug into the books, looking for anything to bring home and convince her father that was why she went to the library. She found a few texts on ancient lost languages and decided they'd be perfect.

She poked around in other rooms and found some information on the black market. Perfect for the Biology assignment that was handed out on Friday. Megan carried her selections to the old living room, which was filled with tables and chairs. A few people were working on research; some hid behind partitions. She left her chosen books on an empty table and went to the front desk.

"Hi," she said to the man behind the counter. "I need to use a phone."

The man looked at her, confused. "You don't have a phone?"

"I have money. I can pay."

"Let me ask." The man went through a door. He returned a few minutes later. "Anyone with a library card can use the phone for ten minutes.

We had to look it up. No one has ever asked before."

The man picked up the phone from his desk and offered it to her. Megan pursed her lips. "Is there another one I can use? I'd like a little privacy. I'm calling the hospital to check on a friend."

"Sure, why not." The man shrugged. He directed her to the back. "There's one in the breakroom."

Megan walked into what used to be a kitchen. An older woman sat at a small table, drinking from a mug and reading a book. "I was told I can use the phone," Megan said to her.

"Right there." The woman nodded to the phone on the wall.

"Thank you." Megan dialed Bonnie's cell number from memory. "Hi, Bonnie, it's me, Megan."

"Why haven't you come to visit?" Bonnie sounded upset.

"I'm sorry, my father won't let me visit or call. I used the excuse of going to the library to call you."

"Oh?" Bonnie sounded both disappointed and intrigued.

"Besides, I did manage to see you once. Didn't your mom tell you?"

"Yea, but I was sleeping." Bonnie sighed. "So, what's going on? If you had to sneak out to contact me, it must be something big. I wish I was there with you."

"Me too. I miss hanging with you." Megan looked at the woman reading and sipping from her mug. "Okay, look, I'm just going to say it. I think you might still be in danger." She licked her lips, watching the woman. "See if you can change the cop at your door to always be female."

"Female? Why?"

"Let's just say Annie has influence over males."

"Do you really think her reach goes that far? To the cops?" Bonnie sounded excited and a little scared.

"I've found evidence that points that way," Megan said.

"You've got to be kidding."

"I'm not kidding. Crap, I have to go. I'm only allowed ten minutes on the phone. Be safe." Megan placed the receiver into the rocker on the wall. She walked past the woman to get to the door. The woman stared intently as she turned the page, her eyes wide and focused on the novel. Megan left the breakroom and went to collect her books.

# Chapter 26

Kevin walked up the stairs and onto the porch of the library. The building used to be a farmhouse and was at least one hundred years old. It had many additions and renovations over its lifetime. Looking at the cobbled collection of architectural styles in one building reminded Kevin of Grandpa Joe, who loved to comment about others' construction skills.

He ignored the people behind the front desk and wandered the rooms and bookshelves. Kevin knew the numbers on the spine meant something. He didn't know precisely what, and he wasn't about to ask. He hoped the decorations and room themes would get him close.

He found books on werewolves, vampires, and the occult after looking for more than an hour. Witchcraft, Christianity, Buddhism, and Voodoo seemed to be in the same area, regardless of what Ruby said about religions. Kevin shrugged. He pulled a few books and brought them to a partitioned table.

He stretched and sat then began to read. One of the books was folklore about sightings of werewolves. The myths spread from medieval England to the modern-day United States. The text included names of cities and towns where the beasts were seen and described the evidence of their existence. Which usually consisted of blurry pictures or a clump of hair that's never identified. One piece of evidence seemed to be controversial simply because no one could decide if the photo was a werewolf or a bigfoot. Kevin laughed then looked around to see if anyone would come over and tell him to be quiet. He closed the book and pushed it aside.

After an hour, two more books joined the discard pile. Kevin opened another book and skimmed. This one seemed to be of general information, most of which he already knew. Werewolves only come out at the full moon and are allergic to silver. To become a werewolf, one must be bitten by another werewolf. A subsection indicated that saliva from a werewolf had to invade the bloodstream of an otherwise healthy person, which implied licking a wound could pass on the contagion without being detected in the usual manner.

He found a short paragraph about a Russian wolf deity that protected the Siberian Forest.

The Wolf of the Woods could transform from wolf to beautiful woman at will. *Safe to say, that's not my problem.*

Kevin knew the moon was at half the night before. He fingered the ring on his pinky. He pulled it off and read the inside of the ring, *Sterling.*

When his mother collected antiques, she always preferred Sterling over any other silverware because it was almost pure silver, not plated. *Stands to reason that Sterling on a ring means the same thing*. The skin of his pinky seemed no worse for wearing silver, no blistering, no hives. Kevin fingered the book and intentionally pulled his fingertip along the page edges. He caught the right angle, and the familiar burn of a paper cut told him he succeeded. His finger bled, and he touched the wound to the ring, holding it there. His eyes closed, expecting the worst.

"It isn't often that you find someone in the library checking for lycanthrope."

Kevin looked up to see Megan standing next to him. Her arms were filled with thick old books. The title of one said *Neolithic Dig Sites*.

"Is that what you think I am doing?" Kevin smiled nonchalantly.

Megan poked at each book then read them. "*Lycanthrope, Medieval Folklore and Ritual, Werewolves and How to Find Them, The Science Behind Werewolves*, and *Movie Wolves*." She looked at Kevin. "You're putting a silver ring into a wound. I'm going with my first impression. For some reason, you think you might be a werewolf."

"Nah, I'm writing a report for English class."

"Bullshit." Megan laughed.

"What are you doing here? Besides stalking me." Kevin folded his arms.

"Looking for some historical information on that stone."

"Why not use the internet?"

Megan smiled. "Some things are not on the internet. Some things need to be dug by hand and researched. Some of these things are sensitive, and it is nice not to have it on your search history. Right?" She looked him in the eye. Her eyebrows raised.

Kevin brushed aside her werewolf accusation. "Have you told anyone else about the stone?"

"I have more tact than that. Mr. Mulligan, my father, and the museum are the only ones who know. Why do you ask?" Megan shifted the book to her other arm. He made out the words *Black Market* as part of the title.

"I can't find the stone. I think someone might have stolen it. But even stranger, my window is broken, and there are scratches in my wall." Kevin looked down at his hands. He wanted to accuse Annie and Tony, but he kept his mouth closed.

"Well, don't look at me. Wait a minute, is that why you think you have lycanthrope? Because of a broken window and some scratches?" A smile crept on Megan's lips. "A branch could have hit your window, or someone might have tossed a brick."

Kevin sighed and rubbed the back of his neck. He waved her to come closer. "I forget things, like parts of the evening. And I wake up naked in places I don't expect," he whispered while scanning the room.

Megan studied Kevin, deciding if he was telling her the truth. She sat next to him, setting the books on the table. "Where did you wake up?"

"The attic."

"You could be sleepwalking."

Kevin pointed to the book that was labeled *The Chinese Black Market*. "What's that book for? Are you going to sell my stone on the black market?"

Megan's eyes widened, then she frowned. "I didn't think about that." Her fingers thrummed on the tabletop as if she were giving the idea real thought. "No." She opened the book and pushed it to him. "I'm writing a report for Biology. About the damage, black market medicines have on the environment and the animals who are involved."

"What?" Kevin looked at the page that had a bookmark. A strange bipedal creature with scales was in a picture. The photo was titled African Pangolin. "That's an animal that really exists?"

"For now." Megan nodded. "People in China think pangolin scales will cure their cancer." She shook her head, suddenly looking very sad. "The demand for the scales is killing hundreds of pangolins every day."

"Do pangolin scales work?"

"Are you kidding me? Of course not." She slammed the book closed. "Those scales are made of the same stuff as your fingernails."

"Then, why do Chinese people buy medicine that doesn't work?"

"I think it's because they're desperate. Nothing else has worked. Maybe they can't afford real medicine. Or they don't trust western medicine. Maybe they're just ignorant." She looked at Kevin. "If I told you taking this medicine will cure your werewolf disease, would you take it?"

Kevin rolled his fingers on the tabletop. "Not if I knew an animal died to give me that medicine."

"People eat steak."

"That's different. You can't get the steak without the animal dying." Kevin raised a finger. "You can shear a sheep. Maybe they ought to try shearing a pangolin."

Megan laughed. "Well, this is an argumentative paper. I ought to give that angle a try." She stood and collected her books.

"You're welcome."

"And Kevin, if you think you're a werewolf, you ought to stay home tonight." She backed away from him. "Stay." She held up her hand as if telling a dog to listen. She laughed then headed for the checkout.

Smirking, Kevin watched Megan leave and then continued to read. Only one of the books seemed to have practical information about werewolves. Almost as if the person who wrote it experienced werewolves. He picked up the books and put them back on the shelves in the proper locations. Kevin carried *Werewolves and How to Find Them* to the front desk and checked it out.

Dinner started, and everyone was seated. The triplets sat across from Kevin and Grandma Ruby. Inez sat as close to her father as possible, which was also as far as she could get from Kevin.

Mom was cutting a chicken thigh on her plate. “Did you hear about the church?”

“I’m at work all day I don’t hear anything,” Dad complained.

“The belfry and the cemetery were damaged.”

“Damaged? What do you mean? How”

“Well, the Smiths witnessed *something* attacking the church and cemetery. The Smiths are elderly, and many of the parishioners think they didn’t have their glasses on. Someone else reported a group of kids in costumes vandalizing the church and its grounds.”

“Poppycock.” Grandma interrupted. “I’ve seen *something* before. And it always turns out to be a monster.”

Kevin turned to look at Grandma and noticed Inez staring at him. Her eyes were wide with fear. What had she seen? *Does she know what I am? Can she help me?*

"Ruby, not now." Mom chastised her mother-in-law. "Father Pat agrees with you. No, not that there are monsters, but on the poppycock sentiment. He is blaming the construction crew who replaced the church roof last year." She returned to the chicken thigh and continued cutting.

"The monster I saw wasn't scary, but a beautiful creature meant to trap the innocent." Grandma Ruby paused for dramatic effect. "A unicorn."

"Do you really think a unicorn damaged the church?" Mom pointed at Grandma with her fork.

"Don't be rude, Donna," Dad said to her.

"It's alright, Jerry." Grandma put a hand on her son's arm. "Donna doesn't like to listen to my stories.

"I have my reasons," Mom said, her eyes flickered to the triplets. "Your stories tend to be on the scary side."

Inez folded her arms. "May I be excused?"

Mom nodded, and Inez moved away from the table, keeping her eyes on Kevin. At the last moment, she turned and bolted down the hall. Mina and Tess followed their sister without asking to be excused.

"What is that all about?" Dad pointed at the seats the girls vacated.

Mom looked at Kevin and Grandma. "It seems that Inez has had some nightmares about Kevin. She said something about a monster. Nothing I understood, of course. I hoped she'd get over it. But as you can see, she hasn't."

"I should talk to her." Kevin stood.

"No," Mom said, grabbing his hand. "She's afraid of you. Talking to her right now won't fix that. She needs time."

"I should go." Kevin collected his dirty plates and brought them to the sink. He left without saying anything and went home, to his room, feeling guilty.

"Kevin, I'm home," Ruby called up the stairs. "Is everything alright? Do you want to talk?"

"I'm fine. I want to be alone." Kevin closed his door and paced back and forth in his room. He had a new window and curtain rod. Maybe he ought to do as Megan suggested and stay put tonight.

He pulled the drapes closed then took off his clothing. He sat naked on the floor and waited.

He thought about the events of the day and wondered what Inez might have seen. Ten minutes passed.

"Nothing's happening," he complained. He looked at the clock and decided to give it more time.

Ten more minutes, then fifteen. Kevin looked at the clock, then leaned back to get his feet under him. Heat cascaded from shoulders to hips. His breathing quickened, then stopped. Pain tore into his spine at his shoulders, rolling down his back. Kevin felt lightheaded, and then he felt nothing.

# Chapter 27

Kragnor opened his eyes. He recognized the bed, desk, and dresser and noted the window was whole again. "I slept in the room above, yet I wake here." In the past, his home was on stable, beautiful high craggy mountains. Lush green hillsides flowed from his perch. Every night he would awaken to see stars. Every morning he would sleep as the sun rose. Sometimes he would stay awake during daylight hours to have conversations with other beings. Kragnor preferred the night. He felt the strongest then. For centuries, his pattern of movement and wake cycles didn't change.

Even when he moved, the new location lasted for centuries. Until humans arrived and created cities, Kragnor lived in the mountains and forests of the world. After humans, most of his time was in cities, on top cathedrals, or other high locations. At first, the towns were small, not much more than villages. At those times, he had a prominent place in a city square or near an important building.

Each time decades or centuries passed before a new location came into his life. This place, although comforting, was not home. Too many things break at his touch. The church felt more like home, but it also was not a place he could stay.

Kragnor carefully opened one of the other doors in Kevin's room and discovered clothing. A wardrobe. He snorted and tried the last door, which opened into a hallway. Sniffing the air, he continued slowly. Kragnor was careful to tread lightly in the delicate house. It was a space for humans, not akitu. Three more doorways crowded the end of the hall, and in the center was a set of stairs.

He stood at the top of the stairs and wondered if he should descend or if going out the window was the better idea. He touched the wall with his claw. The spot was soft and pushed inward, leaving a hole. Kragnor sniffed, billowing white powder. He inserted his claw and scratched the interior of the wall, drawing his finger back with white covering his nail.

A wall made from paper and chalk? He grunted, amazed. No wonder everything broke at his touch.

The stairs had a strange fur-like covering on them. Kragnor pulled at the fluff and freed a single strand. He looked at it and decided it wasn't fur but a form of clothing. He pulled his wings in tight to his back and changed his stance to be on hands and feet, which spread his weight over more area.

The stairs didn't buckle or creak. Kragnor made sure to keep his weight over the riser of each tread, where each stair was strongest. He entered a room that had soft appearing furniture.

A portal to another dimension flashed soundlessly at him. Kragnor looked around for the wizard that could conjure such a fantastic piece of magic. A human female slumbered in a long chair, with the portal pointing directly at her. She must be the originator of the magic.

*Perhaps she is the one who brought me here. If so, why does she ignore me?* Kragnor knelt before the prone woman. But she did not open her eyes. Her eyes fluttered, and she mumbled something incoherent. One arm glowed in the light of the portal. She turned in the chair, her back facing him.

Kragnor snorted, stupefied by her actions. "Why do you ignore me, my lady?"

The woman's head lifted off the chair. She looked from the television to a black rectangle sitting on the table before her. She readjusted in the chair, sitting upright, then looked around.

Her eyes skittered over Kragnor in his kneeling position, but she didn't seem to see him. She reached toward the table and the strange black rectangle. White, red, and yellow marks covered its surface. The woman looked at it, blinking for a long moment before touching a white mark.

Sudden sound filled Kragnor's ears. He jumped to his feet, wings spreading wide, tail whipping around, striking a wall.

The woman's eyes flew open. Kragnor could see her fear and surprise. She pointed the rectangle at him, striking the white marks repeatedly. The portal changed and made strange sounds. Her movements slowed, and her eyes rolled up. She crumpled into the chair, and the rectangle fell to the floor.

Kragnor picked up the rectangle and sniffed. It smelled of metal, oil, and something odd. His lip curled with disgust. It was not natural. It must be a magic weapon. Surely this is another human test. He placed it on the floor where it fell and waited a moment. The woman didn't move. Kragnor snorted and left.

A white feline rubbed on his leg. Its green eyes studied him. Kragnor reached down and petted the cat on its head, scratching under its chin. The cat meowed, turned with tail raised high, moved to its mistress, and licked her hand.

The deep thrumming of the grandfather clock startled him. He crept up on the clock, a feeling of recognition overcame him. The pendulum swung and brought a memory to life. He lived on top of a giant clock in the center of a city for years; the vibrations of the chimes helped him sleep. The tick and thud of the gears of the enormous clock were ever constant, like the hum of mother earth. He caressed the oak surface and smiled, something to remind him of home.

Kragnor entered a room with a white floor and cabinets. An iron rack hung from the ceiling directly over an elevated flat wooden surface. The wooden table smelled of meat, blood, and plants. Inside, one of the cabinets were glass containers. In another were herbs. How strange. Is this a torture chamber or an apothecary? Kragnor's mind flitted back to the wizard woman. This could be where she makes her spells or where she tortures those who do not cooperate. He huffed.

Kragnor looked back into the room where the prone woman still lay. He breathed deep, trying to ascertain her nature. The tip of the cat's tail flicked back and forth. He shook his head, not pleased with the lack of information.

He opened the door with a red and white checkered curtain. It exposed the backyard and the house behind the metal-net fence. The movement of three children was evident through the curtains and windows. He smiled at the antics of the three girls that looked alike, but not alike. One of the girls looked out the window; she waved and shouted for the other two. He felt their eyes touch him for a long moment.

A woman entered the room. One of the girls waved at him shyly then closed the curtain.

Kragnor lifted a hand in response but was uncertain if she saw. At least there is one friendly face. He squatted then kicked off the ground catching air under his quickly deployed wings.

Kragnor returned to the Catholic church, landing on the top of the building. His weight and claws caused the roof to groan and creak. What happened to the strength of churches? The flying buttresses? The stone? The brick? He sighed disheartened. He scanned the church grounds and noticed an area further away from the church which contained tall and stately tombstones. A small building separated the two sections. The building was too small to be a horse stable.

He walked down the peak of the roof, setting the wood into a crescendo of squeaks, grinds, and whines. Some shingles loosened under his talons and skittered to the ground.

"Hey, what do you think you're doing?" A man in black clothing and a white collar yelled at him. The man picked up a shingle. "I'm going to call the police!" The man's voice changed from concerned to angry.

Police must be law-keepers or guards. He looked from one side of the church where the man stood to the other, where the small building was. He jumped from the roof, diving toward the secluded cemetery, away from the man.

"My God!" The man proclaimed.

Kragnor stretched his wings, gliding past the small building and into the small cemetery. He crouched and waited, expecting a commotion of activity. The man in black came around the corner. He looked around the immediate vicinity near the church's base as if expecting Kragnor's jump to result in a corpse.

The man went into the church and returned with a bright directional light. He flashed it on the roof then around the grounds.

Kragnor studied the tombstone that was closest to him. It was a large red granite slab. At least six times the size of the small headstones in the other cemetery. A toran. The stone had a date that read 1820 – 1860. There was another nearby that was black granite; its date was 1804-1820. The surnames on the slabs were the same. It was a family plot and much older, which explained the separation of sections. A flash of light caught Kragnor's attention. The man approached.

Kragnor touched the red stone toran and pushed his hand into it. He noticed a subtle difference in temperature on his hand. He ducked low, pulling his wings tight against his back and sides, and pressed the rest of his body through the tombstone-gateway.

Kragnor's body mingled with the material of the headstone, transferring through, like a doorway. He emerged from another red granite headstone into a cemetery that seemed lost to time. He was somewhere deep in the country with a forest and an unkempt fence. The yip of a dog or wolf broke the stillness.

Most of the headstones in the cemetery were small, and the elements wore away the writing. Kragnor pushed aside the tall plants looking for another large stone, another toran. Going through the red headstone, the way he came out would take him back to the cemetery where the church was. The man would still be there. If he went through the stone from the other side, he could end up somewhere new.

The clearing that held the lost cemetery seemed to have defined borders. Kragnor swept through the weeds and grasses, looking for more stones. He found a large black granite piece lying down, hidden by old grass. Kragnor ripped the dead grass off the stone's surface and wiped it clean. This slab, too, was beaten by time and weather. It didn't matter; it was solid, which would allow him to port through. He saw other mounds of grass and cleared them. He found three more headstones that would serve as toran. Two were marble, and another was black granite.

Kragnor went back to the first black granite stone and touched it, remembering its shape, texture, and voice. He went headfirst through the stone slowly to make sure he knew which way he would emerge on the other side. His stone memory was sharp. Once through, its destination remained with him for life.

He came through a block that was larger than the headstone. He stepped on the floor, which was also small granite squares. Gentle light exposed the black granite walls of the room he entered. A little red light blinked at him from a high corner. Being surrounded by so much stone made him feel at home. He turned to study the wall he came through. It had metal letters raised off its surface *Banco de Mexico*.

The words lighted on his mind like a butterfly. Kragnor recognized the Latin and Arabic influenced Castellano language or, at the very least, the flavors of them all. But this too had changed, like English.

"Bank of Mexico. Where's Mexico?"

Kragnor walked through the room, enjoying the stone surfaces. He touched each slab, wondering where they might lead. Another red light blinked at him from a different ceiling corner. Kragnor stepped through a doorway into a vaulted antechamber. His nails clicked on the floor, echoing off the high walls and ceiling.

Suddenly, loud, pulsating sounds screamed, and lights turned on. His presence was noticed, and he was not welcome. Kragnor ran back the way he came, diving into the slab with the words written on it.

He rolled out of the headstone and across the grass. The tiny cemetery lost to time welcomed him with the chirping of crickets. Seven hundred years had passed. These new magics were unfamiliar and potentially dangerous. He rubbed his ears, hearing the echo of the screams as if he were still in the room.

He snorted. One thing he always had in abundance was time. Kragnor would take his time to explore. There is no reason to rush these things. He watched the stars move across the sky and meditated for a couple hours.

Kragnor ported back through the red stone and into the family cemetery on the church grounds. Where could he go to be safe? How can he explore the world with so much time passing? Things changed. Not just the materials of the buildings being weaker, but magic was bigger and stronger than before. He could be in danger, and he would never know. Kragnor knew he was ignorant. It would be helpful if he had an ally. He must find other akitu or humans to trust. He needed someone to teach him the strangeness of this time. Perhaps he needed to fly to a big city to find his answers.

While he pondered, the sun rose over the horizon. Kragnor slowly hardened and slept.

# Chapter 28

A cold wind whipped across Kevin's naked body. His eyes snapped open. "Aw, come on. A cemetery?" He sat on the ground with his back against a red granite headstone. The tall stone seemed to draw the heat from his body. He moved from a sitting position to a squat, so only the balls of his feet touched the cold ground.

He peeked over the gravestone and saw the church. "Aw crap, it's Sunday morning. I can't stay here, but I can't walk twelve blocks home either, at least not naked."

Kevin was an altar boy at the church for years when he was young. He knew the church and its grounds quite well. In the basement was a small kitchen and a room where the church held donations for the poor and needy. He'd be able to find some clothes if he could get in.

He waited for a passing car then ran to the back door of the church. He pulled the handle. *Damn, it's locked.* The small basement windows looked promising, but they were secured too.

A car passed.

Horrified, Kevin ran around the side of the church, hoping the car didn't see him.

The car tires squealed to a stop. The engine revved, and it turned around.

Near the side entrance to the church was a metal door with the word COAL embossed on it. Above the door was a wooden sign that read "Delicate Packages." Kevin pulled the door open. A laundry basket filled with blankets and pillows was tied to the door and was in the way. He broke the string and shoved it toward the church stairs. There was an old, beat-up, metal slide that went into the basement, probably for coal.

The car slowed and pulled into the church parking lot.

Kevin slid down feet first, pulling the door shut behind him. He let go of the door and slipped the rest of the way into the dark room. An edge of the metal slide tore into Kevin's thigh. He landed on soft fabric, biting his tongue as the pain throbbed.

The car came close to the coal chute door. He heard the engine turn off and a door shut. Kevin moved beneath the slide, hoping to hide in the shadows.

The door opened, flooding the dark room with light. So much light that Kevin briefly wondered how he could have seen before the door opened.

"You there, what's going on?" asked a familiar voice.

The door swung freely and closed. "I saw someone lurking around the church. And after what happened to your roof, I wanted to look." The voice was deep and masculine. "I didn't think you were around this early."

"Mass is in a couple of hours. I turn on lights, heat, and get the Lord's House in order." Crunching gravel and kicked stones skittered near the coal chute door. "What happened? Did you move the basket?" Father Patrick demanded.

"No, I thought I saw someone jump down the chute. They must have moved it."

"You, sir, have done me a favor," Father Patrick said. "Would you please call the police and let them know what happened? Feel free to be on your way; I'll take care of the trespasser."

"Are you sure you don't want me around to help you? You know, to be your muscle?"

"I've caught a few rabbits in this trap, and often it's a young woman escaping a bad situation. That's why the basket is there, for the abandonment of unwanted babies. Better that than an abortion."

"But, Father, what if it's a man who doesn't want to be caught? You could be hurt."

"I'll go inside and wait a few minutes before going into the basement. If the person doesn't want to be trapped, they can leave. The coal door is low enough. No harm, no foul. I forgive trespassers." Father Patrick chuckled at his joke.

"Okay, Father. I'll call the police."

"That would be best, my son."

The car door opened, and the vehicle started. It sat idle for a few minutes and then left.

After the car departed, silence filled the room. Kevin stood. Sure enough, the coal door was low enough to escape back out. He thought about it for a minute, but it would do him no good. He was still naked. He grabbed a blanket off the bed and wrapped it around himself.

Bed?

The coal chute door was still slightly open, allowing light to expose the area. The room was red brick, with a closed wooden door at one end. It had a metal ring where a knob would be. The place looked like a dungeon. *I've never seen a brick wall in the church basement before. Why would a church have a dungeon?* Kevin thought about the predator priests, and his mind whirled. Is Father Patrick McCobbe dangerous? Is this a pedophile cage?

He pushed on the door. No movement. It was locked. Blood ran down his leg as he strained. The cut stung, but the initial pain was gone.

A knock came across the door. “If you’d like to escape, please do so now. I’ll give you another minute or two.” The thick wooden door muffled Father Pat’s voice.

Kevin looked back to the coal chute. He had a blanket now; he could leave.

Father knocked again. “Ready or not, here I come.” The sound of a key in a lock and the door swung outward. Father stood in the doorway with a baseball bat in one hand and the basket in the other.

Kevin scrambled to the other side of the room, keeping the blanket between him and the priest.

“Kevin? Is that you?” Father Patrick leaned the bat against the door jam.

“Yes.” Kevin laughed, embarrassed by the nervous squeak in his voice.

“What are you doing in there?”

Kevin wrapped his arms in front of the blanket. What could he tell the priest?

“What happened? Are you naked? Have you been accosted?” Father Patrick shook his head. “I’m sorry, too many questions.” He backed out of the doorway. "When you're ready, come out."

Kevin straightened the blanket, wrapping it around his shoulders, and walked out of the room.

"What's going on? Why are you in my basement?"

"I don't know. I woke up in the cemetery."

Father Patrick's eyes narrowed. "Are you taking drugs?"

"No, never." Kevin cleared his throat. "Although if I were, it would explain a lot." He chewed on his bottom lip, then stopped and looked Father in the eye. "Wait a minute. Why are you attacking me with questions? You know me." He studied the wooden door. "Why do you have a dungeon in your basement?"

Father lifted his hands and opened his mouth to say something, but then closed it. "I don't need to justify my actions. But to be fair, most of my questions are because of the damage to my roof. A few of my parishioners have suggested teenagers are to blame."

Kevin raised his eyebrows. "Really? That motorist called the police before leaving your parking lot. So, when the cops arrive, and they find a naked…a naked me. And that room…" Kevin trailed off. "After the troubles, the

Catholic church has had with scandal and predator priests." He cleared his throat. "Do I have to spell it out?"

Father Patrick crossed his arms and turned red in the face. "I know where you're going, and I won't participate in that nonsense."

Kevin raised his eyebrows. "Well?"

"Okay. You have me over a barrel. Let me explain. Initially, we had young mothers abandon babies on the church landing, between the outer and inner doors. But then someone dropped a baby down the coal chute. The poor darling died when she hit the cement floor. We didn't know her name, so she was given Kate Sweet." Father Patrick dabbed at his eyes. "As a church, we came together with a solution so that it wouldn't happen again. A way to catch a baby safely." He shook his head. "No babies have been dropped through the coal chute after that one time. Instead, we have caught burglars. Burglars. Can you believe it?"

Kevin shook his head. *What could be stolen from a church? A pew? A candle holder?* Both of which seemed like ridiculous ideas.

"So, we added walls and made sure anyone we catch can get out on their own. We don't have to worry about anything becoming stolen. And if we catch someone in need, they have a place to stay that is warm and dry. They have the option of staying and getting help or leaving."

Kevin nodded. "That explains why there is a bed and blankets in there. I was surprised when I saw it."

"Why didn't you leave when you had the chance?"

"I was naked. And I cut my leg on the chute. But mostly because I felt safer here than out there, so I stayed."

"Cut your leg? The slide is damaged?"

"Yes"

"May I see?" The priest reached for Kevin's leg then stopped.

Kevin winced a little. "I was afraid to look." He sighed and moved the blanket aside.

The cut was wide and shallow, more like a rug burn than a slice. Dried blood created a rivulet down to Kevin's foot.

Father Patrick stood and walked to the coal chute. "I need to examine the slide."

A section was sliced and turned in on itself, like a dagger. "This looks intentional. You were lucky you only got a scratch." The priest pushed the offending piece of metal back. "I'll have to fix that."

"I have a confession, Father. Would you hear it?"

Father raised his eyebrows. "Down here or in the confessional?"

"Here. Now." Kevin felt afraid of what he was about to say. But he had to tell someone. He had to release the shame and fear.

"Let's go in the other room and at least be comfortable." The priest swept his arm to usher Kevin out of the bricked room.

Kevin sat on a sofa. "I think I'm a monster."

Father's eyes glazed as if deep in thought. "All men are monsters. Some men are monsters every moment of every day. Others are only monsters once and a while. What kind of monster are you?"

"Werewolf."

Father Patrick smiled. "Really? But you're in a church, on consecrated ground. You know werewolves and vampires are Satan's minions?"

"No, I didn't." Kevin lifted his hand. "I'm wearing a silver ring too."

"That would be an issue if you were a werewolf."

Kevin nodded. "What about cemeteries?"

"That's consecrated ground too. Like a church. Nothing evil can go there."

"Then what is wrong with me?" Kevin broke and cried. He wanted to say more but couldn't.

"Nothing, my boy, nothing." Father leaned in toward Kevin but stopped. "Oh, my, you're still naked. Have I not offered you some clothes?"

Kevin chuckled uncomfortably. "No."

"How about a ride home? Did I offer that? Or sanctuary until the mass is over?

"No, I'm afraid not."

Father Pat shook his head. "I *am* slipping in my duties." He looked at his watch. "Mass will be starting in fifty minutes. Some come early to help set up." He stood. "You know where we keep the donated clothing. Please take what you need. If you're still here after mass, I'll find you a ride home." Father moved closer to Kevin, placing a hand on his head. He mumbled a prayer and said aloud, "Amen."

The priest moved to leave the room, then paused. "You might want to keep a journal, to keep track of what you ate, how you slept, who you spoke with. Perhaps the answer you seek is within self-reflection." He waved a hand toward the coal room. "My dungeon is always open." Father Pat smiled. "But I prefer we meet in the confessional or something more private. I am available to talk if you have the need."

After Father left, Kevin went into the charity closet. Most of the items were leftovers from rummage sales. He crossed his fingers in hopes that there would be something that would fit and not be outrageous.

Very few of the clothing items were men or boys. Of those items, they were too small or way too large. Kevin looked through the women's and girl's items. Much of the clothing that appeared to fit him had glitter or sequins. In the end, he took an extra-large lime green sweats and a tie-dyed sweatshirt.

None of the charity organizations took underwear or socks. The shoe choice was limited, so Kevin went barefoot.

Kevin jogged on the sidewalk. With every swing of his arms, he cringed, witnessing the bright colors. Kevin could not get home soon enough. He tried to pick up the pace, but barefoot running was hazardous. He watched where his feet landed to avoid rocks and sticks.

Kevin's mind wondered. If I'm not a werewolf or vampire, what am I? Maybe Father is right. I should journal my activity and food. His big toe caught in the folded pant cuff, and he stumbled, sprawling in the grass next to the sidewalk. He checked for any cuts or road rash. The knee of the sweats ripped, but his skin was undamaged. He stood and continued.

Kevin noticed the tan sedan parked outside his house. Johnny leaned on a supporting post talking to Grandma Ruby. She poured coffee in his thermos.

Grandma spotted Kevin and smiled. She said something to Johnny. He turned and watched Kevin walk up the stairs.

"Where were you, young man?" Johnny smiled and wagged his eyebrows.

"Having fun?" Grandma suggested.

"No, no, nothing like that," Kevin said.

"Oh, I remember those days. You know it's a good party when you stumble home in clothes that aren't yours. Unable to remember anything." Grandma Ruby smiled, amusement and memories twinkled in her eyes. She studied Kevin then frowned a little. "Are you ok? Would you like some coffee?"

"All I want is a shower. I feel violated." Kevin squeezed past, noting Johnny's name and phone number on her cast.

After a long, warm shower and changing into clean clothes, he remembered Father Pat's suggestion. He thought about using his laptop but decided against it, pushing it aside. Kevin pulled the composition notebook from a drawer. He read the spell Grandma Ruby chose, trying to remember the night he cast it, then turned the page and began writing.

# Chapter 29

Megan lay back among her blankets and pillows, looking through *The Chinese Black-Market* book. She flagged a few pages with sticky notes. Among the stories of animal and human hardship were mugshots of the people who were caught selling animal parts. These people had horrible stories too, no jobs, no money, and a hungry family. In their minds, who would miss one elephant or rhino? There were no winners in these tragic stories. Megan skimmed the photos of men, women, and children. They all looked miserable, except for a few that had smug countenance. One of which was a Chinese woman that looked familiar. Was that Tai Lu? The same woman who rented the stones to the museum? The name was in Chinese characters, and she couldn't read it.

A gentle knock rattled her closed door. "Nikolai has found some information on the men who escaped the morgue. I'm going to the gym. You have an open invitation to come along."

Megan tossed the book on the bed. “Yes, please. I need to get out of the house. I feel like a caged animal.”

Artem chuckled uncomfortably. He cleared his throat and said, “Grab your shoes and jacket. It’s cold and windy.”

She unlocked her bedroom door, collected a few protein bars, and joined her father in the car. Artem drove the car like a man who’d lost his license and was afraid of being caught. Every stop was complete, and every turn blinked. Megan smiled, knowing his paranoia extended to almost everything he did.

Artem pulled into the gym parking lot. He drove past the normal parking area to the side, where Nikolai’s car sat. They stepped out of the vehicle and entered a side door that was marked, “Emergency exit only, this door is alarmed.”

Nikolai stood waiting for them. “I heard you drive up.” He waved them deeper into the building. “I have found some interesting data on the men Megan killed.”

“I only killed one.” Megan frowned. “And I didn’t do that right, apparently.”

Nikolai chuckled. “No need to take offense.” He led them into his apartment, then handed over some paperwork to Artem. The title on the top of the page implied it was official paperwork from the coroner. Megan leaned into her father's arm and read.

"What the hell does that mean?" Megan pointed to a line that said: *Cause of death inconclusive time of death inconclusive.*

"Look here." Nikolai took the paper and turned it around. He tapped a highlighted paragraph:

"Subject has a combination of living and dead tissues. The subject has a temperature of one hundred point seven a full hour after the time of death. Tissues of the subject appear to function autonomously. Circulatory and respiratory systems appear to be in an advanced state of decay. No blood found in the subject. The nervous system appears to be functioning normally."

Artem raised his eyebrows. "Dead but not dead? Alive but not living? Where did you get this?"

"It is exactly what you think. From the coroner's office."

Artem raised a finger. "Is it the official document?"

Nikolai bowed to his friend. "This document was discarded. The official record is everything you see there, except that paragraph."

"Now, I understand why the cops wanted to know how the men died. They had nothing conclusive." Megan nodded.

"You didn't admit to anything, did you?" Artem asked.

"You've taught me better than that." Megan turned to Nikolai. "I heard the bodies are missing. Is that true?"

Nikolai nodded. "My source tells me the office went home for the evening, and when they returned the next morning, the refrigerated room was open, and those two bodies were gone. No sign of entry, forced or permitted." He raised his hands. "They've had break-ins in the past, so their security is quite good. Surveillance and motion detection covers the entire office, especially the examining room. Lots of contention in a courtroom whether an autopsy was botched or not. Tampering of evidence can start early in an investigation." Nikolai shook his head, amazed someone would sink so low.

Megan looked at her father. "Clearly, this is not the work of Russian mafia."

Artem shrugged. "Nikolai and I have seen quite a bit while we were in Russia, have we not, old friend?"

"Sure, but nothing like this."

A look of betrayal covered Artem's face as if the undead were an everyday occurrence in Russia, and Nikolai wasn't admitting it. "This wasn't the only reason you asked us to come over, is it?" His words came out sharp and biting.

"No. We discovered some data on the people who adopted Annie."

"Seems weird to adopt someone who's eighteen," Megan remarked.

"Actually, it isn't." Nikolai sat on the loveseat. "Let's say you were given up at birth and were adopted. When you're thirty, you find your real family, and they want you to rejoin, for medical or financial reasons. They can adopt you to make it legal."

"Oh." Megan frowned. "So, her parents aren't necessarily dead."

"Right." Nikolai nodded.

"Is that it?"

Nikolai sighed and shook his head. "If you're not interested in listening, you can go home. I will bring Megan when we are done."

Artem sat in the rocker. "I'll wait." He crossed his arms.

Megan rolled her eyes and looked to Nikolai. Her father wanted undeniable proof that Russia was behind the attack on his daughter, and when that proof didn't materialize, he behaved like a baby. "Continue, Nikolai, I'm curious," Megan encouraged.

"Annie's new parents, Mr. and Mrs. Fredrick, have a record of their own. For most of their early career as criminals, they did little things like shoplifting and purse snatching. Petty stuff. Though recently, they have gotten into higher stakes robbery, identity theft, and blackmail. We are not certain if the names, Mr. and Mrs. Fredrick, are theirs. Now, this really isn't a big deal. But they have joined forces with an even larger organization called Order of the Eye and Tooth. This organization has been directing them to manipulate young women all over the country. It seems Annie is only one of many."

"Order of the Eye and Tooth? What does it mean?" Megan asked.

Nikolai shrugged. "We can't find much. The OET is Fate-oriented, as in the Greek Fates. The group appears to be matriarchal in nature."

Megan interrupted, "Matriarchal? As in female-led?"

"Exactly."

"I can see how that would be appealing to some." Megan looked at her, still pouting father. "If this, Mr. and Mrs. Fredrick are helping young women who were raped or hurt by men. Then it stands to reason that they could gather an army."

"And not just by themselves. There are hundreds of camps like the one Annie attended. Nearly ninety percent of those are run by someone associated with the OET." Nikolai offered her a color pamphlet of the camp Annie attended. Emblazoned on the front was the familiar name Distressed and Troubled Teens. Beneath were many young women participating in camp activities. It all appeared benign. Nikolai tapped the bottom corner where there was a distinctive logo of an eye with a sharp slit pupil. "I believe this is the symbol for the Order of the Eye and Tooth."

Megan waved her hands. "Okay, fine. But why? What is the purpose of the OET? What is their end game? Why are they in Avalon?"

Nikolai shrugged. "No one outside of their group seems to know anything. I assume it is like any other religious cult. They could be looking for a new place to set up another camp or church?"

"I heard Annie talking about sisters."

Nikolai nodded. "Sounds like they are recruiting."

Megan frowned. “I’m not so sure. The way she said sisters made it sound like a distinct group. Like a set of twins.” She felt like the explanation was inadequate. “I don’t know.”

Nikolai consoled her with a smile. “It’s hard to see with the eyes and heart of someone you don’t know or understand.”

# Chapter 30

Kevin walked downstairs to dig up lunch when he heard voices coming from the kitchen. He sat on the stairs and eavesdropped.

"So, then, I ran in the room and pulled my gun." Johnny laughed. "But." He snorted, breathed deep a couple of times, then continued. "But the guy was too busy, ah, getting busy."

"Wait a minute, didn't you tell me this was a sex trafficking ring?" Grandma questioned. Kevin could hear the disapproval in her voice.

"Yes." Johnny laughed. "But that was no human he had. You know those rubber dolls you can buy online." He snorted. "He was having intimate relations with it."

"What?"

"I know, I know." Johnny slurped a drink and placed it on the table. "When he was brought up on charges, his defense was that he didn't partake in the *deflowering* of the girls and boys he was charged to oversee." Johnny's tone turned somber. "What a slime. He expected leniency because he didn't rape anyone. He only imprisoned them and took money from the rapists."

"I heard a similar story about a fellow who robbed a bank, but the gun wasn't loaded. So, he received less time than someone who used a loaded gun. I always wondered if those stories were true."

"I don't know about that case, but on this one, the guy got life. He won't be eligible for parole until he is eighty."

"You tell the most interesting stories, Johnny."

"Bah, it's nothing."

"That was when you worked for the FBI, right?" Kevin didn't hear the answer but assumed Johnny nodded. "What does AKG stand for?"

"Asylon Kryptos Gignoskein."

"So, you work for some kind of foreign country?"

"Oh no, it's nothing like that. AKG is in every country. We have unique jurisdictions. The words themselves are Greek. The only word I know for sure is Kryptos; it means hidden. But I think the word Kryptos as more of a puzzle. Like cryptography, where a cipher is used to solve a secret message."

"A puzzle, huh?" Grandma sounded like a lovesick puppy. "I bet you've seen all kinds of strange things. Can you tell me what your job is like now?"

"No, I'm not allowed. Even if we were married."

"Oh, Johnny," Grandma Ruby said, her voice dripping with velvet.

Was Johnny trying to move in on Grandma? Johnny was older, but grandpa old? Kevin narrowed his eyes. He walked into the kitchen and looked in the refrigerator.

"Hi, Kevin," Johnny said.

"Are you looking for something to eat? There's deli meat in the drawer, with lettuce and tomatoes." Grandma Ruby suggested.

"Um," Kevin said noncommittally. He pushed the milk aside, then changed his mind and pulled it out, setting it on the counter. He grabbed the brownies and a knife and started cutting.

"You wouldn't happen to have some ice cream, would you?" Johnny eyed the sweets, a half-smile on his face.

"Oh no, you can't have any."

"Kevin!" Grandma scolded.

"I'm bringing the brownies over to my sisters. I made Inez mad or scared, and I need to make peace. Brownies worked in the past." Kevin begged with puppy eyes.

"So, you're telling me there are only three servings?"

Kevin looked at the pan, with only two vacant spots. His shoulders slumped. "Okay, you're right. There's more than enough." Kevin pulled out two dessert plates and placed a brownie on each. He deposited the plates before Ruby and then Johnny.

"So, Johnny, what are your intentions with my Grandmother?"

Grandma dropped her fork. "That's none of your business."

"We're sharing stories," Johnny said.

"I don't think that's all you're sharing." Kevin glared at Johnny. "You should know my grandmother has dementia. I'll not allow you to take advantage of her."

Johnny took Ruby's hand. "I know. She told me. That is why I'm collecting her stories before she loses them forever." He pointed at his phone on the table. The red light of the recording application blinked at Kevin.

"Oh." Kevin looked at his feet, feeling embarrassed.

"You did the right thing to confront me and protect your Grandmother," Johnny said.

Kevin turned away from Johnny. "I'm going to bring the rest of the brownies over to Mom's." He took the pan and left out the back door. As he walked, he wondered if he should have left Ruby alone with Johnny. That man didn't appear to be everything he said he was. Kevin didn't trust Johnny, but he didn't get a *save your Grandma* feeling from him either.

Mom assembled sandwiches on the kitchen counter. She still wore her beautiful clothes from church. "Hello, Kevin. I wish you would come to church with us."

Kevin smirked a little. "Didn't Father Pat tell you? I was there this morning."

"Were you now?" Mom looked at her son appraisingly. "Still, it would be nice to go as a family."

"I brought over Grandma's lava cake. I want to make up with Inez." He set the pan on the table.

"I'm not sure cake will fix this problem. I don't even know what the problem is." Mom removed a few large carrots from a bag on the counter. She cut them into three-inch sections then halved them into snack-size with a large cleaving knife.

"I don't know either." Kevin turned to walk into the living room. He paused. "You know,

Mom, you were right. I miss my sisters." The knife stopped cutting for the briefest of moments, and Kevin imagined his mother smiling at him.

His father sat on the couch in the living room, wearing green and gold sweats, watching football. He clicked the remote to switch between two different games. He nodded a greeting to Kevin but didn't say a word.

The girls were conspicuously absent. Kevin went to the game cabinet and pulled out *Monopoly*. He set it up on the dining room table for four players, hoping the girls would play a game with him. As he counted out the money, Mom came into the room with a tray of sandwiches.

Mom turned and spoke loudly into the house. "Come and get it."

Dad appeared, grabbing a few sandwiches, and then ran back to the couch and television.

Mom rolled her eyes. "You're welcome, Jerry."

Dad grunted a response. He loved football, and there was nothing anyone could do to pull him from the television. Kevin never got addicted to the games despite his father's attempts. He had more important things to do.

Like, play video games, something he hadn't partaken in since he moved in with Grandma.

"I'm going to change." Mom tugged off her earrings. "Girls, food." She shouted then went to her bedroom.

The girls ran into the dining room, and upon seeing Kevin, they stopped cold. Inez bit her bottom lip, then turned and ran back the way she came. Mina and Tess exchanged a look but continued forward, grabbing plates, sandwiches, chips, and carrots. Tess filled two plates and went back to their room.

Mina turned to leave but stopped. She faced Kevin. "Inez thinks you're evil." She sat across the table from Kevin. "I saw the creature you turned into last night." Mina bit into a carrot.

Kevin blinked in surprise. "What did you see?"

"A monster."

"Oh great, I'm a monster." He tossed his hands. "A werewolf?" He looked down at the game.

"No." She crunched into her chips. "I didn't see any hair. Looked more like a demon." Mina tossed a carrot, hitting Kevin on the head. "Shhh, Mom."

"Mina, I'm scared," he admitted to his sister. He picked the carrot off the table and ate it.

Mom strolled into the dining room, looking more comfortable in jeans, a tee-shirt, and a light jacket. “Where are the other two?”

Mina shrugged.

Mom gave her a stare. “Is Inez still hiding from her brother?”

Mina shrugged.

“This nonsense has got to stop.” Mom raised her voice so everyone could hear her, closed door, loud TV, or not. “You all need to get along. Talk, figure it out.”

Mina’s eyes widened. “But, Mom…”

“No, buts Mina,” she scolded.

“Mom. Stop,” Kevin pleaded. “Mina is talking with me. Please stop yelling.”

“Fine.” Mom turned on her heel. “I am going to Janet’s house to partake in a Football Widow’s Party. Your father will be here. But he is watching football, so he really isn’t here, is he?” She left the dining room and then the house. Her car started, and she was gone.

“Now, that’s melodrama.” Mina rubbed her chin and smiled as if she were taking notes.

“She’s right, you know. I miss you three. I miss the trouble and games.” He gestured with his hand toward *Monopoly* spread out on the table. “But most of all, I miss the talks we’ve had, even when we talk about nothing.” He felt foolish. He changed his tactic. “How about a game? Maybe the others will join us.”

Mina raised her eyebrows. “A game? With me?” She laughed, a deep and hearty belly laugh. “You’ll lose, of course.”

“Maybe.” Kevin picked up the dice. “I’d like to play anyway.”

Mina grinned. “Yes, this will be fun. Tess isn’t a challenge, and Inez cheats.” She shook her head when Kevin offered the dice. “No, you go first.”

“You’re not allowed to have fun without me.” Tess stood in the doorway, hands on her hips. “But she needs a handicap. Five hundred, take it, or leave it.” Tess pointed scathingly at Mina.

“That doesn’t seem fair.” Mina pouted.

“Fair?” Tess yelled at Mina. “What do you know of fair? You never study, and still, you get straight A’s. I study and retake tests, and I’m lucky to get a B. So…If you’d like an alternate handicap, I can hit you in the head with this.” She reached on the far side of the doorway, producing a Louisville Slugger, a maniacal grin on her face.

Mina eyed the bat. “Five hundred seems fair. What about Kevin? Do you think it’s fair for him?”

"He should get an extra…two hundred." Tess tapped the bat against her other hand. "Right, Kevin?"

Kevin looked at Mina, who nodded encouragingly. "Yes, that's an excellent idea."

"Good." The bat skittered across the floor, out the arched doorway, and into the hallway. Tess settled onto a bench, taking an extra five-hundred-dollar bill. She looked at Kevin then nodded to the bank. "Well?"

"Sorry, lost in thought." Kevin reached into the bank and removed two, one-hundred-dollar bills. "This seems like a different side to you. I'm not sure what to think of the threats."

Tess smiled. "Aw, thank you, Kevin. We tone it down for Mom. She gets bent out of shape easily. If we behave, we can have gymnastics lessons for Christmas."

"Speak for yourself. I want Bobby Fisher or Coding lessons."

"And Inez?" Kevin said quietly.

"Martial arts." Mina and Tess said together.

Kevin nodded. That made sense. "Don't you think Dad can hear what's going on?"

"Football." The girls said as if that explained everything.

"Can you keep all this," Kevin waved his hands about, "toned down until Christmas?"

"We have to." Inez entered the room, bat in hand. "It's a form of bribery. Mom gets what she wants." She smiled a humorless smile. "We get what we want."

Kevin felt the urge to run. His sisters seemed older and creepier than just a couple days ago. He took a deep breath, closed his eyes for a moment, trying to find calm. He opened his eyes to see Inez moved closer to his side. The bat was on her shoulder, waiting, begging for use. He cleared his throat. "Um, Inez, would you care to join us?" Kevin was surprised by how calm he sounded.

"No, I prefer to stand right here to make sure you don't hurt my sisters." He could have sworn her eyes flashed red. "Besides, *Monopoly* on a table this long is only suitable for three players.

"I have no intention of hurting anyone." Kevin protested.

Inez looked at him like he was an idiot. "This Kevin," she poked his flesh with a finger, "isn't a problem. It's the other Kevin."

"Other Kevin?" He looked to Mina.

Mina nodded.

"I see." Kevin swallowed. "Inez, Mina, Tess," he looked at each of them. "I don't know what happened or how it happened, but I think you're right. I blackout every night. My clothes get ripped up. Just this morning, I woke up in a cemetery, naked."

Tess giggled at the word naked. Mina lifted her eyebrows, and Inez dropped the bat off her shoulder.

Kevin continued. "At first, I thought I was a werewolf. But Father Pat said a cemetery and a church are consecrated ground, and nothing evil can go there." Kevin shrugged. "Mina told me the thing she saw wasn't furry."

Inez let the bat touch the ground and moved by her sisters. She squatted, and the three talked in their secret language. It was disconcerting watching them as if they had a hold over his actions, his soul. Like they could give him permission or give him death. Kevin shook his head, trying to shake the feeling that his biological sisters were something more. Like Benny or himself.

Tess looked at him, frowning.

Instinctively Kevin knew he should keep his mind quiet. He focused on the little silver game pieces, sitting on the board, noticing how the light bounced off their corners and bumps. He let his eyes blur, making the edges of the silver pieces disappear, and the reflected light grew to gain color, then moved and stretched into surreal shapes.

"Kevin."

He felt his body roll in his chair; someone shook him.

On the far end of the table were the triplets, playing Monopoly. Kevin blinked. The game was in front of him moments ago.

"Kevin."

He looked up. "Oh, hello, Ruby." To his ears, he sounded drunk. "What's going on?"

"I sure would like to know." Grandma looked at the girls.

Mina waved off the accusation. "He's fine. He was meditating, and we didn't want to disturb him. So, we moved the game to this side of the table."

"I didn't know he could meditate." Grandma forcefully opened Kevin's eyes wider.

"We didn't know either. But Kevin does an outstanding job." Inez said.

"I'm hungry," Kevin heard himself say.

"You didn't slip him something? Did you?" Grandma asked the girls.

"Of course not," Inez said. "That wouldn't be any fun."

Grandma Ruby made an unusual noise and then sat next to Kevin. She pushed a sandwich into his hands. Kevin ate mechanically, food in the mouth, chew, swallow, repeat. He continued until the sandwich was gone. He stopped and stared at the game the girls were playing.

"How long have I been sitting here?" he asked.

The girls shrugged in unison.

Kevin ate some carrots, watching the girls. "Um, Ruby." He waited to see if she would look at him.

"Yes?"

"The girls think there is an evil monster in our house," Kevin said.

All three girls gasped then held their breaths, looking at Grandma.

"Bah, I know evil, I've seen evil. I would feel it. There's no monster in our house." Grandma studied the triplets, daring them to say otherwise. "Rapscallion would have warned me if he sensed something. No, I stand by my first impression, nothing evil."

"Maybe it's a monster that's not evil? A good monster?" Kevin proposed. "Is that possible?"

"Why not? Evil is about action, not appearance." Grandma Ruby folded her arms. "You're old enough to know that simple truth." She stared the triplets down, daring them to argue with her.

"Like beauty and the beast," Tess said dreamily.

"Exactly," said Grandma.

"Oh, brother," said Inez. "I can't believe how far our conversation degraded."

"Are you friends with your brother again?" Grandma asked Inez.

"Until he does something stupid," Inez said.

Kevin felt more like himself after eating. What happened to him? Why did he fall into a stupor like that? Did his sisters drug him? Was it a monster side effect? He looked out a window and noticed twilight was setting in.

"I need to get home." Kevin stood. "It's getting late, and I don't feel right."

"Give me a minute, I'll come with you," Grandma eyed the triplets, then went into the living room to talk with her son.

Kevin watched the girls play their game for a few minutes before realizing they made purchases and payments to each other without saying a word.

"Okay," he said. "I've had enough weird for one day. Ruby, I'm going home."

# Chapter 31

Kragnor opened his eyes. He was back in the house, back in the bedroom. He was confident he slept in the cemetery.

On the desk, a book laid open. In the spine was a yellow object that smelled like wood. Kragnor moved it aside and noticed a cup-like-container that held similar items. The pages had blue horizontal lines across them. Someone wrote a paragraph, out of curiosity, he read.

> Sunday, October 18, 2026
>
> This morning I awoke in the cemetery at St. Stephens (naked). After a conversation with Father Pat, he's convinced that I am not a werewolf. He suggested I keep a journal, hoping that with self-reflection, I'll discover what's going on. This is my first attempt, and I don't know what to write.

> Grandma has dementia and sees things—I hope it's not genetic.
>
> I don't know if I am sleeping; I have no dreams.
>
> My sisters are acting strange, even for them. I brought brownies to Mom's, and I believe they like me again.
>
> Hopefully, I won't wake up in a cornfield tomorrow.

The bottom lines were in a shiny grey script while the top was written in deep blue ink. Kragnor looked across the desktop for a quill and inkwell. His eyes lingered on the yellow object that sat in the spine of the book moments before. He gripped the instrument and wrote with the pointy end.

He swept left and right, making circles and geometric shapes. "Fascinating." The cup-container had other objects with a similar design. He dumped it, watching the tools roll across the table. He picked a short one that smelled like candles, placing the tip to his finger. It left a spot of orange on Kragnor's flesh. The soft, creamy texture of the crayon was a delight. He moved his exploration to his arm, captivated by the amount of color left on the rough surface of his skin. The orange crayon broke. He frowned.

Kragnor tried another tool encased in man-made-stone. It marked on the paper, showing blue scribbles, but on his flesh, nothing appeared. He selected a purple crayon and wrote a sentence under the journal paragraph. He continued with the writing instruments, coloring, and drawing as only the curious can.

Kragnor sighed, upset that he allowed the paper and colors to distract. He needed to continue searching for his brothers and sisters. He opened the hallway door and descended the clothed stairway. The woman lay in her chair, snoring. The silent portal displayed images from far off lands. He located the portal-wand and held it in his grasp.

Gently he touched the woman's shoulder.

Ruby stirred, stretched, and then said, "Kevin, are you alright?"

"I am not Kevin."

Startled by the low tambour of Kragnor's voice, Ruby sat up and pulled a blanket over her lap, up her chest, like a shield. Her eyes skated over the bulk of his body. "Who are you?" Her voice was not timid or scared like she seemed the first night he met her.

"I am Kragnor."

Ruby reached out tentatively to touch him. She smiled. "Good, you're real."

Kragnor huffed.

"My apologies, my imagination gets the better of me from time to time." Ruby stood and turned on a light. She stepped back and gaped. She took a deep breath and poked him, moved his tail, then wings, lifting and looking under them. Ruby rubbed the webbing of his wings, gasping. "Feels like dragonfly wings." She babbled with a giddy trill to her voice. "Still, I'm not certain that you exist. You could be part of my dementia. Not that I mind. I have met all kinds of friends. My, you are handsome." She rubbed the side of his face, stopping, realizing what she did.

Rapscallion rubbed on Kragnor's legs and meowed at Ruby.

Ruby picked up the white cat. "Rap approves of you. You're not malicious. Welcome to my abode. What can I do for you?"

Kragnor shook his head, not fully understanding. "Did you summon me, Sorceress?"

Ruby smiled. "Sorceress, I like the sound of that. But, no, I didn't summon you."

Disappointment crossed her features. "If only I could."

"Then, you would not care if I take my leave?"

"You may come and go as you please, but I think I would be happy if you returned," Ruby said. "I feel safe and content with you here."

"As you wish." Kragnor knelt and offered Ruby the wand. "I return your portal-wand."

Ruby accepted it graciously then noticed the purple crayon tucked between his fingers. "Thank you. You are most kind. Would you do me the honor of writing on my cast?"

Kragnor huffed. "What is cast?"

"This is a cast." Ruby showed him her pink arm. "It is used to help a broken bone heal."

"Your bones are broken? And this," he tapped the cast with a claw, "keeps the bone still, like a splint?"

"Exactly."

Kragnor nodded, feeling proud for understanding the external covering but made no move to write on it.

"Would you mark on it for me?" Ruby shoved her pink arm toward him.

With his purple crayon, Kragnor wrote three symbols that Ruby never saw before. "You honor me, Sorceress. Now I must take my leave and find my brothers and sisters." He kept the crayon and waited for dismissal.

"Thank you." Ruby touched the marks. "It's beautiful."

Kragnor nodded then turned, leaving out the back door. He looked to the house behind the metal weaved gate, hoping to see one of the young children. There was a time when children adored him. Did the curtain move? It was hard to see inside the dark room. He looked to the stars, squatted into his strong haunches, and leaped into the sky.

He landed stealthily in the small cemetery near the Catholic church. He looked around, climbed through the red granite headstone, and emerged in the quiet country cemetery.

It was warmer in the forgotten cemetery than the city cemetery. Frogs chirped, and mosquitoes buzzed. He didn't know how far he traveled between headstones. Someday he would find out. But to do so, he would have to talk to the author of the paragraph or the Sorceress. Though he doubted Sorceress would be reliable. She had a powerful spell of forgetting cast upon her.

He entered the same black granite headstone as before. He wanted to track the other stones inside Banco de Mexico. He was careful to enter the room slowly so as not to awaken the magic noises. He stood in the room with granite walls, feeling at home. He breathed deep, taking in the earthy tones of the stone. Each section smelled similar. They probably came from the same quarry. He entered the slab next to the one with the words on it. He came through, appearing in the same bank but out a different wall.

He tried another and felt a change in gravity. He slowly appeared out the top of a countertop sink. Only his head and eyes were above the countertop. The room was beautiful, filled with the same black granite stone walls as the bank. White marble decanters filled with flowers sat near the door. A clawed bath basin carved from white marble was in the center of the room.

A woman relaxed in the tub, her head laid back, and a cloth covered her face. She faced away from the sink. A white statue of a woman holding grapes stood on a pedestal in the corner. The figure moved, indicating to Kragnor that she was one of the brethren. Brethren were works of art created by humans and given life through magic spells. They were not alive like plants, animals, and people. Instead, they appeared more life-like than other statues. To humans, the incantation increased the statue's mystique and value. To akitu, the brethren were like finding lost family or friends. While a stone could share memories with an akitu, a brethren could discuss and converse.

He eased out of the countertop surface. He stepped onto the floor and walked across the tiles, claws clicking with every step. Click. Click.

The woman in the tub sat up, startled. She pulled the cloth off her face and looked around. Kragnor froze, hoping she would not turn to look at him, but she did. She screamed, "Ayudame, Ayudame!"

Two men burst into the room with strange-looking weapons. They saw Kragnor, screamed in terror, and small metal projectiles flew out of their weapons. The pellets hit Kragnor, but they ricocheted off his flesh and flew unpredictably, striking the screaming woman. She dropped back into the water-filled tub. The delicate statue, the brethren woman, fell from the shattered pedestal and broke into many pieces.

Realizing he no longer had a purpose in the room, Kragnor leaped toward the countertop, diving into its surface while projectiles continued to strike his flesh. He entered the bank with such chaos and speed that the magic thrumming noises and bright lights filled the corridor of granite walls. Knowing he needed to leave the bank too, he leaped through the Banco de Mexico wall.

He erupted out of the headstone into the forgotten cemetery, sprawling on the grass. Chirping frogs, singing crickets, and buzzing bugs serenaded him. Kragnor enjoyed the sounds of nature and remembered simpler times before humans.

The magics of this era are strange and incomprehensible. *It seems, from their screams of terror and desire to harm me, those humans never saw an akitu before. What happened to make the world forget?* He sat up and snorted with disgust. *I was a fool to think I could figure everything out on my own. I destroyed that brethren woman. I need allies. The Sorceress has talked with me, even if she is uncertain that I am real. The three children in the other house have shown interest; perhaps I should go to them.*

A fox trotted past Kragnor, nose to the ground. It startled when it saw his movements. "No, woodland creature, I am not a boulder." Kragnor held out his hand, allowing the fox to catch his scent. "But I probably smell like one."

The curious fox sniffed then returned to the trail he was following. "It is time for me to return to the Sorceress's house."

He stood and looked at the small pockmarks that the projectiles gave him. He touched them, surprised by the damage. The wounds didn't hamper his movements or cause much pain. He studied his finger, where he cut the tip on the blade. It was healed. These marks will be gone soon too.

He looked around; this cemetery could be his sanctuary if he needed it. The thought that he had options pleased him. Still, it was best to give Sorceress and the author a chance.

Kragnor entered the red granite headstone and emerged in the newer cemetery near the church. He half expected the man in the black clothing to chase him. But it was quiet, no frogs, crickets, or bugs. It was colder here; the animals must be preparing for winter.

He jumped high before opening his wings, catching the air and flying to Sorceress's house. Within minutes he landed next to the gnarled oak. He entered the house and climbed the stairs to the room with old things. He remade his nest, curled up, and fell asleep.

# Chapter 32

Kevin woke gasping. What the hell happened? Pain coursed through him. He touched his sore body. *Did I fall fifty flights of stairs?* The early light in the attic was not bright. He smiled. At least he was home. He went to his room and turned on the lights. His muscles were tight, pulling with every step.

He opened the closet, which held a full-length mirror on the backside of the door. Bruises the size of oranges covered his body. They were center mass, at least that is what the cop shows called it. He turned to look at the rest of his body. The damage was everywhere, including a cut under his eye. He looked over his body again and noticed another cut on his shoulder and hip.

Kevin poked the bruises then hissed with pain. There were strange marks on his arms. He touched them, but they didn't hurt. Looking closer, they appeared to be squiggles, lines, circles, and geometric designs written in ink, pencil, crayon, and marker. He looked from the bruises to the drawings. *Was I in a paintball fight with a bunch of kindergarteners?*

He closed the closet door and noticed his desk in a state of disarray. The composition notebook contained markings similar to the designs on his skin. Was the monster trying to communicate? Below the paragraph Kevin wrote the night before, in large beautiful purple crayon script, was: *My name is Kragnor. I can assure you that I am not a werewolf.*

Kevin sat on the bed, holding the notebook in shaking hands. He turned the page, licked his lips, and wrote *I am human*. What if this monster doesn't know what a human is? Kevin found a *People* magazine and cut out a *Calvin Klein* model. "You only wish you looked that good," he said. About halfway down the paper, he wrote another sentence: *I think we are sharing one body.* Briefly, he thought about finding a picture of a werewolf to add to the page but decided against it

Kevin dressed quickly and ran downstairs. Ruby sat in her chair, drinking coffee. There were some strange purple marks on Ruby's pink cast. The purple looked like the same hue of crayon that Kragnor used to write in the notebook. *Should I ask her?*

"Good morning."

"Morning, sorry no breakfast for me, I'm late again." Kevin ran out of the front door. Johnny's car was out front, and he was drinking coffee. "Morning," Kevin called as he passed the ugly tan vehicle.

Kevin ran to school at a brisk pace, feeling rather pleased with his ability to keep his speed all the way. The strength and endurance probably came from being part monster. Kevin entered the school just as the first bell rang. He continued running down the hall to his first class.

Tony, Vin, and Chad were in the front row, mocking him. But Kevin didn't care. He was in a good mood. There was no way Tony could make him feel bad. Kevin smiled at Tony and his cronies then took his seat.

Tony seemed upset or disappointed by Kevin's smile. Psychology class started and ended with no other distractions.

Annie stood next to his locker, batting her eyes at him, twisting her finger around her necklace, rubbing the purple stone. Annie was out of her mind. He didn't want anything to do with her, yet she seemed to want him. Annie took his hand and pulled him into the nearby girls' bathroom. She shoved Kevin against a wall and planted a kiss on him. He tried to jerk away, but she pinned him.

"Stop it," Kevin demanded.

"You know you want me. No point in fighting it," Annie said, caressing his face.

"But I don't."

Annie stepped back. "What's wrong with you? Everyone wants me." She caressed her body, rubbing her breasts, hips, and inner thighs. She licked her lips. "Everyone wants what only I can give them."

Kevin looked at her, confused by her actions and his lack of response. Only a couple days ago, he would have killed to have Annie look at him like that. It seemed as if his own body was denying him. Maybe because he realized that she was poison.

Annie's eyes darkened, then hardened with hate and anger. "You're an ass." She slapped his face then ran out the door.

Kevin shrugged off the slap and followed Annie out of the girls' bathroom.

Tony, Vin, and Chad were outside the door. Annie was gone.

Kevin tried to step around them to get to his class. Tony sidestepped, blocking him.

Kevin glowered. "What do you want?"

Tony stepped back and cracked his knuckles.

Vin and Chad punched each other on the shoulder, psyching themselves up.

"Oh, yea," Vin said, drawling the words.

"There's gonna be a fight. I love fights!" Chad shouted down the hallway.

The hallway cleared. Vin and Chad chanted, "fight, fight, fight," and others picked it up. The chant surrounded Kevin. He looked around for a friendly face or a teacher to stop this nonsense.

Tony smiled maliciously. He nodded to Vin and Chad. They grabbed Kevin's shirt and hauled him into the center of the hallway.

Tony put up his balled fists and bobbed around, dodging and weaving. "Poor Widdle Kevy doesn't know how to fight." His smile faded. "How about a lesson?" He stepped back, then quickly forward, landing an uppercut to Kevin's jaw.

Kevin fell backward, sliding on the linoleum floor.

Tony screamed, "What the fuck?"

The chanting stopped. Kevin sat up, mentally prepared for another attack. Someone moved fast down the corridor away from him. "What happened?" He said aloud. "Where's Tony?"

"Shut-up, asshole."

Kevin looked around, getting to his feet. *Who said that?* It sounded an awful lot like Vin.

An hour passed before he realized that his jaw didn't hurt.

The final bell rang, and the students filed out of Russian History class. Most had busses to catch or sports practice to attend. Megan wasn't packing up her books. Instead, she pulled out more. She opened a book titled *Cuneiform Writing* to a page that she marked with a sheet of loose-leaf.

Kevin walked to her desk to see what she was doing. "I tried to decipher some of the inscription myself. But I didn't do very well." She opened the paper, exposing a line of cuneiform and many different words in line under each grouping.

"Why not have your father figure it out?"

Megan looked up, startled. "Oh. Hi, Kevin, I thought you were Mr. Mulligan."

"Does your dad know what the engravings mean?"

"The translation doesn't make sense." Megan pointed to the desk near her. "Sit, let me explain."

Kevin straddled the chair so he could face her across the desk.

"The Chinese people told my father that the engraving reads, *the stone shall protect the bear till the end of time.* But that doesn't agree with the number of marks on the stone."

Kevin gave her a blank stare.

"Okay, watch." Megan pulled out a piece of paper. On it, she wrote a series of lines and triangle shapes. "This says 'I don't know what to write' in cuneiform. It's a direct translation from English." Megan wrote the same sentence in English directly below the cuneiform. She wrote another cuneiform sentence. "That one is 'I don't know what to write' also but translated from French. 'Je ne sais pas quoi écrire.' Do you see the difference?"

Kevin frowned. "There is an extra mark for the French."

"Good." Megan nodded. "Do you know why?"

"No."

"It is the number of syllables. The French sentence has seven. The English has six. The same sentence in Romanian is five."

"Wow. How many languages do you know?"

Megan blushed. "That's not what I was trying to show you." Megan wrote the sentence. *The stone shall protect the bear till the end of time.* "How many syllables does this sentence have?"

Kevin said the sentence in his head and counted on his fingers. "Twelve."

"The cuneiform marks imply there ought to be thirty syllables or words."

"Okay," Kevin said, then frowned. "I'm not sure I understand."

"The people who gave the stones to the museum for the exhibit lied about the translation."

Realization dawned. Kevin's eyes widened. "Why?"

"It's a mystery. That's why I'm trying so hard to find the answer. I like puzzles." Megan shrugged as if to apologize.

Kevin looked at the paper with the rubbing on it. "I thought I might be able to help you translate, but I'm way out of my league." He pushed the paper back.

# Chapter 33

Kragnor picked up the book from the desk. A new purple crayon sat nestled in the spine. He read the first sentence and responded with, "I am akitu." For the second sentence, he nodded. Sharing a body explained how he moved from one location to another while he slept.

Kragnor flicked the image of the man poorly taped to the paper. *As if I didn't know what a human was.* An open magazine exposed a man-shaped hole. The pages flopped in his hands. The book had no spine, and two small metal clips held it together. *The bookbinder ought to be whipped.*

He closed the book and read the cover *People*. He nodded to himself, amused. Either humans have become less intelligent, or they have no idea what their species looks like. He placed the magazine on the desk and slowly rifled through the pages. Images of people in strange clothing covered the pages. Kragnor read the print, wondering who they were and what their importance was. Only kings and queens were written about in such a manner. It seemed ridiculous to have so many royals.

Kragnor closed the magazine. Reading about humans was a waste of time. He had studied humans for centuries. Humans are confusing, plain, and simple. No book, not even one named *People,* would shed any light.

A knock rattled Kevin's bedroom door. "Kevin? It's late. You should be sleeping." It was the Sorceress. She was checking on Kevin, that implied that Kevin was young. How young? What is the relationship between Sorceress and Kevin? Kragnor frowned. Too much was unknown.

Kragnor grunted noncommittally. He heard Sorceress's footsteps on the stairs. She was probably going to bed. He hoped she wouldn't return.

A stack of twelve yellow-edged books was under the desk. Kragnor reached under and looked at one. *National Geographic.* There were animals and cities that Kragnor had never seen. These were stories worth reading.

He set the stack of books beside him and looked at the other magazines on the floor. Most were about humans and the silly games they played. Some wore armor, and others wore almost nothing. But they all chased a ball or threw a ball or hit a ball. Kragnor chuckled.

He discovered a thin, more delicate book than *People* filled with drawings of humans that seemed to be fighting evil. The word *evildoer* was one of the words the man said. Usually followed by the word *sock* or *pow.* The man in the tight black suit looked like an akitu, but he called himself Batman. How odd. It seemed as if akitu disappeared from the knowledge of humans but were still in their collective memories. Only to be discovered when creating art or stories. Kragnor smiled. So, we are not dead to the human world. He liked Batman. He could relate to his belief in protecting the innocent.

There were other similar thin books that Kragnor looked at, but only "Batman" and the yellow-edged *National Geographic* caught his eye. The yellow magazines had fantastic maps and enchanting stories that seemed as if they were real. Some stories Kragnor wanted to be accurate, others were heartbreaking, and he hoped they were just stories.

After he looked at the third yellow magazine, he found an article and map of Paris. A city that he felt was his home. But the pictures showed images that were not familiar. The tall metal tower was not there when he was last awake. Understandably, humans would improve upon the city, but now it seemed foreign. Paris was not his home any more than this house.

Kragnor learned about the world's politics, wars, art, music, animals, cities, and so much more. He was surprised at how much he could learn by reading. This was easier than trying to find information by talking to others. So much had happened since his last emergence on the planet. He didn't find any information about his people, making him wonder if he was the last.

Eventually, Kragnor stopped reading and looked at the beautiful pictures in the magazines. The images were better than any painting from any master that he had ever seen. They allowed him to experience the location in ways he never could before. The artist was a genius. How did they capture the movement and the lifelike aspect of these people, places, and animals?

As dawn approached, Kragnor left more questions for Kevin:

> Do you know how we came to share a body?

I need to find others like me.
Can you help?

I would enjoy more books with
yellow edges.

Are there any gardens nearby?

Kragnor climbed the attic stairs and curled into the pile of familiar objects.

# Chapter 34

Kevin opened his eyes to the familiar sights and uncomfortable lumps of Kragnor's nest. He smiled, pleased that he wasn't three counties away in a cornfield. Kevin poked at his chest, noticing the bruises seemed to have disappeared overnight, but the tenderness was still in the muscle. He ran to his bedroom and checked the notebook.

"What the hell is an akitu? Find more akitu? And gardens?" Kevin tapped his bottom lip. "This Kragnor can't be much of a monster if he enjoys *National Geographic* and wants to visit gardens. Grandma was right. Kragnor is not evil." He sighed, feeling happier.

Noticing the clock, Kevin realized he would be late to school, no matter what he did today. He grabbed his book bag and went to the kitchen for breakfast. Grandma had a plate with pancakes on the table, and they were still warm. "How did you know when I would be downstairs?"

“You seem to get up at the same time every morning.” Grandma shrugged. “Like your father.”

Kevin poured the syrup over the short stack. “Ruby,” he said between bites. “Do you know what an akitu is?

“Akitu?” She sipped at her coffee. “No, I don’t think so.” Grandma drummed her fingers on the mug. “What is it?”

“I don’t know. I was hoping you did.” He finished eating. “It doesn’t matter. I’m sure I’ll figure it out. I’ve got to hustle. I’m late for school again.”

“Well, you were up late last night. It’s no wonder you’re late in the morning.”

Kevin looked at her sideways.

“Don’t you remember me knocking on your door?”

“No, I don’t remember. I was probably half asleep.” He tossed the book bag over his shoulder and headed out the front door. His endurance improved so much he didn’t notice the run to school. Kevin walked into the office to get a truancy note for his first class.

“Really, Kevin?” Mrs. Renfro, one of the ladies in the office, scolded him. “Late two times in a month?”

Kevin shrugged. “Honestly, I have not been feeling like myself lately.” He chuckled, not expecting the secretaries to get his joke.

“Well, if you’re late again, it’ll be reported unless you can get a written excuse from a parent.”

“Can I write it for myself? I am eighteen.”

“I’ll take it up with the principal, but I bet he says no. Best, you be prepared.” Mrs. Renfro handed the note over the counter.

“I understand.” Kevin took the note and went directly to Psychology class. He opened the door, handed the letter to Mrs. Anderson, and walked to his seat. Tony’s chair was empty. If the day went the way he wanted, Tony would be absent all day.

After his first class, Annie caught Kevin in the hall. “Kevin baby, I miss you.” She batted her exaggerated eyelashes at him. “I don’t know why I gave you up for that awful Tony.” She pouted, looking pathetic.

“Why are you playing these games? It’s disgusting.” Kevin turned away from her. He was uncertain why he even liked her in the first place.

Annie bobbed next to him in the hall, following close, hanging on him. Kevin felt a chill roll up his spine. If anything in this world is evil, it's her. He stopped and let her take a few steps without him, hoping she would continue. She turned and looked at him through her lashes, trying to be sweet.

"What do you want, Annie?" Kevin wanted her to go away.

"I want you, Kevin. I always have." She caressed his cheek. "Wasn't it me who asked you for a date?"

"That's right. You did. I forgot."

"I never forget." Annie caressed the crystal charm on her necklace. "I always get what I want." She grabbed Kevin's shirt and pulled him toward the lockers out of the stream of students. "And right now, I want you." She leaned against a locker, reached behind his neck, and pulled him into a kiss.

Kevin smelled strawberries, but it was an off smell like they had gone rotten. He pulled away from her. "I don't want you. You're poison."

Her smile fell, and her eyes flashed over his shoulder.

Kevin noticed her distraction. He pivoted to the left to face whoever was behind him.

Tony smacked Annie with his offhand, bouncing her head off a locker. She grabbed her bloody lip and glared at Kevin.

Kevin looked from Annie to Tony. “What the hell?” Tony’s right arm was in a cast and sling. How did he break his arm?

“What’s wrong, Kevin?” Tony snarled. “Why can’t you love Annie like the rest of us? Do you need to learn by force?” He looked around the hall. Mr. O was only feet away. “You’re lucky.” He pulled a blade from the sling he wore. “Since you won’t take a punch, we’ll have to try steel.”

Vin and Chad were behind Tony. They laughed and pointed at Kevin.

Annie placed her hand on Tony. “Not here,” she hissed.

Tony helped Annie wipe off the blood on her lip. He put his arm around Annie’s waist, and they disappeared around a corner.

# Chapter 35

Megan turned down the hallway and saw Tony, Annie, Vin, and Chad by her locker. Her eyes narrowed. What are those idiots doing now? They moved away. Good. She made it through the crowd and saw Kevin. Of course, it seems that the idiots have found someone to play with. Or torture. She rolled her eyes.

"Kevin, can you move? I need to get into my locker."

"Oh, yeah, sure." Kevin moved, his eyes still on Tony and friends. "I still can't find that stone." He turned to look at her.

Megan rifled through her organized locker. "If your room is messy, you may never find it." She adjusted the books in her arms and closed the door.

"I think maybe Annie stole the stone." Kevin wrung his hands. "Or maybe she had Tony steal it for her."

"What? Those ding-bats?" Megan studied Kevin, pleased to see that his Annie-delusions seemed to have passed. “They’d only use it to break a window.”

Kevin laughed nervously. “Yea, you’re probably right. Still, I think it might be gone forever.” He moved away from her locker, walking to his next class.

Megan followed. Her class was in the same direction. “When was the last time you saw it?”

“Here at school.” Kevin furrowed his forehead as if he were trying to remember.

“Well, yea, that’s when you showed me. But you took it home, right?”

He nodded. “I kept it in my pocket for the day. I walked Annie home.” He shook his head. “Seems like the memory is muddy.” He frowned. “Annie wanted me to stay at her house, but I needed to check on Grandma Ruby. So, I went home.” He paused. “I don’t remember taking it out of my pocket.”

“So, is it in your pants pocket?” Megan asked. “Maybe in the laundry hamper?”

“No, I used it to help Ruby cast a sp...” Kevin stopped in the middle of the hallway. “Oh, shit. Oh shit.” He looked at his hand in horror. He continued to stare, unmoving.

“Kevin?” He didn’t respond. She snapped her fingers in front of his face. “What is wrong with you?”

Kevin blinked, surprised. He grabbed Megan's hand. "I think I know what happened to the stone."

Megan tilted her head. "What?"

"I can't tell you." Kevin seemed to realize he was still holding Megan's hand. He let go and seemed to deflate before her eyes. "No one would believe me."

The bell rang.

"Shit," Kevin said, then ran off to class.

Megan entered the Chemistry classroom a few feet away. *What the hell was that all about. He can't tell anyone. No one would believe him. What could be so embarrassing that he couldn't say or admit to?* Megan took her seat and opened the Chemistry textbook on her laptop. Boys were so confusing. Her feelings were equally perplexing. Why was she even thinking about him? Megan squeaked out of frustration. Her classmates turned to look at her.

She dropped her head to her desk. But still, Kevin would not leave her thoughts.

# Chapter 36

The day flew by like a whirlwind. Kevin couldn't remember what class he went to or even if he ate lunch. Occasionally, he would poke his hand, expecting, hoping the stone would reemerge from his flesh, like some grotesque pimple.

Kevin walked home, lost in thought. He didn't notice the cars pass or even which direction he took. He stopped on the wooden bridge that went over Miller's Pond and overlooked the children's play area.

Koi glided through the water, their white and orange markings vibrant against the pond's deep brownish-green. Kevin squatted and looked at his reflection. The fish moved and traded spaces. Their quick movements blurred their edges, looking more like a mass of wriggling tentacles than many individual fish. He felt that way. Where did he end? Where did Kragnor begin? Was there a difference?

"Hello, Kevin" Annie leaned over him.

Startled, Kevin teetered in his squatted position, looking up. "What are you doing?" he asked.

"Making a statement. No one leaves me. Ever." Annie's eyes narrowed then moved to the parents and children in the park. "It's too bad they're so far away."

Something hard and heavy hit the back of Kevin's head. He wobbled and fell. The water stuck his body with an electric cold. He flailed his arms and legs then sucked in a deep breath before going underwater.

He felt heavy and cold. His arms and legs didn't move with enough speed or coordination to swim. The bottom of the pond enveloped his feet with sand, silt, and seaweed. Koi swam in circles above him. The shadow of the bridge lay behind. Kevin clamped his mouth shut, hoping he had enough air.

He used his arms to stabilize, then took a step forward. He took another and another, eventually breaking to the surface. He gasped for air then realized he was alright. He didn't need it. He continued climbing out of the pond.

"Oh, my. We thought you drowned." A woman came into the pond, hip deep, to help Kevin. She took his arm over her shoulder. "You sure are heavy."

"Wow, you were under the water for an hour," said a young boy.

"That's impossible," Kevin said.

"It sure seemed like a long time," the woman said, helping him settle on the ground. "I saw the woman who hit and pushed you." She patted Kevin on the shoulder. "When the police arrive, I'll let them know."

"Annie."

"Is that her name?" The woman grumbled, "bitch" under her breath.

"I need to go." Kevin stood.

"The police will be here any minute. They'll want a statement."

"I need to go." Kevin ran, blindly following instinct. He rushed into the house, smacking the door against the wall. Johnny sat on the couch next to Ruby.

"What the hell happened to you?" Johnny asked, getting to his feet.

"Are you alright?" Grandma Ruby moved toward Kevin, but Johnny reached his side first.

"Annie tried to kill me." Kevin choked, surprised that tears rolled down his face. He fell to his knees, realizing for the first time that mud covered his clothes, and his shoes were missing.

Kevin blubbered a recount. Johnny helped him out of his muddy jeans, then guided him into the bathroom for a shower.

He was clean, in fresh clothes, and a mug of hot cocoa warmed his hands. He felt somewhat normal. Johnny sat across from him at the small kitchen table. “Did she really say, *no one ever leaves me*?”

Kevin nodded, staring into the brown drink.

“Did she have a lucky charm or piece of jewelry she wore all the time?”

Kevin nodded.

Grandma Ruby rubbed Kevin’s shoulders. “Please stop bothering him. He’s been through hell.”

Johnny threw up his hands, stood, and paced the kitchen. “If I can’t get a statement from him, I have to take him to the police. They know he was thrown into that pond. They know he came home. And they know it was Annie. What they don’t have is a statement and charges against her.”

“How would they know all that?” Grandma crossed her arms.

“It’s a small town, Ruby.”

Kevin sighed. “There were a lot of kids and parents at the pond. Plenty of people to give a statement.” He looked at Johnny. “Why would the police care if Annie had a charm?”

Johnny stopped pacing. “They wouldn’t. The company I work for, the AKG, is interested.” He sighed and knelt next to Kevin. “I was placed in this town to find that charm. But when the church was attacked and a demon was spotted, I got distracted. I should have stayed on target. Then you wouldn’t have gotten hurt. It’s my fault.”

“It’s not a charm, is it?” Grandma stood with her hands on her hips.

“To the casual observer, it is.” Johnny shrugged. “To the AKG, it’s a danger to society.”

“What does it do?” Grandma Ruby’s eyes narrowed.

“You’re not going to let this go, are you?” Johnny looked from Kevin to Ruby. “Fine, it has limited mind control.”

“Really?” Grandma blinked furiously then folded her arms.

“Johnny’s right,” Kevin said, swirling the cocoa. “The day after I saw Benny, I knew what the charm was, or at least I suspected she had control over me like she controlled Tony. But it was broken. Because it didn't work anymore."

"Damn it, Kevin, I asked you to let me know if you knew of anything strange." Johnny threw up his hands. "From the day I met you, I had a feeling you were under some enchantment. Even now, there is something…"

"I was too busy trying to figure out if I was going crazy. Besides, I thought you had your *strange* with the church attack." Kevin frowned. "Wait a minute? Is that why you got involved with Ruby? Were you checking to see if she was controlling me?"

Grandma ruffled Kevin's hair. "You're partially right. He knows I'm a witch. We talked, and he decided that I'm harmless. Me? Harmless?" She laughed, placing her hand on her chest, looking fondly at Johnny.

Johnny didn't appear amused. "I still need a statement from Kevin, or I need to bring him in to give one." He turned the video on his phone and pointed it at Kevin.

"All right. I want to press charges. Annie tried to kill me. She knew exactly what she was doing. It was no accident."

"I see you're not influenced by her anymore." Johnny turned off his phone.

"No, like I said, after Benny, I noticed something wrong with her. She looks wrong; she smells wrong. I can't explain it."

"Who is Benny?"

"Benny is a friend," Grandma said defiantly.

"Friend?" Johnny's eyebrows lifted.

"Oh, would you just tell him?" Kevin shook his head. "He's a gnome."

"A gnome?" Johnny laughed. "You know they can be tricksters. What did he tell you?"

Grandma stared as if surprised that Johnny didn't make fun of her. "He wanted me to read my tarot."

"Tarot." Johnny narrowed his eyes. "Is that all?"

"The cards I pulled made me upset. And I asked Kevin to cast a protection spell."

"I remember." Kevin scratched at his palm. He looked at Johnny. "What else do you know about gnomes?"

"Not too much. Gnomes are the best gem cutters in the world." Johnny tapped his temple. "They like dirt and can help gardeners grow plants."

"That's why people have the plastic ones in their yard," Grandma added.

"You said, trickster. What did you mean?" Kevin felt tricked, but more so by Annie than Benny.

Johnny shrugged. "I remember reading that somewhere, but I can't think of an example."

Kevin looked from Grandma to the back door. "I think I'm going to tell Mom that I'm not coming over. I'm tired. I want to rest. And I know they'll have questions for me. I don't want to deal with it right now."

"I need to put Kevin's report into the police." Johnny kissed Ruby on the top of her head and left out the front door.

"I'll talk to Jerry, Donna, and the girls. You stay here." Grandma put her hand on Kevin's shoulder. "You look like hell."

"Ruby? Can I get more National Geographic magazines?"

"Your Grandpa Joe loved those magazines. What are you going to do with them?"

"Not much. Just look and see if they have any information that would help me with my homework."

"Sure, sure, there are a bunch in my bedroom. Don't cut them." She left out the back door.

Kevin went upstairs. At the top of the landing, he turned left to Grandma's room. He opened the door and stepped inside.

The room was a shrine of sorts; it looked the same way it did before Grandpa died. The bedspread was unchanged. The sports jacket Grandpa wore was draped over the footboard like it always was. Kevin sighed, feeling a twinge of sadness. He missed Grandpa, maybe not as much as Grandma did, but the ache was there.

On the floor near a full-length mirror was an old scale with a dial readout. Kevin took a deep breath, sealing his mind for the worst, and stepped on it. The dial spun, and the red arrow quivered and stopped on three hundred and forty-four pounds. *This explains why I couldn't swim and why the lady thought I was heavy.* He looked into the mirror at his pencil-thin shape and rolled his eyes. "Kragnor must be a big guy." Kevin chuckled to himself. Gazing in the mirror, he pulled off his shirt, poking at his chest and stomach, which appeared unchanged. *Did Tony break his hand when he punched me? Could I be turning into an akitu? Will I wake up someday and be a monster?* He tugged his shirt back on, fears flitting around his mind.

Book shelving covered a full wall, from floor to ceiling. Kevin moved closer to look for the bright yellow bindings of National Geographic. There weren't any. Then he noticed many faux leather magazine holders that looked remarkably like an old novel. The spine read "National Geographic 2002 Jan-June". Kevin pulled the holder, impressed with the weight and strength of the case. He grabbed two more and brought them to his room, where he placed them on the floor.

He sat on the bed, opened the shared notebook, picked up a pen, and scribbled answers to Kragnor's questions.

> I cast a spell of protection for my Grandma Ruby. I used a green stone with cuneiform writing on it. The rock melted into my hand, and I passed out. The next morning, I was in the attic. I figure that was your first night here.
>
> What is an akitu? Can you draw one?
>
> There are plenty of gardens in the area, but the growing season

> is over. Most people plant vegetables. Also, the books you requested are on the floor by the bed."

Kevin took off his clothes and waited for the change.

# Chapter 37

Kragnor's eyes snapped open, settling on the notebook. He read, pausing at the mention of the stone. The stone was important. But why? He shook his head, trying to remember. An image of the bloodstone flashed in his mind then disappeared. He closed his eyes, willing the memory to return. A friend's face. Francois, with his dark brown robes. Friar Francois held the stone in his hand. His mouth moved, he was telling Kragnor something important, but no sound came. The memory faded.

Kragnor sighed, sitting back on his tail. "It will come in time. You've been asleep for seven hundred years, be patient," he scolded. He picked up a crayon and requested Kevin write down the words he remembered from the stone. The engraving would tell him more and perhaps allow more memories to flow.

He looked back to the notebook and chuckled at the idea that people would grow vegetables in gardens. Only lords and ladies had gilded gardens filled with exotic plants and flowers, statues, fountains, and hedge mazes. Peasants grew vegetables in their fields. He scratched his smooth head. "The world has changed in seven hundred years."

The idea that akitu were lost to time made sense. Everyone was frightened upon seeing him. "Why were we forgotten?" Kragnor thought the stone's engraving would have an answer. He picked up the magazine that had the word Batman written on it. He ripped out the cover image. Batman stood on a roof with the moon behind him, cape billowing in the wind, like an akitu. He used the strange adhesive strip to attach the picture to the book. Under Batman, he wrote: "This man looks like an akitu."

A gentle knock rapt on the door. "Kevin, I know you're awake. I can see the light under the door. Johnny wanted me to pass on a message." The handle jiggled, and the door opened.

Sorceress stood in the wash of light, mouth agape. "Kevin?" Her eyes fluttered. She reached for the door jam and steadied herself. "You're not Kevin." She took a deep breath and stepped into the room. Her demeanor changed from helpless surprise to stalwart determination.

"Sorceress. You surprised me." Kragnor stood and bowed. His earlier assessment of her tremendous power was correct. He felt it rolling off her.

"What have you done with my Grandson?" Her eyes narrowed dangerously.

"I did nothing. It was he who did it to me."

The sorceress stepped forward, threatening. "I don't believe you."

Kragnor stepped back, bumping his tail into the desk. He reached back, grasping the notebook, then held it before him. "Read the truth for yourself."

Her eyes skimmed across the page and then lowered. "We made a column of power that night. Johnny and I downstairs, Kevin up here." Sorceress's pleading eyes locked with Kragnor's. "All I wanted was protection from harm." She looked away. "I did this to you and Kevin. It's my fault."

"Sorceress," he consoled

"My name is Ruby," she barked.

Kragnor waved his hand apologetically, indicating she should continue.

"I chose the spell. I gave Kevin the books and tools. I begged him to cast it." A look of shock crossed her features. "Benny!" She paced back and forth. "It all started with Benny telling me to read my tarot cards. That little stinker lives in my backyard." She waved her hands in frustration. “Johnny told us that gnomes are tricksters. He was right.” Ruby sat on the edge of the bed and sighed.

“Gnomes?” Kragnor relaxed, sitting back on his tail. “I like gnomes.” They were an ancient species, almost as old as akitu. They often tricked humans, that was true. But they would never take advantage of an akitu. “If a gnome is involved, then this is a dire situation.”

“Aren’t they trouble?”

“Not to an akitu.” Kragnor huffed. “Although, he did trick you into freeing me.”

“Freeing?”

“I was a prisoner of that stone.”

“Stone?”

Kragnor studied her. Her moment of strength and clarity seemed to have passed. Ruby’s eyes were glazing, her mind turning quiet. “Sorceress, it is late. You should sleep.”

Ruby stood and patted Kragnor’s arm. “Thank you. What is your name again?”

The gargoyle tapped his chest. “I am Kragnor, your humble servant.” He bowed slightly, extended his hand, took her hand, and kissed it.

She blushed. “What a gentleman. I can’t stay and talk. I need to go to bed.” Ruby smiled and stepped out the door, leaving it open.

Kragnor waited, giving Ruby time to fall asleep. The sound from the portal downstairs went silent. He waited a few moments then crept down the stairs and out the back door.

He looked around the raised beds, searching for the gnome. “Benny,” he called. “Benny, I know you are here.”

A toad croaked.

“Gnomes need not hide from akitu.” Kragnor directed his voice to the toad’s location. “Come now. Toads sleep at these temperatures. I know you are a gnome.”

“Fine,” said a deep grumpy voice. “Over here.”

Kragnor moved to the voice and sat back on his haunches. “What is going on that you needed to set me free? Why did you involve humans?”

The gnome climbed onto the gargoyle's knee and sat. “Found out, did you?” Benny wiped the end of his bulbous nose. “Humans have forgotten too much. I knew you were in Ruby’s house, but I couldn’t get in there, and even if I did, I don’t have the power to reverse the spell that put you in that stone.”

“Rapscallion is protecting Ruby from you?”

“Damn cat.” Benny fidgeted and pouted.

Kragnor nodded. A good familiar will protect its master, even if the master is ignorant of the danger. "Why, Ruby? Why now?"

"I could have waited until the cat died, sure, but Ruby deserves to be set free. She's a good human."

"Set free? What are your intentions?"

"I wasn't going to kill her if that's what you're insinuating." The gnome folded his arms defensively. "By freeing you. You're going to set her free." Benny shrugged. "You may have done so already."

Kragnor leaned closer to the gnome. "Explain."

Benny stood and pointed at him. "You are akitu, Ancient of Ancients. Your magic runs deep and true. Your presence is enough to revive those who have become physically and mentally weak. You can break spells that corrupt and hide the truth. I knew you slumbered in that stone; I could feel your strength. Simply by being free from your stone prison, you have rejuvenated this area. Have you not noticed?" The gnome spread his arms wide.

Kragnor huffed. "What have you done?"

"I have done nothing other than influence a human. You did the rest." Benny pointed to the house where the girls lived. “You broke their spell. I didn’t know they had one.” The little man shrugged. “What’s done is done.” He smiled. “At least it’ll be a bit more exciting around here.”

The gargoyle reached down to grab the little man. Benny dove from Kragnor’s stone knee into the exposed soil of the raised bed, disappearing as quickly as if the dirt were water. Kragnor growled, cursing himself for forgetting that gnome ability. He could outwait and outlast a gnome.

He looked at the girl’s house. *I can’t undo the damage I made, but I could tell Ruby. She might be able to correct it. Especially if her mind is becoming whole again, and her power is returning.*

Kragnor returned to the house, entering through the back door. In the room with the silent portal, Rapscallion studied him from Sorceress’s lap. The cat yawned and stretched, indifferent to the gargoyle’s presence. Kragnor had not harmed Ruby. The familiar would have attacked if he had. Perhaps the gnome was right. She needed her power reawakened.

# Chapter 38

Kevin closed the shared book. He closed his eyes, trying to remember the marks on the stone. Was the first mark a short line or long? Did it have one arrow shape or three? The only way to get the *words* that Kragnor wanted was to request the rubbing from Megan. Kevin rolled his eyes. *Oh yes, I can imagine that conversation.* "Megan, can I have that rubbing from the stone? I need to show someone."

"Who?" She'd ask.

"Oh, no one in particular, just the monster I turn into every night."

*She'd call the insane asylum, and an ambulance would take me away.* Kevin pulled his shirt on, grabbed his book bag, and went downstairs.

He cast a glance at the grandfather clock. "Late again."

"It's no big deal," Grandma said. "You have an excuse today. Yesterday you were almost killed. In fact, if you want to stay home, I'll call you in."

"No, I need to be there today." He microwaved a breakfast burrito.

"Well, if you ever need assistance, I can wake you up at seven."

"Seven?" Kevin looked into the microwave and watched the burrito spin. What would happen if Ruby saw Kragnor? Or the change? Would her mind snap? He swallowed. He couldn't risk it. "No, I'll pass and take my chances with the ladies in the office."

"Suit yourself."

Kevin wrapped the hot burrito in a napkin and left out the front door. He ate and ran to school, finishing the burrito as he stepped in the door.

He entered the office. "Good morning, ladies."

"You're late, Mr. Arkis." Mrs. Renfro frowned at him.

"Ah, but I avoided that fate last night." Kevin smirked at his joke.

"Excuse me?"

"Didn't you hear? I figured it would be all over the news and school this morning." Kevin smiled at the women. "Well, then, ladies, let me tell you. Last night Annie Brown hit me in the head and tossed me into Millers Pond. I almost died."

Mrs. Renfro stared at him, not knowing what to say. "I think I heard something about that." Her fingers danced on the keyboard, and she looked at her computer. "Here it is. It says you pressed charges against Annie for attempted homicide. Well, that's not very nice."

Kevin frowned. "Neither is almost drowning."

"She just loves you, dear. You shouldn't take it so personally."

"What?" Kevin cleared his throat. "Can I get a pass, please?"

Mrs. Renfro handed him a slip of paper. "You ought to give Annie another chance. I'm sure she didn't mean anything by it."

He took the paper and turned away. *Another chance? That was the last thing I would ever do.* "Thank you," Kevin said over his shoulder. Why did she always take the girls' side?

When History rolled around, Kevin was relieved to find Megan. He sat directly behind her. "I need the rubbing you made the other day, of the rock."

"I left it at home. I wanted to try a different tactic."

"I found someone who said they could read it."

"Impossible. You know we tried Acadian, Sumerian, and many other languages."

"He seemed certain of his ability."

Megan crossed her arms as if offended that someone could succeed where she didn't. "I'd like to meet them. I'd love to know where they learned Cuneiform. Maybe they can teach me a thing or two."

"I'm not sure you should."

"Not sure of what? That I shouldn't meet him or that I shouldn't learn from him."

"I don't know this guy. He could be a creep."

"A creep who knows how to read Cuneiform?" She laughed. "I think I'll take that chance. I can bring the rubbing over tonight. I'll need your address." Megan looked Kevin in the eye. "This isn't some stupid joke, is it?"

"Not after yesterday." Kevin scribbled his address on a piece of paper and handed it to her.

"The rumors are true?"

"Many of them are. Annie tried to kill me, and I pressed charges against her." He sighed. "Rumors and people suck."

"The first rule you need to know, people are assholes. If you find one that isn't, hold on." Megan smiled at him.

"Thank you," he said, feeling relieved that someone was in a decent mood. "Ruby and I usually have dinner at my parent's house. I'll be at that address by seven." Kevin pointed at the paper in Megan's hand.

"Pizza? That's unusual." Grandma whispered to Kevin. Three white boxes sat on the dining room table. They had a poorly rendered map of Italy on the top. She reached into the box with pepperoni and removed a slice.

Kevin pulled a slice from the works pizza. He took a small bite and dabbed at his mouth with a napkin, trying to hide his comment. "She only orders pizza when she's too upset to cook."

"So, what happened?" Mom asked Kevin, "There are so many rumors going on that I want to hear it from the horse."

Kevin explained how Annie hit him and pushed him into the pond. He watched his sisters as they ate their cheese pizza slices. *Were they blinking in unison?*

"Well, son, you've got to be careful. Some women are dangerous. Isn't that right, Donna?" Dad folded a slice and shoved half of it into his mouth.

Mom stared at Dad but said nothing.

Dad continued eating, chasing the pizza with gulps of beer. “I’m glad you weren’t hurt.”

“Really, Jerry? He was hurt. Do you have any idea what kind of mental abuse that is? His girlfriend tried to kill him.” Mom cut her slice with aggressive sawing motions.

“She wasn’t my girlfriend at that time. We broke up a few days before,” Kevin said. “It was a strange relationship anyway.” The triplet’s eyes bounced from Mom to Dad. They seemed to be enjoying the discontent between their parents.

“Is that why she attacked you?” Mom asked.

Kevin nodded. “I think so. Right before she hit me, she said *no one leaves me*. Like I insulted her by breaking up.”

“I hope that bitch rots.” Mom stabbed the section of her pizza with a fork and put it in her mouth.

“Donna, are you alright?” Dad stared, shocked that his wife would swear.

Mom dropped her cutlery and swallowed. “Someone tried to kill my son. No, I’m not alright. Maybe you should be asking why you’re okay with the situation.”

Dad held his hands up. “I never said I was okay. I’m not happy either.”

"You don't appear upset, Jerry." Mom frowned. "Seems to me you're only unhappy when the Packers lose."

An uncomfortable silence fell over the table.

The girls giggled.

# Chapter 39

Megan climbed into her car and slapped the steering wheel. "Why did I leave that paper at home?" Now she would have to deal with her father. Artem wasn't about to let her go anywhere once she set foot in the house. *I could trick him, drug him, or kill him.* She smiled as her ideas became more absurd.

Megan pulled her car into the driveway, hoping her father wasn't home yet. The garage door opened, and Artem's car was sitting there, taunting her. She squinted at the car. *Great, he's babysitting me tonight.*

She went into the house and set her books on the breakfast nook table. What was her father playing at? Why didn't he make dinner?

"Good afternoon, my darling," Artem called from the living room.

She slowly walked into the room, dragging her feet. "I'm not feeling so good. I think maybe I ate something bad." Megan rubbed her stomach dramatically.

Artem held a mixed drink in one hand. “Is that so?” He rubbed his chin, disbelief etched on his face.

Megan sniffled, rubbing her nose. “I don’t know. Maybe it’s a cold.” She made a sour face. “Oh, my.” Megan ran to the small guest bathroom, next to the kitchen, and shut the door. She made vomiting and hacking noises.

“Do you need some medicine?” Artem shouted through the door.

“Sure,” she said, muffling her voice with her hand. The floorboards creaked as Artem walked away. She waited a few minutes and went back to the couch, hand on her stomach.

Artem was waiting. He handed her a white plastic bottle.

Megan opened it and drank straight out of the container. She made a funny pinched face. “Gross, chalky.” She put the bottle on the end table and leaned forward as if her stomach hurt. “Oh, I forgot to tell you something.”

“Yea?”

“Annie tried to kill a boy last night. The boy survived and pressed charges. She’s in jail for attempted murder.” Megan held her stomach for a second, burped, then took another drink from the bottle.

“Jail?”

She nodded. "There were lots of rumors going around at school. Many of the male students are acting weird, some of the teachers too."

"I wonder if Nikolai knows?"

Megan shrugged. "It all happened last night. I'm not sure who knows."

Artem went into the kitchen but returned a minute later. "Nikolai didn't answer. I'm going to the gym. Want to come?"

"No, Dad, that's okay. I think I'm going to go to bed early. Might need more time in the bathroom." She rubbed her belly again.

"Nikolai might have questions."

"I've told you all I know. I'm no good to you tonight." Megan picked up the white plastic container and walked to her room. "Good night, Dad." She shouted from her door.

"Do you want me to check on you when I get back?"

"I guess, but right now, I just want sleep," Megan said in the whiniest voice she could muster. She closed the door and locked it. He would expect it locked. The book on cuneiform writing was on her dresser; she opened it and put the rubbing into her pocket. Megan pulled some blankets and pillows out of her closet. She stuffed the bed and molded the fabric to make it look like a body. Her father had never checked on her before, but he'd been acting abnormally for a few days.

Megan sat on the edge of the bed, tapping her fingertips on her leg. She double-checked that the paper was in her pocket. From her bedroom, she heard the garage door close, and her father's car drive off.

She went to her window, opened it, and slipped out. Megan had to leave her car; otherwise, her father would notice when he returned. Then he would definitely make good on his threat to check on her. She bent and re-tied her laces then ran to Kevin's house.

Megan climbed the steps, eyes darting around. The porch gave her an eerie sense of déjà vu, but this wasn't Bonnie's house, and no one was lurking about. She reached the door and was prepared to knock when the door suddenly opened. Kevin stood there, but his head was turned. He was in mid-conversation with someone inside the house.

"…girl from school. Megan's helping me with a history project." Kevin turned and saw Megan waiting. "Oh, hi." He stepped aside and waved her into the living room. "Megan, this is my Grandma. She'll insist you call her Ruby."

Megan attempted to shake Ruby's hand, but Ruby sidestepped and pulled her into an embrace. "Oh, no dear, we hug here."

Megan stiffened, feeling embarrassed and a little attacked. She stepped back and moved closer to Kevin.

"I'd like you to meet Rapscallion." Ruby picked up the huge white tomcat and brought him to Megan. "We've had some issues with people lately, so I want you tested before you go any further. Rap is never wrong."

"Ruby. I can't believe you're doing this." Kevin rolled his eyes at his grandmother.

"It's okay, Kevin. After what Annie did to you, I'm not surprised by a test. The familiar's opinion is important to a witch." Megan looked from Ruby to Rapscallion and nodded.

Ruby raised her eyebrows. She set Rap on the floor at Megan's feet. "Kevin told you I practice Wicca."

"Yes, it's a fascinating religion." Megan squatted to get closer to the white tom. She held out her hand and let him sniff her fingers. Rap stepped into her, rubbing his face on her hand. He reared up, placing his paws on her knee, and meowed at her. With both hands, Megan rubbed his sides and bumped his forehead with hers. “What a friendly kitty.”

Rapscallion meowed, then turned and, with his tail in the air, jumped on the couch.

“I think that means I pass.” Megan stood and looked at Ruby.

“You did more than pass,” Kevin said, pride in his voice.

Ruby seemed disappointed, but then she smiled. “I assume you two are going upstairs to work on this project?” She reached into her purse sitting near her chair. She placed a condom into Kevin’s hand. “You better have protection.” She grinned at Kevin as if to embarrass him.

“It’s nothing like that; she’s helping me with my homework.” Kevin tried to give the condom back.

“Right,” Ruby said. She plopped into her recliner and turned on the television.

Megan followed Kevin up the stairs and to the right. She smiled wistfully, wishing her relationship with her father was silly and sweet, like Kevin and his Grandmother.

Kevin opened his door and stepped inside. Megan expected the guy who could read any cuneiform to be sitting on the bed waiting. But the room was empty.

"So, where is the guy?" she asked.

"Guy?"

Megan put her hands on her hips. "You told me you know a guy who can read any cuneiform. I expected him to be here."

"Oh, yeah, right." Kevin looked at the clock. He rubbed the back of his neck and cleared his throat. "He should be here soon." He looked at the clock again, then shot a glance at Megan. "You arrived earlier than I expected."

Megan shrugged. "I had to jog. My car is acting funny." She pointed to the clock. It read 8:42. "So when is this guy coming?"

"He's on his way, right about nine o'clock." Kevin twitched and began to pull at his hands. "Megan, I don't expect you to believe me. And, well, I didn't exactly tell you everything."

Megan closed her eyes and tilted her head back. "You've got to be kidding me."

"Please, wait, and hear me out." Kevin paced the room, keeping an eye on the clock. "I change. I turn into something else. Like a werewolf."

Megan's eyes drew into tight slits, and her hands clasped into fists. "Not this werewolf crap again. I thought you were kidding at the library."

"I wish I was." Kevin sat on his bed, eye to the time. "I feel like I'm trapped. Kragnor comes every day whether I want him to or not." He looked at her with pleading eyes.

Megan folded her arms and raised one eyebrow.

"If I were you, I wouldn't believe me either. Just leave the rubbing. Go, I'll deal with it." Kevin pushed Megan toward his bedroom door. "Quickly, he comes," Kevin finished in a harsh whisper.

Megan handed Kevin the paper and stepped out the door. She turned to say something. But Kevin shut the door. Why would anyone claim something so ridiculous? She put her ear to the door and heard movement. Carefully she opened the door a crack to see what Kevin was doing.

Kevin sat on the floor naked, his back to the door. His skin was smooth and pale, his dark hair a mess. Suddenly he tensed, his arms thrust away from his body. His whole body jerked as if convulsing.

Like some grotesque form of plate tectonics, Kevin's back split up the spine. Blood pooled on his skin but didn't spill out of the fissure. Two enormous grey wings struggled to tear free from Kevin's muscles and tendons.

Megan squeaked and covered her mouth in horror and pulled the door to close it but stopped. Kevin wasn't lying; his transformation was real. She opened the door further and continued to watch.

As if in a trance, Kevin stood. The same rift rippled down his buttocks and back of his legs. His skin rolled away from the opening, sloughing, sliding forward, like a freakish hospital gown. Where Kevin's skin once was hulking, masses of grey material took its place. An earthy smell rolled through the door opening, reminding her of a recent rainstorm.

The creature shook and stretched, appearing to grow in height and bulk with every movement. How did this beast fit inside Kevin's frame? The shape of the creature's broad shoulders and narrow waist made Megan think it was male. It was easily five times Kevin's size and made of what looked like stone, probably twenty times his weight.

The creature moved to Kevin's desk as if expecting something to be there. He picked up the rubbing she brought over and turned it. As he studied the paper, he settled on the floor, getting comfortable. She recognized him, not him exactly, but the creature he was. These creatures were never known to be alive, and yet here one stood. She had seen millions in her time, sitting on the edges of churches and city buildings. She always thought they were marvelous.

Gargoyles.

This couldn't be a coincidence: zombies, witches, the Order of the Eye and Tooth, and now gargoyles. Something unusual was happening in Avalon. Megan opened the door and stepped into the room.

# Chapter 40

Kragnor moved to the desk, expecting to find the notebook. A crumpled piece of paper with a rubbing of cuneiform sat in its place. He picked up the paper and gently straightened it. The words were both familiar and foreign.

The door handle jiggled. Kragnor turned, expecting Sorceress. Instead, a young female approached him, completely unafraid.

"Kevin told me about you. But I didn't believe him." The young woman looked at Kragnor from head to toe. "It's an amazing sight. You burst out of his flesh like a butterfly."

Kragnor blinked but didn't respond.

The young woman crossed her arms, tilting her head to the side. "Kevin told me you could read cuneiform." She waved her hand toward the paper in Kragnor's claw-like hand, then cleared her throat. "Do you have a name?"

Kragnor blinked again, then realized he was behaving rudely. "My apologies, young one." He touched his throat, then cleared it. "Kragnor, at your service." He bowed. "Who do I have the honor of meeting?"

"Megan." She attempted to curtsey but stumbled.

Kragnor hid his smile. "Are you not afraid?"

"Should I be?" She looked at him sideways.

"No. But the humans who have seen me thus far became visibly upset." Kragnor moved away from the desk, towards an open area of the room. He squatted, leaned back onto his tail, and huffed. "I am a protector, guardian, and teacher. I have never hurt anyone in my lifetime." With a flourish, he unfolded the paper. "Would you like to know what this paper says?"

"I would." Megan moved closer to Kragnor. She hesitated for a moment, then continued.

Kragnor patted his knee. "This is where all my students sit for lessons."

Megan stared at him, looking up even though he was squatting. The gargoyle was at least six times her size. He ripped his way out of Kevin's body and could destroy her just as easily. Something beyond science and logic allowed this creature, made of stone, to exist. Despite her training and the constant mantra, *trust no one*, Megan felt instinctively confident that the gargoyle would never hurt her. In fact, if anything, he would protect her. She nodded, then sat tentatively on his knee.

His arms encircled her like a parent reading to a child. He straightened the paper and held it flat in one hand. With the other, he pointed at each of the symbols with the claw on his forefinger. "This sanctuary stone shall keep the soul of this akitu quiet until the unrest is complete." Kragnor huffed and grumbled. He turned the paper over, hoping to see more.

"Is something wrong?"

"Yes." Kragnor looked down at Megan, his golden eyes locking on her brown. He smiled reassuringly. "You are my student. Try to figure out what is wrong. I will give you a clue. I have discovered I slept for close to seven hundred years. And the last city I remember is Paris.

"I don't know." Megan shrugged.

"It will help if you talk it out." Kragnor insisted.

"Cuneiform is three to five thousand years old." She looked at him for approval.

The gargoyle nodded.

Megan smiled, feeling a blush rise on her cheeks. "Seven hundred years ago would be in the thirteen hundreds, which is also near the end of the Renaissance."

Kragnor creased his brows. “Yes, that is what those texts said.” He pointed to the pile of *National Geographic* on the floor. “How many people do you think could read or write cuneiform seven hundred years ago?” Kragnor prompted.

“Well, I’m guessing but, in Europe, probably only a few educated people. In Turkey or the Middle East, probably more.”

“I can agree with that assessment. So, what does that tell you?”

Megan reached out and touched the wrinkled paper. “Well, I have tried to translate it myself using Acadian, Sumerian, and Babylonian languages, but I could not get the words to work. So, I am going to guess that this cuneiform text is in a language I don’t know.”

Kragnor patted her head. “You are right. Humans do not know this language. Humans are forbidden to know. Only an akitu would have the knowledge to carve the stone.” A slight growl rolled in his throat. “I believe one of my people put me into the stone.”

“You believe? Don’t you know? Weren’t you there when it happened?”

“I do not remember. I try to focus, but my mind is clouded.”

“What can you remember?” Megan asked.

"I was born and lived in the high mountains. I spent hundreds of years learning all I could from my fellow akitu. I also learned from my environment, plants, animals, and minerals. Even the stars gave up their secrets. Over time your species arrived. Humans were kind to us early on. We were treated as deities, which is ridiculous." Kragnor paused. Deities. Gods. His mind spun. There was something there, a memory. Something important. He strained, trying to find the connection, but the harder he grasped at the memory, the quicker it dissipated.

Megan touched his hand. "Did something come back? Do you remember?" She sounded excited.

"I thought there was, and I tried to remember, but it disappeared." He frowned. "Let me continue. Maybe it will happen again. Where was I?"

"Mountains and humans." Megan prompted.

Kragnor stroked his chin. "We spent much of our time in the mountains. Many akitu still live there, I suspect. It was easy to hide from anyone or anything. After all, our tissues are very similar to the mountains themselves." Kragnor's eyes glazed with memory. "I built a home there. Nothing like this house, which is for the softness of your kind. My house was stone and torans, nothing more." He became quiet, introspective. "The last thing I remember was Paris. I can't remember day to day things, just Paris." His brows furrowed.

Megan leaned closer to him. She placed her ear to his chest.

Kragnor stirred. "Are you tired?"

"No, I'm curious." Megan poked his chest. "You said you were born and lived in the mountains. Yet, when I touch you, your skin is rough like stone and cool to the touch. I hear no heartbeat, no breathing, no digestion. But you do have a smell, earthy."

"I am not an animal or plant. Nor am I a mineral, not exactly. I don't need sustenance or air. I am different, but I am just as alive as you. That is how I can sleep for seven hundred years." Kragnor patted the top of her head as if she were a pet. His touch seemed to calm her.

Megan stood and walked around the gargoyle. She poked and prodded his wing membranes. She continued her inspection, then stopped in front of him, bouncing on her toes. "What year were you born?"

"Years are not important to akitu. We are very long-lived." Kragnor stretched a bit, moving into a standing position. "Do you know what second you were born or how many seconds you have lived? Do you name the seconds of your day like you do hours?"

Megan looked at him. She cocked her head, then smiled. "Okay, I understand. I don't count seconds because that frame of time doesn't matter to me. Years, months, and days matter to me."

"A day for me is the shortest time I think about. That is like your seconds. The moment I think about it, it is dismissed again. I think of time in years, decades, jubilees, centuries, millennium, and eons."

"How old are you?"

"I'm almost three and a half."

"Not years or centuries, obviously because you have slept for seven hundred. Are you over three million years old?" Megan counted on her fingers. "Are you kidding me? I can't even imagine that."

"Yes, now you understand. But I am not three million years old. I am three and a half eons old."

"Wow. That's the same as a billion, isn't it? Three and a half billion years." Megan touched him again. "You have seen human empires rise and fall. Animals evolve. Mountains grow, and continents travel."

Kragnor nodded, smiling. “It was peaceful before humans arrived. But I have to say life has become interesting now that your kind is here.”

“You called yourself an akitu. Is that like me being a human? Or an American?”

“American?”

“The country we are in right now is America. I was born in a country called Russia, which makes me Russian.”

Kragnor nodded. “I am akitu. You are human. Countries and borders are a human way of thinking. Ownership of land is ridiculous. Lands shift and change.”

Megan yawned. She covered her mouth, then looked at the clock. “Oh, my. I have to get home; it’s getting late.”

“Oh, must you?” Kragnor frowned, wrinkling his face and exposing his lower canines, giving him a ferocious expression.

“Does that make you angry?” Megan asked, holding her hands in front of her.

“No, just sad.”

“You look angry.” Megan motioned to her face. “Your frown looks like a snarl.”

Kragnor chuckled. “Not a snarl, a frown. Will you come back tomorrow? I think if we talk, more memories will come.”

"If I can, I will." She squeezed his hand. "I must go before my father becomes upset."

Kragnor gripped her hand. "Please don't tell anyone of my existence."

"Ow." Megan pulled her hand.

The gargoyle released her. "My apologies, I didn't mean to hurt. If others know, I am here…" He gripped his head. "No, no, I think that fear was old and back in Paris."

"Fear of what? Someone knowing you're alive."

"Yes." Kragnor's eyes lit up. "There was a religious faction who wanted to end the old beliefs. Pope Boniface led them. We, the akitu, were at the roots of the old beliefs. If we were destroyed, then other religions could be forced upon people.

"So long as we lived, old faiths could worship the old ways. The akitu were a threat to the new religious order." The gargoyle sat back on his haunches. "I can remember it now. During the night, while we slept, we were pushed from our perches. Those who were on high buildings or were very young, they broke. Many of my friends and family died.

"Others, like me who were too old to be destroyed by a fall, were captured. Some of the young were deep in catacombs or inside buildings. They were safe from the first night's culling." Kragnor paused, his eyes moist with sorrow and memory.

Megan moved to the gargoyle's side. "Oh my God, you were in a genocide." She took his hand into both of hers. "How did you survive?"

"We were placed separately into metal cages until another death could be dealt to us. We were to be heated over a fire until we glowed and then dumped into cold water. The sudden temperature change would have killed us or shattered us internally. Either way, the process sounded horrible. If we didn't die that way, the Pope promised to find other ways to destroy us. Boniface was certain that we were evil because, to him, we looked evil. What else did you need to determine someone's alignment? We had horns, tails, wings, and our appearance was terrifying, the embodiment of hell's demons." Kragnor slouched. He felt the pain and sorrow as if it were yesterday.

"While we were confined, Friar Francois approached us with an idea of escape. He and Basal had created Akitu Stones. Basal devised a ritual that would move our souls into the stones where we could hide until Pope Boniface's reign was over. Or until the stones were brought to a safe place. At least that is what I assume.

The ritual would have to be reversed, and we would have a new body to inhabit. I can only imagine the worry Basal had, trusting a human to save akitu."

"Why did Friar Francois help? Wasn't he part of Pope Boniface's religion?"

Kragnor smiled. "There are two possibilities. During that time, King Philip of France defied Boniface openly. Either the Friar was faithful to the King before the Pope. I think even some of the faithful saw that his ego drove Boniface to do terrible things. Or the Friar saw akitu as an educational resource. I used to work with the Friar to copy and write texts. We spent many years together. Because akitu knowledge was greater than his, he understood our value as teachers and scholars."

"This genocide went further than France, didn't it?"

"Boniface was compelling. He believed himself above the power of kings and queens. He thought himself second only to God. Even though I didn't see or hear it, I am positive he took his decree as far as his reach would go." Kragnor raised his hand.

Megan paced back and forth, thinking. "I think I'm missing something. Kevin managed to reverse the ritual. Right? That doesn't feel right, but that seems to be where this conversation has led."

"That seems to be what happened. Either Kevin or Sorceress reversed the ritual. Because there was no akitu body for me to inhabit, I went into Kevin. Sorceress said they created a spell column that night. I would like to see what spells they each used."

"Why would it matter? What's done is done."

Kragnor shrugged. "Curiosity. Knowledge. We may have to repeat the spells to put my soul into the proper vessel."

Megan raised her finger and shook it. "Wait a minute. Back in Paris, if the akitu soul was out of the body, wouldn't it be obvious? Wouldn't Boniface know his attempt to destroy you was wasted?"

Kragnor shook his head. "When I sleep, I look like a statue. There is no difference to the human eye. Another akitu would know. We can see and feel the life force of others like ourselves." Kragnor rubbed his chin. "Why do you ask?"

"Maybe the Friar or Basal left something to tell us how to reverse the ritual. But if the Friar was caught in the act of helping the akitu, there probably isn't anything. He probably would have been killed."

"I wouldn't know. Many of the other akitu didn't trust Friar Francois because he was a man of God, just like Pope Boniface. I remember the fear. The confusion. The urgency. So, out of my group, I went first."

"Wow, that took an immense amount of courage. I'm not sure I could have done that."

"You would be surprised what you can do in a time of crisis. But what helped more than anything was what Friar Francois told me and showed me the stone Basal's soul entered. I could see the akitu life force inside it. I knew the Friar was telling the truth. If we can find the onyx stone that contains his soul and release him. Basal would know how to separate me from Kevin."

# Chapter 41

Megan looked at the clock. "Speaking of crisis. It's late. I have to go."

Kragnor looked disappointed. "I understand, child. If you are in a hurry, I could take you." The large wings opened and closed slightly as emphasis.

"You'd fly me home?" Megan closed her eyes for a moment. "That sounds fantastic. I promise to come back tomorrow."

"I will be fractured until you return." Kragnor bowed, emphasizing the dip with his wings. "Please, after you." He opened the door to the hallway.

Megan smiled behind her hand. "Why, thank you, sir." She stepped through the doorway and went down the stairs.

Ruby watched television from under a blanket. Curled on her lap, slept Rapscallion. She smiled when she saw Megan. "You stayed late." Her eyebrows wagged, implying something grander than talking.

"You're right. I'm late. But I got a ride home."

"Kevin's going to take you?" Her mouth fell open when Kragnor stepped out of the stairway. She blinked a few times.

"Sorceress," Kragnor said, bowing to Ruby. "It is good to see you again."

"Kragnor said he would take me home," Megan said. "Kevin is, ah, preoccupied."

Ruby blinked, not saying anything.

"Ruby, are you alright?" Megan moved closer to the older woman. "Ruby?"

"I'm okay, dear." Ruby's eyes landed on the gargoyle. "Good evening Kragnor." Her voice changed from soft and playful to assertive. It was as if she had transformed into another creature as Kevin did, but the physical change wasn't as pronounced.

"Sorceress, while you are lucid, you must know I spoke to Benny last night. He told me that my existence had broken many spells and curses. Including yours and the girls." Kragnor bowed. "My humble apologies."

Ruby's brows knitted. "My curse? The girl's spell?" She rubbed her temples.

"Who is Benny?" Megan asked Kragnor.

The gargoyle indicated with his head. "A gnome who lives behind the house."

"A gnome?" Megan raised an eyebrow, then nodded. "Of course."

Kragnor huffed. "Sorceress, are you alright? You look pale."

"Broken?" Ruby's forehead creased. "That little trickster." She looked from Rapscallion to the gargoyle. "Kragnor, we're going to be busy."

"Sorceress, I promised to take Megan home, she is late, and her father is acrimonious. We must take our leave. We can talk when I return if you wish." Kragnor bowed again and turned to the kitchen.

Megan pointed to the living room. "Shouldn't we go out the front door?"

"No. The back is better. We can move in secrecy." He continued to direct her through the kitchen and to the back door. They stepped out into the dark. Kragnor turned her around and picked her up in his arms, like a superhero. "Are you well?" Kragnor asked. "Your breathing and heart rate have increased."

"I'm nervous," Megan said, embarrassed.

"You have nothing to fear."

"I hope not."

Kragnor sank low into his haunches, then shot them upward. His wings swung open, catching the air, and pushed them higher.

"Which way?"

Megan looked down. "West until there is a pond below you, then north to the river." Kragnor pumped his wings a few times then glided. "Do you have muscles under there?" She pressed her hand on his chest. "I don't feel any movement under your skin."

"I have no skin or muscle."

"Fascinating." Megan pressed her head against his chest as if listening for something.

"Here?" Kragnor asked.

Megan examined the ground, but it was too dark to see. "I think so."

The gargoyle circled, dropped lower, and gently landed next to the river. Kragnor set Megan on the ground.

"How far can you see?" Megan asked. "Nothing looks familiar here."

Kragnor pointed down the river. "I see five small houses near the river." He pointed the other way. "Four small houses that way. Very small. Do humans still keep other humans as slaves?"

"Slaves?" Megan chuckled. "According to our school texts, it's been hundreds of years since there were slaves. But I'm not so sure. Human trafficking has become a problem. Do you see one of those small buildings with a blue roof?"

"Blue," Kragnor repeated. He looked both ways then pointed. "There. Three houses away."

Megan laughed. "Not bad. I've never given directions from the air before." She ran toward the boathouse to be sure. Kragnor galloped on all fours next to her, sounding like stampeding buffalo. "Excellent eyesight, I'm impressed."

"Shall I walk with you? To ensure your safety?"

Megan shook her head. "No, my father will hear. I need to sneak back in on my own." She put a hand on his arm. "Thank you for getting me home."

"Will I see you tomorrow?" he asked.

"You will."

Kragnor smiled at her, then launched back into the sky and flew back to the Sorceress. There was much to discuss with Sorceress if she was still lucid. He landed in the backyard next to the oak.

"You are but a flame, and all the curses come to your light," Benny called to Kragnor from one of the raised beds.

"Benny? Stop speaking in riddles."

Benny's voice came from a different bed. "Do you not know a Wolf of the Woods when you are so close?"

Kragnor frowned. "Benny, what have you done?"

Benny chortled from a third raised bed. "It's all you, my gargoyle friend. If she doesn't know she is the Wolf, she will soon. What is done is done."

Silence filled the night.

Kragnor swept into the kitchen and to Sorceress. She was not alone.

A man stood near her with a metal thrower pointed at him.

Kragnor swept between them, enveloping Sorceress and Rapscallion with his wings. "Your metal thrower will not harm me, but you could kill Sorceress or her familiar."

"I wouldn't be so sure," Johnny said with bravado. "There is more than metal in my bullets."

Kragnor huffed. "It does not matter what you throw at me."

"Johnny, put your gun away. Kragnor is my friend." Sorceress's tone confirmed she was still lucid.

Johnny relaxed, but his metal thrower remained in his hand. Kragnor pulled his wings back and stepped away from Sorceress.

"I have broken another curse, Sorceress. But I can't seem to break my own."

"Call me, Ruby, remember?"

Kragnor nodded. "I remember."

Ruby narrowed her eyes at Johnny. She stood from her chair and stepped between man and gargoyle. "What curse?" She placed her hand on Kragnor's arm.

"Yours, the girls," Kragnor pointed toward the triplet's house, "and now, Megan."

"No." Ruby grabbed Kragnor's face. "What curse do you have?"

"The one Kevin and I share."

Ruby's forehead creased. "Yes, now, I remember. The spell column." She sighed. "Megan?"

"She is a Wolf of the Woods."

"Who told you that you broke her curse?" Ruby asked.

"Benny."

Johnny laughed. "You can't trust a gnome."

Kragnor forgot about the man. He turned his stare to Johnny. "Who are you to determine the trustworthiness of another creature?" He pointed his clawed finger at the man. "Narrow minded vainglories jump to such conclusions." Kragnor didn't care for this human. He gently picked up Ruby and moved her aside.

Kragnor towered over the man. He growled, displayed his wings, and tossed his tail, techniques which would have scared most humans.

"Too late big guy. I saw you protect Ruby and Rap. You'll have to try threatening someone else. I stand by my word. Gnomes are naughty. Besides, I've protections against your kind." Johnny smugly crossed his arms.

"Like what? Holy water?" Kragnor chuckled. He reached for Johnny.

"No. Knowledge. You are akitu. Protector and pacifist."

Kragnor's clawed hands stopped. "You know akitu?"

"Only from textbooks. You're the first one I've met."

# Chapter 42

Kevin scrambled out from the piles of odds and ends in the attic, went into his bedroom, and looked for the notebook. In green crayon was written:

*Talk to Megan.*

*I need more purple crayons.*

Kevin trotted down the stairs, a smile plastered to his face. *Megan stayed; she might be able to help.*

"You look like the cat who ate the canary," Grandma said. She handed him a granola bar and poured a cup of milk. "Why the good mood? Or should I ask?"

"It's nothing." Kevin tried not to smile but failed.

"Right." Grandma Ruby sipped her hot coffee. She nodded to the oven clock. "You're late again."

Kevin shrugged. "Nothing I do seems to make a difference. I guess I'm late." He ate the breakfast bar and slammed the milk, leaving the glass on the table. "Gotta run." He kissed her on the cheek and ran out the door.

Sitting in his old car, Johnny waved Kevin over. "Get in." His eyes were bloodshot like he hadn't slept all night.

Kevin took shotgun. "What's wrong?"

"Many things. But my priority, in this case, is you. Annie is gone."

"Gone?"

"She was not in her jail cell this morning. The cops don't know how she got out, but she had help."

"Did she seduce someone in the police department?"

"The AKG confiscated her necklace, and it was destroyed. She couldn't have used it." Johnny drummed his fingers on the steering wheel. "I don't know if she ran or if she is nearby biding her time. Either way, you have to be careful." He looked at Kevin over his glasses. "Her accomplices and her parents are missing too."

"Wait? What? Her parents? They knew?"

Johnny nodded. "It would seem so. They may have organized her escape. We don't know, and it doesn't matter. The AKG wants me to keep eyes on you. I thought you should know."

"Am I bait?" Kevin turned away from Johnny and looked out the window, not wanting to know the answer. "If I know Annie, she isn't going to be happy that I defied her and survived. She'll try again. The best way to catch her is to use me as bait." Kevin swallowed hard. He wasn't afraid, but he wasn't looking forward to it either.

Johnny pulled into the school driveway. "See you after."

Kevin turned back to Johnny. "Are you going to admit that I'm bait?"

"Nope."

"A lot can happen during the school day."

"I'm aware."

"I've seen many movies where the hero can't tell anyone anything because the government company he works for won't let him. Or, that the hero is there in plain sight, working as a substitute teacher, there to save the day."

Johnny picked at his cuticles. "You've seen too many movies. You better get going. You're late the way it is."

"You're not coming with me?"

"Nope. I figure I'm going to hang out with Ruby." Johnny winked at Kevin.

Kevin smiled. "Right, okay." He opened the car door and went into the school. He looked over his shoulder to see Johnny drive away.

## Chapter 43

Megan grabbed her lunch from her locker and headed to the cafeteria. Lunch hour was so much better when Bonnie ate with her. She hoped Bonnie was healing; she frowned, wishing her father would let her go to the hospital.

Megan watched Kevin go through the lunch line. He seemed smaller and weaker than before. But that's probably because Kragnor was so huge. She tilted her head. How can a creature so large fit inside a scrawny teen boy? Kevin looked in her direction, grinned, and walked over.

"Can I sit with you?" Kevin stood at the edge of the table.

"Sure," Megan said, waving to the empty chairs. "Pick a spot."

Kevin settled next to Megan. "Thank you for staying last night. It meant a lot to me."

Megan leaned into Kevin. "Kragnor is a gargoyle," she said in low tones.

Kevin poked at the food on his tray while he thought. “You know, that makes sense. He told me an akitu looks like Batman.”

“Batman?” Megan laughed. “How did he tell you that?”

“We write back and forth in a notebook. Kragnor tore the Batman picture out of a comic and said it was what akitu look like.” Kevin tapped on the tabletop with his fork, glancing around the room. “Do you suppose there are others of his kind out there?”

“After what he said about Boniface and the genocide he escaped from, I doubt there are very many.” Megan shrugged. “If they’re anything like dodos, Tasmanian tigers, and elephant birds, humans probably killed them off.” She bit into her protein bar. “Humans kill all the cool creatures. Kragnor is pretty damn cool.”

Kevin stared at her. “You’re right. Humans are jerks.”

“I’ve been thinking about the stone. Kragnor said that his soul was inside for seven hundred years. My father borrowed stones from China that look identical to his bloodstone.”

Kevin nodded as he ate. “Yea, I remember you saying something about that.”

“What if those have gargoyle souls too?”

"Do you think it's possible?"

"Sure, from what Kragnor said, it's possible. But how would we know?" Megan ripped open another protein bar and took a bite. "And," she pointed the bar at him, "what if other gemstone books have more boxes hidden inside?"

"That's possible." He pulled his phone out of his pocket and searched for the book title. "It says here that it's out of print."

"Well, we wouldn't want a new copy anyway." Megan rolled her eyes at him. "Maybe we need to check out an antique bookstore."

"Do stores like that exist?"

"I don't know. Probably." She shrugged. "Check with your phone."

"Later." Kevin put his phone away and looked around the cafeteria. "Have you noticed how many guys are missing?"

Megan nodded. "It seems like they are all Annie's."

"Annie's?"

"Yea, her old boyfriends."

"Are you serious? She's been with that many guys? Including Mr. Olsterholtz?" Kevin shuddered, setting down his fork. "Suddenly, I don't feel so good."

"I should say not. You were almost one of them." Megan covered her mouth. "Was that rude?"

"No, it's not rude," Kevin said. "It puts everything in perspective. And well, it makes me sick to my stomach." He looked down at his hands. "It also explains the hate stares."

"The what?" Megan took another bite of her bar.

Kevin continued to look down. "If you look, you'll see a couple guys staring in this direction, and they look furious."

Megan casually looked around the room, munching on her bar, covering her mouth with her hand. "I count three."

"It's not just students. Some of the teachers are angry too." Kevin stroked the palm of his hand. "I wonder if Kragnor saved me from that fate. I see everything differently since he came into my life. It made Annie appear like she had a cloud over her, and her touch was disgusting." He shrugged. "It's hard to explain."

"Does everyone look different?'

He nodded. "You too."

Megan was curious. "How?"

Keven twisted in his chair like he didn't want to say or was embarrassed to answer. "You look clearer, um fresher. Damn, that sounds stupid."

She laughed then finished her protein bar. "I promised Kragnor that I would talk with him tonight."

"Does that mean you're coming over?"

"If it's okay with you."

"Expect Grandma Ruby to give you crap."

"I think I can take her." Megan cracked her knuckles.

They laughed.

"Um, speaking of Ruby, you ought to know, she's acting weird. Even for her."

"What do you mean?" Kevin raised one eyebrow.

"When we first came down the stairs, she was acting like Ruby. But when she saw Kragnor, something inside her snapped. Her voice and demeanor changed. Kragnor called her Sorceress. Then he said, Benny the gnome, told him that Kragnor's presence is breaking spells and curses."

"Ruby knows Kragnor? Well, I guess I'm not surprised. I thought he put a mark on her cast." He leaned in toward Megan. "What did he mean breaking spells and curses?"

"I don't know. Kragnor said something about the girls."

"What girls?"

Megan shrugged.

Kevin frowned. "I'm sorry, I've gotten you into all this voodoo crap. If you're uncomfortable, you don't have to come over."

"No, I want to. I made Kragnor a promise. Besides, I must get out of my house before I go nuts. My father won't let me go anywhere. He thinks I am going to be hurt or killed. I'll have to sneak out tonight."

"Is that because of the attack on Bonnie?"

"Exactly." Megan slapped him on the arm. "I need to visit Bonnie, but, again, my father won't let me." She rolled her eyes. "I know this is a weird request, but can you visit her?"

"Me?" Kevin looked at Megan like that was a ludicrous idea.

"She's had a crush on you for some time. She would love it if you appeared to see how she is doing." Megan held up her hands. "You don't have to. It's a request. I'll still be there tonight for you and Kragnor. I might be late, though." Megan frowned.

"Try not to be too late." Kevin looked down. "Kragnor seems to come earlier and earlier and leaves later. Almost like my body will someday be his alone. And I'll no longer exist."

Megan put her hand on his. "The unknown is always scary. I'll talk to him." She squeezed his hand.

Artem was in the kitchen preparing dinner, spaghetti. A two-quart pot of sauce bubbled and burped on the stovetop. She set her book bag on the chair in the breakfast nook. “Good afternoon, Dad. I’m surprised to see you so early after school.”

Her father danced around the kitchen, adding oregano and other spices to the sauce. “A good meal starts with a good sauce. It all takes time.” He bopped her nose like he used to when she was a child. “Besides, I was worried about you. You don’t still feel ill, do you?” He raised one eyebrow.

“No, I felt much better after vomiting and resting last night.” She kept her gaze steady and stared into his eyes. “What about work? You were home yesterday early too.”

“I’m staying on top of things remotely. Besides, I really don’t do much at work other than shuffle papers, and I can do that here.”

“How long till dinner?”

“I’ve got a new recipe for meatballs that I want to try out; it might be a while.”

"Okay. I'll work on homework in my bedroom. Watching you create a new recipe will be too distracting."

Artem smiled. He swayed around the kitchen, singing a Russian ballad.

Megan picked up her book bag and went into her room. Spaghetti reminded her of a movie. What was it called? It didn't matter. The wife in the story tried to kill her cheating husband by putting sleeping pills in the spaghetti. I don't want to kill dad. In the movie, it didn't work. But that's a movie.

Megan went into her bathroom and opened her medicine cabinet. She had a bottle of prescription sleeping pills, she used them a couple times, but they never worked. Even if she took double the amount. The container said two pills for a restful sleep.

She imagined the servings of sauce in the pot and figured four, maybe six. Megan dumped twelve pills into her hand, then shook out four more, to be sure. She slipped them into her pocket and went back into her room.

Megan finished her math homework, and for a few minutes, she listened to Artem walk around the house. Every so often, he would go to the den, where Megan assumed he did some work for the museum. She went into the kitchen and sat at the breakfast nook, watching and waiting.

Artem was rolling meat into balls. Every few rolls, he would stir the sauce.

"I can stir if it'll help," Megan offered.

"Sure." Artem handed her the wooden spoon. "I would appreciate it."

Megan added one pill and stirred until it dissolved. She continued to add more when her father wasn't looking. She tasted as she added but didn't notice anything out of place.

"Megan," Artem said, startling her. He wrapped his arms around her and kissed her head. "I love you. I don't know what I would do if you were not in my life."

"I love you too," Megan said, suddenly feeling guilty. "Are you drunk?" Artem had never said he loved her before, and it concerned her. Why would he say it now?

He smiled at her and patted her shoulders. "Maybe a little." He shrugged and dug into a cabinet to find a frying pan. Artem turned on another burner and added a small amount of oil. He waited for the oil to heat before adding the meatballs. They sizzled and snapped as they cooked. The smell was fabulous. "Can you get the water ready?"

"Sure." She pulled out a large pot to boil the noodles.

Artem set the table for two, then went into the den. "I need to finish something," he told Megan.

Megan wondered if the thing he had to finish was a cocktail. By the time he returned, the noodles were done and, on the table, along with the meatballs and sauce. Megan drank from her glass of milk, studying her father. His eyes were glazed from the alcohol. For the second time, she felt a twinge of guilt as he poured a large amount of sauce onto his noodles.

She dug into her serving of spaghetti and meatballs, lightly sauced.

After dinner and clean up, Megan suggested an old movie. They settled on the couch and watched a classic, *Terminator*. She loved watching the old movies, where the special effects were stop motion.

About halfway through the movie, Artem started snoring. Megan grabbed a pillow and blanket from his bed and made him as comfortable as possible.

She checked the time, a little past seven. Megan entered her bedroom, locked the door, and climbed out the window. She left her car in case her father woke up looking for her. He would assume she was sleeping in her room.

Megan broke into a jog.

Megan knocked on Kevin's door. Ruby opened the curtain, looked out, grinned, and opened the door. "Couldn't keep away from Kevin, could you?" Ruby went to her purse and pulled out another condom, holding it up.

Megan laughed. "That's not why I'm here. I promised Kragnor I'd be here."

Ruby gave her a quizzical look. "Kragnor?"

"He was with me last night, remember? He called you Sorceress."

Ruby closed her eyes and slowly reopened them. "Good evening Megan. I'm sure Kragnor will be arriving soon." She bowed her head and placed the condom in Megan's hand.

Megan accepted the gift, walked upstairs, and knocked on the door. She heard a lot of fumbling, and Kevin said. "Uh, who is it?"

"Megan."

There was more fumbling, and the door opened. Kevin stood naked with a towel around his waist. "I didn't think you'd make it." He hustled her inside. "Hurry, it's almost time."

"Nice towel." Megan stepped into the room.

"It's too expensive to have him rip up my stuff every time he appears." He shrugged his apologies.

On Kevin's desk was a laptop, open and displaying an old-time camera, used to take celluloid movies. "Do you have a phone I can use to video the change?"

"That's a good idea. Over there." Kevin sat on the floor with the towel over his lap. He pointed to the bedside table where a blue phone with a Celtic knot design on the back sat.

Megan grabbed the phone and got it ready. She focused the viewfinder on Kevin and hit record.

# Chapter 44

Megan picked up clothing from the floor.

"Good evening, Megan." Kragnor felt a warm flush.

Megan threw the clothing on the bed. "Kevin said you show up earlier and earlier every night, and you stay longer and longer. He's afraid that you are going to take over his life, killing him."

"I am a protector. I don't harm others. I never kill. I have no need." Kragnor huffed, putting his hands on his hips. She looked at him and covered her smile.

Megan approached the gargoyle, touching his arm. "His fear is valid. Even though I know you'd never do anything to hurt him."

"Am I really born of his body every night?"

"Yes." Megan held up Kevin's phone. "I took a video."

"What is a video?"

Megan smiled and shook her head. "It's a record of events."

"Like a manuscript?"

"More like a movie." Megan cleared her throat. "You don't know what a movie is. It doesn't matter." She waved her hands around. "It is a visual record. Like a manuscript, but with pictures and sound instead of words."

"I see." Kragnor sat back on his haunches, crossing his arms. Painting a picture took months. Many paintings took just as many canvases, not to mention the paint, the smell, and the mess. Multiply those together and you had a herculean feat. Kragnor looked around the room. No paint, no canvases, no artwork.

"What I'm about to show you will be surprising." Megan pushed herself closer to Kragnor. "Please give me the space you reserve for students." She smiled, waiting for him to adjust, then she sat on his knee. "Now, I am the teacher." Megan tapped the phone. "Watch the screen."

Kragnor craned his head, looking around the room. "A screen for a fireplace or dressing?" He raised his eyebrows.

Megan smiled. "No, no. This is a screen." She tapped a rectangular picture in her hand. In the picture, a young man sat on the floor, with his back visible. He appeared to be naked. The man must be Kevin.

The gargoyle grunted. "I think I understand."

Megan touched an arrow pointing to the right, and the picture came to life. The young man moved, looking over his shoulder. "Am I in the frame?" His voice sounded strained.

Kragnor jumped, startled by the magic. Megan pulled the rectangle to her chest. "I'm sorry." She touched his arm. "I thought this might be hard to understand."

"No, no." Kragnor huffed. "I've seen magic portals before, but not from a sorceress so young, nor a portal so small. I was not prepared."

"It's not magic," Megan said. "Anyone can do it."

"Things have changed," Kragnor stated. *If anyone can use magic, then the world has become dangerous.*

"Are you ready to see more?" Megan dragged her finger across a line on the bottom, reversing the movements of the young man.

The gargoyle nodded, determined to bite his tongue, and let the magic play out. Megan touched the arrow again and the images and sound played. Kragnor heard Megan's voice in the display. He was confused. How could she be in two different places at one time? The young man in the series of images suddenly went rigid, and his flesh tore open. Blue-grey wings emerged first, followed by Kragnor's head and shoulders. He watched himself be born, like every other mammal, blood, and pain. Where did Kevin go when Kragnor was in control? *Was he inside, like I was inside him?* The gargoyle touched his chest and belly, wondering.

"What happens when Kevin returns? Is he born of my flesh, like I am born of his?" Kragnor frowned, wanting to know the answer but afraid.

"I don't know." Megan shrugged, "I haven't stayed long enough to see the method of his return, but I think it's safe to assume so. If I'm around when you turn to Kevin, I'll take a video." She shook the small rectangle.

The small black shape intrigued him. "What is that if it is not magic?"

"It's called a phone. It's a small computer."

Kragnor nodded. A computer was a person who helped solve complex equations, usually under the guidance of an astronomer. He studied the box, trying to understand what math had to do with portals and magic.

Megan stood away from the gargoyle and clicked a button, pointing the box around the room. She pointed the phone at the bed. "This is Kevin's bed, his desk, and his dresser." Megan moved back to the gargoyle. “This is a video.” She clicked the button again, and the video replayed.

Kragnor stared open-mouthed. “Are you sure you are not a witch?”

She laughed. “No. Anyone can take a video, even you. Touch the red dot on the screen.”

Kragnor touched the screen with his nail.

“Try your fingertip.”

Still, the phone didn’t respond.

“It is touch-sensitive, but maybe not rock sensitive.”

“I don’t understand.” Kragnor wondered if she was tricking him.

“Shhh. I’ll touch the dot, and you take the video.” After Megan set up the phone, she placed it in his hand. “Okay, now point it around the room. Look in this area and it’ll show what you are copying. And when you are done, it’ll replay that copy. Good. Let me turn it off and replay it for you.”

The video replayed. Kragnor watched, amazed. “Does that copy of reality exist inside the phone?”

“No, it’s picture and sound. Not a duplicate of reality.”

"Are you sure? What about that, Megan?" Kragnor pointed to the image of the young woman in the video.

"Pretty darn sure. I'm not a programmer or application designer, but duplicating reality that's in the realm of physics. And I don't think they have managed that one yet. That Megan is still me."

Kragnor's forehead wrinkled.

She held up her finger. "Observe. No matter how often I replay the video over, it'll only show the same movements. The words coming out of my mouth are the same." Megan moved the video forward and back and replayed from beginning to end. "Every time. Megan, in that video, is an image. A complex painting, nothing more."

Suddenly Kragnor grunted. "It is like a memory. The phone's memory. It remembers what it sees and what was said." He thought of the headstones he spoke to. The video wasn't any different. The image and sound were better, but the result was the same.

"Well, that's an interesting way to look at it. I can't find fault with your logic." Megan smiled, encouraging.

"The magics of this time are quite complex."

"Magics?"

“Like that object in your hand.” Kragnor pointed to the phone.

“It is not magic. We call this type of object technology.”

“To me, there is no difference between technology and magic.” Kragnor huffed. It didn’t matter what something was called if the result was the same. Humans liked to complicate things with words. That practice, it seemed, had not changed. “What else can that phone or technology do?”

“I can call or text another person.”

“What is call or text?”

Megan smiled. “This might be hard to understand. I can send pictures or videos or notes to another phone or computer.” She clicked a few buttons and waited. Kevin’s laptop made a ding noise. She walked to the desk and woke the computer by clicking on the keyboard. She pointed to the screen. “I sent a message, see?” She held the phones next to the laptop to show Kragnor the duplicate text.

“It would be easier to talk back and forth if you are that close.” The gargoyle tilted his head. “Would it not?”

“Yes. But distance doesn’t matter.”

Kragnor grunted. “Distance is irrelevant? So, if Kevin was in Paris, you could contact him?”

"Yes. But you have to think about the time difference too."

"Time? How can time be different?"

Megan's brow furrowed as she thought. "No, you're right. The time doesn't change; the location of the sun in association to the person viewing it does. So, the person in Paris, the sun would be down, and it would appear to be night. But to me in Wisconsin, it would be morning. It is the perception of time that changes."

He grunted. "Because of the curvature and orbit of the planet. That I understand." Kragnor pointed to the phone and laptop. "Anyone can use these?"

"Exactly, you only need to be taught."

Kragnor paced the room deep in thought. He poked and prodded Kevin's clothes. "I want to break our bodies apart. I'm certain Friar Francois and Basal left instructions to remove us from the stones. But I doubt very much if those instructions could be found. Besides, I'm no longer in a stone. I have a different problem. I wish I could see the stone that held me. Perhaps then I could find the secret."

Megan used Kevin's computer and went to the Field Museum website. "There are other stones that look the same as the one you came from." She pointed to the screen, showing

Kragnor the protection stones the museum had on loan. An onyx was near the center of the picture. It could be Basal's stone.

"Where are these located?" Kragnor leaned in and poked at the picture with his claw.

"The Field Museum in Chicago."

Kragnor looked at Megan, his expression unreadable.

"Um, it's not far. My father works there.

The gargoyle grunted.

"I think there might be gargoyle souls inside. You should come to the museum."

"That is a good idea. Will you talk to Kevin? It is his body, too."

"I'm sure he'll agree."

"Would you show me how to use that," Kragnor pointed to the laptop, "thing?" If it is magic and anyone can use it, then he ought to learn.

"This is called a computer. You push these buttons to compose sentences." Megan indicated the keyboard. "You have big strong hands, so you'll need to be gentle."

Kragnor nodded. "Bring it here, sit, and show me." He felt the excitement of discovery.

Megan laughed. "You're nothing but a big child, aren't you?" She unplugged the power source and brought the laptop to the gargoyle.

Kragnor reclined into his teaching position. Megan guided his left hand to hold the machine and showed him how to type in searches with his right.

"We've already figured out that you can't use the touch screen. I've had some training with shortcuts." She grinned triumphantly at him. "Click this key and that one at the same time. See how this rectangle opened? That is called a window." Megan continued to show him shortcuts, and Kragnor learned quickly. Clicking a variety of keys was slow, but she never had to show him twice.

Once he understood the logic, Kragnor tried to figure things out on his own. Searches were the hardest because he didn't know the proper words for the information he wanted. Megan showed him how to ask the right questions. While videos were entertaining to demonstrate things, Kragnor found that reading was the fastest way to absorb information.

Kragnor didn't hear Megan say goodbye, but she must have. When he turned away from the laptop, she was gone.

# Chapter 45

Kevin opened the curtains; the sun appeared lower than before. He looked at his clock,7:01. He frowned and wondered if something was wrong with Kragnor.

The notebook sat on the bed with an ink message in flowing cursive. "I showed Kragnor how to use your laptop. I hope he didn't break anything." He dressed and went downstairs.

Grandma Ruby and Johnny were in the kitchen, talking over cups of coffee. "Good morning," Grandma greeted him. "Fancy that; you're up at the right time today."

Johnny nodded to him.

"I decided to go to school on time." Kevin shrugged.

"You're not going today." Johnny sipped from his mug.

"Why not?" Kevin wanted to see Megan. He didn't know where she lived or her phone number. How would he contact her if he didn't go to school?

"It's all very exciting," Grandma Ruby said. "The school is closed until further notice. A few students were caught rigging lockers with explosives. They broke in, in the middle of the night, and didn't hide from the cameras or police."

"Who was it?"

Grandma nodded to the man across the table. "Johnny knows."

"Tony Meleta, Vincent Russo, and Chad Allen." Johnny smirked. "Your locker was one of the targets. Surprised?"

"Hardly. The whole school seems to have gone wacko." Kevin turned away from the small table and opened the refrigerator. "Who else was targeted?" He pulled out the eggs and sausage links. The date on the hash browns was tomorrow. He set them on the counter, along with a frying pan.

"Megan Petrov and Bonnie Schumacher."

Grandma Ruby made a squeal. "Megan? The girl that was over last night?"

Johnny looked from Ruby to Kevin, his eyebrows raised.

Kevin nodded. "Yea. Same, Megan." He added oil to the pan and ripped open the bag of hash browns. "Are you guys hungry? We've got to eat these before they go bad."

"I can always eat." Johnny lifted his mug, saluting Kevin.

"If there's no school today, I'd like to go to the hospital this morning." Kevin flipped the hash browns.

"I'm supposed to protect you," Johnny said. "Especially after this. I'd rather you not go anywhere."

Kevin sighed. "Who is going to protect Bonnie? Or Megan?"

Grandma shook her head. "No. I don't like it."

Johnny stood. "Everyone calm down. First, Megan is safe. Her father will make sure of that. Second, I investigated Bonnie's situation. The police have set a guard for her."

"The same police who allowed Annie to escape?" Kevin added the sausage links to the frying pan.

"Touché." Johnny looked at the meal coming together under Kevin's guidance. "I'll make a phone call to rectify the situation at the hospital." He left the kitchen and shouted from the living room. "Save some of that breakfast for me!"

# Chapter 46

"Get up!" Artem's fist on the door startled Megan awake. "Get up!" he shouted again.

"I'm up, I'm up. What's going on?"

Artem didn't respond; he was making noise in the kitchen.

Megan quickly changed into jeans and a sweatshirt. She rushed into the kitchen. Artem struggled to pull a duffle bag up the saferoom's spiral stairs. "What are you doing?"

Artem leaned over, his hands on his knees, huffing. He pointed to the bag. "Heavy." He held up his finger as he caught his breath. "School has been canceled. Some *Tony* person put a bomb in your locker."

"What? My locker?"

Artem waved his hand around. "and Bonnie's." He shrugged.

"He was caught then?"

Her father nodded. "With two accomplices."

Megan looked from the duffle bag to her father. "So, what's with the bag. No, don't tell me. We're bugging out."

To her surprise, Artem shook his head. “No, we are leaving.”

“Leaving? Explain.” Megan folded her arms.

“First,” he waved his hand, “undead assassins try to kill you.”

“Not me, Bonnie,” Megan interrupted.

“Yes, Bonnie,” he agreed, frowning. “And now a bomb in your locker. This little town isn’t safe.”

“Father!”

Artem held up his hand. “Let me finish! We moved here almost three years ago, and Avalon was peaceful and quiet. In the past week or so, hell has broken loose, and it seems that Bonnie is the epicenter. I have a hard enough time protecting us from Russia. I let you stay too long in one place, you made friends, and this is what happened. We are moving away from this nonsense.”

“You can’t blame Bonnie for this.”

“It isn’t just Bonnie. That AKG guy was right.”

“What guy?”

“The guy who came over the other day.” He paused, tapping his bottom lip in thought. “Johnny Conner. He was right. Tai Lu, the Chinese woman that let the museum use the cuneiform stones, she wants the stones back.”

"Did she say why?"

"She accused me of trying to steal her protection stone. I told her that I located another stone with the same inscription. I don't think she believed me."

"So, let her have the stones back. What does that have to do with us leaving?" Megan paced, feeling like her father would never get to the point.

"If Johnny was right about the Chinese. Then he is probably right about the Russians too."

"You want to leave based on a rumor?" Megan felt sick to her stomach. She had six or seven months until she graduated and moved out. She could get away from her father and the chaos he exuded.

"He was right about Tai Lu." Artem shook his head as if explaining his worries was as tricky as defining the laws of physics to a cat. "The Russians are dangerous. They will kill me, and you, if you're lucky. At the very least, they will bring you back to Mother Russia." Artem paused. "Then you will wish you were dead."

Megan sighed. "If you want to leave, then leave. I have no intention of going anywhere." She narrowed her eyes at her father. She would find a way to finish school on her own if she must.

"You don't understand what these people are capable of. No one understands." Artem looked around the room. His face brightened. "Except Nikolai. You'd listen to him, wouldn't you?"

Megan threw her hands up. "Sure, Dad, sure." If someone with more rational thought backed him, then she might believe him. "Why don't you go to Nikolai. Maybe he'll agree with you." She hoped Nikolai would talk some sense into him.

Artem grabbed his jacket hanging by the door and left through the garage. The engine of his car revved to life, and then he was gone.

Megan stood in the kitchen, uncertain of what to do. Should she stay and wait for her father to come back? Should she leave? Megan needed friends, friends that would give her a place to stay.

Megan parked outside Kevin's house. The tan Honda Civic was parked nearby, but it was empty. She looked up and down the street, but Johnny was nowhere to be seen. She knocked on the front door.

Ruby opened the door; a smile crossed her features. "Hello, dear. Come in, I'll call for Kevin." Ruby shouted up the stairs.

Megan stepped into the living room and noticed Johnny sitting on the couch.

"Hi, Megan." He tossed his head in greeting.

Megan felt afraid, trapped, and confused. She looked back at the closed front door.

Johnny chuckled and drank from his glass. Rapscallion lay next to him, perfectly content. "No need to fret, Megan," Johnny said.

"Oh, good, you two know each other." Ruby sat next to Johnny with Rapscallion between them.

Footsteps on the stairs announced Kevin.

Megan rounded on Kevin. "What's he doing here?" After finding her voice, she looked at Johnny. "What are you doing here?"

Kevin grabbed Megan's hand; concern was written on his face. "It's okay. Johnny's all right, even though he spends way too much time with Ruby." His eyes rolled.

Megan took a deep breath and closed her eyes, trying to find her focus. "Fine. Johnny's okay. But what is he doing here?" She looked at everyone, in turn, stopping her gaze on Johnny, her eyebrows raised.

Johnny said, "Annie escaped jail. I've been tasked to protect Kevin until she can be apprehended."

Megan blinked back her confusion. The same Annie that sent assassins to kill Bonnie and her, and this guy, this old man is going to stop her? She couldn't help herself. She burst out laughing.

"What's so funny about that?" Johnny asked.

"She almost killed Bonnie, and if I wasn't there…" Megan shut her mouth and looked around. She should not have said that.

"If you weren't there, what?" Johnny prompted.

He wanted her to finish the sentence. Megan narrowed her eyes.

"Your trick with the steel needles didn't kill that man..."

"Because he was already dead." Megan finished for Johnny. "They both were."

"That's why you should have used silver or jade."

"You said that before. Why?"

Johnny looked over his audience as if making a decision. Then nodded. "You know silver hurts vampires and werewolves. It also can kill undead bodies. Like those men, but their souls could return to animate something else.

Jade is more powerful. It can kill the undead body and trap the soul that powered the body. Jade can kill a ghost or trap a poltergeist. Silver has limitations." Johnny shrugged. "See the difference? Both are powerful against the undead, but Jade has an advantage that silver does not."

Megan stared dumbstruck at Johnny. "AKG, Sanctuary of Hidden Knowledge. There is more to you and your company than you let on."

"The same could be said of you."

Megan felt the heat rise in her cheeks. "You have no idea." She turned to look at Ruby. "How long has that portrait been there?" She pointed to the framed picture above a small desk.

"A few years, why do you ask?"

Megan looked at Kevin. "I never met the rest of your family. I didn't know you had three sisters." She took a deep breath, then continued. "Annie is part of a group called the Order of the Eye and Tooth. She was after Kevin because she wanted to befriend his triplet sisters."

Johnny stood, eyes wide with surprise. Ruby grabbed Johnny's hand.

Kevin stepped closer to Megan. "How do you know that?"

"Bonnie and I were in the bathroom when she received a phone call. The topic was her latest mark and his sisters. I didn't know it was you at the time, but now it makes sense." Megan pointed to Kevin's family's photo, including Ruby and an older gentleman, who she assumed was Grandpa. The triplets stood in front, wearing the same dress, drawing attention to their sameness. "The Order is related to the Greek Fates, and you have three identical sisters. You can't tell me that it's a coincidence."

"Is that why she tried to kill Bonnie and you?" Kevin asked.

"I don't think so. Annie didn't know we were in the bathroom. She discovered we were looking into her background. Her fake parents, her criminal record." Megan sighed, feeling guilty. "We didn't realize what we got into until it was too late." Megan shrugged apologetically. "I would have said something sooner, but I didn't see that picture before today." She looked at her feet. "And there has been a lot going on at home."

"Her parents are not her parents?" Johnny said. "That seems like an obvious thing to look into. Why didn't my people investigate? How did we miss that? Kevin, did you know?"

"Now that Megan said it, yes, I knew." Kevin scratched his head. "I think I always knew. For some reason, I forgot."

"A memory spell," Ruby hissed.

Johnny's lip curled. "This goes deeper than I thought. Something bigger than a charm on a girl who wants revenge. I need to contact AKG and tell them about this Order of the Eye and Tooth. Do me a favor, check on your sisters."

"Johnny," Megan said. "Nikolai has done some digging on Annie for me. You could check with him." She paused. "Wait, my father is with Nikolai right now. And he's kind of mad at you."

The older man nodded, then headed to the door.

"You're supposed to protect me," Kevin reminded Johnny. "That's why you won't let me leave the house, remember?"

"Megan's with you. You're covered." Johnny left the house and went to his car.

"What's that supposed to mean?" Kevin looked at Megan, frowning. "Who are you? Who is Nikolai?"

Ruby laughed. "She's Megan." She ruffled Kevin's hair. "Rapscallion likes her. That's all I need to know. Come on, let's check on the girls." She headed to the back of the house.

Megan watched Kevin and Ruby but remained. If her father left Avalon and she stayed here, with this family, would she be safe? Would they be safe?

"Come on, don't you want to meet them?" Kevin asked.

Megan sighed, then followed them through the kitchen and out the back door. The old oak in the backyard was beautiful. Why hadn't she noticed the tree the other night? Megan touched the thick bark, feeling tension release from her neck and shoulders. She moved closer. The smell of earth and moss filled her nose. The tree's age and ambrosia reminded her of Kragnor. He would protect her and Kevin's family.

"Megan?" Kevin looked at her, his head cocked to one side.

"Leave her be," Ruby said. "That oak is special. It calls to her."

Megan looked at the woman standing at the gate and the young man beside her. She blinked and looked again, really looked, taking in sights, smells, feelings, the slight taste on her tongue. These two, this place, this tree, Kragnor, it all felt more like home than Artem ever did. She shuddered, stepping away from the tree.

What was wrong with her?

# Chapter 47

They walked through the gate and entered the back door of the neighboring house. "Hello?" Kevin called out. "It's us." He continued into the house.

Sounds of cheering and whistles filled the living room. Jerry lounged in a recliner, filling out a roster form with numbers and comments. A football game filled the big screen. He leaned forward as play resumed, shouting at the players and coaches.

"Hi, Dad," Kevin said. "What game are you watching?"

Jerry paused the game. "Monday night two weeks ago, Steelers versus Browns. Looking at replacing my fantasy running back with number forty-three there. What do you think?"

"I'm not going to make that decision. You yelled at me last time I picked a quarterback for you."

Jerry nodded. "I forgot about that. Probably best I go with my gut." He hit play, and the game resumed.

"What's wrong with your dad?" Megan asked.

"Fantasy football, he gets obsessed." Kevin walked into the dining room.

The three girls sat on one side of the table. "Hello, we've been expecting you," they said in unison.

Megan looked at Kevin. "Are your sisters always this creepy?"

"No, it's new." His brows knitted with worry.

"How did this happen?" Megan looked from the girls to Kevin and Ruby.

"The blame lies with me." Ruby sat at the head of the table. "I knew they were special when they were in the womb. Your grandfather and I cast spells and wards to hide them from those who would do them harm. After Joseph died, I hid the information from myself with a spell. Recently, I asked Kevin to cast a spell of protection for me." Ruby looked at Kevin as if apologizing. "That spell released Kragnor."

Kevin stepped to Ruby's side, placing a hand on her shoulder. "You couldn't know what would happen."

"Didn't I? I picked the spell for you as if subconsciously I knew." Ruby's hand went to her mouth. “I set all this into motion.” She looked at Megan and sighed.

“What does Kragnor have to do with all this?” Megan asked.

“Gargoyles are the oldest purest source of magic. Their very presence can break spells, curses, and wards.” Ruby looked into Megan’s eyes then quickly looked away. “The spell I put on the girls is gone. The spell on myself holds on by a thread. Benny’s glamor is gone and…” She licked her lips, then looked at Megan. “And your spell is broken too.”

“My spell?” Megan put her hand on her chest. “What do you mean?”

“The wolf awakens.” The triplets giggled.

“What does that mean?” Megan looked at the three girls.

“Your father has many secrets,” they said.

Ruby narrowed her eyes. “Girls, you understand why this behavior can’t continue?”

The triplets looked down at their hands. “Yes.”

Mina looked up. “The one who was after us is gone. Others forced her to find us, to befriend us, but her heart wasn’t in it. She runs from her keepers.”

“You must understand that there will be others who want to find you and use you.”

"Yes."

Ruby stood and touched the girls on the head, leaning in and hugging them. "Girls, time for games is over. Your lives, your parent's lives, the lives of those around you are in danger."

"But…" Inez started to say.

"Enough! I am not *asking* you to behave." Ruby's eyes flashed. The house darkened and creaked as if under the pressure of a giant hand. "Your insolence will come to heel."

# Chapter 48

"Good news!" Megan rushed toward him.

Kragnor blinked and focused. It seemed being born every night gave him a moment of clouded thought. "You sound excited. Please, tell me your news, young one."

"Kevin and I are going to drive down to the museum and spend the day there."

"Day?" Kragnor frowned. "All day?"

"Yes, it'll be fun. I'll show Kevin all the displays." She touched his arm. "Especially the Halloween one, where the stones are."

"What time would you come back?" Kragnor waited to see if she would see any problems with her plans.

She halted then tapped her lip. "The museum closes at five. With drive time and dinner." She bounced on her toes more. "about seven or eight."

The gargoyle looked at the clock on Kevin's dresser. He flicked his eyes between the clock and Megan until she took the hint and looked at the time.

Her brow creased in concentration. "Oh, crap. I'm sorry. You need to see the stones, and you don't arrive until past six."

Kragnor smiled his approval. She figured it out. "Is there an alternate solution?"

"There is, but I don't like it. My father will have to meet you." Megan fidgeted where she stood, then paced, like a caged animal.

"Your father?"

"He works at the museum. We could stay late because he has keys and access to everything. Then you could touch the stones." Megan chewed her fingernails.

Kragnor watched as her pacing became frantic. "Clearly, bringing your father into this bothers you. Is there another way?"

"No." She stopped then stared into his eyes. "The woman who allowed the museum to borrow the stones is picking them up. I'm afraid if we don't go soon, the stones will be lost to us forever."

"Bring your father tomorrow night. We can work together. I am sure of it. If not, I have another way."

"If you have another way that won't involve my father, we ought to explore it."

Her sweet, upturned face made Kragnor smile. "I will try, but I make no promises."

"You can't just say that and not tell me what the other way is." Megan protruded her bottom lip and pouted. "Please," she begged.

"Most museums have vast marble columns and walls, correct?"

"Yes." She tilted her head as if trying to figure out where his line of thought was going.

"I can use stone to travel."

Megan looked down, thinking. "I don't understand. What do you mean?

"See those bookends? Bring them to me."

Megan stood on a chair to get the bookends. She looked at them, turning them over and poking their surface. She placed them into his open palms.

"These are just stone, right?"

Sensing a trick but not seeing one, Megan narrowed her eyes at the bookends then slowly nodded.

Kragnor arranged the stones as they would have been cut from the quarry face to face. "These stones were cut from the same parent stone, like this."

"How do you know?"

"Through a series of deductions. See how this crack is the same here?"

"Sure, and those two." Megan indicated the bottom section of both stones.

"Right. I also know the stones are siblings because they told me."

Megan held up her finger. "If anyone else told me they talk to rocks, I would call them a liar. You, however, are a rock." She waved her arm around. "More or less."

"More or less," Kragnor agreed. He handed her one of the stones. "Hold it in the palm of your hand, like that. Don't drop it. It has enough fractures. What I am about to show you might make you jump. Compose yourself."

Megan nodded, and she seemed to age before his eyes, becoming more stoic.

"Watch this stone." Kragnor pressed his hand into the bookend. It was too small to accept his entire hand; his fingers disappeared. His fingers should have gone through the rock, but instead, they seemed to be cut short.

"Whoa," Megan said.

"Now, look at the stone in your hand."

Megan swallowed, then looked; Kragnor's fingers stuck out of the stone. She looked from one rock to the other. "That's still you, right?" She poked the dark grey fingers protruding out of the honey-colored bookend. The alabaster rippled like water as Kragnor moved within the stone.

Kragnor wiggled his fingers. “Yes, it is still me.” He grinned. “Most people become scared when they first see this demonstrated.”

She pulled at his fingers as if trying to make more of him come through. “If it were big enough, could your body pass through?” Megan’s eyes closed in thought, then snapped open. “Do you plan on going through a big enough piece of marble and travel to the museum?” Megan’s finger touched, then penetrated the alabaster. She jerked her hand back, startled.

“Perfect, young one.” Kragnor pulled his hand out of the stone, setting the bookend aside. “Your thought is good in theory, but stone-travel is much more complicated.”

Megan kept the bookend and returned to sit on Kragnor’s knee. “I don’t understand.”

“I would be surprised if you did. I can only travel out of the stone that was next to the one I entered. They have to be born of the same parent and cut sequentially.” Kragnor indicated the bookends. “Those two are merely a doorway. In one, out the other.”

Megan picked up the other bookend. She placed it face to face with the one in her hand, the same way they were before. “Your hand went in through this face and out this face.” She touched the outside surfaces of the stones. “What if you entered through the other side? Wouldn’t you exit out a different stone?” She separated the bookends and touched the inner facing surfaces.

“Very good.” Kragnor ruffled her hair. People like Megan did not come along often. She was very bright and quick to understand. “If I put my hand in the other way, you would not have seen my fingers. Not a very dramatic demonstration.”

Megan nodded. “Can you find the marble that will lead you to the museum?”

“Yes,” Kragnor said confidently.

Megan blinked and raised an eyebrow. “In what time frame? Could you do it in hours?”

“Potentially, yes. I know the quarries the Romans and Greeks used.”

“Greeks? Romans?” Megan rolled her eyes and laughed. “Are you serious?”

Kragnor frowned. “I am always serious.”

Megan stood and patted the gargoyle’s cheek. “The world has changed while you slept.” She moved to Kevin’s desk and unplugged the laptop. She punched in a map program then gave the computer to Kragnor. On the display was an image of the earth. “This boot is Italy, where the Romans lived.” She pointed at another part of the map. “This is France. England. And waaaaay over here is where we are right now.” Megan rolled the earth under her finger until the Great Lakes of North America were in the center of the screen.

Kragnor touched the screen like Megan, but the computer didn’t respond.

“I have a gift for you.” She gave him a thin metal object with a soft rubberized end, a stylist. “Use this to move the image.”

The gargoyle used the rubber end and swirled the earth around. “Fascinating. We are currently in the land of the Chippewa, Miami, and Shawnee.”

“You know about Native Americans?”

“I am not familiar with the words: Native Americans. I know of the tribes that lived in this land hundreds of years ago.” Kragnor blinked. “Where is Mexico?”

“Mexico?”

“I traveled there my second or third night. Banco de Mexico.”

“Oh? Really? How?”

“Through the headstones in the cemetery.”

“You think you can do the same to enter the museum?”

"Yes. But…" Kragnor looked away from Megan, feeling embarrassed. "There were magics. I had to leave quickly."

"Bank magics?" Megan smiled and nodded. "The museum has magics like the bank, with guards who wander the halls. And metal gates that could trap you."

"Metal gates? Cages?" Kragnor grunted. He didn't like cages. "My idea doesn't seem so appealing anymore. We must work with your father."

Megan paced the room, thinking. "I hate to say it, we have no choice but to work with my father. If you were caught, Kevin would be caught too."

Kragnor frowned. "Tell me about your father. What do I need to say to convince him of our need?"

"Where should I start?" Megan tapped her bottom lip. "Artem is a simple man…"

# Chapter 49

After Megan got dressed, she unlocked her door and went to the kitchen. Her father and Nikolai were sitting at the table drinking coffee and talking. Nikolai hardly ever came over, preferring to spend time in his gym.

"Good morning," she said.

The men nodded and sipped the hot brew.

"What time did you get in? I went to bed around midnight."

Artem looked over his coffee. "Would you believe, about an hour ago?" He smiled like he had gotten away with murder. He chuckled into his hand.

"Did you two go out drinking?"

Nikolai shook his head. "I don't think he slept. He was worked up when he arrived." The Weapons Master shrugged. "I gave him all the data he asked for then slept while he read. In the end, I think we have come to the same conclusion that you and I did recently."

"What is that?"

"Moving or bugging out is no longer in our best interest," Artem said with a lopsided smile.

"Oh," Megan said in mock surprise. "What changed your mind?"

"Nikolai showed me the intelligence. There isn't any movement from Russia." He shrugged, looking sheepish. "At least no movement that has anything to do with us." Artem took a sip of coffee. "But there's more. Nikolai showed me your training videos, starting from when you were very young. Your skills have come a long way. You're not defenseless anymore. We also have people and contacts from the gym who would help us. Not to mention the fortifications we've made over the years." He flung his arm toward the pantry. "And we know the area. If someone wants to come, I say let them!" Artem smiled.

"That sounds like the bravado of a drunk man," Megan said.

"A tired man," Nikolai corrected.

Artem nodded. "Very tired."

"While you were gone, I received some good news," Megan said to her father.

Artem blinked at her, waiting.

"The boy from school, who has the stone. He found it and wants you to look at it to see if it's real."

"Let's go." Artem made to stand, but his legs were wobbly, and he flopped back into the wooden chair.

"He's busy until tonight, around seven. Besides, you can't even stand." Megan placed her hand on her father's. "The stone isn't going anywhere. You could take a nap?"

"A nap sounds splendid," Artem said, pushing the coffee aside and placing his head on the table.

"That's dedication," Nikolai said. "I would have found a bed."

Megan laughed.

Megan followed Artem up the stairs and onto Kevin's porch. Artem knocked. Ruby opened the door. She seemed surprised to see a tall blonde Russian on her porch. She spotted Megan then smiled. "You must be Megan's father. So good to meet you. I'm Ruby." Ruby encouraged them to enter her living room.

"Please, call me Artem."

Kevin hovered behind Ruby. He shot a questioning look at Megan.

Artem saw Ruby's cast and the purple crayon design. "That's a fabulous design. Who wrote that for you?"

"Kragnor."

"Fascinating. I've never seen Sanskrit in crayon before."

"Sanskrit?" Megan maneuvered for a better look at Ruby's cast. She studied it for a few minutes. "Strength, Straight, Heal."

"Is that what it says?" Ruby asked. "I've been wondering. Kragnor didn't seem to know what to write." She tried to turn the cast to see the Sanskrit better. "What brings you by this evening?"

"Kevin is going to show us some of the witchy things you gave to him. Like the protection stone," Megan said. She introduced Kevin to her father. Artem frowned at the sight of him. Megan understood. Artem didn't like it when she had friends, especially of the male persuasion.

Rapscallion wandered from the kitchen to the couch. He paused, stopping to greet Megan. The white cat stiffened and hissed at Artem, batting at the man and jumping away.

"Oh, my. I'm sorry, Artem. Rap is normally a well-behaved cat." Ruby picked up the tomcat and held him protectively.

Artem waved the cat's disapproval off and said, "It doesn't matter. We won't be here long."

"When you're ready." Kevin headed to the stairs.

"Why don't you bring it down?" Ruby said to Kevin. "Can't you see Artem is uncomfortable about this situation?" Ruby touched Artem's arm. "But don't you worry, I make sure to give them condoms every time Megan comes over."

"Every time?" Artem barked at Megan. "Condoms?" He bristled with anger.

"Father, please, I've never had sex, and I don't know Kevin." Megan looked at Ruby for help. "I was here to see Kragnor."

Ruby nodded. "Oh, that's right, I forgot."

Artem frowned. "What the hell is going on here? Who is Kragnor?"

"We are here to look at the stone, remember?" Megan coaxed him toward the stairs. "We can leave afterward, five minutes tops." She pulled his arm.

"Fine." Artem snapped. "We will talk later." He yanked his arm free and stomped up the stairs. Megan followed.

Kevin went into his bedroom and pointed to the boxes on the other side of the room. He shuttered as Megan passed. His eyes were pools of pain. Kragnor was coming, and Kevin was trying to hold him back.

Megan showed her father the boxes while Kevin stripped off his clothing. Kevin sat on the floor with a towel over his lap.

"What box is it in?" Artem asked, then turned to look at Kevin's naked body. "What the hell?" He tried to push past Megan, but she held Artem in place.

"You would not have come if I told you this is what you would see," she hissed. Artem tried to pull free of her grip but could not.

"Not likely," he snapped. Artem stopped struggling. "What the…?"

Kragnor's wings unfolded out of Kevin's back, their pointed ends having pierced his flesh. As if in a trance, Kevin's body stood. His head rolled forward, combining with his chest. The remaining flesh, muscle, and bone of his human shape sloughed forward. It bundled into a ball, growing ever smaller. It settled at the center point of Kragnor's chest and pushed inward, disappearing into the gargoyle's rocky flesh.

Artem fell to his knees, leaning back onto his heels. He rocked back and forth, holding his hands in a praying gesture mumbling Latin phrases.

"This is not a demon. He's Kragnor, a gargoyle. Open your eyes and look."

"Good evening, Artem." Kragnor greeted Megan's father.

# Chapter 50

Kragnor cleared his throat. "Good evening Artem," he said again. The man opened his mouth in amazement but seemed to be stuck.

He tried again, this time in Russian. "Dobryy vecher, Artem."

Megan laughed. "You never told me you spoke Russian."

"There are many things you do not know about me, young one."

"What are you?" Artem asked. His mouth gaped in amazement.

"I am an akitu. One of the first in my line." Kragnor held out his hand. "I assume handshaking is still the correct way to greet?"

Artem composed himself. He stood and took Kragnor's hand. "I don't know what to say."

"Usually, an introduction ceremony is done." Kragnor nodded to Megan. "Young one, you know both of us. You should do the honors."

"Yeah, sure." Megan moved to her father's elbow. "Father, this is Kragnor. Kragnor, this is my father, Artem."

"I am pleased to meet the father of my friend." Kragnor bowed deep, billowing his wings to make his greeting extraordinary.

"How, how…" The man gaped and tried to talk.

"How did this happen? How am I alive?" Kragnor suggested.

"Yes!" Artem looked from Megan to Kragnor. "Yes, to both."

Kragnor felt the man's eyes travel over his body, like someone purchasing cattle. "My story is a long and tedious one. But my current predicament is short. Megan's friend Kevin accidentally released me from a stone. For some reason, we share one body. Megan heard of our plight. She showed me a picture of stones in the museum that are identical to the one I was in. The idea is to see the stones, to discover a way to separate Kevin from me. Or me from Kevin." Kragnor noticed Artem flinch when the words friend and Kevin were said.

"You came from one of the Chinese protection stones?"

"No," Megan said. "Kevin's grandmother had the stone for years. Remember? We tried to translate the cuneiform?"

Artem blinked rapidly. "That stone?"

Megan nodded. "That stone."

Artem approached the gargoyle. “You.” He used his hands and arms to indicate how huge Kragnor was. “Came out of a little stone?” His hands moved to form a fist-sized circle.

“My soul is not so large as my physical form,” Kragnor explained.

“You have a soul?”

“Why do you find that hard to believe? I stand before you, more than your equal.” Kragnor didn’t like humans who thought themselves superior to other forms of life.

“My humble apologies. I didn’t mean to offend.” Artem bowed.

Kragnor huffed, not sure he could believe Artem. He was manipulated by humans in the past and didn’t want to experience the situation again.

“Where did the stone go?” Artem asked.

The gargoyle studied him with narrow eyes. “What do you mean?”

“The stone that held your soul, what happened to it?”

“We don’t know.”

“We?”

“Kevin and I.”

Artem nodded. “Do you know where Kevin goes when you are awake? Or where you go when Kevin is awake?”

The gargoyle shook his head. “We don’t know much of anything. That is why we wanted to see the stones you have at the museum. Perhaps we can figure out this predicament.”

“You need my help.” Artem raised an eyebrow.

“Yes,” Megan said. “Kevin is Kevin during the day. Kragnor arrives at night, way past museum hours. Like tonight. So, we need to be inside the museum after it closes.”

“I see.” Artem paced with his hands behind his back. “And you need access to the protection stones. There was specific instruction not to touch the stones. I suppose you don’t have fingerprints or oils that might damage them.” He smiled, nodding to himself. “There’s another problem. The Chinese are arriving tomorrow morning to collect the stones. I could misplace them until later in the evening so you can see them.” Artem raised his hand, finger in the air. “Or perhaps their flight will be delayed. Either way, I’ll make sure they are available for you tomorrow.”

“That would be fabulous.” Megan grinned. She went to Kragnor and gave him a celebratory hug. “You and Kevin could be separated tomorrow.”

“Anything for my wonderful daughter and her friends.”

Megan pulled back out of the gargoyle’s embrace; her smile faded. She turned, looking at her father. “You’ve never wanted me to have friends, and now you proclaim your desire to help them. Forgive me, father, but something’s wrong.”

Artem held up his hands. “You’re mistaken; this is a different situation. He is a gargoyle. I’ve always loved gargoyles.” He smiled, but the warm glow didn’t extend to his eyes.

Kragnor leaned forward and whispered into Megan’s ear, “There is marble in this museum, is there not? I can escape if need be.” The gargoyle straightened, leaving his hand on Megan’s shoulder. “Artem, I accept your invitation.”

“Excellent.” Artem held out his hand. “Come, Megan. I have phone calls to make.”

“Kragnor can take me home.” She clutched at the hand on her shoulder.

“Megan, you will do as you are told!”

She stiffened under Kragnor’s grasp. Something broke free in her mind; Kragnor could feel it. “I am glad you want to stay and keep me company. But I will see you tomorrow at the museum,” Kragnor said.

She nodded, turning to look at him. "Alright. Walk us out, please."

"Of course, my lady." The gargoyle bowed.

Artem grabbed her hand and pulled Megan toward the bedroom door, a look of disgust on his face. Kragnor followed them down the stairs.

"Leaving so soon?" Ruby asked.

"Yes," snapped Artem. "I have preparations to make." He opened the front door and stomped onto the porch, with Megan close to his heels.

"Nice meeting you too. You great big jackass," Ruby mumbled under her breath as she closed the door. "That poor sweet child. She doesn't deserve a father like that."

"We don't choose our family. We choose our friends," Kragnor said. "Megan wanted to stay, but her father became upset. I believe I saw a glimpse of the Wolf. Benny was right about her too."

"You needn't worry about Megan." Johnny stepped out of the kitchen. "She can take care of herself. I've seen videos of her training sessions with Nikolai." The older man shook his head. "Quite impressive."

"Good evening Johnny." Kragnor nodded. "Were you hiding in the kitchen?"

"From Artem, yes. You probably should have hidden also. That man is self-serving through and through. Are you sure visiting the museum is the best choice?"

Kragnor nodded. "It is the only way to see the stones and set Kevin and me free."

"Artem will take advantage of that need. He'll exploit you."

Ruby laid her hand on Johnny's arm. "Is Artem that horrible a person?"

"Yes. When Artem lived in Russia, he was an arms dealer. He made many friends with horrible people all for the sake of money. Megan and her father were given asylum in exchange for information and the names of those friends. If he would roll over on some of the most powerful men and women in the world in exchange for asylum, what do you think he would do to you? A walking, talking rock monster, you are a weapon."

"Humans had tried to use akitu as weapons in the past. We are not fighters."

"A dud is still a weapon."

# Chapter 51

Kevin entered the kitchen and saw Ruby and Johnny having a cup of coffee. "Is it going to be like this every morning?"

Johnny looked up. "This is how I protect you."

"But the girls are the target."

"Do you think your parents would buy that, or do you think they would find me crazy? No, you're my excuse, so you have to deal with it."

"I'm going to Chicago for the day and evening. So technically, I won't be here." Kevin dug through the cabinets and found a granola bar.

"Kragnor told us." Grandma folded her arms. "I want your phone for a second."

Kevin chewed the bar and chased it with a drink from Grandma's coffee mug. "Why?" He frowned, then took another bite.

"Don't you trust me?"

"Should I?"

"Yes." Grandma held out her hand.

He narrowed his eyes, pulled the phone out of his pocket, and handed it to her.

Grandma Ruby gave it to Johnny. The older man pulled out a small bag of tools and took Kevin's phone apart.

"Hey. Don't go breaking it."

Johnny added a small item to the electronics, interconnecting it to the phone. He reassembled it and handed it back to Kevin. "I don't trust Artem, and I don't want anything to happen to you." He shrugged. "So, I bugged your phone. Don't say anything you don't want me to hear, okay?"

"Uh, Okay." Kevin put his phone in his pocket. "Wait a minute. Isn't that illegal?"

"A bug is only illegal if you didn't know, and you didn't want it."

Grandma looked over her cup and winked at Kevin. "I want you to be safe."

A car horn sounded outside of the house. "That's probably them. I'll see you tomorrow." Kevin ran for the front door.

"Kevin," Grandma Ruby called. "Be careful."

"I will." Kevin closed the door and trotted down the porch steps, with his coat in hand. Megan sat shotgun. He climbed in the back seat. "Good Morning."

Artem nodded, but Megan said nothing. Kevin wanted to talk but stared out the window instead. They arrived an hour after the museum opened. Artem parked in his designated spot close to the door. Entering the big double doors, a man behind the ticket counter greeted them. "Good morning Artem, Megan." The man waved them through.

"Thank you, Peter, good to see you again," Megan said with a smile. "Kevin is with us."

Peter nodded. "Good to see you too, Megan. You ought to come around more often."

Artem stopped, taking Megan by the hand. "I have work that I need to do." He looked at Kevin and frowned. "Take Kevin and show him around. Come to my office at five." Megan's father turned on his heel and went through a door that wasn't marked.

"Your dad doesn't like me."

"He hates everyone. Don't think that you're special." Megan grinned then walked down a corridor. She turned to look back and coaxed Kevin to follow. "This is the Egyptian exhibit." She took her time talking about each display as if she had dug them herself.

"How do you know all this?"

"This is where I spent my summers and breaks. After a while, you learn everything. It can't be helped." Megan shrugged and looked at her hands as if embarrassed by her knowledge. She led the way through countless displays. Most museum visitors walked in groups or listened to the headphones that provided a virtual tour guide. Kevin had a personal guide with a vast knowledge of behind the scenes data.

Hours passed, and Kevin found that Megan was engaging and knowledgeable. Most of the time, he simply listened as she talked about her childhood, playing hide and seek with the guards, and helping designers decorate the displays. Eventually, their wandering brought them to the lower level, where lunch was available.

Megan used her father's badge number to pay for both meals. The sandwiches were in dire need of spices and condiments. Megan's stories and anecdotes of the museum more than made up for the lack of flavor. Kevin was surprised at how much he liked spending time with her. It was the best first date, without being a date, he ever had.

They continued on to other exhibits. Megan talked about little things as if they had been friends for years. Kevin found it was just as easy to speak to her about problems at home and school. Time passed quickly.

Megan pointed at the Hall of Gems. "I like fire opals the best."

Kevin followed, feeling curious. "I'm not sure I've seen those. What other kinds of gems are there? Diamonds? Rubies?"

"Sure, but you know a diamond is pretty common. Its real value lies in manufacturing. You know lasers and cutting implements."

"You don't like diamonds?"

"No, not really. A nice crystal can give you the same shine without the price tag."

"I thought all girls liked diamonds."

Megan shrugged. "I don't."

The color and shine of the stones and gems seem to call Kevin. "This might sound funny, but I want to touch all of them. Let them fall through my fingers like water."

"Because it's money?"

"No." Kevin looked at Megan. "Because they are shiny, it would be liquid light falling. I suspect I would feel the same if they were shiny pieces of plastic. But it wouldn't be the same. The weight of rock or metal is comforting." Kevin rubbed his hand through his hair. "Ruby says it's because I was a crow in a previous life."

"A crow? What does that mean?"

"Crows love shiny things." Kevin shrugged. "Don't your parents say nonsense from time to time?"

"I suppose." Megan smiled at an internal thought. "There are many legends in Russia to draw nonsense from." She smirked. "There is Koschei the Deathless, Vasilisa, and Baba Yaga. I would call them fairy tales."

"I've heard of Baba Yaga."

"A witch and trickster." Megan turned and looked Kevin in the eye. "Speaking of tricksters, something odd is going on. My father hates it when I have friends. Yet, here you are. Alone with me. Something he would never allow before." She shook her head. "I don't get it. Why is he behaving so strangely?"

"Maybe he finally understands that you're an adult?"

Megan laughed. "That is true. But no, I don't think I'll ever be an adult in his eyes." She turned away from Kevin and walked through an archway. "I don't know what he'll do when I graduate from high school. Will he let me go to college? Will he let me leave at all? Or am I forever trapped?" Megan looked back. "Do you ever get those feelings, or is it just me?"

"No parent can stop you from leaving."

Megan snorted. “I’m not sure that’s true. Do you plan on going to college?”

Kevin thought about her question and decided to be honest with her. “I want to, but I don’t know what I would study. I thought about getting a job and seeing where it takes me. Then going to school a couple of years later.”

“What about your family?”

“What about them?”

“They might need you.”

“Sure.”

“Would you stay to help them? Or would you go to college?”

“If they needed me, I would stay.”

“That is how a parent stops you from leaving. Guilt, honor, or loyalty, whatever you call it, it makes people stay when they would rather go.”

“I suppose we all have an inner dragon to conquer.” Kevin looked around. Tall grasses covered the view forward. “Where are we?”

“It’s been a while. This is either the African Plains exhibit or the Birds exhibit.” Megan walked around the grasses and disappeared. Kevin followed. Behind glass walls were vast arrays of African wildlife. Once through the elaborate displays of the Serengeti, they entered the Pacific Region.

"Holy crap. I didn't think they were that big." Kevin pointed. "Look, it's one of those statues from that island." The colossal statue stared at them with unblinking white eyes. A strange red hat perched on its head. "It's got to be at least twelve feet tall."

"It's a Moi from Easter Island." Megan laughed. "I'm impressed you recognized it." She placed her hand on his arm. "Come on, it's five o'clock, and this is our exit." She pointed to a door slightly hidden by the Moi. A sign on the door said, *no entrance-exit/staff only*. Megan opened the door and stepped through. A man in a security uniform sat at a table, his fingers clicking on a laptop.

"Good afternoon Megan. Your father is in his office."

"Thank you, Ben. Kevin Arkis is with me." Megan indicated Kevin then walked down a well-lit hallway.

"Just a minute, Kevin, how do you spell your last name?" The guard looked expectantly while his hands hovered over the keyboard.

Kevin pronounced and spelled his name, then nodded to the guard and trotted to catch up with Megan.

She knocked on a door and then walked in. Megan held the door open for Kevin to follow.

Inside was a desk and chair near the door. Items and boxes filled the tables and shelving that covered the rest of the room, which was deceptively long and narrow.

Artem sat behind the desk in a high-backed chair. Stacks of papers covered the desktop. Two flat-screen monitors perched on thick books, above the mess.

"Did you collect the stones already?" Megan asked, sitting in a small wooden chair, like something seen in an elementary school.

"They're right here." Artem pulled a briefcase from under his desk. He opened it and exposed a velvet lined case and numerous stones. Most were round, but some were square or rectangular. Each was roughly the same size as the bloodstone.

Kevin reached out.

"Nyet." Artem pulled the case away from Kevin, setting it under his desk. "No one is allowed to touch, remember?"

"I can't seem to control myself. Sorry." Kevin bowed his head and grasped his hands together. The rocks seemed to call to him as if requesting help.

# Chapter 52

A knock fell on the door. Artem opened it. A man in a three-piece suit stood in the doorway. Four Chinese people were behind him. "Good evening, Dr. Martin." Artem stepped back and allowed the people into his office. "Megan, Kevin, this is Dr. Martin, he is Collections Manager."

"Good evening, Dr. Petrov." Dr. Martin shook Artem's hand. "I am here with the Chinese delegation to pick up the items they allowed us to borrow for the Halloween exhibit. I assume they have been collected and boxed for their return trip home?" The director indicated the people behind him with a sweep of his arm. "This is Tai Lu. She owns the items. Her bodyguards, Chen Yu, Bai Wong, and Qiang Li."

Kevin stepped behind Megan. He spoke softly into her ear. "They weren't supposed to be here until tomorrow. Right?"

Megan looked at her father. "Dad?"

Dr. Martin's phone rang. He answered it then said, "Excuse me, I have to take this call." He stepped out of Artem's office.

"If you don't mind, Dr. Petrov, our plane leaves in a couple hours." Tai Lu's English lacked any hint of an accent.

"Yes." Artem nodded and smiled. He walked over to a shelf and pulled a cardboard box. He placed it on a table. "I am sure you would like to inspect the items before you take them?" He directed the question to Tai Lu, ignoring her bodyguards.

The young woman stepped forward. "Yes, I would." She opened a briefcase and pulled out a laptop. She opened a file and pulled up images of the items that were sent to the Field Museum. She said something in Chinese, and two men unpacked the box, laying all the pieces out on the table. She looked at the objects, comparing them to her visual list. "Very good. Pack it up." The men repacked the box, then waited, standing beside it.

Tai Lu strolled to Artem's desk. "I have everything on my manifest, except my stones." She tapped the desktop with her fingernails. "Tick tock, Dr. Petrov."

Artem reached under his desk and produced the case, setting it on the smooth wood surface.

Kevin placed his hand on the case, protectively.

“Please, father, you promised,” Megan begged.

Artem stood and bowed to Tai Lu. “I promised my daughter that her friend could see the stones before you took them. Would you be so generous as to allow them to stay for a few more minutes? Her friend should arrive soon.”

“Your daughter?” Tai Lu studied Megan then grabbed her chin, turning her face side to side. “She looks a little feral to me.” The woman released Megan and laughed.

“Will you permit it?” Artem asked again.

“I will.” The woman sat on the edge of the desk, an amused smile on her face.

“Alone?” Megan asked.

Tai Lu raised her eyebrows then shook her head. “No, my dear. I have a feeling that if I leave my stones alone with you, I will never see them again.”

Megan frowned. The woman seemed to be up to something nefarious. It was as if she could smell the evil on her.

Kevin groaned. His face was pale and sweaty. “Can they leave for a few minutes?” His mouth contorted into a grimace.

Tai Lu's men moved closer to their charge as if protecting her from Kevin. "No, my darling, we're not going anywhere." Tai Lu chuckled gently.

Kevin stumbled toward the back of the room, slowly removing his clothing, trying to hide behind boxes. The Chinese craned their necks, watching as Kevin transformed, amazed and amused but certainly not surprised.

# Chapter 53

Kragnor looked around the room, crowded with shelving, books, boxes, and people. Who were these people, and why were they here? The room used the same chalk board as the Sorceress's house. He could not port through them, but he could walk through them easily enough. He was not trapped, although he felt like it.

Megan rushed toward him. "I'm sorry they appeared minutes before you arrived. I don't know what they're doing here." She picked up Kevin's clothes and brought them to her father.

Artem sat behind an ornately carved oak desk. His steepled fingers rested on his bottom lip. The people near his desk had the same general appearance as the great Genghis Kahn, straight dark hair, silted eyes, and small of stature.

Kragnor smiled at them. He had a soft spot for the people of his homeland. They helped his kind in the past with words of wisdom and actions of kindness.

The people grinned back, then spoke rapidly to each other in their native tongue. Kragnor frowned, trying to remember the sound of their dancing language. He was sure that it too changed, while he slept, like English. He caught a couple of words, but it wasn't enough to make sense of what they said.

The female and apparent leader of the group turned to Artem and continued to speak. Money seemed to be the subject, but Megan's father shook his head. There was a disagreement. The woman turned away from Artem and approached Kragnor.

She stopped a few feet away from him and bowed deeply. According to custom, she was very high ranked to dip so low.

Kragnor returned the bow and made sure he didn't bow lower than the woman.

"I am happy to see an akitu wandering free in the United States." The woman spoke in her native language slowly, purposefully, to be sure the gargoyle understood what she said.

"Thank you. I am happy to hear the name of my people in your tongue," Kragnor said. He wanted to ask if she knew of any others of his kind, but customs were essential to follow.

"Artem informed me that you desire to see the stones." She didn't ask a question. She snapped her fingers, and one of her men brought a case to her. The man held the box flat in his arms so that the woman could access the opening. She turned a dial, releasing the catches. "You may look, but do not touch." She opened the case displaying the protection stones nestled in foam and fabric.

Kragnor stepped forward. The stones glistened, pulsing with life. These stones had akitu in them, trapped like he was. His hand lifted of its own accord and reached toward the case.

The woman slammed the case shut and barked a few words to the man. The man withdrew to where the others stood, taking the case with him. "I told you to look." She narrowed her eyes at the gargoyle. "You displease me."

"My apologies, kind woman." Kragnor bowed. He remained prostrate. "My brothers and sisters are locked inside those stones. I can feel their souls. Please let me free them." He chanced a glance at the woman, but she turned away from him.

The woman spoke to Kragnor over her shoulder. "If you wish to free your people, I will allow it. On my terms. In Shanghai." She made a hand gesture. Her people gathered the boxes and moved to the door.

The woman stopped at Artem's desk., speaking in clear English. "We cannot stay and talk. Our plane leaves soon. It will not wait forever. It has been a pleasure." She inclined her head to Artem and Megan, then bowed to Kragnor. "Another day, perhaps, ancient one." She followed her people out of the room.

Kragnor rushed to the door, his hand on the knob. Voices from the other side indicated people he didn't know. He stepped away.

"What the hell was that?" Megan asked her father. "What did they say to you?"

"They spoke of money," Kragnor said.

"Money? Money?" Megan yelled at her father.

Artem held up his hands. "It wasn't money. It was about Tai Lu's mother, she is ill."

Megan crossed her arms. "Her mother? What do you take me for?"

"It is possible," Kragnor interrupted. "The words money and mother are only an inflection apart. It has been a very long time since I heard their language. I am sorry, Megan, Artem, I did not mean to cause a fight between you."

Megan narrowed her eyes at Kragnor as if the gargoyle stopped a legitimate fight. “Something fishy is going on.”

“Indeed! The airplane,” Artem offered. “A woman of that power and money would never have to wait for a plane. It would do her bidding.”

“Yes.” Megan nodded but seemed disappointed at the same time.

“I would not go to Shanghai, Kragnor. I believe it is a trap. She seemed very interested in you. Too interested.” Artem tapped his fingers on the desktop. “What do you think, Megan?” He pushed a water bottle toward her.

Megan frowned. “I think you’re right.” She sat in the small wooden chair, took a drink from the bottle, then set it down.

Both Megan and Artem seemed to be preoccupied with their thoughts. Kragnor studied the shelving and wooden crates that snugly filled the room. The lid of a wooden container big enough to hold his great size was askew. He moved the loose wooden top and looked inside. Curled and twisted bundles of straw and paper filled the empty cavities. Nestled in wrapped and taped padding was a partially exposed Egyptian statue.

Kragnor moved the straw aside and finished unwrapping the alabaster statue. He turned it over. It was a cat sitting on its hindquarters, ears tall and upright. On the cat's shoulders were Egyptian hieroglyphs. The cat didn't move. It was not a brethren. It didn't have the spells cast upon it, but to Kragnor, it still had special meaning. There was a connection, a familiarity that couldn't be described with mere words.

"What does that stone tell you?" Megan asked, watching him turn the statue in his hands.

The gargoyle knew humans didn't see the statue as he did. Often, he wondered what statues looked like from the human perspective. Did they contain the same mystery and significance? He doubted it.

Cradling the statue, Kragnor brought it to Megan, setting it on the desk. "What does the statue tell you?" he countered.

"I can't speak to stones," Megan said, then drank more water.

"Not literally. What can you deduce by examining it?" The gargoyle cocked his head to the side and studied her.

She shrugged, then stroked the statue, as if petting a living cat. "It's smooth. The craftsmanship is wonderful. I would love to own one."

Artem laughed gently. “We couldn’t afford that statue.” He patted his daughters’ arm. “If only we could.”

“What gives it value?” Kragnor asked.

“It was certified to be from the tomb of Tutankhamun.”

“Was it?” Kragnor picked up the alabaster statue and focused. “The stone tells me that information is incorrect.”

Artem frowned. “Excuse me?” He stood from his chair and walked around the desk. “The stone told you?”

Kragnor nodded. “It tells me it used to be a statue of Anubis in Egyptian times, but recently it was re-carved into Bast.”

“Re-carved?”

“Indeed, the Anubis statue broke, and an artist named Tuku used part of the foot and shin to carve the cat. It sat high on a shelf in an art store between the re-carving and coming here.” Kragnor sunk further into the stones' memories and counted the days that passed as the stone sat on the shelf. “It appears its current form was a recent carving, within the last fifty years, or so.”

Artem laughed. “You would be an excellent partner. If I could spot fakes as easily as you do.” He whistled. “I could command better rates from vendors and a bigger paycheck from my employer."

"If it's a fake. Does that mean I can have it?" Megan picked up the cat statue and placed it in her lap.

"I'm afraid not. The museum believes it to be genuine. They would expect a good price for it." Artem looked at Kragnor. "Let's be honest. They would never believe the information I have or where it came from."

Megan put the statue on the desk. "Well, that sucks." She looked around the room. "Are we here until morning?" She finished her water and left the bottle on her father's desk.

Artem looked at his wristwatch. "In a couple of hours, the rest of the staff will be leaving for the night. We can walk around the museum after they go. We'll have to keep an eye out for the guards, for Kragnor's sake. In the meantime, you can sleep on the couch." He waved his arm to the back of the room. "It's against the wall, probably under some boxes."

Megan sighed, then stomped off to the back of the room. She moved a few boxes before shouting, "Found it!"

"Kragnor, would you look at the rest of the statues in the crate? They were supposed to be from Tutankhamun's tomb. We now know that one was not. I might be able to convince the museum to return them if they are all fake."

The gargoyle moved to the crate and dug through the stuffing. Kragnor's finger touched their alabaster surfaces. The seven other sculptures were siblings with the first. "All the statues came from the same broken Anubis statue."

"Impressive." Artem smiled. "You didn't even look."

"I see with my eyes like you, but I can find knowledge by touch too." Kragnor wiggled his fingers.

"What did the stones tell you about the Anubis statue?"

"The Anubis statue was carved from four pieces of alabaster and stacked outside a building. Millions of people went through the door. The sand's ebb and flow moved like water, which tells me the statue existed for many years. At one point, the flow of sand covered the statue. The darkness of that memory was long, but without the sun, I can't tell you how long. Eventually, the sand moved aside, and people came to uncover the statue. If I could share the memory with you, you might see something I do not."

"That was fascinating," Artem said with awe. "How far back can you go into stone memories?"

"To their birth. Sometimes that is when the stone cooled from pools of magma. Other times it is when they gather sediment and are compacted or heated enough to become one voice."

"One voice?"

Kragnor sat back on his haunches and leaned into his tail. "A tiny grain of sand has a voice, a memory of its existence. A section of sandstone, for example, would have billions of tiny voices. That section would also have a singular voice, the memory of the stone as a unit, not the individual bits and pieces. Eventually, with time, the stone's voice is louder than the voices of the parts that make it up."

"Thus, one voice," Artem finished. "That makes perfect sense."

Kragnor grunted. "In some ways, humans have grown as a people."

"And in the other ways?"

The gargoyle waved the question away. "I dare not say."

Artem laughed, deep and throaty. "That, my akitu friend, says it all." He looked at his watch. "It is getting late. I'm going to take Megan to the lunchroom to get something to eat. If you want to explore the museum, be my guest. Be sure to pretend to be a statue if you see a guard. Oh, I forgot to mention that small crate there has meteorites in it."

"Meteorites? I am not familiar with that term." Kragnor leaned forward, expecting to hear something interesting.

"Atmospheric phenomenon. In this case, space metal and rocks."

Kragnor frowned, unsure if he understood. "Rocks and metal that were born, not of Earth?"

"Exactly."

Excitement coursed through Kragnor. A gargoyle could fly high, but there were limitations. Where the atmosphere ended, so did the utility of wings. He dreamt of entering the black satin of the night sky. He could visit the memories from an alien stone, and he could travel with them through the vastness of space. He went to the crate and pulled off the top.

"We'll be back shortly. I can't wait to hear the memories you discover," Artem said.

Kragnor looked up to see Artem close the door. The gargoyle looked to the empty uncovered red velvet couch. At first, he felt disappointed. Megan always said good-bye.

Kragnor huffed, then turned his attention back to the crate with the meteorites.

Inside were many cardboard boxes packed tightly. The gargoyle pulled one free of its companions. With his claw, he sliced open the box and removed the stone. It appeared to be a fresh piece of magma, but much heavier like pure ore. It had a paper tag tied to it with the number sixty-five handwritten on it. Brief contact with it told him the stone was older than he. Kragnor reclined back on his tail and entered the stone's memories.

As with all stone memories, time went backward. Kragnor witnessed the shipping process, cataloging, and collection of the meteorite. The space rock sat in a crater for years, then it struck the ground with unimaginable force, driving into the soil. Dirt and debris flew into the air. The stone fractured, reducing the meteorite by half. Heat and light covered the rock. It struck the atmosphere of the earth with enough pressure and force to cause a crack. It was on a trajectory to hit the blue-green planet. The bright yellow orb pulled at the stone, drawing it ever closer, ever warmer.

The stone traveled randomly, in cold and darkness. Always, pinpricks of light from galaxies and stars followed the stone.

Kragnor set the stone back in its box. He didn't realize the vastness of the space that surrounded Earth. His head hurt as he tried to wrap his imagination around the thought. The stone didn't finish its story. There was so much more to see. Its story was vast compared to the voices on Earth. Compared to his own story. For the first time in his life, Kragnor felt very small and insignificant.

Heat rolled up the gargoyle's spine. Kragnor blinked, looking for a clock. Where were Artem and Megan?

# Chapter 54

Kevin's eyes opened. Boxes took up most of the space on the floor and shelves. He sat up, noticing he was not in the attic.

The desk near the door looked familiar. It was Artem's. After Kragnor saw the stones, they must have had to wait for the morning. A giant, walking, talking, gargoyle leaving the museum would be noticed. Kevin stood and saw his clothes on the desk. He put them on and waited. Where did Artem and Megan go? Why were they not here when he woke? Maybe something happened, and he was on his own.

He pulled the phone out of his pocket to call Ruby and get a ride home. As he started to dial, the phone rang. It wasn't a number he knew. Might be Megan; she never called before.

Kevin answered it, "Hello?"

"Hi Kevin, it's Megan. Dad and I went to breakfast with Tai Lu. Her car is out front with a couple of her men. They'll bring you to us."

Kevin frowned. “We were all over the museum yesterday. I’m not sure I know how to get out.”

“Ask for the main doors. There are plenty of people who will help you. Please hurry.” Megan hung up.

“Weird phone call.” Kevin shrugged, then made sure he had everything before leaving Artem’s office. He followed the hallway past the empty guard table and into the central part of the museum, where the giant Moi statue stood. Between the maps displayed in the intersections and the wandering guards, Kevin found his way to the front doors.

Just as Megan promised, there was a car parked at the bottom of the stairs. A man in a black suit stood outside the vehicle. He looked like one of the men from the night before. Kevin approached. “Hello, I was told to go with you.”

The man knocked on the top of the car, two men from the back seat got out. One of them stepped aside, opening the door wide, indicating without talking that Kevin should enter. Kevin slipped into the car. The men sandwiched him in the back seat. The black suit standing outside the car sat in the driver’s seat. He started the car and drove away from the museum.

The men didn't look at him or talk to each other; instead, they stared straight ahead. Kevin wondered if their behavior was routine for servants. Maybe the rich didn't like small talk. His phone rang. He reached into his pocket and pulled it out.

The man on the right took the phone and spoke Mandarin rapidly. Did the man sound mad? Kevin reached for the phone. It was his. Why did they take it from him? The driver responded by barking orders. The window rolled down, and Kevin's phone flew out.

"Hey! What the hell did you do that for?"

More Mandarin shouting passed between the three men. Kevin felt the men move closer to him, restraining him in place. *Why do I get the feeling that we are not going for breakfast?* What did they want with him? He'd seen enough movies to know that they didn't cover his head. They had no intention of letting him go. *Am I about to be sold into slavery? What if they intend to harvest my organs?*

They drove into a manufacturing area. Many of the buildings were tagged with graffiti and appeared abandoned. The car entered a concrete and metal structure, like a parking garage. They went down a ramp and around a corkscrew path, eventually parking with a couple of other cars near an elevator.

The men got out of the car, pulled revolvers from under their jackets, and pointed them at him. "Please, come." The driver jerked the weapon, indicating direction.

Kevin held up his hands. "Okay, okay. No reason to get hostile." He scooted out of the car. The men moved him into the elevator. The driver pressed an unmarked button while the other two kept their guns pointed at Kevin. The elevator ran so smoothly it was impossible to tell if they went up or down.

The elevator door opened, and Kevin was directed with the business end of a gun and the ever-present "please." He wondered if the men spoke any English. Most of the building was dark. There were no lettering or pictures on the walls, nothing to indicate a business name or location. Only concrete walls.

The men pushed Kevin through a small concrete opening. They followed one at a time.

"Welcome home, Kevin." The woman from the night before sat on a concrete stool on the concrete floor.

Kevin narrowed his eyes. "You know my name, but I can't remember yours." The walls of the room were dark but also appeared to be concrete. In the center of the room, under bright lights, was a cage made of concrete and iron bars. Was that his new home?

"Call me Tai Lu, your new master." The woman mocked a bow. She looked at the men. "Put him in."

Hands shoved Kevin into the cage. The metal door closed behind him. Inside, rebar showed through the damaged concrete. *She didn't intend for me to live in this, did she?*

"Why am I in a cage?"

Tai Lu smiled. "You've walked into my factory." She tapped her bottom lip. "No. It's more like a slaughterhouse." A smirk crossed her face.

"I knew it. You're going to take my organs." Kevin broke out into a sweat.

"If I wanted your organs, I would have left the rest of you on the street." She approached the cage. "But I do need a piece of you."

"What?"

"Push him."

Behind and out of sight, he heard movement. Someone approached the cage. The zap of an electric charge brought sulfur to his nose. Kevin gasped and turned around. They were not men. They had the body of a serpent with the head and shoulders of a man. Medusa-like. Except the men had bald green heads, not Medusa's signature serpentine hair. The rods they carried went into the cage, with the promise of electric pain.

"What do you want from me?" Kevin shouted.

"Give me your hand." Tai Lu commanded.

Kevin thrust his hand through the bars in her direction. She took it, holding it gently. "You have such soft hands. It'll be a shame to mar them." Tai Lu put out her hand like a surgeon waiting for an instrument from the attending nurse. A snake-man slithered to her side and handed her a set of bolt cutters.

Kevin jerked his hand back into the cage.

"Shock him until he complies." Tai Lu instructed her men.

Kevin looked at the advancing cattle prods. "No, wait. Stop."

Tai Lu lifted her hand, and the men stopped. "Are you willing to cooperate?"

"No, but I have little choice." Kevin put his left hand through the bars.

"There's a good boy." Tai Lu told him. "Chen hold his arm. I want the honors."

The snake-man held Kevin's forearm in a vice-like grasp. The scaley waist blocked his view. Not that he wanted to see his fingers removed. The cold cutters touched his pinky at the joint closest to his palm. He fought the urge to pull away. Kevin knew the cattle prods' pain would be worse, and they would take his finger anyway. He held his breath and felt the blade bite. The pain rolled up his arm. Kevin screamed, pulling his hand back into the cage. He stared at the stump, not wanting to believe. Blood poured from the wound.

A white rag hit him in the face. The snake-man looked through the bars. “Put pressure on it. The blood will stop.”

Tai Lu held up the small finger like she won a prize. “You have made me very proud, Kevin.”

“What are you going to do with it?” Kevin sobbed.

“We,” she indicated everyone in attendance. “Are going to see if it turns to gargoyle when you do.” She smiled.

“And if it does?”

“Then, tomorrow, I will take all your fingers and toes.” She put the pinky on the concrete stool and spun around like a fool. “Maybe your hands and feet too, who knows.” She laughed. “But I can’t go too far because if you die before you turn, then your bits won’t turn at all.” She stomped toward the cage. "And that would make me very, very upset."

"Why are you doing this?" Kevin whimpered, imagining the pain and suffering he was going to endure the following day.

"Do you know how hard it is to cut up gargoyle into recognizable, sell-able bits?" Tai Lu sighed. "It's not easy. There comes a time when a piece of the torso looks like a rock and nothing more. It's hard to convince buyers that it really is a piece of a gargoyle. Now a finger. That always looks like a finger, no doubts from buyer or seller." She spun around again and headed toward the door. "Watch him, boys. I'll be back before sunset."

Kevin fell into a fit filled sleep. His mind fought between the fear of the coming day and the desire for the torture to be over. He'd rather be dead than fear the future.

Tapping rattled the door. "Get up. She approaches." The snake-man seemed to take pity on him.

Kevin sat on the bottom of the cage, arms folded over his knees. His hand throbbed with pain. The scarlet bandage hung over his wound.

His stomach turned every time he saw the blood or the pinky on the stool. He'd heard stories of people willing themselves dead. They must have been in a predicament like this one.

"Aw, my pet is awake." Tai Lu walked into the room, holding a tray. "I brought you something." She set it on the floor just outside the cage bars. If he wanted, he could reach through and take the food. "I promised breakfast this morning, didn't I?" She laughed.

On the tray was a gold plate with a bacon-wrapped filet mignon, potato, and salad. Kevin's stomach rolled, and he covered his mouth. He was not ready to deal with the idea of a last meal.

"When will he turn?" The snake-man asked.

"According to Artem, in just a few minutes." Tai Lu picked up the pinky and held it up to watch the transformation from her vantage point. "Kevin, be a peach and let the gargoyle out."

"It doesn't work that way," Kevin grunted.

"Give it a try," she said quietly through clenched teeth.

"I'll do my best," Kevin said. If he could hold Kragnor from coming, he would. He focused, willing to try anything. The heat and pain that cascaded down his back, heralding the gargoyles' arrival, coincided with Tai Lu hooting with happiness.

# Chapter 55

Megan woke among her blankets and pillows in her bedroom. She moved, stretching, her head pounded in her ears. Her tongue was thick and had a weird coating on it. The sliver of light around the window hurt to look at. She concentrated; there was something important… She grunted, putting her head in her hands. Megan noticed her shirt. She wasn't wearing pajamas; she wore the clothes from the trip to the museum.

The museum!

She sat up. Her head screamed as if it would break in half. Water. She stumbled into the adjoining bathroom and drank as the water filled her cupped hands. In the sink was her bottle of sleeping medication, and it was empty. She opened the medicine cabinet and fumbled to find pain medication. She took three times the recommended dose, chasing it with more water. Megan moved to her bed and laid on top of the covers. She would give it a few minutes. She glanced at the time, three twenty-four.

What happened last night? She remembered the Chinese people. And Kragnor. But the rest was blurry. The bottle of water Artem gave her must have had something in it.

Megan sat up and immediately wished she hadn't. She gently leaned back into the blankets. A few more minutes was all Megan needed. She closed her eyes, rubbing her forehead, temples, and neck.

Megan looked at the clock radio, one-minute past four. Her head still pulsed, but the pain was bearable. She sat up, waited a moment for her head to explode, but it didn't. She stood, paused, and counted to ten, then continued to her unlocked door.

She wandered into the living room and kitchen; both were empty. Megan walked into the den, where Artem sat in a wing-backed chair. He rifled through a box and tossed papers into the fireplace. A few other empty boxes were beside the chair.

He looked up at her approach. He seemed surprised. "You sure slept late today," he said. Without looking, he threw more into the fireplace. The fire, suffocated by the papers, spit out thick white smoke, causing him to cough.

"What are you doing? You're going to set the house on fire."

Artem looked at her blankly and offered nothing.

She looked at the box, written on the side was *Megan*. “Why are you burning my things?” She made to grab the box, but he tossed the whole thing. The fire, already choked by ash and paper, pumped out more white billowy smoke, filling the room. “What is wrong with you?” Megan pulled the smoldering box out of the fireplace, leaving it on the brick hearth. She ran to a window and opened it, allowing fresh air in.

“That part of my life is over.” Artem moved to the window, breathing deeply.

“What are you talking about?” Megan looked at the box with her name on it. What did that mean? Was he done with her?

“I no longer have to run.”

“Didn’t we discuss this the other day? We’re going to make a stand here. Remember?” Megan sat in the winged chair by the fireplace. From the box, she pulled meaningless paperwork and photos. The baby in the picture might have been her, but she couldn’t tell. The small village seemed familiar. She closed her eyes, trying to think. Her head still pounded.

“That will never be enough. I’d still be killed.” Artem cleared his throat and moved from the window to Megan's side, looking over her shoulder at the pictures she pulled from the box.

"The Russian Mafia?" She held up another photo. It was a double-take. Old cameras sometimes shot two pictures over each other, causing a double image. This double-take was over the baby, making her look furry. Megan found the photo compelling and tucked it between her leg and the chair.

"I lied," Artem said in undertones. She barely heard him. He sounded afraid.

Megan frowned. "What did you lie about?" She went through more photos in the box, finding one that reminded her of her mother. This picture looked like a double take too. The woman was tall and beautiful, but her outline was blurry. Next to her was a small old man who looked like an older version of Nikolai. That man could be Nikolai's father or grandfather. She added the photo to the baby picture under her leg.

"Russians are after us, yes. But not just the mafia." Artem shook his head. "If it were only the mafia. Then I'd have a chance."

She pulled another photo, a candid shot of the beautiful woman. The woman looked at something outside the view of the camera. Her gaze was intense. "Who besides the mafia, would come after us?" Megan remembered the fear her father had whenever they bugged out in the past. His anxiety was very real, very palpable. "Who scares you more than the Russian mafia?"

Artem plucked the photo from Megan's hand. "The Wolf of Siberia." A strange smile crossed his face. "I loved her. But I don't think she loves me. I'm not even sure she is capable of that kind of love. She promised me help but was slow to deliver, so I stole what she promised."

"What?" Megan took the photo back. "I don't understand."

"She promised me one of her offspring to protect me. I took you and raised you to think I was your father. So you would protect me because of love. But I see now, my effort was for nothing. You don't love me. You want to escape. To go off to college, to date, to have your own life. But that no longer matters. I don't care if you go back to your mother. I no longer fear her retribution nor that of the mafia." His expression softened into a contented smile. "Everything changed last night."

Megan leaned back in the chair. She looked at Artem, really looked at him. This man she assumed was her father. "What did you do to Kevin and Kragnor?"

Artem stiffened, pinching his eyes shut for a moment. "I sold the boy and the beast to Tai Lu."

"What was your price?" Megan narrowed her eyes.

"My freedom." His expression turned smug. "I'm cutting ties with you and Nikolai."

Megan stood from the chair and stared into her father's eyes. "You sold my friends for your freedom?" She ran from the room and went straight to her bedroom, intending to leave Artem.

On the bed was a wrinkled note she didn't notice before. It read, "My life has no meaning." Was it supposed to be a suicide note? Megan remembered the empty bottle of sleeping pills in her sink. She only used thirty of a three-month supply. Did he put the rest in her water bottle? Artem tried to kill her.

Megan pulled the duffle bag from under her bed, filling it with clothes, toiletries from her bathroom, and the photos. She looked around the room and realized her weapons were missing.

"Where do you think you are going?" Artem stood in her doorway.

"Why do you care?" Megan shook the suicide note at him.

Artem shrugged apologetically. "I need a fresh start." His smile reminded her of a lunatic. "I can't have any loose ends." Artem looked down the hall towards the kitchen. "It is a good headache, though, isn't it? Seems I had one the other day." He raised his eyebrows. "You should have stayed asleep." He slammed her bedroom door closed.

Megan frowned at the door. Loose ends? Both she and Nikolai were expendable. Artem's shoes sounded hollow as he walked around the house. He entered the kitchen and then the pantry. The home defense alarm sounded. "Shit." The panic room was the hub of the defensive systems. Megan ran to her window but couldn't stop the metal curtain that dropped and locked in place. Would he release the gas? Not if he planned on escaping.

She moved to the door. The handle turned, but the door was secured from the outside. It wouldn't budge. Megan traced her hand around the trim, checking for an alternate way to open the door. The metal door felt hot near the top. "I don't believe it! He set a goddamn fire!" Megan went to her bathroom, turning on the tap water. Nothing. Opening the reservoir on the back of the toilet, she dumped her towels inside, splashing water on the floor. Megan packed the wet cloth around her bedroom door, trying to keep the smoke out. She needed to buy time to break out of her room.

Megan looked at her bedroom furnishings with fresh eyes. Four wooden posts made up the corners of her bed. They could be used as a battering ram, but they were much too large to hold in her hand and wield like a weapon. On her bedside table was a lamp with a metal stand. She ripped off the lampshade, removed the lightbulb, and hefted the base like a mace. She swung the weighted square end at the wall, smashing into the lath and plaster with the corner. Megan wiggled the stand free and struck the wall again and again. After pulverizing the plaster, she tore at the wooden straps, throwing debris on the floor. She pulled out insulation, revealing the plywood. Two more layers left.

The metal lampstand was bent and on its last legs. She sighed. It was worthless now. Smoke seeped in between the wall and ceiling. The posts attached to her headboard were longer than the footboard. She threw the bed aside and tore the six by six oak post free. Megan slammed the post bottom into the plywood. The plywood flexed and returned the force, sending her sprawling.

Megan stared at her ceiling. Yellow and orange flames coursed at the edges of her room. *I am not going to die like this.* She grabbed the unwieldy post and attacked the plywood again. The muscles in her back and arms expanded and strained under her shirt, stretching the once-baggy clothing. She screamed with the ferociousness of a wild animal. The plywood gave way from the assault, pushing aside the vinyl siding.

At the sight of daylight and the smell of fresh air, Megan grabbed her duffle bag and muscled through the remaining splintered wall. She ran to the boathouse, looking back at her home. Flames leaped from the roof, the eves, and the hole to her bedroom, bursting free where it could. The whine of firetrucks filled the air. She doubted that any part of the house could be saved. Not that it mattered, she was never going back.

Megan entered the boathouse and found what used to be the bugout bag. It was filled with mundane tools. The weapons, money, and ID's were gone. The bags in her car would be destroyed in the fire. Artem had planned this for days, maybe even weeks.

If he didn't need her anymore and tried to kill her, what would he do to Nikolai? She had no money, no weapons, no car, no phone, and Nikolai's gym was on the other side of town. She flung the duffel bag over her shoulder and ran to Kevin's house. It was much closer, and she could find help there.

The door jerked open. Ruby stood there, staring at Megan. "Kevin isn't with you?"

"No," Megan said, her eyes pleading. "I need help finding him." The emotions of the day hit her hard. She cried, blubbering like a child.

"Honey, come inside," Ruby said. Megan dropped her bag on the floor near the door. Ruby guided Megan to the couch. "Sit, I'll get you some tea."

"Wait, do you have a phone I can use?"

Ruby's forehead wrinkled. She reached into her pocket and handed her phone to Megan. "Don't you have one?"

Megan shook her head. "My *father* forbid it."

Tires squealed to a stop, and stomping feet crossed the porch. Johnny opened the door and rushed in. His eyes fell on Megan. He appeared surprised. "Your house is on fire."

Megan nodded, feeling tears weld. She thrust Ruby's phone at Johnny. "Call Nikolai. Tell him Artem might try to kill him too."

Johnny put the phone on the table and used his own. "Nik, you okay? Megan says Artem is on a rampage. No, I don't." He turned to look at Megan. "She looks like shit, but she's safe. You do that. Contact me in seventy-two." He turned off his phone and put it in his pocket. "He's gone under."

Megan dropped to the couch. "Good." Tears of relief flowed, soon replaced with sobs of fear for Kevin and Kragnor.

"Let's give her a minute," Ruby said to Johnny. They disappeared into the kitchen.

The white cat came to her, rubbing on her legs. Megan sniffled, wiped her tears, and reached out to pet him. Rapscallion, she thought she remembered the name. The cat meowed as if confirming. He jumped up onto the couch next to her. He meowed again, demanding pets. Megan obliged, scratching behind ears and under his chin. She smiled as his green eyes studied hers. "You're the most handsome cat I have ever seen," Megan told him. The cat bonked his head against hers. He leaned into the forehead connection as if he could give her his strength.

“Well, now, I have seen everything.” Ruby stood watching, with two cups of tea in her hands. “Talk to me.” She handed Megan a cup.

“I messed up. It was my idea.” Megan blinked back tears and looked around. “I need Johnny to hear this too. I think he can help.”

“Coming, coming.” Johnny came from the kitchen with a cookie sticking out of his mouth and a mug in his hands.

“I don’t know where to begin.” Megan stood and brought her bag to the couch. “I guess this is the place to start.” She gave the photos to Ruby and Johnny. “I was born in Russia. Some small town in Siberia.” Megan shrugged, then sat next to Ruby.

“Artem told me that he worked for the Russian mafia. But there is nothing in these photos, other than a small village and a few people. Nothing to indicate organized crime. Today he told me my mother is the Wolf of Siberia. When I got mad and ran to my room to pack a bag and leave, he barricaded the door and set the house on fire.” Megan grabbed Ruby’s hand. “He sold Kevin and Kragnor to Tai Lu to protect himself from my mother.”

Ruby gasped, dropping her hand.

Megan nodded. “I’m so sorry. I didn’t know this would happen.”

"Is this you?" Johnny held up the weird double-take baby picture.

"I don't know, I think so. That one is my mom." She pointed to the other double-take photo. "I think the camera jammed."

"No, these photos are real. They were taken with a digital camera." Johnny furrowed his brow in thought. "You didn't know?"

"Didn't know what?"

"You know about Russian folklore but not about the Wolf of the Woods."

Megan shrugged. "Should I?"

Johnny opened his mouth to say something, shot a glance at Ruby, then held up his hand. "We can discuss this later. Tell me about the deal your father made."

Megan curled her lip. "Artem didn't explain much of anything. But, when I did an assignment for school, I'm sure I saw Tai Lu's picture in a book about the black market." She looked at Ruby and Johnny but didn't get the response she expected. "I assume he sold Kevin to the black market through Tai Lu."

Ruby gasped. "Oh, for the love of Pete! Whatever for?"

Johnny grabbed Ruby's hand. "China has an extensive black market where elephant tusks, rhino horns, and other animal parts are sold.

Within that market is a more exclusive market, where more exotic items can be found." He rubbed the bridge of his nose.

"Like what?" Megan asked, feeling sick to her stomach.

"Well, that imbued amethyst Annie had could have been sold there. But what the black market is known for are parts of unicorns, dragons, phoenix, and other lesser-known creatures, like gargoyles." He frowned. "Sometimes, the whole animal is sold. As you can imagine, the cost of a dragon is more than most countries make in a year." He squeezed Ruby's hand. "This is where we get our hopes up. Kragnor and by association Kevin, are worth more money alive than dead." He held up his hand, staving off any questions or comments. "However, it would be much easier to transport bits of stone and rock than an argumentative teenager or live gargoyle."

"I feel faint." Ruby waved her hand in front of her face as if to get more air.

Megan studied Johnny. "How do you know about this rare-items black market?"

"It's part of my job. Find objects like Annie's stone to lock up or destroy it."

"What about Kragnor? Should he be locked up or destroyed too?" Megan narrowed her eyes at the older man.

"No. But to be fair, Kragnor's situation is unique. He and Kevin share a body. Once we discover how to separate them, then he'll be released."

"And Kevin?" Ruby asked. "Do you plan on releasing Kevin too?"

"Of course." Johnny looked at Ruby, then held up his hands. "There is a problem with letting Kevin live a normal life now. He'll need protection from people like these Chinese. He'll need a place to go until we figure out how to separate them."

"You would take my grandson from me?" Ruby's eyes flashed.

"Not permanently," Johnny raised both hands in surrender.

Megan stood, drawing attention to herself. "If we don't do something right now, there might not be a Kevin or Kragnor left. You two can bicker about logistics later."

Johnny nodded. "Megan's right." He stood to leave.

"Where are you going?" Ruby asked.

"I need to talk to my supervisor and track Kevin's phone."

"How long will that be?"

"A couple hours." He shrugged. "I'll come back when I have information. Both of you get some sleep." He closed the front door.

Ruby pointed to the bag on the floor. "I suppose you need a place to stay?"

"I have nowhere else to go. Please, just for the night. I'll figure it out tomorrow."

Ruby sighed. "Rapscallion would be upset if I didn't let you stay." The big white tom hit Ruby's shins with his head. "I already said she could stay," she told him.

Rapscallion meowed in his most resonant voice.

Ruby pointed to Megan. "You can feed him. His food is in the pantry. He gets one scoop." She held up her finger. "Don't let him tell you he is starving because that would be a lie." Ruby thumped Rapscallion on his plump belly.

# Chapter 56

"Hello, beautiful." The woman from the night before reached through the bars of the cage, bumping his nose.

Kragnor shook his head and pulled away. "What am I doing here?"

"You are my plaything." The woman held up a rod of stone.

No, it was one of Kragnor's fingers. The gargoyle looked at his hands, but he had all ten. "What kind of magic is this?"

"The best kind. The kind of magic that will make me rich beyond imagination." She rubbed the finger against her bottom lip. "I cut this off, Kevin, earlier today." Tai Lu snickered. "When you were born, you came with all ten. And this one turned to gargoyle, all on its own."

She held the finger close for Kragnor to examine. It looked like his pinky finger, including the claw. The finger was stone, but it was not gargoyle flesh like she thought. It was just as much gargoyle as any human carved statue.

"Do you know what a pangolin is?" She paused. "It is a small creature that eats bugs and ants. It has scales covering its body. The uneducated in my country believe the scales of a pangolin will cure cancer. They pay millions on the black market for powdered scales. Millions. All I have to do is kill a pangolin." She shrugged. "Or pay for a dead one."

"Who would kill a helpless creature for a cure that does not work?" Kragnor snarled.

"How do you know it doesn't work?"

"Your condescending tone and your distaste for your people." The gargoyle shrugged. "You are taking advantage of them in their time of need. You should be helping your people."

She laughed in a mocking tone. "I do help them. I take pride in giving my clients exactly what they want. You should hear what they pay for gargoyle fragments or unicorn horn." Her eyes glowed with greed. "A few hundred times what they pay for pangolin scales." She waved the finger under Kragnor's nose. "This little beauty is worth one million dollars. And if I break it like so…" She snapped the pinky along the biggest joint. "Now, each piece is worth one million."

The gargoyle flinched at the sight of the broken finger. "Why would I care?" Kragnor looked away from her. Why was she telling him these horrible stories?

"I see." She laughed. "The pet doesn't understand." Others in the room joined her laughter. "You and Kevin are my cow."

Kragnor blinked. "Why must you play this game?"

She waved her hand, ignoring his insolence. "Like any cow, I will harvest a bit of Kevin every day. It is so much easier to cut flesh than carve rock. Even if you have the right equipment." She giggled like a little girl. "And when you appear, the bit I harvested will be back, ready to be retaken. And the next day. And the next." She clapped her hands and jumped up and down. "This is an exhilarating day. No longer do I wake an akitu from the stones and harvest their entire body. No, this is easier. No saturating the market."

"You have killed my brothers and sisters?" Kragnor reached for the bars and noticed the damage done to the inside of the cage. Flakes of granite stuck in the concrete as if an akitu was trying to get out.

"Only six of them. No need to panic." She smiled, clearly pleased with herself. "The pain and suffering your people went through was momentary. Even you…you don't feel the pain of the cut. Kevin does."

Kragnor attacked the cage's metal bars, trying to reach through, trying to grab the petite woman before him. He roared with frustration as she was beyond his reach. She told him her plans because she wanted him to suffer, to feel helpless. She hated akitu, but why?

She knew exactly where to stand to avoid the sharp akitu claws. "Now, you understand. Your damnation will be for eternity. I will pass you and Kevin on to my children, and they will reap the rewards. Over and over again!" She laughed, rubbing her hands together as she walked away. "Come on, boys, leave him in peace with his nightmares."

Kragnor heard a slithering approach and passed the cage. Naga. The men from the night before must have had a glamor or magic cast upon them to look human. They turned off the lights as they left the room.

The darkness enveloped him like a comforting blanket. He was inside a building. Two of the corners in the ceiling blinked red. The walls, floor, and ceiling were concrete. Kragnor could not pass through the slurry of sand and pebble. The doorway the men went through was small and narrow, and it lacked a door. It was so little that they had to shimmy to slide out. He would not fit.

The woman knew akitu, knew their strengths and weaknesses. He growled, feeling like this battle was already lost. *I always had time, but not anymore. Every day, bits of Kevin would be cut away. Every day Kevin would suffer.* Akitu were protectors, but he could do nothing to protect the young man who shared his body. He shook with anger and frustration.

Kragnor growled and punched the concrete and steel of his cell. His tail whipped around, striking the bars. Despite the evidence of the previous residence attacking the cage to no avail, he tried pushing and pulling, but nothing gave. Every corner was solid. Only the door shuttered and twisted when he struck it. Kragnor huffed. The door was too small for him to escape, but Kevin could. If Kevin escaped, so would he.

He dug at the hinges and lock plate, trying to find a weakness. The tip of his nail broke, but still, he persisted.

Kragnor didn't know how long he worked on the metal. But he noticed when he felt Kevin trying to come through. He grunted. Perhaps he could save Kevin by not sharing the body.

He gathered his mind and meditated, trying to hold off the human emergence. He hummed and focused, but he knew he couldn’t hold Kevin at bay forever.

# Chapter 57

"Get Mistress, he's back." One of the snake-men hissed.

A beautiful woman in a white dress disappeared out the door. Kevin wondered if she was a person, or something else, like the snake-men.

His clothes were torn and bloodied, resting on the floor. He forgot to take them off when he turned. He couldn't remember what he was thinking between the pain and fear.

*The pain.* He looked at his hands. His pinky returned, and the pain was reduced to an ache. Kevin made a fist and splayed his fingers. The finger responded as if it was never missing. His stomach rolled as he thought about Tai Lu's delight while cutting it off.

The sounds of feet running made him look up. "Excellent," Tai Lu purred from her side of the cage. "When I saw your gargoyle had all ten fingers, I assumed you would also." She threw a glare at the woman. "Someone told me I should not celebrate until you returned with ten, and the separated finger remained gargoyle." Tai Lu turned away from Kevin and faced the woman. "Happy now, Candali?" She sucked air between her teeth.

The woman bowed to her. "Do you wish to remove all of them today, Mistress?"

Kevin whimpered and backed into a corner away from the woman. He looked at his hands and cried. *All my fingers?* The pain would be unbearable.

"No," Tai Lu said.

"Yes, Mistress." The woman bowed to Tai Lu.

Kevin sighed in relief and sat on the floor of his cage.

"I want his arm." Tai Lu laughed with excitement.

Keven hugged his legs close to his chest. This woman was crazy. "Why?" He yelled at Tai Lu. "Aren't my fingers enough?"

"I'm trying to find your limitations, Kevin. Tomorrow, we try a leg." She smiled sweetly at him.

"Mistress, we can't cut off his arm. He'll bleed out." Candali bowed and stepped back as if expecting Tai Lu to hit her.

"I am not stupid."

"No, Mistress, I never said that, Mistress." Candali continued to bow. "I merely suggest surgery so that we can control the blood loss."

"Prep him and bring him to level three. I do not want my pet to die." Tai Lu slapped the other woman. "Do I make myself clear?"

"Yes, Mistress," Candali said with a bloody lip. "I'll not let your pet die."

Tai Lu stepped away from the woman. "And Candali?"

"Yes, Mistress?"

"If his arm doesn't regenerate, I'll remove yours, without the benefit of surgery."

"Yes, Mistress." Candali's eyes flashed.

"There's a good kitty." Tai Lu turned away from the woman in white and left the room.

A few minutes passed before Candali moved. "I hate her! I wish she were dead! She doesn't deserve to breathe!" The woman screamed with rage, took a few deep breaths, and then approached a snake-man. "Do you have the keys?"

The man grasped his belt and took off a ring of keys. Kevin blinked then looked again. The snake-man had a belt and a bandolier with bullets crisscrossing his chest.

Candali unlocked the top lock. She looked like a beautiful dark-haired woman, but he had his doubts. He focused and noticed a slight haze around her.

"You're letting him out of the cage?"

"Hello? The bitch wants the boy's arm. How do you propose I do that without taking him out of the cage?" Candali crossed her arms. "Well, I'm waiting."

"He could escape."

Candali laughed. "You can't be serious. There are nine naga in this room alone. You all have weapons and skills he couldn't imagine. And there's me, of course. He is so inexperienced. He smells green."

"Hey!" Kevin blinked and took an inadvertent step forward.

"See." Candali pointed. "He doesn't know when to shut up. Green." She continued with the three other locks and opened the cage door. "So, what do you say, Kevin? Are you willing to work with us?"

"Why should I?" Kevin smashed his back into a corner.

"You're right. You don't have to cooperate." She shrugged. "But see those naga behind you? They will force you to comply. Or hit you with enough amps to knock you out, and then we will do what Tai Lu instructs."

Kevin came to that conclusion yesterday. He stood, then quickly squatted again. “Um, I’m naked.” He pointed to his torn clothing on the floor.

“Do you see any pants on the naga? Currently, they are naked too.” Candali raised her eyebrows. “They do not care.”

“What about you?”

“I am not human. The form I currently have is one you gave me.”

“What? How could I give you your appearance?”

The snake-men hissed with laughter. The word *green* seemed to pass among them.

“To encourage others, it is to my advantage to look pleasing.” Candali pointed to the nearest naga. “To Chen here, I’m an engorged female probably with red scales to show fertility. To you, I’m a beautiful young human female in the prime of my life.” She reached into the cage with her hand. “I don’t care if you’re naked. Come.”

Kevin reached up and took her hand. Once outside the cage, he pulled his hand back and stared. “How did you do that?”

“You chose to follow me. Can you go one more step and give me your arm?” She indicated the naga who wore weapons on their backs and hips. “Or do you need encouragement?”

Kevin studied her face, panic in his heart. “I thought this was going to be surgery.”

“It is, but I need to put a drug into your vein.”

“To put me to sleep and for pain?”

“Exactly.” She held out her hand.

Kevin swallowed and placed his right arm into her grasp. She looked at the veins in his inner elbow, pulled a syringe out of her pocket, bit the cap off, and pushed the needle into his flesh. The needle flexed and broke. “Well, that makes things complicated. Where did she cut off your finger?”

Kevin showed her his left pinky, pointing at the joint where the finger attached to his hand.

“Did she pop the joint, or did she cut flesh and bone?” Candali seemed to purr as she smiled.

He looked at her and blinked fast. “I, I don’t know. I was terrified and in pain.”

“You need to pay attention, Kevin. It could save your life.” She bopped him on the nose.

Kevin frowned and studied her. Was she trying to tell him something?

“I’ll need to gas him.” She looked at the nearest naga. “Find the Nitrous Oxide in the medical supplies. And bring a gurney too. Unless someone wants to carry him to level three."

The naga grumbled among themselves. Then two disappeared out the small door.

Kevin turned to the beautiful woman in white. "I've had Nitrous before. It's not meant…"

Candali placed a finger on his lips. "Don't worry, your pretty little head over this." She smiled and brushed the hair off his forehead. "Did you know Tai Lu has her personal quarters on the fourth level? Just one level away from your surgery." Her eyes narrowed in emphasis.

The naga returned. "The gurney won't fit through the door." They thrust the nitrous oxide into Candali's hands. "Give him the gas here."

Candali nodded, then winked at Kevin. She turned on the gas and placed the respirator over his mouth and nose. Kevin inhaled some of the gas, then instinctively, he stopped breathing altogether. His body responded the same way when he fell into the pond. Candali closed her eyes slowly.

Kevin followed her cue and feigned sleep. *How did she know this would happen?* After a few minutes, strong arms picked him up and moved him to a soft surface, probably the gurney. He felt movement and the hissing-talk of the naga around him. He couldn't escape now. The naga would overpower and recapture him.

They took him into an elevator, down a hallway, and into a much larger area that echoed. The naga slithered away. Kevin opened his eyes slightly and looked through his lashes. Four people, wearing blue, milled about the room.

Someone in a chair rolled near his head. That made five. The person in the chair reached for Kevin's neck, resting two fingers. "I'm not getting a pulse," said a masculine voice.

A cold stethoscope touched his chest. "I've got one. It's slow," said a female. The stethoscope moved along the side of his ribs. "But he's not breathing." There was a slight ring of panic in her voice.

"What did those naga do to him?"

"Who cares? We'll be punished."

There were sounds of scrambling and equipment moving along the floor. Kevin panicked. He didn't want anything cut off or things put places they didn't need to be. He ripped the respirator off and sat up.

Everyone stopped what they were doing and stared.

Double swinging doors faced the foot of the gurney. Medical equipment was scattered around, in the process of being moved. He turned to look behind him. The anesthesiologist stood and stepped away.

There was another door.

"Guards! Guards!"

Kevin swung his legs off the gurney. A steady hand grabbed his arm, holding him still. "Sorry, son." A syringe hit his arm, and the needle deflected. The fluid inside squirted onto the floor. "Shit!" The man released Kevin, dropped the syringe, and backed away.

Kevin dropped from the gurney and ran out the side door. The double doors slammed open, and the hissing snarls of the naga urged Kevin to move faster. Beyond the door was an examining room. He shoved the large table against the door, hoping to keep the naga out. He continued through the next door into a hallway.

There were shouts to his right. A man in a guard uniform leveled a gun at him and fired. A bullet zipped past. He ran to the left to the next door, but it was locked. The gun fired again, and burning heat exploded on his thigh. Fear drove him through the hollow core door. Kevin landed on the floor and looked at his leg. There was a round wound that dripped blood. Underneath was a purple circle. The bullet didn't appear to penetrate his muscle.

He was in an office, behind the desk, a window let in the afternoon light. Shouts and running feet came down the hall. Kevin went to the window, opened it, and climbed out onto the small ledge. Below the window was a line of rolled concertina wire atop a fence. Above him appeared to be a balcony. Kevin reached up and grabbed the floor. He heaved and climbed over the metal railing.

Kevin leaned against a wall, out of sight of the office window. His leg stopped bleeding, and the pain lessened. The surface of the wound had already scabbed over, like a rug burn. *Am I bulletproof?*

The door leading onto the balcony was partially open. Kevin slipped inside. A case sat on a coffee table and a long black leather jacket laid over the back of the white couch. He narrowed his eyes. *Was that the case with the stones inside?* He clicked the latches and flipped open the lid. The stones drew him in as if they had cast a spell. He closed the cover and smiled.

Did Candali tell him about Tai Lu's apartment so that he might take the case of stones? Or something more sinister? The woman wanted Tai Lu dead.

Kevin grabbed the jacket and put it on. There had to be more windows in the apartment, maybe another balcony. If he could escape the building and wait until night, then Kragnor could fly them home. The living room had a huge bay window with a view of the Chicago skyline, but it couldn't open. Kevin thought he saw a Play Station and Xbox under a television that covered a wall.

Down a hallway, he found a bathroom and a bedroom. The bedroom had a set of katana blades, a bastard sword, and a mace hanging on the walls.

The front door flew open, striking the wall. "No, I'm not letting those dirty naga into my home. Yes, I see. He came in through the balcony." Tai Lu screamed with rage. "That bastard took my stones and my jacket! No, I don't need help. This is the fourth floor. He can't go anywhere."

He quietly closed the bedroom door, shoving a chair under the handle. He tried the window, but it wouldn't open. Kevin rolled his eyes. On the dresser were numerous mythology books, held in place with crystalline bookends.

The katana blades looked menacing, but he didn't know how to use them. Odds were high that Tai Lu had a gun or other stunning device. Kevin thought about the cattle prods the naga had. He shook his head, the decision made, and tossed a bookend through the window.

Feet pounded down the hallway. "Kevin, darling, what are you doing?" She rattled the doorknob.

He picked up the other bookend and rubbed it on the window's edge to remove all the broken pieces.

"We are on the fourth floor. You'll die if you jump." The door creaked as if she were leaning or pushing on it.

Kevin put his legs out the window, sitting precariously on the edge, case of stones in his lap. "Are you worried about Kevin or your investment?" he snarled.

"Damn it!" She shot into the door, trying to break in.

The ground below Kevin's bare feet was cement. He thought about his new-found athletic skills, running, holding his breath, the needle breaking, and the bullet failing to penetrate his flesh. He closed his eyes, took a deep breath, and jumped.

# Chapter 58

Johnny knocked on the door, waking Ruby from her chair and Megan from the couch. Megan slept in her clothes, only taking off her shoes. Ruby launch herself to the door, flinging it open.

Johnny stepped into the living room. "Megan, we need to go."

Megan touched her chest. "Me?"

"You, and if you have any weapons, bring them." Johnny waved her toward the door. "Come on, we don't have time to dilly dally."

"Dilly-dally? Seriously Johnny?" Ruby tapped her foot.

"I'm always serious." He looked at Ruby then Megan. "If you want to save your friends, you need to move now." He turned and left the house.

"Gimme a second," Megan complained, rubbing the sleep from her eyes. She stopped long enough to take her shoes.

"Bring Kevin back!" Ruby hollered at them from the porch.

Megan opened the passenger door of the Honda Civic and jumped in. The bright colors of the sunrise made the eastern horizon glow. She shot a glance at Johnny. “You were gone most of the night?”

He revved the car and took off. “I had a lot to report.”

“Did you find Kevin’s phone?”

“No, it was turned off, or it's out of power. But we did find its last location.” Johnny turned down a side street and headed toward I-90-39 to Chicago.

“That seems like it wouldn’t have taken that long.”

“It didn’t. The longest part of my report was you.”

“Me?”

Johnny nodded. “The Wolf of Siberia is a mythical deity. She lures poachers by seducing them with her womanly ways. Then changes form into a wolf, gigantic in size, and kills them. She loves nature and protects what she loves.”

“She is supposed to be my mother. Does that mean my father is delusional?”

Johnny sighed. “No, he’s not delusional. I’ve had my suspicions that you were witchy. Whether you knew it or not was another story. You might think being a demi is unusual, but not in my line of work. In fact, I would dare say it's normal. I suppose some of my equipment brings the unusual to me." Johnny jerked his thumb over his shoulder, indicating some items in the back seat.

"What? Demi? As in demi-god?" Megan swallowed. "I just woke up. And you're going to throw that kind of information at me and expect that I understand?" She shook her head, imagining the feats of Hercules. He knew he was half god. His strength made it obvious for anyone to see. "I'm just a girl. There's nothing special about me."

"That's your upbringing. You were raised human, and no one treated you special. It's expected that you don't know or believe." Johnny raised his index finger off the steering wheel. "Well, that isn't one hundred percent true. Nikolai treated you special. I talked to him a few weeks ago, he told me about one of his students. He was always impressed by this person, but Nikolai refused to give me a name. When my job brought me into town, I took the opportunity to stop by his gym. I figured I could find the special student he bragged about. That was the night you saw me and bolted."

Megan laughed. “I saw you the evening before on the street. I thought you were stalking me.”

“I was. Sort of.” Johnny shrugged. “I was looking for magic sources, expecting to find one in all of Avalon. I found three distinct sites. And a few others that were weaker.”

Megan closed her eyes. “For the sake of argument, what if my mother is the Wolf of Siberia? Why would my father hide it from me and make me think she was dead?”

“The Wolf is a protector with supernatural abilities. If he told you that he is your father and your mother was killed by the Russian Mafia, you would protect him as no other person could, especially from the Russian Mafia. Demons could not defeat you. You’re the perfect shield.”

“He *did* convince me that he was my father.” Megan turned to look out the window. “But now, I doubt everything.”

“Good, you should doubt. That’s healthy. Believe with your eyes, heart, and mind. Don’t take anyone’s word.”

“All right, let’s say I am the daughter of the Wolf. Why would you talk to your superiors about me?”

"First, I needed authorization to bring a civilian into a potential fight with Chinese Nationals. Second, I wanted to offer you a job."

"A job?"

"Kevin and Kragnor will need protection. You seem to care for them, so it's a perfect fit. You're also a guardian of the forest. By your very nature, you'll sense special animals and objects. You're a divining rod for the supernatural. Your skills, even untapped, are exactly what this company needs."

"You're crazy!" Megan folded her arms across her chest.

"Am I? Didn't you sense danger before Bonnie left her house? You knew who was going to attack and warned her."

"She didn't listen."

"Irrelevant. You may not have known how you knew, but you acted upon it. You also knew I was *stalking* you. You sensed it."

Megan sat in silence. She broke the hold the man had on her and killed him. She pulled that from somewhere, too. Megan also knew Annie was *off*. She frowned. Was she making something out of nothing? Would she have seen that man because Nikolai taught her to be suspicious? Or did Nikolai capitalize on her awareness and taught her to pay attention? He taught her how to focus and use more than her senses.

She stared out the window watching the buildings become more abundant and the traffic heavier. They'd be in downtown Chicago soon. Mentally she marked the museum as north of their current location, ten or fifteen blocks.

"This is where we figured Kevin's phone was last active."

All the street parking was taken. Garbage skittered along the gutters pushed by the wind. "How do you propose to find it in this mess?"

"I'm not. You are." Johnny smiled at her.

"You're serious?"

"All you need to do is focus. Focus on Kevin and Kragnor. Focus on their smell or their appearance. Whatever you need to feel their essence."

"Essence?" Megan raised her eyebrows.

Johnny nodded. "Do you want to find them or not?"

"Of course, I do."

"Get out of the car, breathe in the air, extend your feelings and focus. Trust your skills. Believe in yourself. I'll drive around the block. There's no parking here."

She held up her hands in surrender. "All right. I'll give this a shot." Johnny slowed the car, and Megan stepped out. She tried to focus on the cologne Kevin wore but couldn't bring it to mind. Her brain kept flitting to Kragnor's rough skin and his earthy smell, like a rotten log or freshly turned boulder. She felt a tug, like the directional pull of a magnet.

She remembered using the same technique to find her lost keys. The distraction caused the pull to waver. She sighed, then refocused on Kragnor. There, down the street, at the corner, under that car. She checked the traffic and ran. The phone was near the back tire, its glass face smashed. The protective cover was still attached; it had the Celtic knot design.

The Honda Civic double-parked. "Get in." Johnny stopped traffic. Megan looked at the angry drivers behind him, opened the back door, and climbed in.

"Is it his?" Johnny asked.

"I think so. The case looks like Kevin's, but it's smashed."

"How do you feel about your skills now?" Johnny asked smugly as he drove forward to appease the other drivers.

"Wiseguy." Megan shot back. She felt pride in finding the phone. "Now what?"

"You found the phone. You know you have the skills. Now apply that knowledge, find

Kevin and Kragnor. You have the phone. You can use it to focus on."

Megan frowned. A phone was one thing but a person? She turned the phone over, tracing the design on the back with her finger. She wafted the phone, catching a slight musky odor. "What if this isn't Kevin's phone?"

"Let me get this straight. You focused on Kevin and Kragnor, and that focus brought you to that phone. Which looks like Kevin's, but now you think it might be someone else's. Are you serious? Do you know what the odds are against that?" Johnny sighed, then drummed his fingers on the steering wheel. "Okay, I understand. I told you a lot today. You need to process. Let's get some lunch."

Megan's stomach twisted. Kevin and Kragnor could be hurt or dying. "Lunch? No, I'll eat tomorrow." She climbed over the seats into the front, buckled, then closed her eyes, and pointed. "Go that way."

# Chapter 59

Kevin landed on the cement, rolling into a summersault. A spider web of cracks marked where he fell. The case was open, and on the ground, two recessed cavities were empty. He closed the lid and pocketed the stones that bounced out.

After looking out Tai Lu's bay window, Kevin knew which direction would lead to Chicago. If he followed that route, he might find people and help. Kevin jogged, his bare feet slapping the concrete. He pulled the jacket around him as a cold wind whipped off Lake Michigan.

A large building blocked his path. Its thin metal walls were worn and rusted. He jogged around it and found another building and a tall fence hindering his progress. There would be no straight line to downtown Chicago. He turned back the way he came, only to see eight men in suits and Tai Lu. The men glistened, like a mirage. Kevin thought he saw a hint of green.

Naga.

He glanced at the building. A door stood slightly ajar. Next to it was a broken window. Jumping through the window would be faster than opening the door. Kevin squinted at his options, not pleased with either.

"Give me the stones, and I'll let you go, peacefully," Tai Lu shouted.

"Bull shit," he muttered under his breath. He looked at the case. If he tossed it in the opposite direction from the door, he could buy time, but he couldn't do it. The stones were too valuable. Kevin darted toward the building.

Tai Lu screamed unintelligible orders, and bullets zipped past Kevin's head.

He leaped at the window, using his shoulder to finish taking out the glass. Kevin landed, sprawled on the garbage-covered floor. He scrambled to his feet and ran away from the door, knowing the naga would charge through at any moment. Cars and trucks in various levels of disrepair and dismantle filled the warehouse. Everything appeared to be covered in fifty years of dust and grime. Was that an airplane engine?

Kevin weaved around an old tanker when he heard gunfire and a couple of ricochets. He felt a massive blow against his back and a hot burning between his shoulders. Kevin stumbled but kept to his feet and moved faster. Reaching up and back, he touched a hole in the jacket. His fingers returned, covered in blood. He wiggled his shoulders and was surprised by the lack of agonizing pain. Kevin hurdled the next car in his path, not wanting to slow and weave around. The case struck his leg when he landed and popped open. The stones vibrated in their compartments but didn't bounce out. He reached for the lid and slammed it home.

An open overhead door beckoned at the end of the building. Beyond looked like a train yard. He willed his feet and body to move faster. Some of the tracks had cars and engines sitting on them. He followed a set of tracks that appeared to lead in the right direction. As he ran, he placed his feet on the wooden ties. The subgrade rocks looked like sharp pieces of flint. Even though his body seemed bullet resistant, he was unwilling to try the stones against the soles of his feet.

*Stones!* While running, Kevin opened the case, and one by one dropped a protection stone between the ties. The shadows thrown by the massive wooden beams hid the round among the pointed. He closed the case and continued running. The track he followed split into two. One way went back into the abandoned buildings, the other over an arched metal truss toward a lakefront factory. Kevin chose the bridge.

The closer he came to the bridge, the more exposed he felt. There was no cover, no buildings, no train cars, nothing. He heard the zip of a bullet pass, followed by the echoing bang. He'd played enough war video games to know that he was being shot at by a sniper. He was out in the open, a prime target.

Kevin tossed the case toward the bridge and ran down the sharp rocky slope of the embankment. He slipped and tumbled to a stop. He took a couple of moments to catch his breath, then he stood.

Was that a car?

He ran toward the sound and found a road, but the car was long gone. He trotted on the blacktop, headed toward Chicago, or so he hoped. A tall chain-link fence rose to his right.

The sun was setting; Kragnor would appear soon. It was almost over.

He heard a car headed in his direction. It squealed around the corner and stopped. The window of the ugly tan AKG vehicle came down. "Get in."

"Johnny?"

"Hurry!" Shouted Megan.

"Megan?" He had never been so happy to see the ugly car in his life. Kevin ran to the vehicle, opened the door, and dove in the back seat.

Megan looked back at him. "You look like hell. Are you okay?" She gasped. "Are you naked? Again?"

"I've got a jacket." Kevin straightened the front making sure his lap was covered. The jacket was not designed for a man. It was too high in the waist, a problem that was evident while sitting. "Tai Lu wanted to cut parts of me off to sell on the black market. There's a huge market for gargoyle parts. She implied that your father…"

"He is not my father. He betrayed me, you, and Kragnor." Megan growled. "If I ever see him again, I'll kill him myself. He sold you to gain protection from the Russian Mafia, among other things." She grunted. "Now that you're not in Tai Lu's hands, he won't be protected."

Kevin narrowed his eyes. He wasn't happy with Artem either, but something else must have happened for Megan to be this upset.

"Shit. Another dead end." Johnny spun the car around, speeding back the way they came.

"Don't you know where we are?" Kevin looked out the window.

"No, Megan got us to you more or less by scent. Getting back out of this mess seems to be more difficult than I expected."

"By scent?" Kevin looked at Megan. "What?"

"I'm a Wolf of the Woods." She shrugged. "Actually, my mother is."

"Wolf of the Woods? I read about that in one of the books on werewolves. Remember that day? When you gave me crap about lycanthrope?" Kevin laughed. "You're a werewolf."

"Shut up, Kevin, don't make me give you back to Tai Lu." Megan looked over the seat with mirth in her narrowed eyes.

"I'm serious. The book said a Wolf of the Woods could turn from a beautiful woman to a wolf at will."

"That's good to know if it's right," Jonny commented. "Would you two pay attention and help me get out of this stupid maze? It's starting to get dark, and I don't want to spend the night here."

"Why not just go back the way you came?" Keven suggested.

"Because getting here wasn't a direct route, and nothing looks the same going backward," Johnny said.

“There, I didn’t see that road.” Megan pointed.

Kevin looked out the window. The area looked hazy. “That’s a glamor.” But it was too late. A building rose before them, blocking the path. Johnny turned the car around. But the road out was gone.

Bullets ricocheted off the ground on Johnny’s side. “Get out!” He pushed Megan toward her door. “Use the car as a shield.”

Kevin climbed out of the car naked, leaving the jacket behind. A bullet struck his shoulder with enough force to push him into the car. He fell forward onto his hands and knees. *If Tai Lu is right, I need to will Kragnor to come now.* He took a deep breath and mentally screamed Kragnor’s name.

Pain exploded from every extremity. Either he was dying, or Kragnor heard the call.

# Chapter 60

The door slammed. Megan turned and saw the empty back seat, except for the long black jacket. She looked around and saw Kevin's pale flesh as he fell to the ground. Kragnor tore his way out of Kevin. It appeared as if the gargoyle exploded forth, and Kevin was no more.

Bullets bounced off Kragnor and struck the car, tearing at the metal on the driver's side with a squeal. "What can we do?"

"Fight back." Johnny leaned over the seat and gave Megan a long thick roll of fabric. The cloth fell away, exposing two long curved blades. "Nikolai said you're good with a blade. These are treated with gold, silver, and platinum to give certain creatures a quick and final death. They'll dispatch a normal human too, so watch where you swing them."

"What are you going to use?"

Johnny held up two pistols. "Don't worry about me. I'm quicker than I appear. Go!" He shoved Megan out the passenger door. "Focus!

Become the wolf!" He crawled toward her, intending to come out her door.

Kragnor landed in front of them, wings outstretched. Bullets ricocheted off the car. Some struck the gargoyle with enough force to create chips and gouges.

"Stop them," Megan said.

"I am a teacher, not a killer," Kragnor grumbled.

"They killed your people," Megan said. "They have every intention to kill me, Johnny, Kevin, and you. You are a protector and sentinel, not just a teacher. Those titles require fighting. But fighting doesn't require killing." Megan licked her lips, remembering who Kragnor thought he looked like and smiled. "Batman doesn't kill."

Kragnor huffed, his brow knitted. "You are right. Batman does not kill. Stay low; I will remove the threat." He stood tall, wings open, moving toward the gunfire.

Megan peered over the car hood, waiting for bullets to sound off since she showed herself. Nothing, other than the sounds of shouts in the distance. Was that metal twisting? Megan turned and looked at the old factory face of the building. She stood between building and car. Someone could sneak up on them from the building, and they wouldn't know. Glass crunched under someone's foot. Megan focused. *Become the wolf.* More sound came from the building, but lighter, like paw pads on cement.

Her lip curled. She felt more than heard a growl come from her throat. Megan followed the sound of paw pads with her eyes. Johnny finished sliding out the door, putting his back toward her. She felt and heard Johnny move around but didn't turn or look. She was confident of his movements. Megan sniffed the air, sensing Kragnor, even though he was a few buildings away. She glanced at her arms, surprised to see human flesh, not fur. Wasn't she supposed to turn into a giant wolf?

More sounds came from the building, but it was difficult to determine what made the noise. Felines appeared in Megan's mind. Something bigger than a house cat and more than one. The sounds came closer. She shook the blades free from the fabric. Two white cats slipped out of a hole in the building. They walked shoulder to shoulder, tails held high above their head. Four tails, but two cats. Was that all she sensed? Cats? Was she hypersensitive because of her canine heritage? Megan frowned. They didn't feel like ordinary cats, regardless of what they looked like.

“Cats,” she hissed to Johnny.

Johnny peered over her shoulder. “Not cats, nekomatas.”

“What is Neko-whatever?”

“Cat demon. They will try to seduce you then suck your spirit.”

“Shoot them.”

“Bullets don’t hurt them. You have to kill them with your blades. Prepare. Be one with the wolf.”

The cats transformed into beautiful men, wearing finely fitted white clothing. “Hello, Megan,” they said together, harmoniously.

She stared at them. So beautiful. The scent of cinnamon wafted from them, her favorite fall time smell.

“Come to us, Megan. We can make all your fantasies become a reality.” They talked in unison with slightly different tones, making their voices musical, beautiful, sensual.

She walked forward to be with them. *What are these swords doing in my hands?* She dropped them. The clattering of steel on cement was barely audible. Nagging in the back of her mind made her look back.

Johnny was waving his hands, screaming at her, terror written on his face. “Go to them, Megan. They will love you forever.”

Johnny seemed to think it was safe. Megan turned back and allowed the men to take her in their arms. She was immediately at ease; these men were nothing like her father. They would never betray her. With these men, she could finally be happy. They loved her.

A hot ripping sensation cut into her upper thigh, which caused her vision and thoughts to clear. The men didn't appear as fanciful as before. They leaned over her, holding her hands and sniffing her skin. Megan ripped her hands free. The men hissed at her in anger and tried to grab her.

Megan rolled away from them, toward Johnny. The movement caused the wound to pulse and scream. The men called her name, sounding melodious with their two-part harmony.

A sword skittered toward her, bouncing off her hand. She gripped the hilt and swung the weapon at the beautiful men, holding them off. Their glamor shimmered and broke, revealing white domestic cats. The cats hissed and ran into the abandoned factory.

Johnny walked, staggering, to Megan. "It would be ideal if we could catch them before they cause havoc in Chicago." He laughed.

"Aw, hell, who cares? It's Chicago. No one will even notice." Johnny giggled and snorted

Megan smelled the freshly spent gunpowder. "I can't believe you shot me!"

"It's just a scratch." He covered his mouth with his hand, his eyes wide with delight. "I had to do something before you offered to have children with those cats. Uh, men. Pain seems to be the best way to redirect thought. Especially thought that is coerced. Sometimes it works when the subject is possessed." He hiccupped.

"Possessed?" Megan stared at Johnny. "What the hell have I gotten into?"

Johnny smiled slyly, waving his hands. "The mysteries of the universe."

"Tell me, Johnny, what did those cats look like to you?"

He grinned. "Beautiful red-haired women." Johnny twirled his guns. "They had sinewy muscle, lean, and long. Flexible." He wagged his eyebrows and whistled a catcall.

"Are you drunk?"

"That's the side effect of a nekomata. It helps control their prey." His eyes rolled, and he fell into a seated position. "But there were two of them, so it's much, much stronger."

"Why didn't I get drunk? I was closer."

"You're not human." Johnny chuckled again. "Give me a few minutes; it'll wear off. Unless you have some coffee in your pockets?" He snorted at the absurdity of the idea. "Or chocolate?"

"Why weren't you seduced like I was?" Megan asked.

"I've got a charm against manipulation." Johnny pulled an array of necklaces out of his shirt.

"But it doesn't protect against the drunk feeling."

"Nope," he said, shaking his head clumsily. "It would be a lie to say I wanted a charm to protect me from the drunken effects." He laughed, then frowned. "Aw, it's going away." His bottom lip protruded in a fierce pout.

"Is it always like this?"

Johnny blinked, not understanding.

"How many creatures are out there? How many charms? Side effects? Death? How do I prepare for something when I know nothing?"

Johnny placed his hand on Megan's arm. "We all started like you, totally ignorant. We learned and adapted. You have an advantage; you have the blood of the wolf."

"Funny. It didn't feel like an advantage when the nekomata were draining me of spirit."

Megan thought for a minute. “What does that mean anyway? Spirit? Is that the same as a soul?”

Johnny shrugged. “Probably.”

“We ought to be helping Kragnor,” Megan said, feeling guilty for not doing something sooner. It seemed as if night had fallen entirely while she was distracted by the nekomatas. “How long has he been gone?”

Johnny shrugged. “Can you find him?”

Megan focused and then pointed. Her senses, dulled by the nekomata, seemed to be working again.

“Help me up.” He thrust out his hand.

Megan heaved, then let Johnny lean on her for support. She picked up the remaining sword. Together they walked toward the car.

# Chapter 61

After Kragnor left Megan behind, he launched into the sky, knowing the attackers were above him. He didn't know Kevin. They never met, but he knew Megan; he would protect her. He would fight for her and for the akitu in the stones.

Metal struck his horn, driving his head downward. Kragnor flew higher, pleased to draw their attention away from his friend. He calculated where the shooters were and sped towards them. The metal projectiles came from a building that was covered in scaffolding. The arm of a crane swayed above the building.

Kragnor landed on the rooftop. Two men standing on a platform behind a metal wall greeted him with fast-flying projectiles. Kragnor stepped toward them, wings wide, keeping their attention on him. As he approached, other men and weapons appeared, shooting the gargoyle from behind. Kragnor stopped, confused as to which way he should go. Who should he disable first?

"Now!" Shouted a voice.

A bulky metal net fell from the overhead crane and dropped onto Kragnor. His knees buckled under the immense weight. Squatting, Kragnor adjusted the chain mesh, sitting back into his powerful tail and pulling his feet under his body.

"No point in struggling that net weighs…well, more than you can move." The men from the tower slithered toward Kragnor. Where legs should have been were muscular coils. Yellow and green scales glinted in the moonlight. They carried metal throwers on the shoulders, looking pleased with themselves.

Naga were creatures known the world over for their archery skills. It made sense that they used metal throwers. Two more green and yellow naga joined the first pair.

"See, I told you the net would work. Once an akitu is trapped, they never fight." The naga then turned to Kragnor. "Isn't that right?"

The gargoyle flexed his legs and tail, noticing most of the net's weight was now on the roof, not on his head and shoulders. Plus, the net was not as heavy as the naga claimed. He stopped moving and looked at the men. "What are your plans when the akitu are gone, and Tai Lu starts harvesting naga scales?" The men flinched as if the thought wasn't new.

"Don't listen to him." A feminine-shaped gargoyle stepped out of the darkness, but she wasn't akitu. She was something different, something dangerous.

Kragnor sniffed the air, catching feline ambrosia. "Nekomata, you are not immune either. Tai Lu will come after your kind too."

The female gargoyle smiled. "I don't care. It's been worth it. The souls of akitu are ancient and powerful, worth everything I've done." She snarled. "Everything!" She licked her lips. The nekomata moved closer to Kragnor, inhaling the gargoyle's scent, then shuddered. "So tasty."

"Enough. Naughty kitty." Tai Lu came into view. "I told you we are not killing this one. You will protect him." She stared down the female gargoyle until it turned into a white cat with two tails. The woman spun and looked at Kragnor. "Where are my stones?"

She lost the stones. How? Kragnor smiled. Kevin. "What a shame. You cannot kill more of my people."

The woman shrugged. "Perhaps not those specific akitu, but I know where there are more."

Kragnor stiffened. She would never stop. "Even if I gave Kevin and myself to you, to cut and sell for eternity?"

The woman picked her way across the tangled metal net and came close to Kragnor, tapping her bottom lip. “If I had an unlimited source of akitu parts. I might stop hunting the ones that are out there.” Her eyes sparkled with mirth and lies.

Kragnor felt his anger rise. This woman and others like her had done all they could to eradicate life for their own benefit. He was on this planet long before her kind showed up. Why did she think she had the right to destroy what she did not create? The insolence and the absurdity that not one akitu stopped her. Are we not protectors? “What then, Tai Lu? What creature would you hunt? Who has the most expensive parts? Dragons? Unicorn? Kraken?” Kragnor shot a glance at the men. “Naga?”

Startled, the men slithered away from Tai Lu and off the metal net. Kragnor’s hand shot through the netting, catching Tai Lu’s throat. He didn’t squeeze or choke but merely held her captive. She grasped his wrist, dangling, and supporting her body weight.

The men shook their tails and leveled their metal throwers at the gargoyle.

“Idiots, if you shoot him, you will only hit me. Besides, he won’t hurt me. Akitu have never hurt me, no matter what I did to them.”

Tai Lu smiled at Kragnor as if he were an unruly child. "What are your plans? Do you think you can hold me here, infinitely?"

She was right. Kevin would appear in a handful of hours, and his grip now would mean nothing. If he were complete, he could hold her until she starved. Although he doubted his fortitude. She would convince him to let go sooner or later. Kragnor dropped his arm until Tai Lu's feet touched the ground. "I must do what others of my kind will not." The men lowered their weapons. Kragnor tossed Tai Lu high into the air towards the edge of the building.

Tai Lu screamed, "Candali!" The white cat jumped, transformed into the female gargoyle, and flew toward the plummeting woman.

With no direction, the naga stood dumbfounded. Kragnor reached down and heaved the chain net off himself and onto the snake-men. Naga curses and random gunfire were thrown at him as he ran to the edge of the roof and jumped. Kragnor deployed his wings and searched for Tai Lu and Candali.

The female gargoyle held Tai Lu with both arms but struggled to maintain lift. The woman wiggled and screamed with fear.

"Let me take her. You are a nekomata your strength in the form of an akitu is less than a fraction of my own." Kragnor hovered next to them as Tai Lu wrestled to get a better grip.

"Don't let him." Tai Lu begged Candali.

"I must do as she says," Candali said in the way of an apology.

Kragnor nodded, dropped below them, then flew upward, taking Tai Lu from Candali's grasp. He held the woman to his chest with one arm and flew away from the naga infested area. Buildings and roads sped beneath him. The unhindered female gargoyle flew next to him.

"Why do you follow?" Kragnor watched the gargoyle.

"Curiosity," she purred.

Streetlights and buildings filled the night sky with illumination. The glow hid the stars. In the distance, he saw a gap in the light, darkness. "What is over there?" he asked the nekomata.

"One of the great lakes, Lake Michigan," the female gargoyle said.

Kragnor flew closer until the sound of water breaking on the shore was louder than city noises. Tai Lu wiggled in his grasp. "I am a strong swimmer," she said defiantly.

"Water was never in my plans. Although in these temperatures, you would probably succumb quickly." Kragnor huffed. He glided toward a beach and landed on the sandy surface. A cold wind whipped off the lake, the woman shivered. The nekomata touched down beside him, watching, following, curious.

Kragnor strode toward the sound of crashing water. Before him lay a large bed of boulders, used as a break to help stop the shoreline's erosion. One had defined black and white granite stripes. Good, evil, right, wrong, the colors fit the purpose.

He held Tai Lu high for the world to see and judge. "For all the animals and people you killed. For all the offspring that suffered and died in the absence of their parents. For all the lies you told. I sentence you to the fate you deserve." He laid her across the arch of the boulder. He loosened his hold on her throat and moved his enormous hand to her sternum and held her still.

The woman struggled feebly then calmed. "Only I know how to release the akitu from the stones. Only I can help you." Her eyes begged and pleaded with him.

He looked away from her, afraid he would become weak and let her go. Kragnor pulled strength from deep inside, a resilience, a logic that told him this woman would never change.

"You did not release me. Kevin and Ruby did." Kragnor placed his left hand on the boulder next to her shoulder and felt himself fall in tune with the granite.

The rock softened like quicksand beneath Tai Lu. Her eyes bulged with panic. Before she could speak, before he changed his mind, he pushed her into the stone, enveloping her body. She thrashed against him for a few moments until her strength and air ran out.

He withdrew his empty hand and stumbled away from the boulder, splashing into the edge of Lake Michigan. The stone appeared no different than before. No one would know what lay in its center.

"What have you done?" the nekomata asked, her voice thick with awe.

"What others should have…but could not." He fell to his knees, the guilt, sorrow, and shame weighing heavily on his shoulders. *This is what it is like to kill. If only the woman felt this deplorable with every life she took.*

Kragnor leaned over frigid Lake Michigan water and wept.

# Chapter 62

Kevin rolled over. The heavy quilt was warm and cozy. He sighed. *It's great to lay in bed and do nothing.* He sat up, startled. The blankets fell away, exposing the bright yellow pajamas his mom bought him for his birthday. The ugliest bit of clothing he owned. *Was it all a dream? The crazy girlfriend, Kragnor, Megan?* Megan. Kevin smiled, hoping she, at least, was real.

The ball of white fur at the edge of the bed rolled over. Bright blue eyes blinked at him. "You're not Rapscallion," Kevin said.

"Of course not. Do I look like a tomcat to you?" The feline curled her lip as if disgusted. She clambered to her feet and stretched. Both of her tails waved gently.

"Did I die? Is this a dream?"

"You're not dead." She licked her paw and wiped her ear and face.

"Kragnor? Is he dead? Is that why I'm in bed?" Kevin rubbed the mattress. He forgot how warm and soft it was.

The cat narrowed her eyes. “Perhaps, part of the akitu died. But most of Kragnor is still in there.” One of her tails pointed at Kevin’s chest. The other curled around her legs.

“You’re not a cat, are you?”

“You know me as Candali. I’m a nekomata, a demon.” For a brief moment, the cat transformed into the beautiful woman he met in Tai Lu’s prison. Just as quickly, the cat returned to cleaning her paws and face.

“Uh, okay.” Kevin slipped out of bed, not wanting to believe his eyes or ears. “Why are you in my bedroom?”

“Tai Lu commanded me to protect you, both of you. It was one of the last things she ordered me to do.” Candali’s blue eyes dilated.

“Tai Lu is dead?”

“And the world is a better place.” The cat smiled and purred.

Kevin’s head hurt. Too much happened over the past few days, and he only understood a small amount. “If she is dead, then why are you here?” He waved his hand. “I know, I know. She commanded that you protect us. But there was a time where the naga were trying to kill me. Where were you then?”

The cat shrugged and tilted her head apologetically. “I’m a demon.”

Kevin sat on the edge of the bed and laughed. “Does that mean you’ll protect me when it suits you?”

Candali curled into a ball and stared at him. “Purrhaps.” She closed her blue eyes and seemed content.

Hanging on the hallway doorknob was Tai Lu’s long black jacket. He slid out of bed and checked the pockets. Inside were two fist-sized stones. “At least we saved two.” Kevin thought about the stones he dropped between the ties of the railroad. He needed to tell Kragnor or Megan. He set the jacket on the bed and went down the hall to the bathroom.

Voices rolled up the stairs. Instead of getting dressed, Kevin investigated. Grandma Ruby was in her recliner, with Rapscallion in her lap. Megan and Johnny sat on the floor, pouring over a Russian map.

“What are you doing?” Kevin asked.

Megan looked up, a big smile on her face. She jumped to her feet and ran to him, throwing her arms around his neck, giving him a quick kiss. Megan stepped back. Her cheeks turned crimson. “Are you feeling alright?”

Kevin ran his fingers through his hair, unsure how to respond. He reached for Megan’s hand and gave it a gentle squeeze. “I think so. Except

I woke up wearing these ugly things." Kevin grabbed the front of his bright yellow shirt.

Grandma laughed. "That was my idea. Inez found them in your old bedroom closet."

"There's a reason I didn't bring them with me when I moved." Kevin found it hard not to smile at his grandmother. "Does that mean they know what happened?" He nodded in the direction of his parents' house.

Grandma shook her head. "I told them you weren't feeling well. Donna and Jerry think you have the flu. But the girls know." She shrugged. "I'm not sure I can hide anything from them."

"Are you hungry?" Johnny asked. "We can make you something, you know, if you want." The older man squinted at him.

"What's going on? How long did I sleep?"

"You've been out for two days," Johnny said. "We've been taking turns checking on you."

"Just me? What about Kragnor?"

"Kragnor hasn't appeared." Megan bit her lip. "Since we found him near Lake Michigan. He was incoherent and upset. He begged us to allow the nekomata to stay by his side. Then he gave the body up. You appeared, but you were cold to the touch and shaking. We put you in the back of Johnny's car and covered you with the jacket. It wasn't enough. You didn't warm. If it weren't for the nekomata, you'd probably have died."

"The what?"

"The cat."

The demon, Candali. "How did she save my life?"

"She transformed into…" Megan turned to Johnny. "What did she change into?"

"I think it was a salamander. But I've never seen one with fur." Johnny shook his head. "It was a crazy night."

Visions of snake men assaulted Kevin's memories. He shuttered. Crazy was an understatement. "For the sake of argument, the salamander you're talking about isn't an amphibian, is it?

Megan blinked a couple of times and shook her head.

Johnny laughed. "Hardly, no. It's more like a fire serpent."

Kevin rolled his eyes, nodding. "Of course."

"You have a lot of catching up to do," Megan said. "The other night was a taste of what is out there. Dragons, phoenix, unicorns, everyone knows what they are. Naga, and nekomata, those were new for me."

Kevin sat on the couch. “I think I am missing something.”

“There are people and creatures that need our help.” Megan looked at Johnny and nodded. “You and Kragnor were going to be sold on the black market.”

“Yea, for eternity.” Kevin rubbed his pinky finger. There was no pain, but the memory was vivid.

“Other creatures are being sold on the black market every day, and they need our help. Special animals like dragons.”

“And things,” Johnny interjected. “Don’t forget the objects.”

“What?” Kevin looked at Johnny, hoping for an explanation.

“The imbued amethyst Annie owned that controlled men. Something like that is sold every day on the black market. The body parts of magical and non-magical creatures are sold on the market. These things need to be confiscated, protected, and sometimes destroyed. That is what the AKG does.” Johnny folded up the map that was on the floor and placed it on top of his briefcase.

“Two questions. What does a gargoyle part do? Are Kragnor and I being protected or destroyed?” Kevin narrowed his eyes at Johnny.

"That's fair." Johnny raised a finger. "Gargoyle parts are traditionally used to break curses and spells. A small piece worn as a charm will prevent anyone from casting a spell against you." Johnny raised a second finger. "Both of you need to be protected until we separate you, then you and Kragnor can go your own way. By then, you won't need protection. At least that is the goal. We have no intention to destroy either of you."

Johnny stood and stretched. "I've been authorized to offer you a job." He flinched and shook his head. "That's a lie." He looked between Megan and Ruby. "I can't do this. It's not fair." Johnny paced.

Megan took Kevin's hand. He felt his heart skip. "My father did you a disservice by selling you to Tai Lu and the black market. Now you and Kragnor are known to many people, many unscrupulous people. You'll be hunted."

Grandma frowned. "And if they discover your sisters while hunting you. I could…we could lose all of you. It's bad enough you almost died."

"You must go into hiding at AKG. They said you could work for them while you're there, but it isn't a job. It's more like working for room and board." Johnny shook his head. "Think of it as a sanctuary."

"Do I have to make a decision now?" Kevin felt like he was trapped. "What about school? What about Mom and Dad? Ruby? And the girls?" His eyes landed on Megan. "Megan, what about her?" Kevin stood and paced, thinking hard.

Johnny held up his hands. "First of all. This isn't a decision to make. If you want to keep your family safe, you have no choice. You must go." The older man looked at Kevin with sympathetic eyes. "I'm sorry." Johnny held up two fingers. "Second, your Mom and Dad will receive a letter explaining your acceptance to a private college, tuition-free. That'll be your alibi while we figure out how to separate you and Kragnor."

"And if they want to visit or call?"

"We have that covered, including a backdrop for video calls."

Kevin nodded. "Of course you do."

Grandma Ruby patted the arm of the couch, inviting Kevin to sit. "We've talked with the high school and the teachers. We haven't told them everything, mind you. They said if you finish some online work that you will have enough credits to graduate in December. A full semester early."

Kevin sat on the couch. "That sounds promising."

"It is," Ruby agreed.

"But?" Kevin prompted.

"There isn't a but."

"You wanted me to sit. There's a but." Kevin raised his eyebrows in anticipation.

"It's not a *but*." Ruby sighed. "Johnny's moving in to help keep an eye on your sisters. Which will also alleviate any problems with your Mom wanting to keep an eye on me."

Kevin nodded as if expecting as much. He looked at Megan, who sat on the floor, watching but keeping quiet. "What about you?" he asked her. "What are your plans?"

"I'm going to finish school." Megan looked at Johnny and Ruby. "Ruby said I can stay here until graduation." She reached for the map on the briefcase. "Like you, the AKG hired me." She shrugged. "My first assignment is to travel to Tunguska for training." Megan pointed at the map, then crossed her arms. "I'm going to meet my mother."

To Kevin, she looked terrified.

# About the Author

RJ Ladon is a nightshift writer (by choice) and a dayshift design engineer (by necessity) to pay for the aforementioned writing addiction. She is a self-proclaimed tree-hugger and animal-lover. If she is not in her garden, pasture, or woods you can find RJ watching movies or reading books. She lives with her husband, children and a variety of animals on a farmette in Wisconsin.

Writing a novel has always been on RJ's radar, and it will soon become a reality this year (2020) with the first book in the series Bloodstone (new adult, urban fantasy). In the meantime, you can find her stories in multiple anthologies. Two horror stories; *Gwen's Gamble* and *The Poppet* in Sha'Daa – Toys. One military science fiction; *The Felix* in Tales from the Lyon's Den – Stories from the Four Horsemen Universe (Book 4). One non-fiction *Invisible Battles* found in Impossible Hope. And *The Ogre's Brownies*, in When Valor Must Hold. A list of books, anthologies and other oddities can be found at www.RJLadon.com On Twitter @RJLadon, Pintrest @rjladon7437 and Instagram rjladon